Also by D. C. Shaftoe

*Forged in the Jungles of Burma*

# Assassin's Trap

D.C. Shaftoe

iUniverse, Inc.
Bloomington

Assassin's Trap



This is a work of fiction. All of the characters, names, incidents, organizations, and dialogue in this novel are either the products of the author's imagination or are used fictitiously.

All Bible quotations were taken from the King James Version.Verses quoted: II Corinthians 5:17; Psalm 23:1; Psalm 116:1,2; Nehemiah 8:10; Ruth 1:16,17; Hebrews 11:1; Ephesians 5:22; Psalm 46:1; Psalm 121:1,2,7,8; I John 5:14-15; Mark 9:24; Romans 8:1,2; John 8:32; John 14:6; John 8:36.
*Kiss Me Again* written by Henry Blossom, 1905. Public Domain.

iUniverse books may be ordered through booksellers or by contacting:

iUniverse
1663 Liberty Drive
Bloomington, IN 47403
www.iuniverse.com
1-800-Authors (1-800-288-4677)



ISBN: 978-1-4697-0057-1 (sc)
ISBN: 978-1-4697-0059-5 (hc)
ISBN: 978-1-4697-0058-8 (e)

Printed in the United States of America

iUniverse rev. date: 1/11/2012

To my parents, Keith and Gloria Fidler,
For teaching me the things I needed to know.
To Dad for showing me the wonders of God and
To Mom for showing me that Jesus could be my best friend.

*Therefore if any man be in Christ, he is a new creature: old things are passed away; behold, all things are become new.*
II Corinthians 5:17 (KJV)

# Contents

## Acknowledgments

My darling husband, Crispin.
My wonderful children, Nate and Jared.
My siblings Diane, Wes and Dwight for their encouragement.
My nieces and nephews Sade, Tyrone, Danille,
Joshua, Natalie, David, Vanessa.
Beth Dube and Carolyn Culliton for marketing
*Forged in the Jungles of Burma.*
Terri Payk, Julie McNamara and Pastor Michael
Krause for editorial assistance.
Anne, Mariette, and all those who read my first novel, *Forged in the Jungles of Burma*, and encouraged me to write more. Thank you!

# Prologue

Pistol in hand and soldiers at her side, Maryn Dale addressed the people of the hidden village, the menace of her intent carrying across the silent crowd. She was a woman of striking beauty—a beauty magnified by the moonlight when the reflected rays glistened off her raven hair and the grey of her eyes deepened to an ebony hue reflecting the darkness of her heart.

"You will tell me now where John Brock has gone!"

"Or what?" The elderly man spoke with steel and determination in his voice.

His blue eyes pierced her veneer of authority, and she couldn't hold his gaze. Turning away to hide the fact, she pulled out her pistol and rotated back to point it directly at the old man's heart. Chambering the first round, she cast her gaze across the people of the Katafygio, refugees of oppression and citizens of this haven of rest.

"Tell me, or I will shoot your precious leader!" she cried. The cold steel in her hand matched the frigid winter of her heart.

Brother Phillip faced Maryn Dale with a look of peace in his eyes as the shot rang out. Echoes of his last words—"I forgive you"—lasted beyond the reverberations of the gunshot.

Upright in bed without even realizing she'd moved, Maryn Dale woke in a panic, sweat sliding between her shoulder blades, her heart pounding like the percussion of Blue Man Group. Swinging her legs over the side of the bed, she sat, head in hands. *Why do I keep dreaming about him? What power does he have over me?* Pushing off the edge of the bed, she padded out to the kitchen, pouring herself a large glass of double-malt Scotch. Downing the drink in four gulps, she savoured the burn in her throat. *This is all John's fault. I need to find a way to make him pay!* Stripping down, she made her way to the shower and tried to scrub away her conscience once again.

# Chapter One
# Bombs, Plots, and Terrorists

SHARDS OF GLASS SCATTERED across John Brock's chest. Pain seared through his shoulder. *Blast!* He couldn't tell if his shoulder was broken or not. And he didn't take the time to check, because through the shattered window, someone was groping for his keys … first a pry bar, now the hand that wielded it.

While wrestling with the disembodied hand, John swung his aluminum travel mug up and over his throbbing shoulder, ecstatic that he'd taken his coffee to go. The mug hit with a solid smack, and John grinned in satisfaction at the grunt of pain that followed.

Not pausing to weigh the options, John accelerated directly toward the gunman positioned in the building ahead, spoiling the shooter's aim, and then slammed on the brakes. A body hurtled past and onto the asphalt. *Gotcha, you git!* Reversing, John spun the car 180 degrees, grinding the protesting gearshift straight to second as the staccato of automatic gunfire obliterated the rear window.

John wrenched the steering wheel sharply right, bouncing off the curb but continuing forward. He glanced in the rearview mirror. A blue sedan pursued him. *Crap!* With the sedan behind and a fire engine blocking the street ahead, he was trapped. So when he noticed the narrow alley on his left, he turned into it.

Shifting his Volvo C30 to the left of the alley, John accelerated straight at a blue rubbish tip. At the last second, he cranked hard on the wheel, spinning and bouncing the car off the far wall of the alley. The airbag punched him in the face. Through the ringing in his ears, he could still hear the blue sedan crash headlong into the tip.

After clearing his vision with a shake of the head, John tore his Glock from the glove box, disengaged the safety and chambered the first bullet. Holding his gun at the ready, he moved in slowly, scanning the seats in the vehicle. He saw only the driver slumped groaning over the steering wheel, loosely holding a submachine gun. John disarmed the man easily, tossing the SMG beneath his own car.

"Raise your hands. Step out of the car," John said, adopting his best military voice, the voice that clearly conveyed that refusal was not an option.

"Hah!" A chuckle bubbled from the driver's frothy lips. "Y'all are dead, Brock," he said in a lazy Texas drawl. Then he raised his left hand slowly like a 6-year-old playing cowboys. "Bang bang." The chuckle morphed into a bloody cough, and John stepped back to avoid the crimson spray. *Yick!*

Wheezing in a breath, the Texan continued. "There's more a-comin'."

*More?* John's anger ratcheted up a notch. "Who are you working for?" The Texan sneered derisively, and John repeated the question, the heat in his voice freezing to a deathly chill. "Who are you working for?"

But it was too late to find out. The blaggard was dead. *Blast!*

John checked through the car and searched the man's pockets to find … nothing. No identification. No clues. Nought of any use.

And then it started to rain. *Of course it's raining! It's London in winter.* John slapped his hands down on the roof of the blue sedan in an uncharacteristic release of temper. "Aargh!" Flipping open his mobile phone, he called his second-in-command.

"Horace Hibbert." The man's deep bass tones filtered through the phone, and John could picture the affable giant running his fingers through his neatly trimmed afro.

"Hibb, I need your help. I'm in an alley just west of Aldersgate somewhere near St. Bart's Hospital. Are you still at Carter's campaign office?" John said.

"Things're fine down our end. It was a small bomb, not much damage," said Hibb.

"It's not that. I've been involved in an …" John paused, looking for a benign word to describe the situation. "Incident."

"Do you want me to send the plods over?" John could hear the concern in Hibb's voice.

"No, only you." John rang off. *There's more coming.* The threat replayed in John's mind as the rain poured down his already soaked body, the chill on his skin matching the chill in his heart.

When his mobile rang, he checked the caller ID. It was his wife. If he let the call go to voicemail, she might worry—and frankly, he could use a little Caroline about now.

Pausing to wipe the water from his phone, he answered, trying to keep his voice easy and light. "What's up?"

"Hi, sweetheart," Caroline said. "The Home Secretary called. He wants to meet with you when you're finished at the campaign office."

"Cheers," he replied.

"John. What's wrong?" Of course his wife would hear right through the attempted calm.

"Nought. The car's broken down, but don't worry, Hibb is on his way to me."

"Darling, what happened?" He heard the edge that accompanied the concern in her voice. This past year, since John had begun going on operations again, they'd argued endlessly, it seemed, about disclosure; she wanted to know where he went and what he did on his operations, and he refused to tell her, hiding behind the Official Secrets Act. John simply couldn't put Caroline at risk by revealing classified information that would likely only put her in danger or terrify her and send her running from him—information such as the fact that assassins had just attempted to terminate his existence using a pry bar, a blue sedan, and an SMG.

"John. What happened?" She sounded annoyed by his hesitation in responding.

"A spot of car trouble, but I'm all right, I assure you. Do you think you could get a clean suit ready for me? I'll meet you on the third floor in the medical suites," he said.

"John." He could hear the frustration in her voice, and then the moment when she gave in. "Okay," she said. Her voice quavered, but he couldn't tell which emotion set it to quake—anger or anxiety. "How long?" she asked.

"Not long. I'll need to drop the car over to the panel beater, I'm afraid," he said.

"The what?" she said. Normally, he would have chuckled at what his wife termed the English-Canadian Vocabulary Gap, but there was no humour in him.

"Body shop," he clarified.

"Oh. That's fine. Are you sure you're all right?" she asked again.

*Oh, just tickety-boo.* "I'm fine. I'll see you shortly," he replied.

Within minutes, Hibb arrived, carrying an umbrella to cover them both. At his approach, John straightened, framing his emotions into a look of confidence and control.

"I take it this was no simple crash," Hibb said, gesturing at the Glock in John's hand.

*Outstanding deduction!* John swallowed his sarcasm, replying instead with a decisive, "Correct." Providing Hibb with a rundown of the events, he quickly moved on to a plan of action. "I need to get an ID on this fellow." *And then I need my wife.*

"How did he know where you'd be?" Hibb asked, clearly puzzled.

"Bomb in London. Political target. Not difficult to guess that I'd make my way here eventually." *If he somehow knew that I was the Head of Counter-Terrorism for MI-5.* "The plods and fire services have all other accesses blocked, making this the most likely route," John said. It all sounded so reasonable until you realized that only a handful of people actually knew what John did for a living.

"John, do you think he …" Hibb nodded at the dead Texan "… had summat to do with the bombing of Carter's campaign office? Could he have planted the bomb to draw you out?"

"Let's find out," John responded fiercely.

"You're looking ragged," Hibb observed, eyeing him up and down. "Need a lift to Casualty?" John shook his head and then froze at Hibb's next question. "What are you going to tell Caroline?"

Holding his section chief's gaze, John replied tonelessly, "That's not your concern." And then, for some reason he couldn't fathom, he continued, "I told her I had a spot of car trouble."

"You really think she's going to be satisfied with that?" Hibb asked.

*Why did I even answer?* On most days, John was glad that Caroline had agreed to be his administrative assistant. She was a brilliant analyst, well-respected and liked by her colleagues, unfortunately to the point now where they had become quite protective of her. On other days, like today, John wished he could return to the time before Burma when he'd been the undisputed autocrat of his section: *Ironheart*, the ultimate spy, his emotionless life neatly compartmentalized.

"You're my officer, not my counsellor," John grumbled.

Hibb muttered something unintelligible in response—unintelligible, but clearly spoken with intent.

John rose threateningly. "What did you say?" Heat flushed his cheeks.

Unperturbed, Hibb replied, "I said, that would be an underpaid job." And then he opened his mobile to ring for a clean-up crew to collect evidence and sanitize the environment, returning it to backstreet London normal.

The "sanitation unit" arrived, and John briefed them on the evidence he wanted collected. Then he hitched a ride with Hibb back to Thames House, headquarters of MI-5. Caroline met him on the third floor, wearing black slacks and a cream-coloured blouse. John thought she looked both angry and concerned … and beautiful.

Her chestnut hair was swept into the new hairstyle she was trying out, a "fred" or a "wedge" or some such. Her round face held a softness. In fact, her entire body and her spirit held a softness he loved, and his hands itched to touch her familiar curves. But the expression on her face held him in check. Even though she stood several inches below his six feet, she was nonetheless very intimidating with her hands on her hips. Her deep brown eyes looked annoyed—but always, always, he could see her love for him written clearly within them.

"Car trouble?" Caroline asked, and her scepticism was blatantly evident in her voice and manner. "John, what happened? You've got a cut over your eye. Your shirt's been shredded by …" She scanned his clothing, looking up to meet his gaze. "Broken glass?"

"An accident. The airbag deployed." He supplied the minimum required information, always hoping that she wouldn't ask for more.

He didn't miss her sigh as she stepped closer and slipped off his ruined blue silk tie and his suit jacket. Her warm fingers brushed his skin as she undid the buttons on his powder-blue shirt, revealing the long welt across his chest and shoulder.

"That … was not caused by the airbag." Her fingertips gently traced the bruise, and he was tempted to hum happily at the tender contact. "It looks like someone hit you with a baseball bat or an iron bar," she said. Really, she was much too clever to dupe, so rather than argue or lie, he remained silent. She might suspect that he was attacked, but if he didn't confirm it, she didn't need to feel the fear of danger. "John!" She clearly wanted to question him, interrogate him really. "Wha—"

And then he just didn't want to argue, so he began to sing. "'Safe in your arms. Far from alarms…'" He moved minutely closer to her. "'Kiss me again…'"

"I don't know that one," she said, and the grim line of her mouth relaxed just a little. "Didn't Boyzone sing that?"

"No, my love. It was written by Victor Herbert and Henry Blossom for the Broadway show 'Mlle Modiste'." And he held his hands out palms-up in a gesture of surrender, begging her for comfort. "Please?"

He watched her struggle for a moment more, and then her arms were around him, her love erasing the fear and frustration from his chest.

"Never mind. I'm glad you're okay." She pulled his head to her shoulder. He slid his arms around her waist, sighing against her and kissing her neck. For a moment, he was fascinated by the trail of goosebumps his cold lips left behind.

"I love you, Caer," he murmured against her skin.

Shivering lightly, she stroked her fingers through his wet and sweaty hair. "I love you too, my bear."

Pulling back, he let her remove his shirt. He waited patiently as she washed his cuts, applied a butterfly bandage above his eyebrow, and kissed his bruises better. Everything felt better when Caroline took care of it.

"Why won't you tell me what happened?" Caroline asked. Her voice was soft and sad.

"It's nothing you need to worry about," John assured her. "I'm fine."

"You know," she said, "just because you say that, doesn't mean I actually stop worrying."

Sighing morosely, he pleaded with her, "I don't want to argue. I hurt. I have a headache …" He knew she saw the sorrow in his eyes, because he didn't bother to hide it. And because she really was incredible, she let him off the hook. He pulled her close, so relieved to have her in his arms, loving him. Loving him in spite of all it took to be married to Ironheart, the ultimate spy.

Soon after, bandaged and dry, John rode in the back of the service-pool car on the way to Whitehall, the centre of Her Majesty's Government. As they wove their way along the Embankment, the grey clouds even parted for a moment, revealing a rare glimpse of the sun's rays shining through the London Eye.

"Shall I wait for you, sir?" the driver said.

"Yes. I shan't be long," John replied, stepping out of the car. With a nod to Big Ben, England's famous clock tower, John walked past the wrought-iron fence and on into the Cabinet Office to meet with the Home Secretary, Sir Desmond Stanway.

"Good afternoon, Mr. Brock," said Sir Desmond, simultaneously offering his hand in greeting and undoing the straining button on his suit jacket to make room for his hefty belly before he sat.

"Good afternoon, Home Secretary," John replied. He remained standing out of deference. "I have a preliminary report on the Carter bomb. The explosion occurred today at 5:45 a.m. in the campaign office of Nigel Carter of Her Majesty's Loyal Opposition. Three casualties. No fatalities. Four groups have stepped forward claiming responsibility, but none is credible."

"I want you to make this a priority. I've arranged with Commander Winters of the Met to coordinate your efforts with Counter-Terrorism Command. I'll expect you to offer your gratitude for his cooperation in person," Sir Desmond said.

*Excuse me?* "Of course, sir," John said. *How much manpower is necessary to investigate one simple bomb? And why am I expected to glad-hand the Met?*

"Very good," Sir Desmond said, gesturing for John to sit before he continued. "Before you leave, I have an urgent matter to discuss with you. The Chairman of the Joint Intelligence Committee passed this information on to me. Apparently, MI-6 intercepted a communiqué that originated in Mumbai, India, and terminated in Drammen, Norway. They believe the receiver to be one Tor Grendahl, a known—"

"Mercenary," John said. "What is the message, and how does it concern MI-5?"

Silently, John took the sheet of paper the HS offered. It read: "Locate: Pet Badger. Very Precious. Reward If Found Dead." And beneath the heading was

John's own picture, taken in Moor Mead Garden from the looks of it, likely when he was walking their dog, Rufus.

Steeling his expression and releasing no emotion, John replied, "Thank you, sir. I'll look into it."

"I have spoken to Special Branch and been assured that they will organize protection for you and your wife," Sir Desmond said. "You live in Twickenham, do you not? They can have a security team in place within the hour. You are a fine officer, Mr. Brock. The Crown has no desire to lose your services."

"Thank you, sir, but I'll organize my own protection." *That way, Caroline will never have to know.*

The HS watched John silently for a moment, and John could read his concern plainly in his eyes. "Very well, Mr. Brock. It is your prerogative."

John rose, shook the man's hand, and departed, returning to the pool car. *This is why, against the culture of English security and law enforcement, I always have a handgun at the ready.* John sank into thought, not even noticing when the car stopped.

"We're here, sir," the driver said as they arrived at the Millbank entrance to Thames House.

John pulled himself mentally back to the present and exited the vehicle. He walked through the door with the tourists, making a left and then a right to the door marked "Staff Only," swiping his security pass and entering the restricted zone. He mounted the few steps, paced along a corridor and then passed through the bulletproof security pods and onto the Grid, the office space for Section G, Counter-Terrorism.

Aubrey Davies met him with a statement that was likely meant to be a question.

"There's been some chatter from our assets in the Indian arms trade during the last forty-eight hours," said Aubrey, a long-time veteran of the Security Services. His domain was the technology of espionage and counter-espionage. His brilliant intellect stood side-by-side with his social ineptitude within a 55-year-old body complete with hunched shoulders and squinty grey eyes permanently lined from spending too much time chasing down ones and zeroes.

"And we're only hearing about this now?" John asked.

"Shall I pass the information on to MI-6?" Aubrey said, reaching up to scratch along the edge of his receding hairline as though to stop the glacial decline of his youth.

Something about Aubrey's manner warned John that his question had a deeper meaning. "Should I assume that you're not content with that course of action?" John asked.

"It seems to me that, given the dodgy source of the rumours and the information Caroline uncovered about the Jammu Kashmir Liberation Front, there may be a connection here that MI-6 might overlook," Aubrey said.

John released an internal *ah*. "Very well. Keep a copy of the information and pass along the Indian rumours. Agreed?" John said, gauging Aubrey's reaction, knowing he'd guessed right when the man released a satisfied smile. It was important to let his officers feel appreciated, something Caroline was seeking to teach him.

But rather than return to work, Aubrey remained, alternately tapping a pencil against his trouser leg and his lower lip.

Eyeing the graphite stains, John furrowed his brow to express his impatience with the man's stalling. "Out with it, Aubrey."

"Well," Aubrey began slowly. "I understand that Caroline's had her issues with the telephone system, but ..."

*Issues?* John mused. That was an understatement. Caroline consistently disconnected the Home Secretary and, on more than one occasion, had set off the emergency shutdown protocol when she was meant to transfer calls.

Aubrey cleared his throat and continued. "Er, Caroline ... well, stone the crows! She has an uncanny ability to see to the heart of people and the issues surrounding them. We could make much better use of her talents as an intelligence analyst rather than an administrative assistant." John felt his gaze tighten, and he noticed Aubrey hesitate before continuing. "Er, remember the Smythe case? None of us understood the significance of what she detected in his banking patterns. What about the ex-minister Sheldon? She sussed him out the first time she met him ... and informed us all that the man was having an affair ... which turned out to be the truth. And with the mistress of the ranking Russian officer in London, who was a KGB agent."

"They're called the FSB now," John reminded Aubrey tersely for the umpteenth time.

"Nevertheless. She's very bright," Aubrey said. His voice was suddenly sure and definite.

John frowned, belying his next words. "I'm grateful, Aubrey. It's not really possible for me to promote my own wife." *And don't think for a moment that I would ever allow her to be involved operationally. She is much safer as she is, answering phones and typing reports.*

John's gaze drifted across the room to the desk where Caroline sat, mercifully oblivious to the danger of a hit man. John had made a long list of enemies in his time, first with Special Forces' Maritime Terrorism Command and then with MI-5. His enemies were not the sort to cringe at the thought of using his wife as leverage against him. The very idea chilled his heart.

"I don't mean to waffle on about it … but, there! I may have a word with the DG," Aubrey said.

*Sir William Jacen has always had a soft spot for Caroline. Will he listen to Aubrey?* "Anything else?" John asked, eager to end this conversation before his wife overheard them talking about her. The last thing he needed was for Caroline to decide that she wanted a more active role in the defence of the realm. When Aubrey shook his head, John asked, "Have you seen Hibb?"

"Nipped down to Human Resources to get Ryan's new badge sorted," Aubrey said.

"He's lost it again?" John inquired, feeling the familiar thrust of annoyance that Ryan Carstairs' ineptitude always seemed to elicit. He would never understand how the young man came to be recruited. If John hadn't been in Burma at the time, Ryan never would have been assigned as a field agent on his team. The young ginger-headed blighter was a liability.

"Indeed," Aubrey replied. "Hibb should return shortly." Aubrey retreated to his lair, the computer and technology laboratory of the Grid.

Crossing the Grid to Caroline's desk, John paused to watch her studying the computer screen before her, every measure of her body immersed in her task. Fear rolled through his belly. A contract on his life was nothing new, but he'd never before had something to lose—never before that one remarkable day in a dingy, terrifying prison in Burma when he'd met Caroline … and loved her. Defying all the odds of his hard and lonely life, she'd loved him in return. She'd married him, taking his name, taking his life as her own.

For a moment, he gave in to the need to have her attention focused on him. "Could you please …" he began, leaning forward on his arms. Watching her eyes shift from the computer, he saw the furrow of concentration ease from her brow. And she smiled at him. She could smile with the greatest joy. As her gaze settled on him, though, her smile reversed into a frown.

"What's wrong now?" she asked.

Her question took him by surprise. "Nought, sweetheart," he replied, but he knew that she didn't believe him because she narrowed her deep brown eyes in scepticism. How she could see through him was a mystery. He had earned the nickname Ironheart in part because he maintained complete control of his emotions and was adept at hiding them from others. But somehow, she always knew.

"John." She interrupted his thoughts, warning in her voice. "I can tell there's something wrong. And don't give me that 'nought' crap, because it won't fool me." And he thought he loved her more in that moment than ever before, because she could always somehow find the "real John Brock." However, he did *not* want her to worry about him. After escaping with him through the jungles of Burma, she deserved a little tranquility. So he fobbed her off.

"Operational issues. Nothing for you to worry about," he replied. But she frowned at him and his heart sank within him. *Is it lying if I'm only keeping the information hidden for her own good?* Hoping to deflect her mood, he changed the subject and made his escape. "Could you please send Hibb in when he arrives?"

She nodded, but the frown didn't shift. Covering a heavy sigh, he tucked his anxiety away. The truth was, he never wanted to go back to life before Burma, before Caroline. He would never survive it.

Ten minutes later, Hibb knocked on his office door.

"Come," John said, inviting Hibb into the glass-walled heart of the Grid.

Sitting behind his modern oak desk, John motioned for Hibb to shut the office door and take a seat, which he did, settling his gigantic frame into the straight-backed wooden chair across from John. Horace Reginald Hibbert—the name was as large as the man. An enigma to the majority of his colleagues, Hibb somehow managed to maintain a transparent Christian world view amidst the shadowy translucency of espionage. John had quickly detected within Hibb the character of a good man, and promoted him. Hibb fulfilled his role as Section Chief perfectly, because everyone trusted Hibb.

"Bad news from the Home Sec?" Hibb asked. His voice was easy and light.

Without a word, John retrieved the folded sheet from his pocket and handed it over. Hibb seemed unfazed by the message, refolding it and raising his eyes to meet John's.

"Badger-Brock. That's twee," Hibb said. "This the third contract you've had on your life?"

"Fourth, actually, but that's not my concern," John replied.

"Is Special Branch providing security? I don't suppose you'll be moving into a safe house or anything convenient like that?" Hibb asked.

And here was where things got tricky. John carefully kept his face void of emotion as he said, "I don't want Caroline to know."

"Aye?" Hibb's eyes widened in astonishment. "Why?"

"That's not your concern," John said. "I want this to stay between you and me, and I want you to liaise with Special Branch to organize discreet security. You can put a couple of blokes on me if you like, but I want Caroline and the house covered. Understood?"

"Aye, sir. Wouldn't it be safer to simply tell her?" Hibb said.

"No. She's either with me at home or safe on the Grid," John said. *If I'm careful, she'll never know.*

"And when you're on assignment?" Hibb asked.

"I'll deal with that when it becomes necessary."

# Chapter Two
## *Red Datsuns and City Cows*

John opened the morning briefing. "Nigel Carter of Her Majesty's Loyal Opposition. The Home Secretary demands that we put all energy into punishing the perpetrators of this 'atrocity'—his words, not mine. Tell me what we know. Then tell me what we think."

"The device was Semtex, exploded using a remote device," Aubrey reported.

"Three casualties: one secretary hospitalized with second-degree burns, two cleaning staff with ruptured ear drums," Alexa Donnehy added, flipping through the file before her.

"Motive?" John asked, struggling to pay attention. Caroline's knee pressed against his leg in a pattern of twos, each a coded *love you*. When he looked at her eyes, they sparkled with mischief. Exactly how was he meant to pay attention when she was doing that?

"Unclear," Hibb said. John nearly laughed at the double entendre, covering up with a cough. Hibb finished his report. "Nothing was taken from the office, and nothing of importance was destroyed."

"Perhaps there was a deeper motive," Caroline suggested. "Maybe it was set to draw attention to something or someone."

His humour wiped away, John hid his shock at Caroline's analysis of the situation, so close to his own suspicions. If Hibb was correct and the bomb was set to draw him out … John shut down those thoughts. "Alexa and Harry, I'll need you to accompany me to New Scotland Yard to meet with the Met's Counter-Terrorism Command." John saw Harry exchange a look of bewilderment with Alexa. "The Home Secretary insists," John explained and then changed the topic. "Ryan, how are you coming with the Plaza Bombers?"

Ryan sat up tall, adopting an arrogant expression. "If the CIA would be more forthcoming, we'd be further along. There's a meet at Tiffany's Bar we need to monitor. That should give us what we need."

"Fine." John was unimpressed. *Just do your job, little ginger.* "Dismissed. Hibb. My office."

John greeted his Section Chief with a terse, "Close the door." Complying, Hibb sat across the desk from him. "Any news on my attacker in the blue sedan?" John inquired.

"Aye," Hibb said, pulling a sheaf of papers from his back pocket. Hibb was a shirt-and-tie sort of bloke, but he despised suit jackets, stating that they only came in "wee man" sizes, so reports were carried beneath his arm or folded into his back pocket. Hibb passed the folded pages over. "Our hit man is one Wade Shafto. Texan. Suspected to be affiliated with Tor Grendahl, a Norwegian fixer. Grendahl is likely our organizer. Complicating the issue, Grendahl has a stable of twenty or twenty-five assassins he's known to call upon. John, if Grendahl's in charge, then this is a right dog's-breakfast. One failure won't slow him down, he'll keep at it."

This wasn't news to John. "Any sense of who's funding him?"

"No, not as yet. The trouble is, there doesn't seem to be any real sense of who Grendahl actually is. There are no confirmed photographs, no known addresses, and no witnesses accidentally left alive. There are rumours linking him to the drugs trade, other rumours of involvement with the Albanian mafia. The Norwegian Politi are even rumoured to have tried to bring him in on tax-evasion charges. Nothing. He's just a name on a page from Interpol." Hibb gave a snort of atypical frustration. "This would be a lot easier if you would let me assign the team to it. Only me and a helper isn't much."

"No. I don't want Caroline to know," John said, confirming his earlier orders to Hibb.

"Why, John?" Hibb's voice was strident, clearly telling John that he found this situation frustratingly incomprehensible. "It's daft. You need to tell her."

"She's safer not knowing," John replied in a tone of voice that clearly said Hibb would agree if he were any sort of intelligent man.

Clearly disagreeing with John but unwilling to press his case, Hibb sighed in resignation. "I simply canna ken your reasoning, John. Have you truly considered the implications of keeping Caroline in the dark?" Hibb asked before departing.

*Considered the implications? What does he think I spend all of my time doing? She doesn't want to be afraid again. After Burma, fleeing pursuit, the constant peril and privation, what would she do if she felt she was in real danger again? Here in London? I don't want to lose her. Father, please. I don't want to lose her. I can't.*

Caroline stretched out her back, closing the update report on the Plaza Bombers that she'd been formatting for Ryan, who was hopeless at typing. She tried to help him out from time to time. He was always so certain of John's condemnation—and, if Caroline were forced to admit it, John did tend to be quite hard on the young agent.

Stepping over to the tea room for a break, Caroline mused, *Everything here is about tea. Yuck! After all the tea we drank in Burma, I prefer coffee. Double-double. And poor John. Sometimes he has no choice but to have a cuppa-tea. I think he'd be happy if a dragon came and burned to ash all the Darjeelings of the world.* Caroline chuckled at her own private humour, but the sound of her name brought her laughter to a halt.

"...Caroline to finish your report?" *That sounds like Alexa.* Caroline had known Alexa Donnehy since she and Harry Blake had arrived at the Deputy High Commission in Kolkata, India, to question Caroline and John about their escape from Burma. *How does she know about the report?*

"Where are we going to find an unknown to monitor the meeting at Tiffany's Bar? Aubrey says there's a book with a hidden camera we can use, but the bar's a known CIA hangout. Any of us would be tagged instantly." *That's Ryan.* Ryan Carstairs was a hotshot. That was the best description Caroline could come up with for the sulky, blue-eyed 24-year-old. The other men called him "little ginger" because of his red hair, which he insisted was plainly brown. A junior field officer, he'd been recruited a year-and-a-half ago from a local football club.

"We often use support staff for these kinds of things," said Alexa.

"Why don't we ask Caroline to do it?" Ryan said. "She would be an unknown, and with her Canadian accent, she might be able to go unnoticed in a bar full of Americans, at least more than anyone else in this building!"

"That's bonkers, Ryan. Take some advice for a change," Alexa said.

*Why is that crazy?* Caroline wondered.

"She's great at typing," Ryan said. "Is she not good for anything else?"

"This is fair warning, little ginger, let it go ..." Alexa paused and then continued, "And don't let John hear you talking like that."

"Must be nice to be the boss's wife," was Ryan's bitter parting shot.

Caroline slipped away. *Is that all I do? Am I just taking up a job they could hire a properly qualified individual to do? I don't want to be "just the boss's wife"! There must be something I can do to earn my spurs, to gain a little respect.*

Rounding the corner, Caroline spotted John through the windowed walls of his office. *Yes! All I have to do is talk to him about helping on Ryan's operation.* She gave a little *knock knock* on his door, although it was slightly open.

"Come," John called, welcoming her with a smile that quickly faded.

Caroline said, "Ryan—"

"No," John said before she got any further.

"No what?" Caroline said.

"No, you cannot go out in the field as an observer on Ryan's op," John said, dropping his eyes to the reports on his desk.

"Oh." *How did he know what I was going to ask?* "I would only have to sit at a table and read a book," Caroline explained. *Then maybe people would begin to take me seriously around here.*

John looked up at her again, obviously calculating something from her stance, and then returned his gaze to the report he was reading. "You are not a field officer. You don't have the training."

"I see. So I'm just your secretary ... just the boss's wife," Caroline replied, using the very words that had upset her earlier.

John sighed and put down his pen. "You are not *just* a secretary. You are an administrative assistant. But you are not a field officer." He returned to signing his report and then finished with, "Could you please get me the final report on Smythe by home time today?"

Caroline watched him narrowly for a few moments and then exited the office, leaving the door open. As she sat back at her desk, Caroline was fuming inside. *Who does he think he is? The boss of the world? It would only be a little field work. I'm not that incompetent. I can do more than type and collate.* Though she didn't mind the more mundane aspects of her job, she didn't like to be treated as a menial.

Shuffling through the day's memos absentmindedly, she stopped at a Human Resources document asking for any staff interested in field training to download and submit a Request Form 32A. The request had to be approved by the officer's Section Head. Inspiration lit Caroline's features. *If I had field training, I could gain a little respect. If I had field training, I'd feel more deserving of my job.*

Logging on to the intranet, she downloaded the form, completed it in record time, and then finished the report on the Smythe case so that she could try the good-news-bad-news strategy with John. If she timed it just right, she could slip it all to him just before home time.

"John, it's time to head over to New Scotland Yard," Harry Blake said in his soft-spoken voice. "Better bring your brolly. It's raining again."

A thirtysomething bachelor, Harry was a quiet man who thought much more than he spoke. He kept his light brown hair buzzed short to hide the growing bald spot on the top of his head, a fact that Caroline found quite humorous. *How do you cover up baldness by shaving your head?* An amateur chef, Harry had recently taken on the role of caring for his ailing mother and his eldest sister, Clara, who had Down syndrome. They had quickly become willing victims for his culinary experiments.

Alexa stood by the security pods awaiting John and Harry. John watched the pressure to speak her mind building within her. She managed to hold her irritation in check until John was close enough that she didn't have to shout. "Why are there so many resources assigned to this fairly minor incident?" she asked.

Never one to mince words, Alexa was the yin to Harry's yang, ready with an opinion and no compunction about being heard. With deep brown eyes and broad shoulders inherited from her Nigerian mother and fair, freckled skin inherited from her Irish father, she was also a thirtysomething bachelor, preferring life on her own and friendship to commitment and love.

"A bomb in a politician's office is clearly considered the gravest of offences to the Home Secretary," John said. Alexa released a snort of disgust. "I don't understand it either," John acquiesced. "However, I will need you and Harry to liaise with the CTC team assigned to the case while I glad-hand the Commander upstairs. Just close your eyes and think of England." John caught the surprised look that passed from Harry to Alexa. His officers were still not used to any humour from him.

Crossing the Thames, the driver took them along Victoria Street past Westminster Abbey to New Scotland Yard, a striking Commercial Modernist building, all glass, granite and steel. Holding the umbrella, John led Harry and Alexa past the security officers patrolling the grounds, through the various concrete and metal barriers, and then inside.

Flashing his badge, John checked in with the desk sergeant. Chief Inspector Bill Perkins appeared almost immediately. He was a striking figure—tall, lean and angular. Nature had obviously compensated for complete baldness by gracing him with abundant facial hair comprised of grizzled auburn eyebrows and a long drooping moustache. The harshness of his features was dispelled whenever he smiled.

"Mr. Brock. Good to see you," the CI said. "We're pleased to coordinate on this matter."

"Pleasure," John said, accepting the greeting and falling in step with Perkins. First introducing Harry and Alexa to the CTC team assigned to the case, Perkins then led John upstairs to the Commander's office. Knocking first, Perkins opened the door in response to the terse "Enter" from inside.

"Commander Winters, this is Mr. Brock from Thames House. If you recall, the Home Secretary asked our agencies to work closely on the matter of the Carter bomb," Perkins said.

John stepped forward to shake the Commander's hand. "Just let my people know how we can be of service," John began, but Winters cut him off.

"John Brock? Of MI-5?" Commander Winters said. His voice was as sour as his lined face. He might once have been a handsome man, but fifty years and something very like bitterness had erased any trace from his features. "You were involved with Maryn Dale, weren't you?"

Suppressing his shock, John replied, "That was a long time ago." *Blimey! Where did that come from?*

"She despises you," Winters said, and spite virtually radiated from him. "Something about Southeast Asia."

John wasn't surprised by this news. Twenty years ago, he and Maryn had been lovers. When he had refused to take her with him to set up his Southeast Asian network, she'd thrown him over for a senior MI-6 officer … and a promotion. What did surprise John was that Commander Winters should choose this venue to air Maryn's grievances.

CI Perkins moved closer to John as though in empathy. "The, er, footy was excellent on Saturday," he said, clearly trying to shift the topic of discussion. John shrugged. He didn't watch football. Winters continued to glare at John.

"How long will the rain last, do you wonder?" Perkins tried again, his voice soothing and companionable.

"Weather's always the same here, Perkins," Winters responded tersely, his beady eyes still matching John stare for stare.

"You were recently married, weren't you, John?" Perkins said, trying again.

"Yes," John replied, allowing his gaze to slip away from Commander Winters and rest on CI Perkins. *Caroline.* "About a year and a half ago."

Perkins chuckled. "So there's hope for us veterans yet?"

Rounding his desk, Commander Winters stepped up to John, menace in his voice and manner. "What does Maryn think of that?"

John's smile quickly faded. "I don't give a toss." Bile burned the back of John's throat, but he kept himself still, steadily holding Winters' gaze. *Will I ever be free of the mistakes of my past?*

The telephone rang, interrupting the standoff. Perkins took the opportunity to escort John out of the office and into the hall.

"Never mind him," Perkins said. "His wife discovered his relationship with Maryn a few months ago and gave him the heave-ho. Of course, once he was free, Maryn bade him farewell as well and sauntered off to India. He's a little bitter."

"Maryn has that effect on people," John said. Needing to escape the acid of the encounter, John shook Perkins' hand, preparing to depart. "Tell my people to find their own way back to Thames House," he said.

"Certainly," Perkins agreed.

John strode downstairs, eager to get away.

"John, mate."

John stopped abruptly. There were only two men in the world who dared call him *mate.* He spun to come face-to-face with one of them: Rory Duncan, formerly John's Warrant Officer in the Special Boat Service. After resigning from the SBS, Rory had signed on with the Met while John had been recruited into MI-5. Rory always reminded John of an artist's depiction he had seen as a boy of Tecumseh, the great Native American leader. Willowy and tall, Rory had straight black hair, black eyes and a ruddy complexion.

John smiled. He couldn't help it. "Rory. It's good to see you," he said. "How are you?"

Rory clasped John's proffered hand in a firm grip. "Fine. And you, John? Are you well?"

"Of course," John replied.

Silently, Rory studied him, and John felt strangely vulnerable beneath the man's penetrating gaze. Rory frowned. "Come with me," he said. "Mick's out and about. We'll join up with him."

Dodging the raindrops, Rory led John to his car. Generally a man of few words, Rory surprised John by opening a conversation.

"Wasn't sure if you'd forgotten about us," Rory said. "You've been back in the country over a year." Before John could reply to the accusation in his friend's voice, Rory continued, "Mick wants to know if you're coming back to rugby."

John grimaced. "I'm married now. Things are different."

"What's she like?" Rory asked quietly.

John sighed happily, not bothering to hide a wistful smile from his oldest friend. "She's incredible! She's so strong and yet so gentle. And stubborn. Blimey, can she be stubborn."

"Tenacious," Rory said, smiling.

John chuckled. "Yes. She never loses hope. You know that's why they put us together in the prison in Burma? It was punishment for her because she was giving the other prisoners hope." He smiled wistfully at the memory. *My darling wife, the bane of the prison warden.* "And joy. She can find joy in the most mundane events. The other day I bought her a jumper she'd admired. She was so pleased, thanking me and putting it on immediately, modeling it for me." The wistful smile was back again.

"I've never seen you happy before," Rory said.

"I don't think I've ever been this happy, not even as a child. Even when things are …" John paused, looking for the perfect word. "Hmmm … strained between us."

"How is she coping with your job?" Rory asked.

John grimaced. "She hates the disconnection between our lives—that I can't tell her where I'm going or what I'm doing when I'm on a mission."

"So tell her," Rory said as though the answer was that simple.

John struggled with the thought and then surrendered. "I can't. If people come to believe that I tell her everything, she'll become a target; my enemies will see her as a weapon to use against me. I have to protect her."

"You'll figure it out," Rory said.

"I hope so. She is formidable when she's angry," John said.

Rory turned onto King William Street and then onto Bush Lane, pulling up outside a pub, the Belle of Maidenhead. The rain had stopped.

"Yo, Leffftennant Brock!" Mick drew out the pronunciation of the word.

John turned at Mick Adair's voice. John's corporal during their days with the SBS, Mick was an outrageously gregarious man—charming, self-confident, always the centre of attention wherever he went. He was a man of indistinguishable height and girth. He simply seemed to fill whatever space was available with his massive shoulders, belly laugh, and crazy brown hair that, combed or not, stuck out in spikes all over his head. That hair had given more than one sergeant apoplexy back in the day.

Mick immediately engulfed John in a bear hug. "Mate. It's been a day and a time since we've seen you. Come into my office, and we'll see what mischief we can make." Pushing open the thick oak door of the whitewashed half-Tudor building, Mick seemed to scan the dark oak walls, deep booths and lead-glass windows to find just the perfect table.

Uncertain how to jump back into friendship after essentially abandoning his relationship with these two men, John instead diverted to a neutral topic.

"What can you tell me about this bomb in Mr. Carter's office?" John asked. *When did we ever discuss anything but work and rugby anyway?*

"There's a great deal of pressure on this one, John," Rory informed him. "Our investigation is definitely being channelled in a clear direction."

"Somebody wants a specific solution, and we're meant to hand it over with peas and escargots on the side," Mick said.

Rory turned a confused expression to Mick, quoting, "'Peas and escargots'? Seriously? That's your choice of metaphor?"

John wanted to laugh but held his emotions in check. It was strange dealing with his past when, at that time, he'd been a certain kind of man and now he was ... something new. "Have you nothing else for me?" John said.

Rory, still shaking his head at the wildly grinning Mick, turned to John. "I don't see—"

Shattering, the glass window over the booth rained in pieces upon them, and the three men instinctively ducked beneath the table. Rising to a crouch, John peered cautiously over the window ledge. A second bullet narrowly missed his head. *Blimey!* He dropped back down, but not before he glimpsed the muzzle of a Vapensmia sniper rifle withdrawn behind the opaque tinted window of a black Lexus.

"Who's that?" Rory said as though asking the identity of the new bloke answering phones at the information desk.

"My assassin," John replied, heading to the door. Mick and Rory followed him. "I need to get him."

"Rory. The plods," Mick said, unfazed. "John, follow me!"

Leaving Rory behind to coordinate with the police, John followed Mick across the street to the man's dearly loved and heavily abused supercharged red Datsun 1600. As soon as John approached the passenger-side door, Mick slid behind the wheel, firing the engine—a sound once likened to a 747 preparing for lift-off. The Datsun revved into motion, accelerating with the characteristic wheeze and clunk of a reconditioned engine. John cringed. *I hope it runs better than it sounds.*

"Follow or acquire?" Mick asked.

"Acquire," John replied, his voice sure and definite.

A wolfish grin encompassed Mick's face as he complied. "Excellent."

*Oh no,* John mused. *This could be bad.*

Spinning an automotive version of a pirouette, Mick pulled aggressively into traffic, following the Lexus in the direction of the A4. As John bounced off the passenger door, he grasped the seat belt and wrenched it across his middle, securing himself to the seat—which itself wobbled violently.

A hard right turned the red Datsun down an alley, scraping the edges of a rubbish tip as the space converged toward the busy street on the other end. Abruptly, Mick turned down a narrower alley, soon emerging into a skateboard park. The Datsun bounced down the steps to the bottom, youth scattering in alarm. *Oh, crap!* John planted one hand on the roof of the multi-coloured car and wrapped one around the armrest on the shuddering door.

"Where are you going?" John shouted at Mick.

"Watch and learn, mate!" Mick replied. "Watch and learn."

Lurching up the first grind, Mick cranked the steering wheel hard to the left to avoid the much higher second grind. And then, hauling the wheel to the right, he flashed through the entrance to a bowl-shaped area, accelerating into the curved basin, gradually spiralling higher with the centrifugal force of the geography until they shot over the top, crashing down hard, John's teeth slamming together with the force. They careened down the grass on the other side, lurching onto the road at the bottom. A hard left and then a hard right barely slowed Mick's progress. The whine of the engine made John's ears hurt. Another hard left thrust John shoulder to shoulder with Mick, who elbowed him sharply back toward his own space.

At the Slough, Mick turned right, coming onto the M4 heading east, the speeding crimson bullet dodging around the traffic.

John's mobile rang. "Brock." John shouted to be heard over the roar of the engine.

It was Rory. "What's your 'twenty'?"

"East on the M4 just off Slough Road," John said.

Shouting into the receiver, Rory confirmed, "I've a chopper on the way. Tell Mick to keep that piece of—"

"Thanks, Rory!" John cut him off.

"What did he call my car?" Mick roared. He reached forward and patted the dash of the car. "Don't listen, baby. Ye're a bonnie lass."

John shook his head at Mick. The black Lexus appeared before them.

"I see him. Mick, there he is!" John pointed.

"Who's the Man, Brock?" Mick exclaimed in triumph.

Whooping in exhilaration, Mick stamped his foot to the floorboards, though John didn't note any change in acceleration. The road was far from deserted, but the congestion didn't seem to bother Mick in any way as he weaved and bobbed around the vehicles, pausing only briefly when he was in danger of being boxed between three delivery trucks: milk, flour and raisins. John pushed away the thought of the gluey mess they'd be mired in if the trucks collided.

Mick slowed and hooked to the right, accelerating again to speed around the dried-fruit bearer and then cut across the bow of the flour conveyance, causing the driver to nervously hit the brakes. A squeal and a crunch followed them, and John wondered at the destruction they'd left behind.

The Lexus accelerated, warned by the crash behind him, shooting past London Heathrow Airport. Turning south, pursuing the assassin, Mick shot onto the Great Road, rounding the traffic circle, leaving a trio of fist-waving drivers behind him. Following the Lexus, Mick was forced to slow as he navigated around the slower vehicles unhappily obeying the traffic rules in the congestion. He flipped 50p out the window at the angriest of the victims, shouting, "Call the traffic commissioner. This is appalling!"

John chuckled ... until Mick shot to the right, heading south, leaving the assassin heading east away from them.

"What are you doing?!" John said, shouting over the roar of the engine.

"You'll see," Mick replied mysteriously.

"Corporal?" John pulled rank.

"Aye aye, Leftenant," Mick said, exaggerating the pronunciation. "He'll try to lose us in the green space. Watch and learn."

John would have chewed his lip in anxiety except it was much too risky with this wild man at the wheel. So he held on for dear life and prayed. Finally, after what felt like ages, Rory called again.

"The chopper's got the Lexus on Kew heading for Richmond Park and the Roon City Farm. You should come out just ahead of him in two," Rory said.

"Woohoo!" Mick said, celebrating his success. Two minutes later, they shot onto the same street as the Lexus, directly in front of it. The black car faltered for a moment, slowing, and then turned sharply onto the shoulder of the road and off onto the grassy verge and across a field toward the Roon City Farm. Mick was in hot pursuit. The Lexus, however, didn't have what it took to cross the uneven ground and was slowing considerably, tail-end swerving.

"Back off, Mick. We don't want a tour of the boot," John instructed.

Mick lifted his foot a little from the accelerator. John watched the hapless Lexus spin and weave and buck until, there across the field, six head of mismatched cattle came lumbering into view. They were led by an elderly cattle herder, fit with green oilskin coat, high-top black wellies, and a gnarled walking stick. Because of the loose friction provided by the sodden grass, the Lexus was snaking a path directly at the little bovine parade.

John and Mick exchanged a glance before returning unbelieving stares at the slow-motion drama before them. Mick slowed the Datsun. Ahead of them, the Lexus barrelled forward.

The farmer finally seemed to notice the two cars racing toward him across the grassy field. Stopping and waving his stick, he bellowed curses at the barmy drivers so far from the asphalt. The Lexus spun one last time, turning the front of the car directly at the farmer, bearing down on him at arthritic speed. The farmer was unmoved by the trajectory until, finally, the driver must have panicked and cranked the wheel hard to the right. But on the slippery ground, the car was pulled inexorably left, lifting the lead cow up and onto its hood, the cow rolling with legs extended toward the clouds, thumping against the windshield. John heard the windshield crack loudly. The car lurched to a stop, propelling the cow forward and back onto her feet. She seemed to shake herself off and, giving the loudest bellow of disgust, lumbered, uninjured, over to the farmer, who petted and patted her like a pup.

Mick reached across John, extracting a pair of handcuffs and a Smith & Wesson from his glove box, and the two made their way over to the black Lexus. They worked in tandem toward the car, finding the driver slumped against the steering wheel, dazed, a crimson stain spreading across his forehead. Without a word of warning, Mick socked him one, knocking him out. Dragging the driver from the vehicle, Mick balanced him over the bonnet.

*Thwack!* "Bloomin' 'eck!" Mick shoved John back as a walking stick came down again, narrowly missing his head. The farmer loudly scolded the men, who tried to placate the cowherd and still keep the assassin under control. Finally, Mick handed over 50 pounds, and the man wandered away with "mine poor caff."

The police helicopter landed in the green space, and John reluctantly handed his would-be assassin over to the Met.

When they were alone again, Mick finally asked, "You have an assassin?"

John sighed. "Several, actually."

It took a lot to faze Mick, but his eyes widened at the news. "What does your wife think of that?" Mick said.

"I haven't told her," John replied.

"Really?" Mick said, clearly astonished now.

"Yes, really. Why is that so shocking?" John asked impatiently.

"Mate, you gave up *rugby* for her," Mick said, as though that were the greatest sacrifice a man could make. "Aren't you willing to tell her the truth?"

"Why does this idea get everyone's knickers in a twist? I'm only trying to protect her," John exclaimed. *Why can't anyone see that this is for her own good?*

"Wouldn't it be easier to protect her if she knew that someone was trying to kill you?" Mick asked.

John's chest tightened at the intense fear he always felt when he thought of losing Caroline. "Mick, she doesn't want to be afraid. When we were in Burma, I held her sobbing in my arms, and she told me she wanted to feel safe again. If I tell her, it's hardly going to increase her sense of security, is it?"

"But John—" Mick began.

John cut him off with a gesture. "I don't want to lose her," he said, his voice terse.

"Well, it's your life, man," Mick said. "But believe you me, it's difficult to hold on to truth with lies. And if I were you, I wouldn't faff about deciding."

John rode with Mick to New Scotland Yard to oversee his assassin, deeply desiring to interrogate the man. Flashing his badge to the desk sergeant for the second time that day, John signed in and followed Mick to the detective assigned to the case.

"Detective Inspector Connors, I'm with the Security Services. I would like to interrogate your prisoner," John said, his voice carrying his authority.

DI Connors turned slowly from his desk, where he was enjoying his cup of tea, and glanced over John's shoulder to see Mick Adair standing behind. Reading Connors' face, John easily detected that the man did not like Mick. Checking in with Mick, John could see that Mick enjoyed the fact. *Brilliant!* John would have groaned, but he resisted the urge. *Caught between antagonists … and I need to interrogate this bloke.*

"I'm not clear … ah … Mr. Brock?" Connors' voice rose to question the validity of John's name. "As I said, I'm not clear on why a member of the

Security Services would be interested in a lowly Met case," Connors said, not even trying to camouflage his sarcasm.

"There is an active threat against an MI-5 officer, and we believe that this man has information that would be of interest to us." John neatly avoided the conflict of interest that arose from the fact that the threatened officer was himself.

"If ..." Connors paused and then drawled onward. "As I said, if I could verify that you are indeed who you say you are, then I could perhaps allow you to listen in. That's as far as I'm willing to go."

Handing over his identification for the detective's scrutiny, John agreed, suppressing his frustration. "Thank you, DI," John said.

Giving John a quick up-and-down before nodding, Connors settled back at his desk, sipping his tea. Mick wandered away. Connors carried on with his tasks for the next twenty minutes before finally motioning for John to follow him. Neatly boxing away his irritation, John arrived at the interrogation room with Connors, only to find it empty.

*No. This is not possible.* "Where is he?" John asked, a sense of foreboding descending on him.

Looking legitimately bewildered, Connors raised his hands palms-up to convey his ignorance. He called down to the front desk and then to Chief Inspector Perkins.

"He's already been released on his own recognisance," Connors informed John, looking as stunned by the news as John felt.

"What do you mean?" John felt his blood chill in his veins.

"His counsel appeared ... as I said, his counsel appeared with a writ from a judge ordering his release," Connors said.

"Who was the judge?" Grabbing Connors' arm, John demanded an answer, his control slipping minutely. "Who?"

"I don't know." Suddenly Connors seemed to shake himself alert. "But I will find out."

"Take my card," John insisted, handing over a simple business card with his name and his office number. "I have a few calls of my own to make."

Heeling about, John barely resisted the urge to storm from the building. Once outside, he called the Chairman of the JIC, Louis Trevena.

"I know what you're going to say, Brock, but it's legal and aboveboard,"

Trevena said. "There was no cause to arrest this man. Speeding and annoying a farmer are hardly reasons for incarcerating a man."

"Excuse me?" John protested. "The man shot at me." *How does the Chairman know so much about what's going on? And how did he learn it so quickly?*

"Can that be verified?" Trevena inquired.

"Of course! There were two members of the CTC present," John said. *And suddenly my word is not enough for you?*

The Chairman was silent for a time. "We'll look into it, Mr. Brock." And then he rang off.

John was livid, but he knew that losing control of his anger would serve no purpose. Instead, he froze his emotions to contain his fury. Frustrated and hoping for an escape from the day, John had Mick drop him at Thames House. He was desperate for some quiet time alone with Caroline to feel that there was still something right about his world.

Caroline impatiently awaited John's return from New Scotland Yard. He'd been gone for hours. She'd completed the Smythe report and bundled it together with her application for field training. Both were sitting on his desk.

Finally, he arrived, looking frustrated and dishevelled. *What on earth happened at the Yard?*

"Caroline," he began quietly. "We'll leave for home soon?"

Tenderness swept through her, but she clamped down on it. *I can't let him use my emotions against me.* "That report you wanted is on your desk. Once you're finished with it, I'm ready to go," she said. She heard him sigh as he turned to his office. *Hang tough,* she admonished herself. *He's just fine. He was only liaising with the guys at the Met. If I wait until he's not sad or angry or intense or worried or whatever, I'll never have the opportunity to do more than type reports.*

Minutes later, John walked out of his office. He handed her a crumpled sheet of paper. "Shred this, and we'll leave." His voice was tight, and his face was hard as he spoke. As she opened the document to place it in the shredder, she saw that it was her application for field training. *Oh no you don't, John Brock!*

"Shred it!" His voice was firm. Caroline scanned the room and saw that there were still four or five people around, too many to deal with this now without undermining John's authority. As tempting as that felt, Caroline had never embarrassed John in front of his staff, and she wasn't going to start now. *But later? Watch out!* Slowly, she flattened the sheet and put it through the shredder, and then she grabbed her purse and walked out through the security pods without once acknowledging her husband.

In the car, she waited for him to explain, but he didn't.

"Why—" she began, but he simply reached over and turned up the radio, George Harrison's "Isn't It a Pity" blasting through the car. "Fine!" she replied to his obvious evasion. *If that's the way he wants it. Fine. He thinks he can just "yes/no" me with no explanation! We'll see about that.*

Once home, she stormed upstairs and spent the next thirty minutes in the shower using up all the hot water in the tank. When she exited the bedroom, John was sitting at the dining table reading the evening newspaper. She heard him sigh as she stormed past. When he emerged from the bedroom a short time later, she was finishing a plate of scrambled eggs and a cup of coffee. She heard him sigh again, presumably because there was no supper for him and only an empty coffee pot. Her angry resolve began to weaken when she snuck a peek at him standing alone in the kitchen with his head bowed and his hands on his hips. *Well, maybe I should—*

Abruptly, he spun on his heel and sharply announced, "I'm going jogging. Do you want to come?" Reacting to the tone of his voice, she shook her head, refusing to speak to him. He took a deep breath, and Caroline saw something switch off in his face. "You are *not* going into the field," he said and then turned away, gathered the dog's leash, and departed.

# Chapter Three
## Secrets, Suspicions, Lies

Caroline was feeling grumpy, not at all enjoying being at odds with John. Three days of her silent treatment had made no change in his demeanour. *How does he do that? He just shuts down his emotions. And he's so stubborn! He absolutely refuses to back down. I don't know how to win an argument with him.* And to be honest, she missed him. When he went jogging, he stayed out longer and then followed up with what felt like hours in his workout room at home. Rather than sad or mad or contrite, he was just … distant. He held himself back from her behind some sort of shield. And she missed the intimacy. *He is an infuriating man!*

Ryan's arrival on the Grid interrupted Caroline's reflections, and his instant flirtations with the clerk gathering registry files set Caroline's teeth on edge, the young woman's responding giggles grinding along her grumpy nerves. Ryan scuttled off when John and Hibb arrived on the Grid.

John walked straight past her without looking, tapping twice on her desk. *Love you? Was that intentional or just a fluke?* Caroline sighed in irritation. *This is simply the most frustrating argument I've ever had. Nothing I do moves him.* They had only been married for a year and half, three months of which they'd spent escaping through a foreign country, and she was still learning … well, *him.* He was not like any man she had ever dealt with before, not like her father, her brothers, not like Henry. *Impossible man!* She rooted through her purse and retrieved two acetaminophen tablets. *I have such a headache!*

"Meeting room," John called out half an hour later, and the team trooped in behind him.

He opened the meeting by pinning his youngest officer to his chair with a glare. "Ryan, have we put the Plaza Bombers to bed?"

"Er, not quite. I thought we had enough evidence with the camera at Tiffany's, but Legal is saying it's not adequate." Ryan ducked his head. Caroline flinched internally at the mention of Ryan's op. *So they found someone else to do it anyway.*

"Did you check with Legal before you had the perpetrators arrested?" John asked.

"Er, well ..." Ryan muttered, immediately flushing red.

"Er, well ... no, I take it," John filled in sarcastically. "That was a rookie error, Ryan. From now on, you check with Hibb before you make any move on any suspects." John was silent until Ryan nodded. "Fix this. Immediately." John glared at Ryan until the younger officer finally realized his boss really meant *now* and scuttled from the room.

"John," Caroline said softly, laying her hand on his arm. "He is a rookie."

He turned to her and asked, "What's next?"

She sighed, replying, "The Summit."

John nodded. "The G20 is a recently reformulated group of the world's principal economic leaders. While the grouping has existed for over a decade amongst international finance ministers and bank governors, the heads of government began meeting in 2008 following the economic crisis. The upcoming Annual Summit of the G20 nations is to take place in Vancouver, British Columbia, Canada—" He cleared his throat, and Caroline smiled in spite of herself at the mention of home. "On September fourteenth and fifteenth. The PM and the Chancellor of the Exchequer will be attending. The DG has asked for a team to be assembled to provide security. Our role at the present time, however, is to conduct background checks on the deputy staff, which will be accompanying the Prime Minister and the Chancellor. Caroline and Aubrey, I'm afraid that unsavoury task will eventually fall to you. Anything else?" John asked Caroline.

"Aubrey has new phones for us," she replied.

Aubrey took over, rhyming off the technical, unintelligible reasons why they were each assigned a new mobile phone. John asked Jade for her final report on Smythe, congratulating her on a successful mission, before he dismissed the meeting.

Jade's return to the Grid signalled the end of the Smythe case, as it had been her undercover work that had finally resulted in his arrest by the Metropolitan Police Service, the Met. A stunning brunette of Serbian origin, Jade Kovic was confident, beautiful and bright, a deadly combination in any operative. She was neither thin nor stocky, and her body tapered elegantly from broad shoulders to a slender waist. She kept her dark brown hair cut short but stylishly shaped around her heart-shaped face. Her deep-set black eyes and full pale lips conveyed a look of intensity at all times.

Caroline remained behind after the meeting to speak to John, but he pre-empted her, his voice calm and pleasant.

"As lovely as it was to finally hear you speak to me, it doesn't help Ryan to be coddled," John said.

Annoyed by his unwillingness to even hear what she had to say before defending his treatment of the young agent, she pressed her lips into a grim line. "You're too hard on him. He is very young. He was an athlete, for goodness' sake, hired for his reckless willingness to try new things, not his attention to detail."

She harrumphed and left the meeting room, taking an excuse to return some files to the Registry, anything to get off the Grid for a few minutes. *Exactly what am I accomplishing here except to make myself miserable? Will I ever figure out how to get through to him?*

Releasing a long, sad sigh, she decided what she would do. *He doesn't seem to care whether or not I speak to him, so I might as well have my say and then put it aside. This pain in my heart isn't worth it.*

Back at her desk, she found one of her pink sticky notes on the top of her files with a message written in John's handwriting. She smiled to herself. He could be as immovable as a napping bison, but he truly was sweet. The note said, "Called away. Back Monday. Love You, John. YFA." *Yours Forever Always.*

"What?" Caroline exclaimed. *Called away? I can't believe it!* "I was only gone a few minutes. Horace Hibbert! Are you in here?" *John's gone? Without even saying goodbye?*

Hibb approached from the tea room. "What's wrong?"

"John's gone? Without an explanation?" she asked. In spite of her best attempts to sound reasonable, she knew she sounded as frustrated as she felt.

"Aye. It was an emergency, Caroline. He had to leave immediately," Hibb replied.

She lowered her voice, hoping a more calm approach would get her more information. "Where has he gone?"

Hibb shrugged, eyebrows raised. "Out of the country?"

She paled, exasperated. "I can't believe it."

Hibb cleared his throat. "Er. Hu-hmm. John asked me to tell you … ask you, I suppose he meant … not to walk the dog while he's away."

"Oh really," she replied sarcastically. *I can't believe it! We're in the middle of an argument and he just trots off to … I don't even know where he is! Aughh!*

That night, Hibb drove her home through the evening fog. The drive was interminable because he didn't know the shortcuts around the stadium traffic that John naturally used whenever there was a rugby game at Twickenham Stadium. Hibb seemed to take it all in stride. Caroline? Not so much.

"I'm sorry I canna invite you over for supper, but the girls have a dozen activities tonight. Katie and I are both on duty, and I'm not sure when *I'll* get to eat," Hibb said.

Hibb was a family man, a rarity in the Security Services. He had been happily married for twenty-three years to Katie, a petite and gentle woman of Korean heritage. They were the proud parents of six daughters. Caroline had once heard someone ask Hibb why he and his wife kept having children. Was he trying for a son? Hibb laughed a loud guffaw and asked why he needed a son. He was going to have such fun with the boyfriends presented to him by his six bonnie lasses. Perhaps, he wondered, his wife and he should try for another lass!

The car halted, interrupting Caroline's thoughts. "It's okay, Hibb. Thanks for the thought. I'll be fine," she said.

"He'll be back soon," Hibb said. He hesitated and then added, "Be safe."

Wondering at the uncharacteristic warning, Caroline stepped out of the car, entering the house to find Rufus excitedly welcoming her with his doggy tongue lolling and his chocolate-lab rear end wiggling a jig. She let him out into the backyard and then went upstairs to change into more comfortable clothes. Feeling too down to cook, she ordered Indian food, paying the exorbitant delivery charges because she hadn't yet become confident driving on the wrong side of the car on the wrong side of the road.

After a depressing meal in front of a boring movie, she decided to take Rufus for a walk to escape the loneliness of the house. Feeling very hard done by, Caroline pulled her hoodie on against the chilly damp of a London night and grabbed the dog's leash, letting them out the front door. She sighed wearily at the overgrown evergreens guarding the corners of the house. *No matter how many times I ask John to trim those bushes, he never does. I feel like I'm living in a piny fortress.*

Crossing the street, she led Rufus through the green space across from their house and to the walking paths beyond. She stopped to admire the silken spikes of the Rosebay Willowherb and the velvety petals of the purple lobelia scattered here and there through the longer grass. *It is nice to find some beauty here in the city. Oh, Father. What am I going to do about John? I can live here in the city. I can handle giving up the beauty and nature of home—but if John is gone, then what's the point? I hate this new compartmentalized man. I miss the closeness we shared when we were first married.*

Pulling to the right and barking, Rufus dragged her attention from the indigenous flora to her domesticated fauna, who was demonstrating very unusual behaviour for their usually obedient pup. As the barking increased, Caroline determined to return home, a sense of panic pushing at the edges of her mind. As she turned, the leash slipped from her fingers, and Rufus bolted like a fox for a hare.

"Rufus!" she called, taking two steps toward him and then retreating as a man in black appeared before her, hands outstretched. "No! What do you want?" she cried, backing away, real fear spiking through her belly. The man lunged and she ran, falling face down on the grass as he snared her ankle. She kicked back at his face but he caught her other ankle and flipped her, slapping her, light exploding behind her eyes. The assault angered her as much as it terrified her. She hated men who slapped women.

Snarling, Rufus returned, launching himself at the attacker, forcing a cry of alarm from his lungs. And then, suddenly, there were two men dressed in matching black suit jackets pulling her attacker from her. But even their combined efforts couldn't prevent the man's escape. As one man gave chase, the other approached her. He stood back to give her time to take hold of the dog's leash before completing the journey to the bench where she'd retreated.

"Are you all right, ma'am?" he asked, his voice deep and confident.

"Yes. I think so. How did … where did you come from?" she asked, her breath still coming in gasps, her nerves unsettled, her emotions fluttering between anger, fear and relief.

"We were passing and saw him grab you. Shall I call the police for you?" he asked.

"Yes, please," she confirmed.

"Is there someone else we can call for you?"

*Father, who do I call? John's away. Hibb?* She nodded at the man and then shook her head and nodded again. "Yes. A friend. I'll call." Caroline pulled out her cell phone and called Hibb.

"Caroline?" Hibb answered. His voice was immediately alert and wary.

"Hibb. I was mugged," she said. "I'm in the field across from the house. Some men helped me. Can you … do you think you could …"

"I'll be right there. Caroline, have you called the police?" Hibb asked.

"The men … one of them … he said he'd call," she said.

"Good. Stay right there. I won't be long," he said.

One of the men retrieved a thermos of coffee from his car that was parked nearby and gave Caroline a cup. The unsweetened brew was bitter, but the heat helped to calm her nerves. *It's lucky those men were nearby.* She stilled at the thought. *Why were they nearby? Why did that fellow have a thermos of coffee in his car?*

The police arrived soon after, and Caroline gave her statement to a constable whose name she never took in. Hibb arrived sometime later, spent a few minutes speaking to the men who'd saved her, and then escorted her and Rufus back across the street. So much danger so close to home.

"Caroline, I'd feel better if you'd pack a bag and spend the weekend with us," Hibb said. "Katie and the girls would love to see you."

"That's not necessary. It was just a mugging. Sure it scared me, but I'm okay," she replied.

"Katie will never forgive me if I don't bring you home. Spare a poor husband the wrath of his wife," Hibb said as though pleading with her. But she knew Katie better than that. Katie and Hibb were devoted to each other.

"Don't be ridiculous, Hibb. I'll stay here," Caroline said—quickly adding, as soon as she saw Hibb open his mouth to protest, "But I won't walk the dog again. Okay?"

Looking up, way up, she felt like she was watching the Friendly Giant's grumpy brother frown down at her. "Aye, all right. But please be careful, Caroline."

"I will," she replied.

Thrust from the closed coolness of the airplane, John was assaulted by the intensity of transition from rainy England to the humidity of South Asia. *Why was the humidity of Burma so much easier to tolerate than this?* Unfortunately, John's heart had an immediate answer: *Caroline was there with me.*

Stepping out of the Indira Ghandi International Airport in Delhi wearing his white long-sleeved khurta and dhoti, looking like he was clad in bleached pyjamas, John willed his persona to shift to that of his legend—a man with no wife, no beautiful wife who was angry and silent—and his sensory system to acclimate post-haste to the somatosensory overload that was India: the essence of curry, cow dung, wealth and poverty.

Today, he was Ugo Ducley, British born of an Indian mother and Italian father, a mole within Her Majesty's Home Office for the Devangari, reputedly the world's oldest intelligence agency. Ugo was MI-5's spyglass pointed directly at the heart of Indian intelligence.

Hailing an auto-rickshaw, John traveled to the Middle Circle where he caught the Metro to the Red Fort, continually assaulted by the olfactory chaos of the city, the exhaust from the morass of vehicles stinging his eyes and making his throat hurt. The vast structures of the fort, teeming with turrets and bastions, sat on the banks of the river Yamuna.

Like any tourist, John entered through the Lahore Gate and into the white marble of the Emperor's Hall of Audiences and on into the Hall of Wives and Mistresses, a palace crowned with gilded turrets, delicately painted and decorated with an intricate mosaic of mirrors. Exiting the palace, John scouted the area carefully, making his way around the Hayat Bakhsh Bagh, the "Life-Bestowing Gardens," to the location of the meet: the rear right dome of the Pearl Mosque, Moti Masjid, built for Alamgir, Conqueror of the World, the sixth Mughal Emperor of India.

Crouching in the shade of the smooth white stone wall, his mind wandered to the Great Game played by Kipling's *Kim*, born Kimball O'Hara but raised in the streets and bazaars of Lahore, India. Kim, the boy who had learned espionage at the feet of an English spy and self-sacrifice at the knee of a Tibetan Lama who was seeking escape from the Wheel of Things, the Buddhist cycle of birth, decay, death and rebirth. *Has the Game changed so very much from Kim's day to mine? We both walk the line between truth and lie, duty and betrayal. God, grant me the wisdom to know the difference.*

Early as usual, but not as early as John, Colonel Chandrakala arrived. John often wondered how, with the Colonel's height—he was hardly taller than Caroline—and his slight build, balding pate and dark, curved moustache, he could carry such threat. But he did. A wholly intimidating man, his black eyes held the glint of violence held tightly in check.

"Mr. Ducley. I am pleased to see you in the country again. You have news for me?" Colonel Chandrakala opened the conversation.

"I do, Colonel." John removed a flash drive, handing it over to the Colonel. "In three weeks, an attack will be launched by the JKLF on the head offices of the Bank of India here in Delhi and regional offices in Mumbai, London, New York, Paris, Tokyo, Hong Kong and Singapore. It is expected to be a coordinated attack. The mastermind, a Jaabir Jones of Birmingham, is here now, according to the MI-6 station in Delhi. I'm not certain how he slipped past you and into the country, but he is expected to remain here until the day before the attacks." The nationalist policies of the Jammu Kashmir Liberation Front called for a free Jammu and Kashmir—free from the governance and influence of both India and Pakistan.

Chandrakala's eyes flashed, but his body remained still. "You have done well, Mr. Ducley."

"Thank you, sir," John said.

"When do you next travel home?" Chandrakala asked.

"Home? This is my home, Colonel," John replied patriotically.

Chandrakala smiled without humour. "Britain then. We have word of a team of assassins hired out of Mumbai targeting a top man at MI-5. A surprising move. What do you know of this?"

*Ah, now this I want to hear.* "Very little, Colonel. What intelligence have you garnered about this plot? No penny-a-shot assassin is going to take on an intelligence agent."

Chandrakala studied John intently for a moment more before finally breaking away to gaze into the middle distance. "We believe the project to be affiliated with the redoubtable General Akram of the Naxalites."

*Interesting.* The Naxalites were Indian Maoist Communists operating along the Red Corridor of India on the eastern edge of the country. Considered a terrorist organization, they'd been recently named the greatest threat to Indian internal security.

John unconsciously quirked an eyebrow but then suppressed his facial expressions once again. "Do you know the name of the assassin?"

"Not as yet," Chandrakala said. "This is what you will assist us with. Ducley, find me the names of both the assassin and the target."

*I was hoping Chandrakala would know more. This news about Akram is very interesting, though.* "Of course, sir. I will be returning to the UK within the week."

"Tomorrow," Chandrakala said.

"Yes, sir," John agreed.

"Very good, Ducley."

John shook the man's hand and touched his forehead in respect. "Until we meet again."

"*Namaste.*"

John endured the transit squish of the bus back to the Middle Circle. His mission complete, his mind travelled back home. *Caroline is so angry with me. She's never given me the silent treatment before. I find I don't much like it.* Stepping down, he planned to take a taxi but halted his hail when he noticed a battered blue Vespa motor scooter approaching him. He'd seen it outside the Red Fort, and here it was again. Oddly, the driver wore a black helmet with a concealing tinted visor. Most people here didn't wear any kind of helmet.

Abruptly turning on his heel, John walked swiftly in the opposite direction, drawing closer to the Vespa, hoping to gain some useful information as to the driver's intent and identity. The Vespa continued on its way, not acknowledging any interest in him. *My imagination is getting carried away with all this talk of assassins.* In the pursuit of surety, John slipped into a restaurant, a Ruby Tuesday, requesting a table by the wall where he could see out the front window but not be easily viewed from outside. He perused the menu with half his attention as he surveyed the street for the Vespa.

Placing his order, he began to relax … until the blue scooter raced back into view. John didn't need any other evidence of hostile intent. He fled, striding through the steam-filled cacophony of the kitchen, ignoring the chef's protests, bursting out the delivery entrance, and jogging to the end of the alley, peering around the corner.

Brake lights engaging, the blue Vespa halted at the large bay window of the Ruby Tuesday John had vacated only a moment ago. While the driver was occupied scanning the restaurant, John strode along the street, as inconspicuously as possible, dodging both dogs and the homeless living the harsh realities of poverty beneath tarps strung across the sidewalks. Passing a particularly large tent structure, John spun to the left, brushing past a woman exiting a flat of apartments. Racing up the central stairs to the next floor, John paused, watching and listening for following footsteps. He heard none. *It couldn't be that simple, could it?*

An elderly gentleman stepped out of his door, and John, pushing past, strode through the man's flat and then climbed out the open window to the fire escape. A visual sweep of the alley behind the flats revealed no immediate menace in the form of a blue Vespa. However, John did not yet relax. Climbing up the fire escape to the roof, he jumped across the space between the buildings, one and then the next, descending by the fire escape, checking carefully around corners before jumping out to hail a nearby taxi. *Free and clear.*

Disembarking at the local bazaar, he moved from the crowded streets lined with people, cars, bullocks, carts, rickshaws and any other conveyance of the modern day and days past into the claustrophobic crush of the market. Immediately, he was surrounded by a kaleidoscope of colour, a symphony of sound and a bouquet of fragrances. *Ah, the real India: beauty and claustrophobia.* John smiled as he began to relax, walking up and down the stalls, employing the age-old counter-surveillance techniques perfected during the Cold War. He could detect no pursuit. *If only I could avoid my feelings as easily. What do I do about Caroline? I tried to apologize with the song on the radio, but it only seemed to aggravate her.*

Drawn toward the silks of one stall, John caught the eye of a woman beneath a palmyra umbrella, sitting in a rickety, obviously long-in-use wooden chair, her long, shiny black locks pulled back into a single braid lending maturity to her young face. Gracing him with a perfect white smile, she laid before him a deep blue length of silk adorned with pale pink roses and trimmed in gold thread. On the top, she placed five golden bangles.

She addressed him in Hindi. "Sahib, for your beautiful wife."

John's startled gaze darted to the woman's face, studying it for intrigue but finding only desire … a desire for profit. He pointed out the blue silk sari and the golden bangles and, in a totally uncharacteristic move, bought them for his beautiful wife, not considering the risk of any personal action taken whilst he was undercover, only considering the pleasure it would give Caroline, a moment of rebellion against the constraints of spying.

Moving past the next stall, he spied a small elephant made of kadam wood, hand-carved by the little man behind the man who was working the cash. The trunk of the little elephant was raised and curled, a symbol of good fortune, and the fine carving showed the eyes, ears, nose and tusks, as well as the pattern of a fine howdah blanket and cap. The little creation fit in the palm of John's hand. He purchased it. He wouldn't tell Caroline where he'd been, but maybe he could give her a little hint. It would be worth it if it would get her to speak to him again.

More relaxed now, his hunger belatedly piqued by the savoury odours of Ruby Tuesday, John bought a curry nestled on a chapatti from a woman crouching beside a fire at the bazaar. He ate it with his fingers before making his way to the airport. Finally, he found himself on the airplane. Only eight hours and he'd be back with Caroline. *Except, what exactly is waiting for me?*

Rufus's dance at the front door told Caroline that John was home, and before long her husband did indeed appear at the top of the stairs. Rufus seemed to immediately pick up on the tension in the room, wandering off to lie on the rug, his head on his paws, a mournful look in his eyes.

"Hi. Everything all right?" John asked, a cautious smile briefly flitting across his face. "Did you have a safe weekend?"

Unable to control her angst, she exploded verbally. "Don't you ever do that to me again! Do you understand? Don't you ever leave the country without telling me! You don't leave the country. Don't leave the city. Don't leave the *building* without telling me. Ever again!"

His eyes widened as though she'd taken him by surprise. And he sounded contrite as he apologized. "It was urgent."

"John," she warned.

He slumped down onto the couch beside her … but not too close. "I should have found you. I'm truly sorry. I didn't think." He subsided into silence, his smile absent from his deep brown eyes, his face growing blank to hide his emotions. It was never a good thing when he hid his emotions from her. "I guess you're still angry with me," he said, and she could hear the piteous sorrow in his voice.

"I guess so," she said. "I want to talk about field training."

He sighed morosely. "I thought that argument was finished."

She furrowed her brows. "How could it be finished when we never discussed it?"

John groaned. "I just got home. I don't want to argue," he said, clearly exasperated. "What made you even ask in the first place?"

"I heard Ryan and Alexa talking in the tea room and it just made me feel … oh, I don't know, useless. They risk their lives for other people, and all I do is answer phones and type reports." Her voice lost energy as she spoke.

John's face was thoughtful as he asked, "Is that all you do?"

She shook her head and sighed. "No. I know that my job is necessary to help you do your job, to help you make decisions that save people's lives. I guess it just hurt my pride to think that the others saw me as a 'do-nothing,' just the boss's wife." She bowed her head in part sadness and part chagrin.

"Doesn't my life count?" he asked gently.

She looked up in surprise. "What do you mean?"

"You say the others risk their lives to save people. Don't I count? You risked your life to save me twice. You rescued me from the prison when I was unconscious. I still don't know how you managed it. Then you gave up your chance at freedom to stay with me and nurse me back to health. And then when Li and his soldiers took me, you came for me and rescued me. I know you still have nightmares about that …" He paused, brushing his fingertips lightly along her jaw. Resting his arm along the back of the couch, he leaned closer to her. "And you did so much more than that. You showed me that my life had meaning apart from my job. You showed me that God knew me, the real me, and loved me anyway. In my opinion, you could sit in our home watching television for the rest of your life, and you would still accomplish more than Ryan, with his vastly superior opinion of himself, or any of the others expect to accomplish in their entire careers."

"John, I would do it all again, you know," she said, quietly affirming her commitment to him.

She was surprised by the relief she saw in his eyes but quickly forgot her reaction as he leaned over to kiss her. *Mmmm.* His warm breath feathered her cheek as he kissed a line from the right corner of her mouth to her ear. Then he gently turned her head to reach her left cheek. *Ouch!* She flinched at the pressure on her cheekbone.

Drawing back in surprise, John reached to the lamp beside the couch, flipping it on and studying her face, his voice tight as he saw the bruise.

"What's this?" he ground out.

Instinctively, she knew that her explanation was going to cause an argument. "I was mugged," she answered slowly. "I was walking Rufus in the green space across the street—"

"You walked the dog? I told you not to!" He sounded furious, and she just didn't understand.

"What do you mean you *told* me not to? Was there some agreement I signed that made me your obedient servant rather than your wife? And why are you so angry? I know you said not to bother. Well, you told Hibb to tell me not to. Thanks for that, by the way." Sarcasm tasted bitter in her mouth. "And frankly, I took it as advice, not an order. Since you don't follow my orders, I don't see why I have to follow yours." His face was grim and he didn't respond, so she continued, filling the silence. "I've walked the dog alone before when you've been away. Why are you so mad?"

She watched him calm himself, slowing his breathing and wiping away the expressions from his face.

"I'm not angry with you. I'm merely upset that you were hurt," he replied evenly.

Abruptly, she pushed him away, standing up. "I don't understand your reaction. There is something you're not telling me. You promised that you would never lie to me, John. Have you forgotten?"

Standing up, he stepped toward her, stopping dead when she held up a hand of warning. His control slipped, anguish darting across his visage.

"I've forgotten nothing," John assured her, his voice intense.

And then he began to fidget with his clothes, and she watched him in confusion. *What on earth is he doing?* Finally, he produced from his front right pocket a carving of an elephant. Tentatively, he held it out to her.

"I bought this for you," he said. "While I was away."

"For me?" she asked. *He thought of me. He actually thought about me while he was away on a mission.* So maybe his life wasn't as compartmentalized as she sometimes felt. "Oh, John. Thank you." Tears welled up in her eyes.

"You're not going to cry, are you? I thought you would like it," John said, clearly distressed by her tears.

"It's my elephant, and I'll cry if I want to," she said, stomping her foot.

His face contorted and she froze, preparing for his response … until he burst out laughing. "I'm not certain that's how the song really goes."

He opened his arms to her, and she walked into his embrace. Pulling her close against him, he held her so tightly she could barely breathe. "I, er, didn't like being away knowing you were unhappy with me," he said, murmuring the words against her hair.

Then he kissed her lightly, tracing the shape of her mouth so that she could taste the coffee and cashews he'd consumed earlier. Pressing closer, she sunk her fingers into his hair, tilting his head in order to deepen the kiss.

Clearly feeling the changed emotion in the room, Rufus moved closer, pushing between them, lifting his canine head, arching it almost backwards to reach up to John's hand, his doggy body bouncing and wiggling around until John and Caroline had no choice but to give him some attention. Laughing at the dog's antics, they broke apart.

"I am glad you're home," she said.

"Home," John said, looking thoughtful. "You know, I never had *home* before you. This was only a place I slept … when I could sleep."

"Well, welcome home," she said.

He smiled. "Would you like to go out for supper?"

"No. Well, yes. John, you can't just kiss me and hope to avoid every difficult topic," she said.

"What if I kiss you like this?" he said and pulled her against him, one hand on her hip and one buried in her hair, cradling her head. He seared her mouth with a kiss of longing, a kiss of love and passion, a kiss that made her toes curl. Linking her arms around his neck, she opened herself to his exploration, holding nothing back.

When he finally pulled back, she had to steady herself by gripping his arms. "That will definitely buy you some indulgence," she said, her voice husky.

He nuzzled her cheek as his fingertips traced circles on her back. "Supper?" he said, his other hand sliding down her arm to finger her wedding ring.

*I wish I knew what he was thinking.* "Okay," she said, following him to the car, her little elephant still in her hand. She sat in silence for a time as he drove them east along Twickenham Road through Richmond and Hammersmith. Finally, she realized that he wasn't going to be forthcoming with any new information. "If I ask you what happened, will you tell me?"

"I don't want to argue with you," he replied, and he sounded so weary. She could see his wretched reflection in the rearview mirror.

"It's not an argument if you simply tell me about your day," she said.

"Caroline," he protested.

"Why won't you tell me anything?" she protested right back at him.

"Look at the elephant," he murmured.

"Why?"

"Please."

She studied the intricate carving. "It's Indian." Meeting his gaze, she said, "You were in India?"

He didn't respond. "Caroline, look over there, a Ruby Tuesday," he said. He was very subdued.

"That's nice, sweet," she responded. "Not a very subtle redirection."

He still hadn't looked at her. "Would that do for supper?" he asked.

"O-kay." She sighed. "But, John, why Ruby Tuesday?"

He seemed to struggle for a time, looking off into the middle distance. And then he capitulated. "I was in one in Delhi. Yesterday. The food smelled great, but I couldn't stay to eat."

"Thank you, John," she said, and emotion choked her. *A tiny piece of classified information, a little progress.*

"Don't cry," he said, sounding so mournful that she actually laughed.

"What am I going to do with you, Bernard John Brock?" she asked.

He shrugged and looked so sad and forlorn that she simply took him by the hand and led him into the restaurant. After a rib-eye steak and a chicken Florentine, the waitress offered coffee or tea, and they declined both. Tea, the English made with supreme skill. Coffee? Not so much.

"Would you make a pot when we get home? Cream and two sugars?" John asked her quietly.

"Double-double? Sure," Caroline replied, smiling. She scanned his features, suddenly concerned. "You're looking a little grey," she said. "Are you okay?"

"Hmmm. Sort of. My stomach's a bit wobbly. Maybe we should head off," John said.

"Really? Do you think you could make it to dessert?" she said. "I was hoping to share a Death by Chocolate."

"I'm not certain," he said.

"John, honey, you're sweating an awful lot," she said. "Are you—"

He lurched to his feet, cutting her off. "I need to be sick," he said, his voice urgent and tight.

She raced around the table, reaching for him. He propped himself on her shoulders. Just at that moment, the waitresses and waiters arrived with cake, candles and a cheery birthday song for a nearby customer.

"You need to empty … my stomach." Confused, she couldn't understand why he said that, and with the song ringing in her ears, she couldn't process a question to ask him.

Pushing off her shoulders, John lurched to the waiter carrying the cake, grabbing his lapels, chocolate frosting flying.

"Belt *up*!" John said.

The shock on the waiter's face brought Caroline to John's side again as he began to tilt. She struggled to support him around the chest as he slumped against her.

"Stomach," John murmured as he slipped to the floor.

"John? John!!" *Oh, Father. Father. Help us.* Alarmed, Caroline turned to the others beginning to look and watch and whisper, choosing one among the crowd. "You. Call 911. No! Call 999. Now!"

As the woman she had pointed to quickly pulled out her phone and dialled the triple nines, Caroline leaned over to check on John. His carotid pulse was fast and his breathing sounded tight. Turning him onto his side, she forced him to throw up before he slipped into unconsciousness. He lost his steak, salad and guacamole onto the dining-room floor. The customers squealed and shrieked. *Oh, shut up, you morons!* She rolled John away from the mess. A waitress came over offering a tablecloth as a blanket, and Caroline draped it over John's body. She grabbed a sweater off the back of a neighbouring chair to fold and place under his head and then quickly changed her mind and placed it under his feet instead.

"John, baby. Wake up, darling," she said, beseeching him. As she brushed the hair back from his face, his eyes fluttered in response to her touch. His colour was improving; he looked faintly beige now instead of grey.

"I'm a doctor," a stranger announced and knelt beside John, rolling him onto his back and checking his pulse. The doctor reached into his bag and pulled out a syringe, loading it from an opaque glass phial. Suddenly, two men in black jackets arrived. One man grabbed the syringe and phial from the doctor's hand as the other socked him in the face.

"What are you doing?!" Caroline hollered at them. "Stop!" She couldn't understand their actions. The first man quickly subdued the so-called doctor, pinning him to the floor of the restaurant. Caroline reached for the second man who had pocketed the syringe and phial. "Who are you?" she demanded to know.

"A friend," he replied mysteriously.

The arrival of the paramedics ended the discussion, and soon Caroline was forced back as the professionals knelt down and set to work, examining John and calling in the details. As they strapped John to the gurney and wheeled him away to the ambulance, Caroline turned to the second man.

"If you're my friend, take me to the hospital," she said. He looked to his companion, who gave him the nod and then nodded at her. She gave him the keys to their C30 and he drove her to West Middlesex University Hospital, disappearing again once he'd escorted her to the waiting room. Caroline found a quiet corner and prayed for her husband.

"Mrs. Brock?"

Caroline rose and approached the doctor. "How is he?" she asked, wiping the tears from her eyes.

"Your husband is going to be fine," he assured her. "We believe he suffered food poisoning. We've pumped his stomach and done an EKG, and everything looks good. We've given him something to help him sleep, and I think it best that he stay overnight. He'll be fine in the morning. He may need a bland diet for a few days until his body tells him he's ready to eat normally again."

"But we shared the food. How could he be so ill and yet I'm fine?" she asked. The doctor merely shrugged. She searched his eyes, but there was no more information forthcoming. "Can I see him?" she asked.

"Of course," the doctor said.

Following a nurse, Caroline stepped into John's hospital room. *Oh, baby. Father, he looks so weak and vulnerable.* His colour was better, but he still looked pale. She hadn't seen him sick or injured since the Chin village in Burma where she'd nursed him back to health after the brutal torture he'd suffered there. The feelings of those unhappy days washed over her.

Pulling up a chair, she leaned over to stroke the hair from his forehead and kiss him there. He muttered unintelligibly in response but remained asleep.

"Maybe I don't mind so much if you won't tell me anything. I'm just glad you're okay," she said, even though she knew he couldn't hear her.

Settling beside him, she rested one hand on his hip and twined the fingers of her other hand with his, which seemed to instinctively grasp hers. She stayed with him through the night.

John woke to his wife's muffled cries of distress. Opening his eyes, he saw the stark white walls of what could only be a hospital room. Glancing down the length of the bed, he saw Caroline asleep with her head resting on the bed beside his hip. She was whimpering in obvious distress. Ever since he'd started going on missions again, about six months after they'd settled in London, she had been having nightmares, a variety of visions of the soldiers' pursuit in Burma.

John reached down to gently stroke her hair. *Oh baby. Will I ever be able to make you feel safe again?* He used his thumb to wipe away a tear from her cheek.

She startled awake. "Where?"

"The soldiers?" he asked, gesturing for her to sit on the bed. She did, leaning forward to hug him around the shoulders. "'The Lord is my shepherd,'" he whispered in her ear. She nodded, stroking her cheek against his cheek and neck.

"Will this ever go away?" she asked mournfully.

He nodded. "In time." He set his palm flat against her chest. "You have a tender heart. You were simply not made for brutality." He pulled her down against him and kissed her forehead.

"Hu-hmmm." Aubrey cleared his throat to make his presence known. Caroline sat up, but John took her hand so she remained sitting on the bed. "Well, stone the crows, you look positively shattered!" Aubrey said. John didn't respond, blanking his gaze.

"He's doing much better," Caroline replied, glancing slowly between John and Aubrey and then finally resting her gaze on Aubrey. "They said it was food poisoning, but we shared our food."

"The guacamole dip?" Aubrey inquired. John remained silent, narrowing his eyes at the other man. *Keep your trap shut, old man.*

"No, I suppose not. We each had our own. How did you know?" She looked up in suspicious curiosity.

Aubrey shrugged as though any genius could have deduced the source. "He'll be fine now."

"What about the two men in black jackets?" she asked him.

John gestured to Aubrey, giving him a clear message: get out before you give it away. Aubrey just shrugged in response. Caroline murmured in disbelief. "The doctor?" she asked. When Aubrey didn't answer, she turned to John. "The doctor?"

"How am I meant to know?" John said, sounding more defensive than was wise. "I was unconscious, if you remember."

"Aubrey—" she began, but John cut her off.

"Goodbye, Aubrey," John said. He sent a clear warning that any word or deed that made Caroline angry with John would result in Aubrey's slow and painful demise.

"Good day," Aubrey said and departed abruptly.

"John? What is going on?" she said.

"Can you help me to the loo?" John asked instead of answering her question.

"Aargh! It's a good thing you're sick, or I'd crack you over the head," she said. He gazed back at her with an expressionless face. *Don't let her see you sweat.*

"Fine. Come on," she said, wrapping her arm around his shoulders to lever him up and out of the bed.

A low groan escaped him. *Blimey, my chest hurts.*

She kissed him on the temple. "Oh, sweetheart. How are you feeling?" she asked.

"Blaah," he replied, uncharacteristically using one of her exclamations. "My muscles are stiff, my throat hurts and my stomach feels like it's doing a slow waltz. Other than that, I'm just peachy."

She chuckled, and he would have been annoyed except that it was so good to hear her laugh. He let her help him to the toilet and back again, but rather than getting into bed, he immediately retrieved his clothes and dressed.

"Are you sure you're ready to go home?" she asked.

"Mmhmm," he replied. "Could you please fetch the nurse with my discharge papers?"

"Are you sure?" she asked again.

"Yes," he said firmly. "I want to get out of here," he said. *I want to get you out of any place public enough to be dangerous for you.*

"Then will you tell me what the heck is going on," she said.

Her question took him by surprise. Frantically, he searched for a way to put her off the track. "What did the doctor say?" John asked.

"Food poisoning. You know that," she said. "But who was the doctor at the restaurant—"

"I don't remember any doctor," John replied. *You mean medici mortis and his death-tipped syringe?*

"John," she said, warning in her voice.

"I just want to go home," he said, turning his back on her in frustration. *Why won't she just trust me to keep her safe?*

"Aargh! You can be so infuriating at times," she exclaimed.

He pled exhaustion. "I need to go home and get some sleep," he said, his emotions once more tucked away. She was silent as he finished dressing, and then while he signed his discharge papers. *I am more than ready to leave this hospital room.*

"John," she said, and he gave her some kind of noncommittal response. "Do you still love me?"

"What?" Shocked, he spun to face her, pushing aside the dizziness that assaulted him at the sudden movement. "Yes, I love you. I love you more than my own life."

"Then what is going on?" she asked, her voice strident and high. "Where is the man I married?"

*What?* "I don't know what you mean. I love you, Caroline. More than the very breath I breathe," he said.

"More than your job?" she said quietly.

"Yes," he replied. "A thousand times, yes. Why are you doing this to me?" *Please don't doubt me. I can stand anything the world throws at me but not the loss of your trust.*

“Me? Why are you doing this to me? I miss you,” she said, and she began to cry.

His heart twisted in his chest. *Father, help me.* “I’m right here.” He reached for her and she came into his arms. “Can we please hold off on this until tomorrow?” *Or never.* “I really need to sleep.”

“I’ve waited and I’ve waited,” she said, and she sounded so weary and sad.

“Please just give me a little time. But, Caroline?” He brushed the hair back from her face, holding her tenderly. “Never doubt my love for you.”

“I miss you,” she repeated.

“I don’t know what that means. I’m right here,” he insisted.

“No. No, you’re not. Only a part of you is here.”

## Chapter Four
# The Mistakes of My Past

MARYN DALE KEYED IN the prearranged number and spoke the password to reach Tor Grendahl.

"Five-two-nine-one," he answered the call.

"Three-seven-eight," she replied. "Update Badger."

"Three fails."

"Reason?" Maryn's agitation spoke through her voice. *Three botch jobs? Is it possible?*

"Counter-surveillance on two. Lack of accurate intelligence on one. Didn't know he was out of the country. Gave the wife a scare."

"You gormless—Pah! Intelligence," she said with derision, altering the semantics of the word. "Clearly lacking! Akram will be disappointed," she warned.

"We need more direct intelligence, up close and personal."

"I'll see what I can do." Maryn rang off.

Three failed attempts. There was something dodgy here. *It's almost as though he's been warned.* Tor Grendahl was reputed to be one of the best, the "Carlos the Jackal" of the twenty-first century. If his little minions couldn't get the job done, she might need to splash out, raise a little capital, and hire the man himself to do the job.

Moving to the large bay window of the flat, Maryn gazed out over the city of Beijing, the panorama of lights sparkling brightly in the midnight air.

In the distance, she could just see the lights on the pavilions and temples of the Summer Palace.

Long before she was prepared to return to bed, Maryn felt a warm body behind her. Calloused hands slid down her arms and back up, abruptly pulling her back against the body of Colonel Shing.

"Hsin darling, I do wish you would keep your hands to yourself." She propelled her elbow into his girth and was rewarded with a grunt of irritation.

"What keeps you awake, *Wūyā*?" Colonel Shing asked in Mandarin, using the term of endearment Maryn despised: Raven, as though she were some comic-book character.

Maryn responded in kind. "*Huān*."

"Badger? Brock!" Shing said the name as vitriolic acid. "His capture has not been accomplished?"

"We don't want him captured, my pet, we want him dead. And if you don't lighten your grip on me, your death will also occur prematurely." From Maryn, no threat was a joke.

"I want him captured," Shing insisted. "Information is still leaking out of China."

"What? Information that you're conducting espionage against your allies?" Maryn said.

"Semantics." Shing lightened his grip, stepping back and to the side. He was finally growing cautious. "You arranged it with that fool Akram?" he asked.

"You know I did, Hsin," she said.

She sensed him watching her warily for a few more minutes, and then he returned to bed, muttering hotly along the way.

"I did," she mumbled, remembering well the journey to the little compound on the eastern edge of India that she and her man, Sonam Narayan, the Tibetan she had rescued from a Chinese laogai, had made. She remembered the little cinder-block house and well-groomed tennis courts, illuminated with stadium lighting. Chuckling viciously, she also remembered the transparent fear of Akram's mistress after Maryn had tied her to the foot post of the bed, ensuring that her terrified eyes met him as he opened the door.

"Was that really necessary, Maryn?" Akram had asked as he'd stepped over to the younger woman, pulling out his dagger to cut the bonds that

Maryn had attached to the young woman's wrists and ankles. He'd removed the cloth gag from her mouth and pulled her to his chest, murmuring comfort while keeping his eyes always on Maryn Dale.

"You her punter, Qasim? Or is she the scrubber? And Pakistani? An unusual choice for an Indian Communist."

Akram had forced the girl's head up to meet his eyes. "Aarya. Aarya!" He had demanded the young woman listen to his words. "Aarya, go and make some tea. Now." Still shaking from the shock, she'd nodded, her eyes beseeching him. But he'd insisted and she'd left. Only then had he turned to Maryn. "Was there something you wanted or did frightening my mistress provide enough entertainment?"

"Well," she'd begun, sauntering over to face him, stretching her arms upward as though in exhaustion, watching Akram's eyes trace her curves. "It was fun, but that's not why I've come. Are you still interested in John Brock?"

"Is that the Englishman who escaped you in Myanmar, my beauty?" Akram had stepped forward, placing his hands loosely on Maryn's hips. She'd thrust her pelvis toward him, tracing one fingernail lightly around his ear, noting the shiver that passed through his frame.

"If you had been with me, we would have succeeded. I did the best I could with the rubbish that Shing provided. I ask again, Qasim, are you interested?"

Slipping his hand to the small of her back, he'd pressed against her. "I have only your word for it that he has any intelligence that may be used against me."

Maryn had lithely reached to his waist, removing his dagger and planting it against the fly of his trousers, enjoying the velocity of his retreat. "You doubt my word?"

He'd quickly gathered himself into a look of confidence again, but he'd kept his distance. "What do you want? Tell me plainly."

"You're new here, aren't you?" A sultry voice addressed the top of Caroline's head where she sat at her desk.

Distracted, Caroline replied without looking up. "Hmm? Fairly. Can I help you?" *Go away! I have enough to think about with my husband keeping secrets from me.*

"Perhaps. I'm looking for John Brock. Do you know where he is?"

Caroline raised her eyes to meet the gaze of one of the most stunning women she had ever seen. The woman was tall, only a few inches shorter than John, with raven locks shimmering in the fluorescent lights and an intense look in her deep grey eyes that belied the nonchalant timbre of her voice. Slim and curved in all the right places, the woman wore an alluring sleeveless lavender chiffon dress adorned with black roses across the bodice, an amethyst pendant, and matching bracelet and earrings. This was Maryn Dale, MI-6 operative, suspected traitor, former lover of John Brock.

All the air was squeezed from Caroline's lungs. Before even attempting to speak, she drew in a steadying breath. "I believe John is meeting with the Home Secretary," she replied, forcing the words past the lump of anger now forming in her throat. *Why are you here? To see John? My husband, John.*

"Do you know John well?" Maryn asked. "I suppose you must if you work for him. I heard he's gotten himself a piece on the side, brought her in as his secretary because she's ... let me think. What did I hear? Thick as two short planks."

Caroline flushed with a red-hot blaze at the commentary on her abilities, a commentary so like her own recently fed insecurities. Her retort was cut off by the arrival of John and Hibb through the pods.

Maryn floated gracefully over to John, stroking her hand up along his arm as she leaned in to kiss him. Clenching her fists in vexation, Caroline heard the papers crunching in her hand, and part of her mind wondered how she was going to explain the damaged document to Nigel in Registry. *My husband's gorgeous former lover showed up and called me stupid?*

Caroline glanced over, but John's face was blank. He stood there. He just stood there while Maryn kissed him on the cheek. And then he invited her into his office? Passing by without a glance at Caroline. *No! Oh no! This is not happening!*

When Hibb closed the door behind John and Maryn, Caroline was stunned, motionless but not emotionless. *Why now, Father? This is too hard for me.*

What was happening on the other side of that door? What secrets would he keep from her this time?

John was shocked. He'd walked through the pods and there was Maryn

Dale, leaning up to kiss him, smelling like…? He paused to consider. A toxic lover. There was nothing John remembered fondly about his time with Maryn. But duty came before personal feelings. Tucking his emotions behind a professional mask, he let her kiss him on the cheek and then led the way into his office. He walked straight past Caroline because he knew that if he stopped to look at her, he'd be tempted to fall on his knees and thank her for loving him. At the last minute, John motioned for Hibb to follow him. There was no way he was meeting with Maryn Dale alone.

Without introduction, John began. "What can I do for you, Maryn?" He wanted to get this encounter over with as soon as possible, and then he was going to take Caroline out for lunch and tell her how much he loved her, how grateful he was that she loved him … even if she thought that a piece of him was missing, whatever that meant.

"I dropped by, John, to see if you were well after your misfortune in Myanmar." The words were clearly meant as a threat. She smiled as she said them but the smile didn't reach her eyes. When Maryn moved toward John, he passed behind Hibb and took up his usual place, standing behind his desk.

"Thank you, Maryn. Your concern is always welcome," John said in a tone that implied it never was. "I've survived quite well as you can see. I've come out of Burma with more than I ever imagined possible." *Caroline. Salvation. Love.*

"I hear the government is trying to gain some political capital with the elections there. Perhaps you'll be able to return and meet up with some old friends," Maryn said. There, again, was the threat. Maryn could use the most benign words to threaten you.

A rap on his office door pulled John's attention away from the cold darkness of Maryn's stare.

"Come," he said. Before he'd finished the word, Caroline strode in. He smiled at her but she met his gaze with steel in her eyes. *Uh oh! What's happening here?*

"Who is this, John?" Caroline asked, stepping forward and offering her hand to Maryn.

He hesitated, uncertain how to read his wife's behaviour. "Er, Caroline, this is Maryn Dale, MI-6 operative. Maryn, this is Caroline. My wife," John replied.

Nonplussed, Maryn held Caroline's hand for a split second and then abruptly released it. "Oh, it's you. The secretary."

John watched fire ignite in his wife's gaze. *Poor Caroline.* Her every thought was written in capital letters on her face. "She is my administrative assistant," John clarified, knowing that the title *secretary* seemed to bother Caroline for some reason.

"Ah," said Maryn. "Assistant." And John almost heard the hiss of a serpent in the word. He shook his head to shift the thought. Maryn continued, "Will she be traveling with you to Myanmar? Or perhaps you would need someone with a little more … experience."

Okay, now Caroline was really going to lose it. He needed to end this encounter PDQ.

"At the present time, there aren't any plans," John said. "Thank you for your concern, though. Was there anything else? We actually do have work we need to accomplish today."

A brief flash of annoyance at being dismissed crossed Maryn's features, but she quickly hid it behind a shake of her head, her raven hair swirling around her shoulders. She turned to leave the office, stopping with her hand on the door frame and turning back. Obviously not getting the reaction she was seeking, Maryn let loose one last verbal jab before she left. "Well, cheerio! Keep a close eye on him, *Catherine.* He has a tendency to wander."

Clenching her teeth in blatant irritation, Caroline responded with a grace that John could see clearly impressed Hibb where he stood by the door. Truth be told, it impressed John as well.

"I always enjoy keeping an eye on John," she said. Then Caroline actually managed to smile—smile!—at the wicked Maryn Dale.

Clearly annoyed, Maryn departed in a flounce, and Hibb followed her out, escorting her to and through the pods. John closed his office door behind them.

He turned to Caroline, exclaiming, "You are a wonder to me." But before he could finish the phrase, she slapped him on the chest.

"What?" he asked, shocked by her behaviour.

"Burma?! Burma, John? You are *not* going to Burma!" She advanced on him. He retreated a step in the face of her fury. "Do you not remember what they did to you there? Don't you remember?!" She shoved him and his back met the wall. "I remember. I remember what they did to you!" She clasped the fabric of his shirt, hauling at the material. "Should I show you what they did? The scars on your back? Should we take an X-ray to count your broken ribs?"

He grabbed her fisted hands, trying to remove them from his clothes. "Caroline! Stop! Caroline, you're hurting me!"

She stopped abruptly at his words, backing away, squeezing her arms around her body. *What is going on here?*

"You are *not* going to Burma," she said, dark heat lacing her voice. "I won't let you go."

"Won't let me go?" His independent heart rebelled. "I don't answer to you operationally. You have no say in what operations I am assigned or where I am asked to travel!" The chill in his voice had thawed and fired to an angry white flame by the end of the sentence.

"Oh no?" she asked. Her thoughts seemed disordered, clearly angry but disorganized. "How could you let something like this happen?"

*Okay, okay. This is getting out of hand. She has no right to speak to me in that manner! I won't stand for being treated like some*—But he never got to finish his thought, because Caroline was clearly nowhere near the finish line of this conversation.

"What is Maryn Dale doing in London anyway? Visiting you? Why has she not been arrested, the treacherous cow? How can she get away with what she's done? She arranged with a Chinese colonel to have you abducted and tortured in Burma." Caroline stood toe to toe with him. "Have you even spoken with the DG? You know, your boss, the Director-General of MI-5, Sir William Jacen?"

"I'm aware of the man's name and title," he replied coldly.

"Or maybe you don't really want to," she said.

*Now what is that supposed to mean?* "That's enough, Caroline. Calm yourself. We're at work, and in case you haven't noticed, my walls are transparent." He gestured around them.

"And this means what to me? Just tell me, have you spoken to Sir William?" she said, insisting on an answer.

Reluctantly, he replied, "Well, yes and no." She made a noise surprisingly like *hmph* and turned her back on him. Now he was really getting angry. *I haven't done anything to deserve this!* "Officially," he gritted out the word, "I can't speak to him without evidence. If an accusation is brought against her without proof, Maryn will swan away even stronger than before. I have to be careful. Maryn has a lot of influence in the bedrooms of the Security Services ... and the government, for that matter. Because of our—er ..." Okay, now maybe John was beginning to understand Caroline's reaction. "... history together, any move I make against her would be interpreted as a personal vendetta. However," he added quickly before she could gather steam again, "Sir William is not under her influence, and he seems to feel that my capture reflects badly on his authority as the Director-General of MI-5."

Exasperated, Caroline gestured toward the pods through which Maryn Dale had exited. "What did you ever see in that woman?"

"Who? Maryn? Oh Caroline, I don't know. She was attractive and she wanted me, for a while," he said, humiliation flooding him as it always did when he remembered his foolish relationship with a woman of such shifting morals. He was worth more than that. Caroline had proven that he was worth more than that.

"Blah." She stuck out her tongue to show her opinion of the woman.

Caroline's unexpected response broke into his thoughts and he wanted to laugh at the comical expression on her face, but he didn't dare. He reached for her, but at that moment Alexa burst into the room, interrupting their conversation.

"John, you need to see this," Alexa said, spinning about and striding away.

Quickly following her out onto the Grid, John was immediately drawn to the news report on the television:

"... was an explosion at the Embassy of the People's Republic of China thirty minutes ago. The cause is unclear, and preliminary reports indicate that five people were in the area at the time of the explosion. There has been no indication as to whether this was a terror attack. Reporters on the scene ..."

Caroline followed John and Alexa onto the Grid still feeling furious and terrified. *Burma? Oh, Father, please don't let him go back to Burma. It's so dangerous for him there. He just went to India. Would he go back to Burma? Without me? Without even telling me?*

John's mobile interrupted her thoughts. "Yes, Home Secretary ..." His words trailed off as he re-entered his office and closed the door.

The television news report continued, finally capturing Caroline's attention.

"Harry, what do you think this means?" Caroline asked, still feeling out of her depth at times in this world of bombs, plots and terrorists. She tried to put aside her distress for the moment in view of the current crisis. It was difficult. She simply didn't have the experience John had at compartmentalizing her life.

"If it was a terrorist bomb," Harry began, clearly following his own train of thought, "we've had no warning. Terrorists typically like credit for the chaos and destruction they cause." Harry began to chew the inside of his cheek.

Hurrying through the security pods, Jade stopped and pivoted, scanning the room, her eyes finally lighting on John's returning figure. All eyes followed hers because of the wry tirade issuing from their Section Head.

"What does he think, that we keep the good intelligence secret until the bomb goes off? Wh—"

Jade interrupted him. "John! Where is Hibb?"

"Ryan, fetch Hibb," John ordered. Ryan glowered at his Section Head before complying. Caroline caught his look. *Yeah, Ryan, that's about what I think of him at the moment too.*

Jade launched her explanation immediately, not waiting for Ryan's and Hibb's appearance. "I met with a Chinese asset today. We've been meeting more frequently recently to discuss a new wave of espionage. She feels there's some sort of information network that's bleeding industrial secrets out of the UK and into China. She was very frightened. Said that employees at the Embassy were disappearing."

"What's happened?" Hibb inquired in a stage-whisper to Alexa.

"A bomb. At the Chinese Embassy," Alexa informed him.

"What?!" Putting a startling halt to Jade's explanation, Hibb's question conveyed so much more than a desire for clarification of the facts.

Blinking once in surprise, Jade continued. "Each of the missing assets was tracking MSS surveillance of government agencies in London."

"MSS?" Ryan said.

"Ministry for State Security. China's intelligence agency," Jade explained in barely concealed disgust and then turned to the others. "Hibb, it looks to me as though the five reported as dead are our assets," she said, clearly moved by their demise.

Aubrey appeared as if out of nowhere, as though he intuitively sensed the need for information. He launched into an explanation without preamble. "Current intelligence reports indicate that China employs approximately one million intelligence agents worldwide. Many of these agents are engaged in industrial espionage, the use of clandestine methods to acquire secret information for commercial advantage. Most companies don't like to admit their own weaknesses, but GCHQ estimates that the UK loses one billion pounds a year to cyber-espionage. In the past, the impact of industrial espionage could be devastating but was much less pervasive. Now, with our reliance on technology and networking, with our global economy, with our outsourcing of production, with the focus on profit margins, we are uniquely vulnerable," Aubrey explained. "Economic spying allows countries to save billions in their own research and development. The three countries most hotly accused of industrial espionage are Russia, Iran and—"

"China," Hibb filled in the blank.

"Yes," Aubrey said. "China seeks to be the world's leading economic power by 2020. Economic spies take on many forms: foreign students and scientists, business delegations, immigrants, journalists ... and diplomats. The Germans have estimated that of the five hundred official staff members at the Russian Embassy in Berlin, one hundred and fifty are suspected intelligence agents."

John's face had gone blank and, sounding anything but proud—in fact, sounding positively nauseated—he said, "Thank you, Aubrey. Well done, Jade. I'd like a report on your findings, PDQ. No copies. Thank you. Caroline, Hibb, Alexa, my office, immediately." Turning on his heel, he marched back into his lair, leaving confused glances all around.

John began speaking as soon as the door was closed. "Caroline, I need you to take minutes." He looked back to Alexa and Hibb as Caroline scrambled to pull out a pen, searching around for paper. *Oh, fine, back to secretary.* John pulled a pad of paper out of his desk, handing it to her as he directed his attention to his Section Chief. "The Home Secretary has informed me that, as the Chinese government is a great ally to British industry and commerce, a threat to their embassy is to be treated as a threat to national security. Hibb, I want you to put a security detail on the Chinese Ambassador, and I want you to personally assure him of our support in locating the bombers. Meeting done. Don't move. Caroline, I want you to type up those minutes for my signature, immediately." Before she could move, he continued speaking. "Alexa, I want you to find a way to contact all of our—" Caroline began to write again. "Put down the pen," he instructed tersely, and Caroline looked up in surprise at his tone of voice, placing her pen on his desk. *What the heck?*

John continued. His voice was hard and his manner terse. "Where was I? Oh yes, I want contact established with each and every asset presently in the UK who has any association with China or Chinese interests ... off the radar. And I want them warned off. Use Jade. There is something filthy going on here, and I want to know what it is. This meeting is adjourned. Caroline. The minutes."

Hibb asked, "John do you think this is related to your as—"

*Slap!* John smacked the table with his open palm, silencing Hibb. Caroline narrowed her eyes at her husband, suspicious of his reaction. There was definitely something fishy going on here. *First, Maryn Dale appears at Thames House, then I find out that John is considering returning to Burma, and now this ... "as" ... whatever that stands for.*

"Close the door on your way out," John instructed as he began to dial his phone.

"John—" Caroline began, but Hibb took her firmly by the elbow, leading her into the privacy of the tea room, despite her protests, and closing the door behind them.

"Don't question our man, Caroline," Hibb said. "Trust him."

"Hibb, I'm not some airhead, you know. I'm not going to blab about important issues, but I won't be treated that way," she said.

"This is work, Caroline," he said.

"Hibb." She repeated his name in three syllables, lacing each with sarcasm. "I get that he wants to keep work and home separate. I don't understand it, and I don't like it. I mean, he won't even talk about what he wants for supper while we're at work. But he needs to know that he crossed a line today."

"I—well, I'm the last person who would want to interfere in someone's relationship, but ... I don't think you're aware of who your husband truly is." Hibb's voice lost volume as he finished the sentence, his eyes dropping with it.

"I know who he is," she insisted hotly. *Don't I?* When she had met John in the prison in Burma, he had been cold. A hard man. A little cruel. And, yes, he had frightened her. But then over time, a long time, a veryveryvery long time, she had come to see the man beneath the façade. A man who was kind. And brave. And sweet. Would that man return to Burma without telling her? Perhaps. *Burma. China. Maryn Dale. What next?*

"Caroline? This John you've seen in the last five minutes? He's the warm, fuzzy Brock compared to the man I knew before his abduction." Hibb's eyes were full of compassion for her. *And isn't that positively irritating?* "Everyone's been waiting for Ironheart to reappear," he said.

Grimly, Caroline responded, "Thanks for your advice, but—"

Resting a hand gently on her shoulder, Hibb seemed determine to explain. "There's summat going on, and he's trying to protect the rest of us from it. It'll be fine. Do as—"

"Caroline!"

John's voice interrupted Hibb's explanation, or non-explanation as far as Caroline was concerned. She pursed her lips in annoyance, but Hibb shook his head, giving her a nudge out the door and toward her desk, the geographical source of the bellow.

"Yes, your majesty," she mumbled when she was close enough that only John could hear.

His eyes narrowed, and she saw a spark in his flat gaze. "Minutes."

"Right away, your majesty!" she said in a mocking voice, low enough that it didn't travel far. She wanted to give him a mock salute, but the room was too full. For the moment, she decided that she didn't care about China and bombs and espionage. He was not going to get away with treating her this way.

John stood over her as she typed the minutes. "E-mail them to me with copies to Hibb and the DG," he instructed. She glared back at him but complied with his request. *Has he already forgotten everything I've said to him? Well, I haven't. Compartmentalized doofus!*

"Do you want a hard copy as well?" she asked in a very stilted voice.

"Yes." She printed off a copy and handed it to him. "Now, delete the report from your computer," he said.

"Why?" she asked.

John tapped once on her desk, very hard. "Delete." She made a great show of erasing the e-mail and deleting it from her hard drive.

The telephone rang, putting an end to the fiery-frigid staring contest between them, the dragon and the abominable snowman.

"Yes, Sir William, he's right here. Of course." She turned to John. "The D—"

John cut her off. "Put it through. Correctly." Her eyes narrowed as he spun away to his office, closing the door firmly behind him. He emerged a few minutes later. "I'll be in meetings for the rest of the day. Call George at the front desk to arrange a driver when you're ready to go home tonight—straight home, mind you. No stops." And then he was gone.

Caroline didn't see John for the rest of the day. She went home at six and fixed supper. Promptly at eight, their usual time to walk Rufus, she received a text from John telling her that under no circumstances was she to walk the dog alone. She texted him back with a few choice words, but he didn't respond. Frustrated, she flung the cell phone onto the couch, watching it bounce onto the dog, causing a yelp and a doggy dive under the coffee table.

Caroline spent the next fifteen minutes coaxing Rufus out and reassuring him. By that time, she had decided it wouldn't be worth defying John's infuriating bossiness by going for a walk anyway. But he was going to hear about this. No question! Refusing to tell her what happened during his operations was one thing. Treating her with disdain was quite another!

Her anger dormant in repose, she was roused from sleep sometime in the middle of the night to feel him crawl into bed beside her, too sleepy to bother resisting when he pulled her close, sighing against her. When she woke at seven the next morning, he was gone. She sent him a text, stating that she wanted to speak with him, but he never replied.

John had finally convinced the Chairman of the Joint Intelligence Committee, Louis Trevena, to institute surveillance on Chinese-owned companies in the UK. Hibb had been lobbying for tighter control on the MSS presence in London, and John was now convinced. Convincing Trevena had been more of a trial. But with the upcoming Summit, Britain's allies had been uncovering more and more intelligence linking the Chinese government to industrial espionage and influence peddling. John had a great deal of respect for the director of the Canadian Intelligence Service, CSIS, who had bucked his government and released a public statement of warning about that very topic.

CSIS … Canada … Caroline. Time to go home. *I need my wife.* John walked onto the Grid, his eyes fixed on Caroline as he approached her desk. *I need Caroline, solitude and a good cup of coffee.*

"Home time," John informed Caroline, his heart sinking at the angry glare she was sending him. "What's wrong?" he asked as he held her coat for her, hoping for his favourite word.

"What do you think is wrong?" she muttered angrily, snatching her coat from his hands, grabbing her purse and just managing to hold back from storming through the pods and down to their newly repaired Volvo in the dank and gloomy parking garage.

"What's made you so prickly?" he asked, thoroughly confused by her manner.

She just glared at him, and he shut down his gaze, returning to blankness. *Fine. You don't want to explain? That's fine with me! I guess I'll have my quiet evening after all,* he mused ironically.

But rather than stepping into the car, she exclaimed in obvious exasperation, "You can be so infuriating at times!"

"What do you mean?" he responded, shocked by her statement, panic flirting around the edges of his consciousness. *What now? I finally get everything settled, and now this.*

She glared at him for a few moments and then sighed in curt resignation, "Never mind."

That was John's favourite phrase from Caroline, because it meant that whatever the problem was, she would resolve it and return things to a state of happiness. *Perhaps the conflict is finally past.* John got into the car and moved into traffic, on the road home.

Turning onto Kew past Chiswick, John noticed a black C4 Citroen following them. Scanning the traffic quickly, he made an instant decision, making a quick left then right then left again, heading them into the maze of inner London. The buildings slipping past changed from low-level residences to high rises.

"Where are you going?" Caroline asked. Her voice was heated.

"Want to go out to supper?" he asked, his eyes glued to the rearview mirror. He took a left, accelerating, weaving his way around the cars, putting distance between their Volvo and the Citroen. "You wanted to try out the Mango Tree. We could go there. Thai food."

"No, I don't want to go out for supper. John, slow down! What is wrong with you?" she said. If anger could ignite a flame, he'd be incinerated.

"Nothing. We could ride the London Eye?" She glared at him wordlessly. *Definitely not. She'd probably chuck me out.*

John took a right and then another right onto the Ring Road into Hyde Park, hurtling past the carefully manicured lawns, the sprays of water fountains and the dazzling flower beds. And then, spinning into the parking lot of the Park Admin office, he lurched to a halt. Noting the angry set of her shoulders, he remained silent, oblivious to the patter of a ground squirrel across the roof of the car and the angry squeal of brakes-on-rims as an irritated cyclist detoured around them.

"What are you doing?" she gritted out.

"Sorry. I got turned around. You don't want to go out?" She just stared straight back at him. "No problem. Let's go home," he said.

Silently, she seethed for the rest of the journey home, and somehow her anger trumped his, disheartening him. Once through the door of their house, John made his way directly to the bedroom, offering only a pat in response to Rufus's excited greeting. He needed to report the make, model and partial plate number he'd memorized to Hibb, get the plods to pull it. *Was it the gunman from the Belle, the false doctor/poisoner or someone new?*

Caroline stood at the top of the stairs, everything about her body posture making her anger clear to him. "Where do you think you're going? You can't just pretend nothing happened," she said.

"We'll sort it out later, after we've had a shower and some supper." He kept his voice calm and even. He wanted to get into the bedroom and make the call in private.

"John, you just drove us around London at top speed! That's not the way I wanted to see Tower Bridge. And I have a watch." She tapped her wrist angrily. "I don't need to drive past Big Ben twice to know the time."

"I apologized for that. I got turned around," John said.

"Bollocks!"

"Caroline, that's not a very ladyli—"

"You are being obstructive," she said, speaking right over his words.

Breathing deeply to calm his frustration, he tried to reason with her. "I'm knackered. All I want is a shower, some supper and a quiet evening. I don't want to argue with you," he said. *Someone is trying to kill me. I don't need this aggravation right now!*

"I want to talk about it!" Caroline insisted hotly.

His mind went cold. "Cheers then. But later." He heeled about and walked into the bedroom, shutting the door behind him. Pulling out his mobile, he called Hibb, reciting the make, model and license plate of the car that had followed them.

"What is going on?" John heard Caroline shout at the closed door. He pressed the phone against his chest until she subsided.

Deciding against a shower, he started to change his clothes. He wasn't at all certain that he was willing to risk the vulnerability that nudity would allow at the moment. On one such frosty occasion, she had reefed up the hot tap on the kitchen sink while he was showering, dousing him in a frigid spray. He sighed. *I certainly do seem to have a talent for annoying her.*

As he buttoned his jeans, his mobile rang. It was Hibb. "You'd better come in, John. We've got a possible sighting on your tailgater."

John sighed wearily. "Fine, I'll be right there." Grabbing a suit jacket, he pulled it on over his golf shirt and walked out of the bedroom. Caroline was standing in exactly the same spot.

"I don't want to argue," he warned her. "I have to go back in."

She ignited at his words. "That's not fair, John! You can't just win every argument because you get called away."

"Fair? I don't even know what I did. I took a wrong turn. Sorry," he apologized, very unrepentantly.

"Something!—is!—going!—on!!" she shouted, her voice cracking on the last word. He just stared at her. "Listen to me carefully, John. You are not going to Burma."

"Burma?" John dug his fingers into his hair in frustration. "I am not going to Burma. I was never going to Burma." Now it was her turn to stare. "What?" he asked. "Maryn Dale tells you one thing and suddenly it's true?"

Caroline's confusion seemed to cool her anger. "Why didn't you just tell me?"

"When? When was I supposed to do that? When you were shouting at me? When you were giving me the silent treatment?" His anger was making her angry again, but he didn't realize it in time.

She stomped her feet like an angry toddler. He definitely wasn't going to point that out right at this exact moment. "Then what is going on here?" she asked. "You're avoiding topics. Refusing to tell me what's bothering you. You're aloof and controlling, telling me what I can apply for and what I can't, what I'm allowed to know and what I can't." The pace of her rant accelerated. "Telling me when I can walk the dog and when I can't. Suddenly, you're this different guy, completely closed off from me. You tell me it's operational, nothing to be concerned about." He started to reply but she spoke right over him.

"I've been patient," she said. "I've given you time. I've swallowed my fear and fury until I feel like I'm going to burst. If it's your job that is making you act this way, then I want no part of it! I quit!!"

John's jaw dropped in shock. *If you're quitting, are you leaving me?* "Quit? You can't quit over an argument!"

"If you don't explain yourself, then just watch me!!" she insisted.

Regret puddled in his belly. "Look, I'm the Head of Counter-Terrorism for the UK. I can't make operational decisions based on what may displease my wife." He was pleading with her, but she obviously heard only the words and not the message.

"Fine. Then this isn't going to work," she said.

He blanched. "What? Us?"

She shook her head. *What does that mean?* he wondered. He reached for her hand, but she pulled away, fixing him with an iceberg of cold, to his titanic regret.

His mobile rang. "It's the DG," he said, letting the call go to voicemail. "I have to go in," he said. "Please. Don't do anything rash." Turning on his heel, he departed.

# Chapter Five
# *Ephesians 5:22*

John's heart was aching in his chest. *What is going on? How can she say that my job is the problem when all I'm truly trying to do is protect her? My entire career, everything I do, is filtered through her safety. How can she do this to me?* John made his way to his office, bellowing for Hibb along the way.

"John, the DG's on the line for you." Harry called to him as he strode past.

"Have it transferred to my office," John said. His voice sounded strained even to his own ears. Closing his office door behind him, John inhaled a bracing breath and answered the telephone.

"Sir William," John greeted the DG tonelessly.

"I have an e-mail here from your administrative assistant tendering her resignation. What is going on over there?" Sir William was anything but amused. John's heart dropped into his stomach like a clay tile from a roof. *Caroline resigned? How do I explain that?* "Mr. Brock, your wife has resigned?"

John cleared his throat. "Apparently."

"Why?" Sir William inquired. *Why? I don't know why.* "John, what is going on? Your wife is too valuable to lose. I'm prepared to offer her a promotion if she'll return ..." Sir William paused. "Is this a personal matter or an operational one?"

"Er, can I get back to you, sir? Would you be willing to hold her resignation for the time being?" *What is that animal that stings its victims, the blue-ringed octopus that kills you by paralysis?* John felt the bite in his heart, but the paralysis was quickly spreading.

Sir William was silent for a long minute. When he spoke again, his voice was softer. "I understand that this ... er, situation ... is unusual in the history of the service. Have I made an error?"

"No, sir, but I believe I have," John replied mysteriously. *Only, I don't know what it was.* "Can I get back to you, sir?"

"Mr. Hibbert tells me that you've not informed Caroline of the current danger. An assassin has you in his sights, John," Sir William said.

Heat reversed the numbness. *He'll pay for that!* "She's safer not knowing," John replied, knowing how feeble that sounded.

"Are you certain? I'm afraid I have to question your judgment in this matter," Sir William said.

John's reply was fuelled by anxiety and angst. "Let me deal with it my way. Sir."

John heard the DG sigh down the phone line. "I'll be waiting, and I will hold the resignation." He rang off.

John buried his face in his hands. *What do I do now?* He had to admit that he was afraid to go home and face this. Keeping news of the assassins from her was in her best interest. Wasn't it? Or was it his interests that were taking precedence? Groaning, he tried to—

*Knock!*

"Come," John called, and Hibb entered, closing the door behind him. John shot to his feet, pounding a fist on the desk. "Don't you dare go over my head again!" John said. Hibb's eyes widened. Abruptly, John changed the subject. "What have you got on the Citroen?"

Hibb responded slowly at first, clearly disturbed by John's vicissitude. "The plods located the car outside a pub. Fortunately, the villain panicked at first sight of them, or so it seems. They ran him down and pulled him in. He's in the local nick."

"Who is he?" John asked.

"Guess?" Hibb replied.

John slammed his hand down on the desk. "I don't have time for games!" He could feel the curious glances directed at him from the Grid. *Blast!* Just what he needed: an audience for his hissy fit.

"John," Hibb began. "You need to calm down."

*Calm down?* Hibb was using his soothe-the-wild-beast voice. John hated that voice. "Hibb, you jerk!" Hibb's eyes widened in shock, and John would have blushed if his cheeks weren't already flushed in anger. Although ashamed at losing control enough to shout childish names at his colleague, John refused to back down. "Get out of here!"

The telephone rang before Hibb rose. "What?" John's voice held tones of barely leashed aggression.

"Mr. Brock," the Chairman of the JIC said.

*Blast it all!* John struggled to calm his voice. "Mr. Trevena," he replied, blowing out a breath. "What can I do for you?"

"I understand the police have arrested a man at your instruction? On *probable cause*? They have no reason to hold him," Trevena said, his voice crackling with disgust.

"He was to be picked up on terrorism charges," John said.

"The police tell me the man hasn't actually committed a crime yet," Trevena said.

"He was following me, sir," John said.

"That is not a crime, Mr. Brock. I've instructed the Met to release him," Trevena said.

"But, sir—" The Chairman rang off, ending the conversation.

Slamming down the phone, John encountered Hibb's concerned gaze.

"Get out of here!" John ordered, gesturing wildly.

Hibb complied, shaking his head as he departed. John slumped into his chair again, dropping his head into his hands.

Caroline rose from the home computer after sending her e-mail to the DG. She was filled with regret but uncertain which part of this horrible situation she regretted. *What is going on with John? He's being controlling, distant. Oh, Father, what is happening between us? Burma. But wait, he was never going to Burma, was he? That was just some trick of Maryn Dale's. Oh, Father, I smacked him for nothing. Poor man. Knowing how his father treated him when he was a boy, how could I do that to him?* Caroline sighed loudly enough to startle the dog. *But John has been acting so strangely.*

Rather than weep, Caroline grabbed the leash and took Rufus for the longest walk he'd ever had, longer than even a happy Labrador could possibly enjoy. Up and down the narrow sidewalks of the high street they walked, closed in by the line of four-storey Victorian buildings. They walked past Clarks Shoes, the HSBC and WH Smith, dodging the suspended London transit signs that announced *Bus Stop* in huge letters on the street. They wove around the perpetual movement of commuters, tourists and shoppers.

*Today it's sunny!* she mused wryly. *Today it should be miserable and grey. Oh, Father. I don't want to feel this way anymore. "I love the Lord, because he has heard my voice...Because he has inclined his ear to me...I call upon him as long as I live." I hear you, Father. That was the verse in my devotions this morning. And you have been with me. You carried me through my grief at losing Henry and the children. You brought me to a new life where I can experience hope and joy once again. I am grateful for that. What was the rest of the Psalm? Something about repaying the Lord for his goodness to me? Vows?* She gulped. *Oh yeah, fulfill my vows. Oh, but Father. It hurts. "The joy of the Lord is your strength."*

Caroline walked and walked and finally realized that she hadn't brought her purse, so she would need to walk back. No purse, no money for a taxi, no cell phone to call for a ride. *I don't even have a coin or a card to use in a public phone.*

A thrill of fear spiked through her when she realized that a black Citroen had passed by three times. She desperately hoped she was just being paranoid. Checking behind her through the reflection in the shop windows, Caroline moved along the street. When the Citroen returned, she slipped between The Lion and The Unicorn Bookshop and The Alianti Sandwich Shop. Jogging to the end of the alley, she turned right and took a different route home, one with no alleys and plenty of busy stores along the way. *I can walk away from bookstores and black cars, but I can't walk away from you, Father. What do I do? Father, tell me what to do. Please. I don't know what to do.*

Once she arrived home, she fed the dog and collapsed on the bed, falling asleep almost immediately. *I haven't felt this exhausted since ... well, since Burma.*

Caroline woke alone, fully dressed as she'd dropped onto the bed the night before. It felt as though her mind, however, had stayed awake all night. *Fulfill my vows ... Marriage is a commitment to love even in the unlovely moments ... but it's not enough to stay together, you have to find a way to be happy as well, even if it kills you.* Caroline smiled. Weren't those the very words she'd said to John? What exactly was there to understand? She could surrender to unhappiness or endure the hard things and persist; stay and fight for her marriage, for the man she loved—because she did love John.

Checking the clock, she could see that it was four-thirty in the morning. *Where is John?* Some of her anger had dissipated in the night, and she was ready to go in search of him. She found him snoring on the couch in the clothes he'd worn yesterday, his shirt open and rumpled, his longs legs stretched out across the coffee table and his neck craned sideways against the arm. He looked aggrieved and uncomfortable.

Rufus quickly diverted her attention, wiggling his backside in a furious need for the outdoors. *He must have slept through just as I did, poor beast.* Descending to the back door, she let the dog out. When she returned upstairs, John was just beginning to rouse from sleep. Pity pulled at her heart, and she knelt beside him.

"Hi," he greeted her cautiously, his voice husky and full of sleep.

"Hi. It's still early. Come to bed." She stood, reaching out her hand to invite him to join her, admonishing him as he rose. "I thought we agreed that no matter how bad the argument, we'd always sleep together."

"Wasn't my idea. Fell asleep," he replied. His voice was sharp, but Caroline knew that he was hiding his true reaction, so she just took him by the hand and led him to their bedroom, removing his shirt and trousers and then her own. "I'm sorry," he murmured.

"I know. We need to talk this through," she warned.

"After we sleep?" he asked hopefully, pulling her into his arms and sighing against her hair.

"All right. If you give me your word."

"I do."

Caroline gradually emerged from sleep into the music of Neil Diamond as John sang of her name. "Are you singing to start the conversation or avoid it?" she asked, opening her eyes to see John watching her carefully.

"I don't know a song with the lyrics 'please forgive me because I'm a prat,' but I thought this one might do," he said.

She softened her gaze. "You don't have to sing me an apology. You could just tell me what is going on," she said.

"It's easier to sing. I never realized how much easier it is to … er … express … er …"

"Emotions? To convey your deep intentions? I love that you've found your voice, John. But we need to talk," she insisted.

"All right," he said, sounding defeated. "What have I done?"

"I don't understand what's been going on lately, why you've become so obstructive and controlling. I don't like it," she said. When he didn't respond, she sighed, trying to control her frustration. *At least we're in the vicinity of the topic at hand. Well, here we go!* "Do you know that passage in the book of Ephesians that talks about wives submitting and husbands loving?"

"Not really," he replied, his eyes downcast. "I know there's some verse about submission that makes feminists very angry."

She released a dry chuckle. "Yes. When I was a young woman, it used to make me angry, too. It seemed incongruous with what I knew of God and what my father expected of my sisters and me. My parents taught me that women and men had equal value in God's eyes and that a woman could be anything she wanted to be." She paused, and John pulled back a little as though to study her face, interest and query in his eyes. "As I got older and experienced more of life and marriage and parenthood and the professional world and God, I began to see those verses in a new light. The Bible doesn't ask us to submit to slavery imposed by our husbands—"

"Slavery? Caroline, I can't believe that God ever asked a wife to be a slave to her husband!" John said, clearly astonished by the idea.

"No, I agree." A smile escaped her, but John didn't return it, probably too tense at the topic of discussion. "When the Bible speaks of husbands as the head of the home, Paul actually seems to be using the same term used for the head of a river, the source from which the river is fed rather than the headmaster of a school. It's not about bosses and servants. I mean, first, God asks husbands to love their wives as Christ loved the church and gave Himself up for it. Christ was tortured and executed, nailed to a cross, for the church. That's an amazingly tall order. All the wife is asked to do is submit to the husband who loves her in this manner. If you love me enough for that, you're never going to ask me to do anything against myself, against who I am. I only have to give respect, you have to love sacrificially. What's not to respect about a husband who loves his wife in this manner? I think, perhaps, when the husband fulfills his role, the wife's is a cakewalk."

"What made you think of that?" he asked, and his voice was gentle.

"I feel like I'm submitting, but you're not loving," Caroline replied.

Clearly startled by what she'd said, he pulled back, his gaze slamming shut just after she glimpsed the intense grief behind his eyes. "You're saying that I don't truly love you?" His voice sounded angry, but she knew it was really sorrow speaking.

Resting her hand on his chest, she sought to prevent his emotional escape, to open his mind again with her tender touch. "That's not what I meant. You love me very much, just as I love you. What I mean is that you expect me to passively submit to your need to keep me divided from your reality. This meets your needs but not mine. Where's the rest of the verse, John? 'The husband shall love his wife.' Can you not imagine what I go through while you're away on a mission? How it feels to know that you are keeping things from me? Lying is lying." She rested her forehead against his. "I don't know what you're doing or why, I just know that you're hurting me. In fact, this current situation hurts a whole lot," she told him.

Silent for a time, she wondered if he would respond, and was almost startled when he finally spoke. "Do you remember when we were in Burma? When you were attacked by the leopard?" He moved his hand to rest on her right shoulder, stroking his thumb lightly across the scars there.

"I'm not likely to forget it," she said, shivering at the memory.

"I was terrified," he said. "It was my job to protect you, and I couldn't. I was powerless to save the most important person in my life." His breath catching in his throat, he paused, drawing her minutely closer. "You opened my heart. You led me to God. I was desperately in love with you but still hadn't told you. I was terrified that I would lose you and all the good would flow right back out of my life."

She scanned his face, looking for a hint as to what he meant. "I don't understand what you're saying to me," she said.

"Come back to work. Forget about resigning. Be my admin assistant again. You can have a raise—a new office—the DG wants to give you a promotion. Take it. Forget about field training," he said, and he almost sounded desperate.

"Forget?" she said, utterly confounded by his words. "Are you crazy? Do you think I'm just a petulant child having a tantrum to get her own way? How dare you! Is this really what being married to you is going to be like? You think you're the boss and I'm the employee? You say and I do?"

"No!" He shook his head vehemently, denying her charge. "No, I …" He faltered into silence.

"What, John, what?" she yelled.

He groaned, rolling abruptly out of bed and toward the bathroom. "Please don't be angry with me, Caroline. I can't stand it."

Dismayed by the depths of his grief, she followed him. "John! John, stop and talk to me. You gave me your word."

He halted but remained turned away from her, his arms crossed as though to protect his aching heart. "I don't know how to tell you what I mean."

"Just say it. Plainly," she said. "Say something."

"I don't want you to resign."

"Why?"

"I … I … Blast it, Caroline! I love working with you. You keep me grounded, and there's nothing sweeter than returning from a meeting with the JIC and seeing your smile. You smile at me. You're happy to see me. Please don't leave me," he begged her as he turned toward her.

"Oh, John," she said. Stepping into him, she wrapped her arms around him, and he leaned down to rest his head on her shoulder. "I don't want to work in a situation where we are constantly coming into conflict. I won't let my job ruin our marriage. Our marriage is too precious."

"Then please just tell me what I have to do. I don't want to lose you. I'll do anything," he said.

"Tell me what is going on," she said.

He pulled back, and she thought she glimpsed real fear in his eyes. "I can't."

"Then you're not really willing—"

He clutched at her arms, almost in a panic. "If I tell you everything, then you'll become a target," he said in a rush.

Utterly confounded, she repeated his words, trying to make sense of them. "A target? What do you mean?"

Releasing her, he walked to the other side of the bathroom. "If people come to think I tell you everything about the operations I go on, then someday, someone will use you to get to me. I don't want you to be hurt. I can't let you be hurt … for me," he said.

*Now I understand, but …* "Well, that's just silly!"

Brow darkened, he spun to face her. "Silly?"

"Yes," she said. "If someone wanted to use me against you, it wouldn't matter what I did or didn't know." He clearly didn't understand her meaning. "Sweetheart, I think we make it pretty obvious that we're in love. Who exactly do you think you're fooling?"

His eyes widened in understanding and a slow smile crept across his face, quickly replaced by a deep frown. "Then there's no way I can protect you."

She strode quickly to him, resting her palms against his chest. "You protect me by loving me. I don't need any other kind of protection, darling. After all we've been through together, did you really think I was looking for a simple, safe life? I just want you."

"Caroline." His love hung heavily upon her name. Stroking his right hand lightly up along her arm to her cheek, he traced her features gently with his fingertips. Leaning down to meet her mouth with his own, he tenderly kissed her, the weight of his love pressed against her lips. When he pulled back, her eyes fluttered open to see his eyes filled with love and adoration, only for her. She opened her mouth to speak, but he gently pressed his fingertips against her lips and pulled her close. They remained in that position for a long time. Finally, he spoke again. "What did I ever do to deserve you?"

She smiled against his cheek. "Something very nice, I'm sure. Now, tell me why Mr. Bossyboots has suddenly appeared." She continued when he hesitated. "You are keeping something from me, something important; something that is not truly operational. What is it?" She watched the rise and fall of his Adam's apple as he gulped. "John." She admonished his hesitation, her voice rising in agitation. "I'm so afraid of what's happening between us. I would rather be back in Burma with Captain Li chasing us than have this distance between us!"

She watched the thoughts and emotions warring behind his eyes until finally he seemed to make a decision.

"Come," he said, quickly adding, "Please." She followed him out to their desk, where he removed a folded piece of paper from the back of a bottom drawer and handed it to her.

Feeling very uncertain, she opened it. "Badger? Why is there a picture of you?" she asked, clearly confused.

"Badgers are called brocks here," he said. "This is a contract, for a hit."

"A hit?" she said.

"Someone has hired an assassin, well, a group of assassins to kill me." Her eyes widened in shock and then flooded with tears.

He pulled her close, brushing his fingers along her cheeks, tucking her hair behind her ears. "Don't cry, baby. Please don't cry," he begged.

She sniffed back her tears. Burrowing into his chest, she spoke into his shirt. "Assassins. No wonder you've been acting so weird! I wish you'd told me. Why did you keep it from me?"

"You told me that you didn't want to feel afraid anymore, that you only wanted to feel safe," he said.

She chuckled mirthlessly. "I would rather be afraid of … of an assassin, than afraid of losing you. You can move forward on that assumption, okay?"

He nodded, declaring, "I love you. I'm sorry I've been such a—"

"Bossyboots," she said, filling in the blank.

He released a wry chuckle. "Yes. That."

She sighed, relief expanding within her. *I don't know how I can feel relieved that there's a killer after my husband, but this is a situation we can face together. I would rather have this than the heartache of losing him.* "I love you, too. Please don't ever keep something like that from me again," she said.

"I won't. I'm sorry." He kissed her forehead.

"Um, John? Who are the men in black jackets who keep appearing to help me?"

"Your security detail," he replied.

She laughed. "You've been protecting me without my knowledge, haven't you?"

"Of course. Er, Caroline?" He began to fiddle with her wedding ring. "I am sorry."

"I know."

Arriving at work, John immediately called Hibb into his office. Ten minutes later, the big man emerged, walking past Caroline's desk shaking his head and murmuring "about time" and "pillock." The DG was the next to arrive, making his way directly to John's office, sparing not a word of greeting for anyone else.

"Mrs. Brock!" Sir William called as he exited John's office some time later. His words were so abrupt and unexpected that Caroline jumped in her chair.

"Yes, Sir William," she replied breathlessly.

"Would you please accompany me to my office." He had the same knack John had, of asking questions that sounded like orders.

Following along, Caroline descended the steps from the Millbank exit of Thames House and ascended the steps of the Horseferry entrance. She soon found herself greeting Janice Goldbloom, the keeper of the DG's time and space. A well-chosen guardian, Janice was polite, efficient and wholly intimidating.

Nodding once to Janice, Sir William escorted Caroline directly into his office. Motioning for her to sit in one of the ornate green velvet chairs, he settled behind the oversized carved mahogany desk.

"Did your husband inform you of the promotion I have planned for you?" Sir William said.

"Yes, sir. But I submitted my resignation," she said.

"Your husband asked me to hold it." Knowing she should probably feel annoyed by John's interference, she simply nodded, grateful in the end. She waited for Sir William to continue. "I would like you to become an intelligence officer on Mr. Hibbert's team. I have it on good authority that you are a natural analyst. However, if this is to work, you and John will need to resolve this issue between you."

She nodded affably. "Could I still work for John, Sir William?"

"It makes no nevermind to me if you continue to keep his diary. However, I believe we should find someone else to answer his phones, preferably someone who doesn't cut off the Home Secretary." His eyes lanced into her.

She bowed her head in chagrin. "Yes, sir. I suppose that would be best. I'm sorry for wasting your time over the e-mail. Thank you for holding it."

"I never consider it a waste of time to help you, my dear." He handed over a blue file folder. "Now, while John is out of the country—"

Lurching upright in her chair, she demanded to know, "Out of the country? Where is he going?"

"Mrs. Brock, I cannot tell you that."

"But if it has something to do with the assassin …" she began and then faltered.

Sir William leaned back in his chair, and Caroline thought she detected relief in his eyes. "So he's finally told you."

"Yes, the sweet idiot," she said. "I would like to help."

Smiling paternally, he said, "You can help best by doing as I ask."

"Oh really," she replied indignantly. "Well, perhaps I could help best by saving my husband's life."

This conversation was far from over. She was determined that Sir William would at least hear her out and then she would abide by his decision ... well, probably.

Returning to the Grid, Caroline joined Jade in the forgery suite—the room that contained costumes, fake passports, driver's licenses, credit cards, and anything else needed for undercover officers to maintain their false identities, their legends.

Walking into a hive of activity, Caroline searched the room for John, finding him dressed in a suit—but not one of his own. Perhaps the word *suit* was overstating his attire. He was wearing jeans, desert boots and a suit jacket that looked as though a patchwork quilt had procreated with a tartan, creating a hideous mix of coloured lines and boxes known as madras. His arms were raised as one of Aubrey's apprentices fitted an electronic device into the lining of his jacket. Beside them, Alexa loaded a wallet with credit cards and other identification.

Aubrey gestured for Caroline to approach. He set about fitting and calibrating a listening device and earpiece. As these activities proceeded, Caroline could sense John's gaze following her.

"What's happening here?" John walked toward Caroline, a couple of Aubrey's apprentices trailing behind, still connected to him by wires.

"I convinced the DG to let me come along on your mission," Caroline replied quietly.

"You did *what*!?" John's wrath and incredulity boomed across the Grid, and the room froze into silence. Not a sound could be heard except the whirring of the computer calibrating the surveillance equipment. Hibb's shocked face appeared at the door to the suite.

Glancing about, finally noticing everyone staring at him, John ground out "My office" before spinning away, catching the paralyzed apprentices by surprise, finally disentangling himself and shoving his jacket into one of the men's shaking hands.

Sighing, Caroline carefully handed the equipment back to Aubrey and followed John out of the room. As she passed by Hibb, he gave her pause with a hand on her arm.

"Are you going to be all right?" Hibb asked. "You want me to come with you?"

Caroline smiled sadly and shook her head. "Hibb, the last fellow who tried to interfere in one of our arguments got punched in the face."

"Caroline. He's brassed-off," Hibb said, and she could read his concern plainly on his face.

"I know. I'll be fine." She patted his hand reassuringly and finished the journey to John's office, entering and closing the door tightly behind her. John had lowered the blinds on the windows by the time she arrived.

He was pacing the dusky green carpet in front of his desk, his fists tightly clenched and tapping a furious rhythm against his leg. Yes, he had quite a lot to say to her.

"John, I know you're angry—" she began.

"Angry? You think I'm only angry?" He stopped pacing in order to face her. "So everything I said to you meant nothing, did it? You simply had to have your own way."

Irritated by the accusation, she retorted, "This is hardly about getting my own way. I'm not a child." Breathing deeply, she sought to calm herself. "The DG said that you just needed someone to play your lover and to sit in the hotel room and conduct computer searches. I can do both of those things. There's no risk involved."

The heat in his voice ratcheted up a notch. "No risk except that I'm travelling to the home town of the mercenary who's been contracted to arrange my death."

Taking a half-step closer to him, she admitted, "That's why I want to come."

His voice was high and explosive, each word launching from his lungs. "To get caught in the crossfire? Caroline, I sliced my heart open for you, and this is how you treat it? You throw the pieces back in my face?"

Confused, she took another half-step toward him. "What do you mean?"

"You went over my head for permission to go out in the field even after I told you that I'm in mortal danger and my greatest fear is losing you," he said. "Don't you even care how that makes me feel?"

Caroline sobered. "I didn't think of it that way. I just saw this as an opportunity to come with you. The role only required someone who could sit in the hotel room and provide a little analysis. I'm sorry. I won't go."

Astonished by her words, he cocked his head as though unable to believe what he'd just heard. "What do you mean?"

"You're right. I didn't listen properly. I'll stay behind," she said.

Stock-still, he stared at her, a completely novel expression on his face. "You'll stay?"

"Yes," she said. "I'm sorry for making you feel betrayed. I just didn't really think it through."

John watched her carefully, as though trying to understand. "But when I refused your request for field training, you wouldn't speak to me for days."

She shrugged as though the difference was obvious. "Well, you were just being controlling. You didn't explain."

"How could I explain?" he asked. "You weren't speaking to me."

"No. But I would have listened," she said. "I just wanted an explanation."

"And today?" he asked.

"You explained."

He snorted. "I will never understand you, woman."

She poked him in the chest. "Watch it, Buster. I am a woman, true, but the same one who cooks your supper and cleans your shirts and shares your bed."

Drily, he replied, with a lopsided grin, "I usually cook supper."

"True," she agreed, and then she smiled. "You're a good cook."

Visibly relaxing, he leaned back against his desk. "Come here."

Hearing the invitation in his voice, she walked over to stand between his knees. "Back to Bossyboots, are we?" she said, grinning crookedly. Then she wrapped her arms around his shoulders and began playing with the hair at the nape of his neck. His breathing deepened in response to her familiar touch.

"Why do you want to come?" he asked, resting his hands on her hips.

"Aside from the fact," she said, "that your legend is a philandering world-traveler who has picked up a bored socialite in London to play kissy-face on the train?" He grinned broadly, and she considered smacking him on the shoulder but decided he'd probably been more bruised already than he deserved by her callous disregard for his feelings. "If someone is going to try to kill you, I want to be nearby. Maybe I can help."

He sobered. "I don't want you to be hurt."

"Trust me. It would hurt a whole lot more to become a widow again. Especially, always wondering, if I'd been there, would I have been able to save you? You know, when Henry and the boys died in that plane crash, I hated most that I'd been left behind. Part of that was because I would have preferred just to be in heaven with them. But part of me always wonders if I'd been there, would I have been able to save them?"

Drawing her closer, he traced his lips along the shell of her ear, murmuring soberly, "I'm grateful that you were left behind."

"I know you are," she said.

"If you come, will you obey orders?" he said.

She shone him a crooked grin. "Yes, boss."

"Caroline," he warned.

"Yes. I will dutifully kiss you senseless on the train ride there and then sit in the hotel room searching for … whatever I'm supposed to research while you go out and meet contacts. Does that mean you don't mind if I come?"

"I would always rather have you with me," he said.

"Thank you, John."

"Pleasure," he murmured against her lips.

Inhaling deeply of his spicy aftershave, she kissed along his jaw, adding between pecks, "There's just one little thing." He froze, his hands gripping her hips tightly. "Do you think we could have Aubrey change the legend to a married couple?" she asked. "Then I don't have to take off my wedding rings."

He released his breath on a gasp and a laugh. "You are one of kind, Caroline."

Caroline followed John back into the forgery suite. All conversation ceased immediately, and everyone turned to watch them.

John ignored the glances and said with all authority, "Jade. The blue dress with the larger bag thingamajig. Aubrey, hook her up and teach her how to use the tracker. Hibb, Caroline will need to be brought up to speed on Grendahl."

By the end of John's instructions, the entire room had been mobilized into action. No one dared comment on his about-face. Caroline simply smiled to herself. Her husband wore a hard shell around his heart, but the heart itself was full of love.

# Chapter Six
## *Is Grendahl Home?*

"What on earth is that?" John heard Caroline exclaim as they emerged from the Oslo Airport in Gardermoen into a sunny Norwegian day.

"What?" John asked, glancing up from the map he was reading. *She sounds so excited.*

"That!" she said, indicating a large metal sculpture that, through long observation, resolved into the figure of a man in the process of throwing a paper airplane.

Amused, John replied, "That, my dear, is art. Now come, before we miss the train." He took her hand, releasing it only to hail a taxi to the Eurail Express.

*Aubrey, son, you chose the perfect legend for my dear wife's first undercover operation,* John mused as they settled onboard the train into Drammen. He smiled against Caroline's lips. She was thoroughly enjoying herself. And they were clearly making the other passengers ill with their affection. If she didn't slow things down, he was going to have to drag her off into a corner somewhere before they even made it to the hotel.

"Pay attention," she murmured, turning his head to give her better access to his ear.

He swallowed a moan. "Slow down," he whispered. "Or I'm going to haul you into the loo and have my way with you."

She pulled back sharply, and he thought he'd shocked her. "Yeah?" she said, her eyes sparkling with mischief.

He laughed aloud, drawing even more attention to them. "We're working. Remember?" he whispered.

Grinning broadly at him, she began to draw circles on his leg. "Am I overdoing it?"

"Not if you want me to combust," he said.

She laughed. "Sorry. I'll slow down. It was great fun, though."

"Don't mistake me," he said. "But I'd enjoy it a whole lot more if there weren't thirty people watching us."

She laughed again and settled in his arms. "Love you," she murmured.

"Good," he said.

Finally, they arrived at the Comfort Hotel, Union Brygge, a massive modern structure, all polish and glass, half a block and a warehouse away from the banks of the Drammenselva River. Arm in arm, they paced the lobby slowly so that John could enjoy Caroline's blatant curiosity as she examined the indigo columns and puerile green art-deco benches. Up the metallic amber-striped elevator, they found their floor and then their room. He laughed once at the gasp she emitted as they entered, getting her first view of the garish swirls of the wallpaper and the vibrant stripes of the bedding on the queen-sized mattress.

John quickly turned his back to the bed and set to work arranging to meet his assets. *We're working,* he reminded himself. Kissing him once and then again, Caroline also set to work activating the specialized equipment Aubrey had sent. John breathed a sigh of relief. *Work.*

"You remember your remit?" John asked.

"I'm to use the codes Aubrey gave me to trace any possible links to Tor Grendahl including his tax records, local police record and an address that is a possible home location. We're trying to locate him and find evidence that can be used against him by the local politi. So the dirty rotten piece of filth can be arrested and stop sending assassins to try and … and kill you." Her eyes filled with tears.

"Steady on, sweetheart," John said, meeting her gaze. A lone tear escaped from her eyes, and he caught it tenderly on his thumb, continuing to stroke her soft skin. "We have twenty-four hours, at the outside, before he gets word we're onto him. If we can link him to crime in any way, Interpol will coordinate with the local politi to pull him in. Once word gets back to him, he'll simply disappear."

"I'll be okay. It just makes me so mad that he would do this for money. Without regard for who you are," she said. He watched her carefully. "And you can relax, sweetheart," she said. "I can do this. I promise. It just ticks me off."

"Are you certain?" he asked.

"Yes. Absolutely. It really ticks me off." She managed to smile.

"I mean are you certain—"

"I promise I'll be fine," she said, hooking his belt loop and jerking him toward her for a kiss.

Smiling, John kissed her once and then got down to the game. "I have three contacts to make. I'll stay in touch by text between each one. Call me if you need me. Text me if you have any leads. I'll check back in a couple of hours."

"Got it," she replied confidently.

"Caroline? Whatever you do, do not leave this room, and do not let anyone in. Activate the security devices Aubrey sent, and don't take any chances. If the alert on the computer sounds, it means you're being tracked, and you need to disengage immediately. Understand?" he said.

"I do." She moved over to him. "Be safe."

"I will," he said, kissing her once and then again before stepping through the door. He waited until he heard the click of the deadbolt.

John passed by the glossy metal sphere of the River Harp, caller of the legendary Nøkken, whose beautiful music enticed his listeners to a watery grave. Pausing not even a moment to enjoy the cultural significance of the myth, John boarded the baby-blue trolleybus and then disembarked, disappearing into the Torpedo Bokhandel. Mildly surveying the bookshelves first, he slipped out the back, reversing his colourful jacket to plain grey and attaching himself to the back of a group of local commuters.

Hailing a Drammen Taxi to the Assiden Upper Secondary School, empty at this time of day, John disappeared unnoticed behind the gymnasium. Young Reidar was there and waiting in his faded green jean jacket, the odour of reefer hanging about him like a cloud over Charlie Brown's friend Pigpen. That was a good sign. Reidar would know what he was talking about when it came to the Norwegian drugs trade.

John got right to business, asking the young man to give him the information he sought. "*Fortell meg hva du vet.*"

Reidar nodded and replied, "*Ungdom regler.*"

John chuckled lightly. *Youth rules. Clever.* John quickly sobered and got right to the point. "Tor Grendahl?"

Reidar switched into heavily accented English. "He has not the … uh … *narkotika* … Vegard gives to us … this time … in the present."

"Is Grendahl an associate of Vegard?" John inquired carefully.

"No." The lad stopped speaking and reached out his hand, palm up. "*Penger.*"

John handed over an envelope of cash as requested. "*Takk,* Reidar." *So Grendahl is no longer embroiled in the Norwegian drugs trade. We won't be able to get him that way.*

The beep on his mobile alerted John that a message had been received, registering the text *Ypsilon Bar.* Locating the restaurant on his mapping GPS, John took a taxi back to the Union Brygge and, crossing the impressive cable bridge over the Drammenselva, found the Ypsilon Bar. As he approached the patio umbrellas, a patron exited the restaurant and the scents of coffee and fresh bread wafted out, filling his senses. *Mmm. I wish I could bring Caroline here for lunch … simply as tourists. Father, why is my life so complicated?*

Entering the restaurant, he soon spotted his contact in the Politi, the Norwegian police, Constable Gunnar Mats, looking suspiciously unobtrusive in the back corner booth. John strode over and sat. Gunnar made a great show of slipping a document beneath the table, and John suppressed the urge to laugh at this very young man who had obviously watched too many American spy films.

Gunnar whispered hoarsely, "He has *plettfri vandal,* clean record. Pays … *avgifter* … taxes in addition. He is not wanted by us."

John nodded, passing over the football tickets for the upcoming Rosenborg match, a highly sought-after commodity. Who wouldn't want to see first-hand the best team in Norway?

*Why are successful hit men always such good citizens, paying their taxes, avoiding small crimes?*

Popping back to the hotel, John couldn't resist the urge to pull his wife into his arms for a brief break from spying.

"How goes it?" he asked.

Extracting herself, she pulled him over to the computer. "I've located three possible addresses for Grendahl. But unfortunately, none has given me anything useful."

"Good work," he said, kissing her on the cheek. *I should have known this couldn't possibly be that simple.*

"You know," she said. "You don't have to pretend everything is hunky dory."

John relaxed, letting his frustration show. He paced the hotel room from swirl-covered wall to plain white wall.

"I don't suppose we could make out for a while?" Caroline inquired coquettishly, completely breaking his mood.

John stopped pacing, his astonishment quickly morphing into a leer. "What did you have in mind?"

"Oh, just a little ..." She paused, and he watched her expectantly. "Foot massage. My feet are killing me."

He laughed. "You've been sitting on your behind all day."

"Okay. If you're offering."

He grinned broadly at her. Never in his entire life had he met anyone with her capacity for joy and playfulness. She never ceased to amaze him. "If I start that, you know we'll be out of commission for more than the twenty minutes I have before I leave to meet with Georgie." That was going to be a tricky job. Georgie was an established MI-6 contact in the local Albanian Mafia, the girlfriend of a foot soldier of one of the clans.

"True. Oh well, next time we come to Norway," she said.

He pulled her to her feet, twirling her into his body. "Next time." He kissed her deeply. He never tired of kissing her. But before the warmth in his heart traveled lower, he pulled back, taking her place at the computer and scanning the information she'd uncovered. "You are quite good at this job, you know?"

"Kissing?"

He laughed. "Yes. Kissing. And analysis. Aubrey was right. You were born to be an intelligence analyst."

"Did he say that?" she asked, and John nodded to affirm his words. "Cool!" she exclaimed, a broad, proud grin on her face. He chuckled at her obvious glee.

The church bell down the street chimed. "I'd better go. Georgie's the last contact and then, unless you turn something up, we're done for now."

Walking into the alley behind the wedge-shaped glass-walled Papirbedden Vokser, the new centre of knowledge in Drammen, John studied the bleached-blonde who stood there nervously fidgeting with her cigarette. She wore a tight black miniskirt and red faux-fur jacket. He walked directly to her and offered her a light. When she flinched at the appearance of the lighter, suspicion reared its ugly head in warning.

John used a conciliatory tone, hoping to put her at ease. "Hallo, Georgie. *Hvor er du*?" She was definitely not fine. She was fussing with her clothes and her cigarette, shifting from foot to foot. Her eyes darted around the damp darkness of the alley, and she never more than glanced at his face.

"*Mørk fremmed*? Dark stranger," she said, her voice quivering in concert with her hands.

"Do we have a connection between Tor Grendahl and your boyfriend?" John asked, narrowing his eyes to study her response.

Voiceless, she rubbed her arms briskly as though trying to escape the chill of intrigue.

Grasping her elbow, John jerked her closer. "Georgie, what's wrong?" His voice was hard, firm, clearly telling her that he expected an answer … *now!* When she still didn't respond, he shook her once. "What is going on?" Gritting his teeth, he emphasized each word and then repeated it in Norwegian. "*Hva som skjer*?"

"Stop! *I vrasin ju!*" The threat speared unexpectedly through John's ears as the cold steel of a revolver pressed against the back of his head. He cursed himself for missing the man's approach. "Ve vant nussing to do wiss yer assassin. You verk for Grendahl, I kill you." Grinding the pistol against John's skull, the Albanian mafioso held John's shoulder in a vice-like grip. He was all bulk and intimidation wrapped in the smell of crime. John was not going to let this man kill him.

With suddenness born of training, John dropped to a crouch, spinning and then driving his fist against the man's knee, hearing the crack of the patella with grim satisfaction. Screaming in agony, the mafioso collapsed, clutching his leg, the pistol forgotten on the pavement beside him. John socked him one in the solar plexus, winding him. Kneeling on the man's stomach, John quickly checked his pockets, emptying them of his wallet, his keys and a mobile phone. Pocketing these, he regained his feet and spun to meet Georgie's open hand. *Ouch!* The slap burned but did no permanent damage. However, when she wound up to slap again, John grabbed her arm, jerking her close to his chilling face. *Not again, lady!*

"Don't you dare slap me!" John said, and Georgie's eyes widened. She tried to pull away but he held her firmly, forcing her to meet his gaze until she nodded twice. Then he released her. Stepping back, she fell to her knees beside her man.

Disgusted, John strode out of the alley, making his way through the maze of twists and turns until he was, at last, pointed back to the hotel and finally began to feel calm again. *There has got to be a better way to make a living.* He sent off a warning to the local MI-6 station that Georgie was no longer to be trusted as an asset. Grendahl? The animosity of the local Mafia could come in handy but ... how did an assassin manage to steer clear of law enforcement *and* organized crime?

Texting Caroline, he made his way into the hotel restaurant, settling in the bar, frustrated with his lack of progress. For Caroline's sake, he'd been hoping they'd find the answers they were seeking to make an end to the contract. She texted back that she would "tidy up" and then meet him for supper in the hotel restaurant.

"*Kaffe*," John ordered, holding up two fingers.

"*Krem*? *Sukker*?" the bartender asked.

"*Ja*," John affirmed.

Suppressing a surge of frustration, John blanked his expression, mentally reviewing everything they'd learned, or not learned, since arriving in Drammen twenty hours ago: Grendahl had no fixed abode; he wasn't in with the drugs scene; and he always paid his taxes. Personally, the man was clean. Professionally, he stank!

Startled from his musings, John flinched instinctively when a meaty hand slapped down on his shoulder. *How did he get so close? I must be losing it.*

"Get off!" John said and then translated, "*La meg være i fred!*"

Standing slowly and turning, determined to meet aggression with strength, John came face to face with the biggest, meanest Viking he had ever seen: grizzled eyebrows, a thick matt of wiry hair and a tangled blue beard thick enough to disappear in. The Viking ground his thumb against

John's collarbone. John gritted his teeth against the pain. *Ruddy X, that hurts!* Shifting suddenly, John ducked under the Viking's grip, crouching to attain the best balance possible while looking around for a weapon.

"Brock *det grevling*. Badger." The Viking spat onto the floor. "*Lite grevling*. You *er* mine."

John felt a shot of panic through his guts. They'd found him. He'd come sniffing after Tor Grendahl and found nothing. But Grendahl had found him! This was no simple brawl; this was deadly serious.

Without warning, the Viking fisted John's shirt, jerking his body too close to his foul breath and disposition. John shook his head in warning, refusing to back down.

"Leave off," John warned in his most chilling voice, the voice that sent most opponents running. The Viking was unimpressed. *Uh oh. Father, keep Caroline away. Please, keep her safe.*

The Viking swung his fist. Dodging, John sank to a crouch and then drove an uppercut into the Viking's ribs. Two more men joined the fight, grasping John's arms. The young man on his left was about his height, skinny with what could only be described as a double Mohawk of bright orange hair atop his smooth, hairless face. On his right stood a shorter, younger man, perhaps five-seven or five-eight, clad in black sweatpants and a torn green-and-blue sweatshirt. His head was shaved, revealing a skull tattoo emblazoned across the peak of his own skull. *This is not good.*

John pivoted, simultaneously dragging Double Mohawk forward and slamming Skull Tattoo back against the bar, yanking his right arm free as it loosened in the young man's grip. Slamming the heel of the loosened hand into Double Mohawk's chin, John didn't pause to see the man's eyes roll into the back of his head. Pivoting, John drove a fist into Skull Tattoo's solar plexus, leaving him gasping and clinging to the bar, more concerned about his xiphoid than John's escape. *Hah! Take that, you blighters.*

Before John could draw breath, the Viking's meaty fist was back, tangled in the front of his shirt. Buttons tore free from their thread and torpedoed around the space, even pinging off the mirror behind the bar. John was still recovering from his battle with the bad-hair blokes, and so he couldn't fend off the Viking's punch. The blow snapped John's head back, and he battled the black swirls in his vision threatening to carry him under. Relaxing for a moment, John used the momentum of the blow to lift himself onto the bar, freeing his legs. He kicked the Viking in the stomach.

Pausing for breath, John felt his hand nudge his cup of coffee. Today, more than ever, he was overjoyed to be a caffeine addict. Picking up the cup, he brought it down on the Viking's nose. The Viking staggered back a step, bringing his hand up to wipe away the blood and creamy coffee that dripped down his upper lip. Now the mighty Viking was truly annoyed. No—more than *irritert*, he was downright *rasende*. Furious. John's eyes widened in dismay. *Oh crap!* The Viking growled, the sound morphing into a bull roar as he charged John, gripping him tightly around the ribs, trapping his arms at his side. Struggling to breathe, John knew that he needed to do something quickly before he blacked out. Closing his eyes, he smashed his head forward, connecting with the big man's nose once again. The grip loosened, but the bull roar was back, making John's ears hurt with the noise of it so close to his tympanic membrane. And then suddenly, John was flying across the room, landing on his ribs against a table edge, the contents of the table spilling across his back. He was certain he felt his ribs crack.

Down, gasping on the floor, all he could smell was vinegar and cheap wine. All he could hear was the buzzing in his head and the sirens of the Politi. *How am I going to extract myself from this situation without being pulverized or arrested?*

John spied a set of car keys protruding from a white leather purse. He reached over and fisted the keys, keeping them out of sight until the Viking approached with murder in his every movement. Driving his fist into the man's kneecap, using the trick he'd employed earlier in the evening, John was shocked when the Viking kept coming. *Oh crap oh crap oh crap.* Fear was beginning to take hold when John suddenly noticed a chair arcing toward his attacker's head. The Viking lurched forward, and John watched the man's eyes roll back in his head. And then a familiar voice was urging him up and a familiar, beautiful hand grabbed his.

"Caroline!" he gasped in astonishment.

"Come. Now!" she ordered, and he obeyed.

Clutching his ribs as he ran with her to the stairs, he ascended to their room, running while he still could. Still numb from shock, John couldn't yet feel the pain in his face and chest.

Because her hands were shaking so badly, John removed the card-key from her grip and slid it through the slot, moving them into the meticulously tidied room. Their house never looked this tidy!

"How?" he asked incredulously, inquiring about the rescue, not the room.

"I packed everything and came down to meet you." She panted, speaking in a rush. "Then that giant threw you across the room, and I saw the pain in your eyes and I had to stop him. We have to get away!"

Turning to her, he saw the terror edging into her eyes. "Now's not the time to panic. We need to grab our things and then a taxi and find somewhere to lie low until our train departs." He gripped her shoulder firmly with one hand while the other braced his ribs. "All right?"

She nodded, and the panic seemed to fade enough to allow her to act. Gathering the bag with their gear, John took her hand. Scanning the corridors, he listened for sounds of pursuit and, hearing none, led them out of the room and down the back stairs, exiting by a rear door. He scanned the environment again, noting the arrival of the Politi to the front of the building. Walking quickly away from the hotel, he led her to the next street over, where he hailed a taxi to take them to the rail station, John purchased a ticket for Stockholm once they arrived.

"Why are you buying tickets? Didn't they give us tickets? Didn't they give us a way to get home?" Her voice rose stridently as she spoke.

"Caroline. Stop!" Calmly, he explained, "The other tickets were purchased under our legends. It won't take the Politi long to trace us to the fight and then locate our travel plans. We need a different way to get home."

Her eyes wide, she stared up at him. "But ... but you were the victim. Won't the police help us?"

"We definitely don't want to be tied up with the local police. If they trace my activities here, it's going to look more than a little suspicious." Weaving his fingers into her hair, he pulled her head against his chest. "Listen, sweetheart, that fellow knew my name. It wasn't a random brawl. It was an assassination attempt. You saved my life."

As she pulled back to see his face again, tears sped to her eyes. "Really? It was good that I came along?"

"It was very good. Thank you." She nodded, and he continued speaking just to keep her from crying. "We'll have a connection to make in Lillestrom, but we won't be in Oslo as they'll expect. I used a backup legend to purchase these tickets and paid in euros. Once we get out of Drammen, we should be free and clear."

Nodding slowly, she seemed to be processing the information, visibly calming. "How long will it take?" she asked.

"Five and a half hours to Stockholm, and then we'll catch a Lufthansa or KLM flight to London," he said.

"What about your injuries?"

"We can look after them on the train," he said. "There's no time now."

Nodding once, she followed him, clinging tightly to his hand as they queued and then found their seats. As soon as they were settled, she insisted they go into the loo.

"Take off your shirt," she commanded and, tearing one of his T-shirts into strips, bound his ribs, easing his discomfort.

"Why, Mrs. Brock, you do seem to enjoy getting me out of my clothes," he teased, trying to lighten her dark panic, but the words served only to release it. She burst into tears. "Oh, sweetheart," he murmured. He braced his hip against the handrail to protect them from the buffeting movement of the train and then pulled her into his arms. "It's all right. We're safe now."

Back in their seats, he wrapped his madras jacket around her and took her hand, intertwining their fingers and leaning down to whisper in her ear, "You saved my life once again."

Tentatively, she smiled, resting her head against his shoulder. This train journey was so different from the last. There were no kisses and whispered seductions, only fear and memories of danger.

Maryn Dale woke in a panic, immediately flipping on her bedside light to ensure it had all been a dream. Her pounding heartbeat accompanied her heaving breaths as she pushed off the edge of the bed and made her way to the kitchen past the snoring bulk of Sonam's new recruit, Augustus Doon, sleeping peacefully on the couch. Reaching far into the back of the freezer, she retrieved the vodka she kept hidden there for emergencies. Well, what *she* considered an emergency. She filled the shot glass and downed the contents once, twice, three times. Then she drew an ice pack from the freezer and held it against the back of her neck.

*Sleep without dreams. That's all I'm seeking, is sleep without dreams.* She had brought her man, Sonam Narayan, to bed, trying to ensure a complete night's sleep. The nightmares were usually unpredictable, but she'd had one two nights in a row, and she simply didn't want any more. *How did that … Brother … whatever … Brother Phillip … feel such peace? I ordered him to give up John to me for capture. I threatened to shoot him. How could he smile when I killed him? What devil is this man?*

The sweat dripping between her shoulder blades tickled, and she shuddered at the sensation. She needed to exorcise this man from her mind, from her conscience. *John is to blame. He was the reason I met that man. John and his wife are going to pay. Tor assured me that they would pay.*

"John, the Chairman of the JIC is on line three for you," Caroline said. She could have used the intercom to let him know about the call, but she wanted to check on him. He'd insisted on coming in today even though she felt it was much too early to be back at work. And he'd refused to see either his own doctor or the duty physician about his injuries.

Confirming her suspicions, he winced at every movement as he reached for the phone. She stayed and watched rather than moving back to her desk.

Grimly, he sighed "Very well" into the receiver and then rang off. "Louis Trevena wants to see me before the meeting of the Joint Intelligence Committee … to discuss China. I'm hoping he's planning to narrow things down a bit. I'm off to Whitehall." He sounded so weary.

"John? Why don't you go home after your meeting—or, better yet, go and see a doctor? West Middlesex isn't far from there. Or we could go on the way home. Honey, you're obviously in pain," she said.

Shaking his head, he wrapped an arm across his ribs and rose slowly from his chair. Immediately, the colour drained from his face, causing the bruises there to stand out more dramatically against his pallor. "I'll be fine," he said. "See you later."

But she wasn't convinced. "Will you end up as sick as you were in Burma when your ribs were broken?" she asked quietly.

A weak smile of reassurance tried to pull past the grimace on his face. "No. I was badly injured there, weak, dehydrated. I'll be fine," he said.

She nodded, trying to prevent the sorrow she felt in her heart from sliding down her cheeks.

"Can you please let Hibb know where I've gone?" he said.

"Of course," she replied as she watched him bury his pain behind blankness, ease himself fully upright, and pace wearily through the Grid and out the pods.

She didn't see him again until he returned—exhausted, drawn and limping—at the end of the workday. She lurched from her chair when she saw him.

"Oh, sweetheart, let's go home," she said.

Shutting down her computer, she pulled her purse from the drawer. As he limped around to face the security pods, she slipped her arm around his waist, helping him walk to the car. *I know he's hurting if he'll let me help him.* Pity filled her as she watched him struggle to fold into the driver's seat.

"John darling, I'll drive," she offered.

He stood, leaning against the roof of the car. "You don't like to drive here on the proper side." His voice was strained and breathy as he attempted humour.

"You can watch for oncoming Brits," she suggested, laughing softly.

He groaned. "Don't make me laugh. It hurts." He passed the keys over to her, giving her hand a grateful squeeze after she'd reclined the passenger seat and clipped his seatbelt. "Thank you," he said.

She drove as quickly as she could manage and as slowly as the traffic would allow, John calling out the occasional "veer left" or "right a bit."

Once home, Caroline sent John off to bed. Soon, however, he reappeared, limping and holding his ribs.

"Sweetheart, you need to rest so you can heal," she said, giving him a stern look of disapproval.

"My ribs don't feel any better lying down than standing up, so I'd rather be in here with you," he replied.

She softened. "You are sweet. But if you're going to be out here, I want you to sit down," she said.

"As you say, boss," he replied, giving her a small salute.

"Very funny," she replied wryly. Caroline gathered cushions of all shapes and lofts over to the couch and propped them hither and yon.

"What's this?" he asked.

"A cocoon. Sit down, and I'll arrange it until you're comfortable. Then you can relax and watch the news." He looked at her dubiously but sat slowly against the pillows. She cajoled him into providing instructions until she saw the pain fade from his eyes and heard a sigh of contentment. Handing him the remote control, she returned a few minutes later with an ice-cold glass of ginger ale and the newspaper.

"Okay?" she asked.

He hmmmed. "My feet are hot." She rolled her eyes at him and removed his socks.

"Anything else, your highness?" she inquired sarcastically.

He wiggled his eyebrows at her. "Maybe later," he said.

She smiled. "Perhaps, unless you're too disabled." He returned her smile.

Once the commotion was settled, Rufus came over, planting his head on the couch beside John's leg at perfect petting height.

After supper, Caroline puttered away at the computer as John sat on the couch watching the television, occasionally dropping his hand to Rufus's head to scratch the devoted canine's ears.

"John, what is the SBS?"

"Special Boat Service," he responded, eyes still fixed on the television.

"Special Boat Service?" she said. "What's that?"

"You've heard of the SAS?" he asked.

"Yep. That survival guy was in the SAS, the one who launches himself into deserts, ice fields and the wilderness, picnicking on juicy grubs and slugs," she said.

John chuckled lightly. "Like the SAS, the SBS is part of Special Forces, but their remit is to complete missions that require specific naval skills."

"They only work on the water?" she asked.

Glancing briefly at her, he grinned. "Normally they function in water operations, but they also operate inland. They've completed operations in the mountains of Afghanistan and the deserts of Iraq, wherever they're needed."

"Why would you receive a message from Corporal Mick Adair of the SBS?" she asked.

"I was in the SBS—the Maritime Terrorism Command, specifically. I'm still in the reserves. Mick was in my patrol," he replied.

"You were in the Special Forces? Why didn't you tell me?" she asked.

Turning his head to look back over his shoulder, he said, "I did. In the jungle, you asked me how I knew how to do all that survival stuff, and I told you I was in the Special Forces."

"Oh, yeah. Very cool!" she said.

"Cheers." He chuckled at her obvious delight.

"Mick wants you to play rugby. He says you can bring your 'bit of stuff.' What is that supposed to mean?" *What "stuff" would you bring to a rugby game?* When John didn't answer immediately, she continued, "When did you play rugby? At university?"

"Before we were married," he said.

She walked over to the couch and sat on the coffee table beside his bare feet, resting her hand on his crossed ankles.

"You used to play rugby? Why did you stop?" she asked.

He shrugged again, tilting his head to see the news around her shoulder, his fingers drumming a rhythm on his leg. That percussion clearly told her he had something to say to her.

As she spoke, she watched his fingers. "I never asked you what you did before. When we got married, I just assumed that life started today."

Stilling his fingers, he reached out to lightly touch her face. "That was my old life."

"This is another one of those submit/love paradigms, isn't it?" she asked. She had his full attention now, probably because he had no idea what she was talking about. "Well, you've loved me by changing your activities for me, but I haven't been submitting to your need for leisure. Except for Rufus and church, we've allowed our life to become consumed by work. You don't do anything for pleasure."

He gave a crooked half-smile, and she felt a blush rise up her cheeks as a direct result of the glint in his eye. "There's one thing in particular that brings me a great deal of pleasure. And you too, I hope."

"Oh yes, my love. Me too," she said, grinning from ear to ear.

The telephone interrupted their innuendo, and Caroline rose reluctantly to answer it.

"Hello?" she said.

"Er, hello," an unfamiliar female voice said in what sounded like astonishment. "I'm looking for John Brock."

"This is Caroline. John's indisposed at the moment. Can I take a message?" Caroline said. John tilted his head back to look at her, and she could feel the blush returning at the passion still present in his gaze.

"Are you his housekeeper?" the voice asked.

"Housekeeper?" Caroline said, surprised, back to her caller. "I'm his wife."

"Wife? John's married?"

Caroline watched John's brow furrow and tried to wave him back to the couch, but he rose and came to her anyway.

"Um, who is this?" Caroline asked, feeling she'd already given away too much information to an unknown person. Not good tradecraft, Aubrey would tell her.

"This is his sister, Sharon."

"Oh, hello, Sharon," Caroline replied, and John froze in mid-step. "John's—" But he gestured wildly to let her know he didn't want to take the call, moving so rapidly he ended up folded over his ribs in pain. Caroline frowned severely at him, pointing back to the couch. He complied.

"I wanted to let John know that Dad's been having chest pains; they've admitted him to St. Mary's Hospital. They're doing tests to see if he's had a heart attack. He should get off his high horse and come and visit him," Sharon said, her voice angry.

"Who?" Caroline asked. "Your father or John?"

"I beg your pardon?" Sharon replied indignantly. "They think it may be my father's heart."

"I wasn't aware that he had one," Caroline said. Then she held out the telephone toward John. "She hung up."

"What was that about?" John asked.

"That was your sister, Sharon. She says your father is having chest pains. And he should get off his high horse and come and … wait, no it was your … frankly, I don't have any idea what the difference is between a high horse and a low horse," Caroline said.

"My father's had a heart attack? Humph, I wasn't aware that he had one," John replied.

"That's what I said." Caroline walked back over to the couch, straddling John's lap. She watched as a mask of blankness took over his features. "John, sweetheart? Are you okay?"

"Fine," he said in a calm, emotionless voice as he gazed off into the middle distance.

Touching his chin first, she traced her fingers along his features, his forehead, his ears, his lips, until his attention was focused on her and the blankness retreated. “John. Stay with me, please. Tell me how you’re feeling.”

He sighed sadly. “Hearing from her … him … it just brings back old memories. None of them good,” John said, his voice soft. Caroline could see the wretched grief in his eyes.

Gently, she wrapped her arms around him. “I love you, John. God loves you. He is your real father. Charles Brock was just a man who provided sperm and bad memories. You didn’t deserve any of that abuse.”

“I know,” he said, pulling her closer, burying his face against her neck. “I don’t want to talk about it.”

“I know, baby, but it will never get any better *unless* you talk about it. Would you rather speak with a counsellor?” she asked. Pulling back abruptly, he looked at her like she was crazy. “Then you’re going to have to trust me.”

“I trust you, Caroline,” he said. “I simply don’t want to talk about it.”

“Please, John? It would help to talk about it,” she said.

“It hurts,” he murmured, and she just held him, refusing to move away until he let her soothe some of the pain in his heart. He seemed to struggle for a long time, and then she felt the tension relax minutely. “All right … if you’ll stay right where you are.”

“Agreed,” she said, smiling against his shoulder.

“What do you want to know?” he asked.

“What happened after your mother died?” she asked.

“I went to boarding school,” he replied.

“I thought most Brits went to boarding school much earlier than that. You were eleven, almost twelve,” she said.

“There was a middle school across the way, and so I attended that as a day student,” he said.

“Did your sister go away as well?” she said.

“Sharon?” he asked.

“Yes,” she replied slowly. “You only have one sister, don’t you?” she asked, not at all certain that she was correct.

“Yes,” he said.

“She stayed home?”

“Yes.”

“Why?” she asked. He shrugged in reply. “You’re not going to make this easy for me, are you?” she asked, pulling back to look him in the face. “This is not an interrogation. It's okay to give away more information than I'm asking."

He looked down between them and released a sad sigh. "She stayed home and I was sent away. Sharon, in many respects, was my father's child and I was my mother's. My sister could do no wrong in my father's eyes and I could do nothing right."

"Did Sharon ever try to help you?" Caroline asked.

John looked as though he couldn't understand the question. "Why would she? My father's wrath was not something to tempt."

"So, she never helped you," Caroline confirmed sadly.

"I never expected her to," he replied.

Caroline nodded. *Oh, sweetheart. No wonder you expect so little from those around you.* "What happened at boarding school?"

"The first two weeks at the new school were a nightmare. I started after the term had begun, and so I was behind already. I was reprimanded on my second day for not having my coursework completed."

Slowly she asked, afraid of his response, "When you say reprimanded, what do you mean?"

"Caned."

"Oh, John." She hugged him tightly to her in sympathy. "I thought corporal punishment was banned."

"It is banned … now. They didn't use the cane in the grammar school I attended, but it was still used in many of the private schools," he said.

"Oh, sweetheart," she said, breathing her sorrow against his skin.

"I was caned again the next week for some prank or something, I don't really remember," John said. "After that, I met Professor Lewis. He hauled me into his office, and I expected another reprimand for whatever. I didn't even know what rule I'd broken, but that had never mattered before, so I awaited his judgment. He sat on the edge of his desk watching me for the longest time. I decided to wait him out, but he had more patience than I did.

"Finally, I asked what I'd done. I'll never forget what he said." John adopted a particular accent and tone that Caroline assumed mimicked his teacher. "He said, 'John, you are a bright and talented young man.' Well, I wasn't used to compliments of any kind, particularly not from teachers. He had my attention then, I can tell you. He continued, 'Great men learn to comply with the expectations of those around them without conforming to their world view.' After that, he moved around to the back of his desk and took his chair, pulling out his reading glasses and opening a book in front of him. I was baffled, intrigued. So I asked, 'What do you mean, sir?' He replied, 'You bring trouble down on your head for no purpose. You are an intelligent lad and could excel here if you could learn to comply with the rules: complete your coursework on time, maintain self-discipline, follow the rules of the school.' He removed his glasses and shifted forward across his desk. 'I will make a bargain with you. If you will learn to comply but not conform, meaning that you obey the rules, do your work but still allow your own ideas free reign, then I will take you with me, along with my two nephews, skiing in the Swiss Alps over the holiday break.'

"I was gobsmacked. I'm certain that nowadays he would have been up on charges for inappropriate and unprofessional behaviour, but it wasn't abnormal for professors to take students on holidays in those days. He told me that if I could keep my marks up and avoid the cane, then he would speak to my father and gain permission for me to go skiing with him. Then he dismissed me. He didn't wait for my agreement. He simply left me to decide. Well, I decided that I truly wanted to go. It was a way to avoid spending Christmas with my father, and that was enough motivation for me. I threw myself into school life. I joined every team and club available and found I was quite good … at all of it. I completed my coursework and discovered that I was quite bright, just as Lewis had said. I began to make friends who weren't delinquents and achieve success, and for once in my life, there were adults around me who liked me, who thought I was 'good' at things."

"What happened?" she said.

"Lewis took me on the trip, and I had an incredible time. I was never reprimanded at school again, and I did well. I won a scholarship to Eton and then to Oxford," he replied.

"What did you study at Oxford?" she inquired. "I've never asked you," she added in chagrin.

"Oriental Studies," he said.

"Ah, now some things begin to make sense," she said, pulling back to smile at him. "What happened back home?"

"Home was home. I managed to avoid seeing my father for the next two years. For my fourteenth birthday, some well-meaning fool decided I should be allowed home for the weekend as a reward for my hard work, the last place I wanted to spend my birthday." John's face grew distant.

"What happened?" she asked quietly.

His face turned back to her. "My father had started drinking very heavily."

"Was he an alcoholic?" she asked.

"Definitely, though that's not something one is really permitted to discuss around here. But I don't quite recall when the drinking shifted from social to addiction or when the violence and neglect came to be associated with it. My home was simply a nightmare that I avoided whenever possible," he said.

"John, sweetheart," she breathed his name, her heart full of the pain of sympathy for his unhappy childhood.

"Do you want me to stop?" he murmured against her hair.

She shook her head. "No. I'm sorry, I'm just so sorry for the pain you've suffered." She pulled him close.

"Caroline?" He pulled back from her to meet her gaze, cupping her face gently in his hands, stroking his thumbs across her lips. "You've given me only happiness. All that pain is in the past. You're my here and now."

"I love you so much." She burrowed against his shoulder, kissing him and wrapping herself around him. "I'm sorry for all the times I'm grumpy and grouchy and—"

In a flash, he covered her mouth with his hand, stopping her speech. Replacing his hand with his mouth, he kissed her sweetly and tenderly.

"Don't do that. Don't try to make up for my past. Be yourself. You know that your supposed 'grumpiness' means nothing to me. Don't start being anything but who you are, for you are perfect," he said.

"John." She spoke his name in the deepest assurance of love and devotion possible between a man and a woman. "All right. Please go on." She wrapped her arms around his shoulders again, playing with the hair at the nape of his neck.

"Where was I?" he asked.

"Fourteenth birthday," she said.

"Ah yes. I took the latest possible bus and arrived at my house around eight in the evening, immediately turning around and finding the local delinquents I used to hang with. As I left the house, my father hollered after me, 'Be in by ten.' I tried to decide, as the time passed, whether coming in at ten would qualify as complying or conforming, and then I decided that the Professor would likely tell me to comply, so I did. I made it to the house right at ten, but the doors were locked and I couldn't get in. As little as I wanted to sleep in my old bedroom that night, I needed someplace to sleep, so I began thumping on the door, calling for my father. He answered about ten minutes later, drunk. He was furious. As soon as I crossed the threshold, he started in on me, yelling and cursing and telling me what a useless—" John stopped speaking, and then resumed. "Well, you don't need to hear what he called me. And Sharon was there beside him, trying to get him back to bed and get me to apologize to him for being late...and rude...and born, I suppose. When he called me a son of a..." He looked at Caroline again. "Well, you know. Something inside me snapped and I told him to shut up. He stopped for a moment, and I'll always remember the way his eyes shifted from shock to rage in under a second. He reached for his belt. When he came after me, I decided I'd had enough. I'd had enough of being bullied. At school, I had learned that I was intelligent, athletic and well-liked. I was at the top of my class and a rugby star. I didn't have to put up with this anymore. He obviously thought of me still as the skinny, underfed twelve-year-old he'd sent away. But I wasn't any longer. I was taller than him by at least two inches, and I was fit from sports and good, healthy food. When he advanced on me, I socked him one."

"Did you? Oh, really, did you?" Caroline pulled back from him with excitement and approval on her face.

"I laid him out, flat on his back. You approve of that?" he asked, clearly surprised.

"John, someone once said that we have no choice about being brought into this world and so all we owe our parents is respect. An abusive or neglectful parent forfeits their right to respect, so what's left? You don't owe your father anything. He forfeited his rights to you when he abused you. You don't owe him anything. I'm glad you decked him. He certainly deserved it," she said.

"Well, it certainly changed things for me. I walked away from him and went to bed for the first peaceful sleep I'd had in that house since my early childhood."

"Where was Sharon when this happened?" she asked.

He shrugged. "I don't know. She was there at breakfast the next day."

"What happened in the morning?" Caroline asked.

"My father didn't refer to the incident. Nor did Sharon. But Dad sported a beauty of a shiner…and he never tried to hit me again. I still spent as much time away from home as possible, but I was no longer worried about being there," he said.

"So, you've really dealt with your father?" she said.

"I don't know about that. Merely the mention of him still makes me angry," he said.

"Are you going to go and see him?" she asked after a moment.

"I don't know. I suppose I have to," he said.

"Why?" she asked. "He broke the relationship. He should repair it."

"Now that I'm a Christian, I'm not really certain how … what … I don't know," he said, sighing against her neck.

"If your father chose to apologize, would you accept it?" she asked.

He shrugged. "Don't know. What does the Bible say?"

"Let's find out. One thing I know from dealing with Henry's family is that the church often misjudges a Christian's role in an abusive family." She held his face gently in her hands. "We'll read and search and figure it out—"

"Together."

# Chapter Seven
# *Hide and Seek*

*Boom!*

Caroline's sleep was shattered by an explosion. Before she had finished processing her fear, John had rolled her onto the floor and under the bed. She heard Velcro rip and looked over to see him bending down beside the bedside table, reaching inside against the edge, appearing for a moment with his Glock and then bending again. Another rip from under the bed and he produced a loaded magazine, slamming it into the pistol grip until it clicked and then pressing the slide release button, forcing the slide forward, chambering the first bullet. Reaching up, he grabbed her cell phone and handed it under the bed to her.

"Stay here," John said. Emitting a distinctive whistle, he ordered Rufus under the bed beside her. "Call the Grid and then emergency services." Standing, he gripped his ribs, but she still heard his barely suppressed groan of pain.

"John," she called, and his feet paused. "Be safe."

Affirming, he limped out of the room, closing the door behind him. Calling into the Grid, Caroline told them what she knew: they'd been awakened by an explosion, and John had gone to investigate. And then she called the police.

It seemed like hours before Caroline heard sirens outside, but it couldn't have been more than 15 minutes. Much more time passed, though, before she heard footsteps in the house.

"Caroline?" She heard Jade Kovic's voice. "Caroline? It's Jade. John sent me. He said to tell you Y-F-A. Don't know what that means. Do you?"

Pushing the seriously quivering Rufus out before her, Caroline crawled out from under the bed. "I'm in here, Jade."

The door opened slowly, and then Jade's handgun appeared around the corner followed by her head. "Are you well?"

"I'm fine," Caroline said. "What happened?"

"Well, no one seems certain at the moment, but it looks like someone planted a bomb with a timer under Carlisle's car, which was meant to explode with John in it on the way to Thames House. Aubrey seems to feel that Ziegler's new handheld tablet computer may have prematurely triggered the bomb."

"Are they okay?" Caroline asked.

"No word yet," Jade said.

"John?" Caroline said.

"Fine."

"What happens now?" Caroline asked.

"John's ordered me to take you to a safe house," Jade replied.

"Fine. Is he still wearing his shorts and T-shirt?" Caroline asked.

"Yes. Nice legs," Jade said.

Absurdly, Caroline chuckled. "I'll send some pants for him."

"Pants? He's got pants," Jade said.

"Trousers," Caroline said, once again stuck in the Canadian-English Vocabulary Gap. "Does he want a suit?"

"You would know better than I," Jade said.

Caroline set out a suit, tie, shirt, socks and shoes for John and tucked them into a garment bag. Then she went into the bathroom to shower and change.

"What can I do with Rufus? Can I bring him along?" Caroline asked.

"I don't think so," Jade said. "John told me to send him over to Hibb's."

"Do you think I could go in and speak to Katie Hibbert on the way?" Caroline desperately wanted to talk to her best friend about John and his father. She knew that Katie and Hibb had wrestled with their own share of issues that resulted from Hibb's alcoholic father and mentally ill mother. Katie always had good advice. But it was difficult to hold a serious conversation over the telephone with her little ones always needing attention.

"That wouldn't be a good idea, Caroline. It could put her and the children at risk. I'll send the dog over with Lawrence," Jade said.

Disheartened, Caroline agreed, not wanting to bring any risk to her friend or her wonderful daughters. "Okay. I want to speak to John."

"He's with the JIC right now. They're very concerned that this assassin is starting to endanger civilians," Jade said.

"Oh, so it's okay for the assassin to kill John but not anyone else," Caroline said, and gall rose in her gorge. "Sometimes I don't understand why he works for these people," Caroline muttered bitterly. "Jade, take me to the Grid. I don't want to go to a safe house."

"John ordered me to take you to a safe house, Caroline. I don't think I can disobey a direct order," Jade said.

"Is John going to a safe house?" Caroline asked.

"Er, no," Jade replied.

"Then neither am I," Caroline said. "Take me to the Grid. I'll be safe there."

"Caroline, please don't put me in this position. He gave me a direct order." The usually implacable Jade looked positively nervous. "I think he only means it to be for a few hours."

Caroline pulled out her cell phone.

John answered after two rings. "Brock."

"I want to go to the Grid, not a safe house," she said.

"Fine," John said. "Tell Jade."

"You tell her." Caroline passed the phone to Jade, grabbed her windbreaker, and walked to the car. Jade met her in the car and handed the cell phone back to her.

"He says to take you to the Grid," Jade said. "Lawrence will take Rufus over to the Hibberts'. I guess Hibb's not too happy about it."

"No. His daughters love Rufus and always pester him for a puppy after he's been over."

Maryn Dale spoke to the shadows, knowing that her little man, her mole inside the Security Services, would be waiting as ordered. She lifted her arms seductively, combing her lithe fingers through her raven locks as she watched him move forward into the shadowy light of the alley. His eyes deepened with desire at the sight of her.

"Itinerary?" she asked without preamble.

"Of course," he replied, handing her an SD card. Hearing his breath hitch as she neared, she leaned in slowly to kiss him on the cheek, high, very close to his ear. Fingertips lightly touching the crimson imprint, he continued, his voice husky with desire. "They're increasing security because of the last failed attempt. He's finally scuttled off to a safe house," he said.

She swore vehemently and then quickly regained her cool. "Well done, my pet. You should return to work now." When he didn't immediately depart, she snapped at him, "Go!" He flushed hotly, turning away. "See you soon, my pet," she added, and he looked back once, the raw desire returning to his eyes.

Caroline scanned the oddly familiar Tesco, seeing the cavernous space, barely filled with fifteen-foot shelves stacked high with bins, boxes and produce, uncovered ducts and struts visible across the ceiling. They were now staying in the second safe house of the past three weeks, first one in Guildford and then one in Reading. This was the fourth grocery store they'd used, trying to keep from repeating any activity to prevent their enemies from once again getting close.

Looking over toward the entrance, Caroline saw the now familiar security officers, Daffy and Bugs, surveying the street outside the Tesco, watching for any lethal intent. There were so many security personnel suddenly a part of their life that she couldn't remember all their names and had taken to giving them more memorable nicknames.

"You know, this new shopping routine is simply smashing," Caroline said in her best British accent. John chuckled at her as he loaded groceries onto the conveyor belt. "Waiting while every aisle is cleared before going down it," she said. "The forty-five minute tour of Richmond to lose any tails was simply fascinating. How many times did we drive past Hampton Court Palace and the Royal Botanical Gardens today?" John shrugged, still smiling at her. "Assassins are quite annoying, aren't they?"

"Annoying?" John chuckled again. "You certainly have your own unique take on life, don't you, darling?" John wrapped his arm around her waist, nudging her back against him.

Paying and moving out to their Volvo, Caroline couldn't resist teasing, "Boot or bonnet, my love?"

"Boot," he replied gamely.

"In the real world, that is called a trunk," she said.

"Elephants have trunks, darling. Even in the new world," he said.

She laughed at his words but could see that he was plainly distracted by the garbage truck parked in the grocery-store parking lot.

"Garbage truck." She pointed as she labelled the vehicle.

"Bin lorry." He flicked a glance back and then patted the roof of their Volvo. "Car?"

"Yes," she confirmed, sliding into the passenger seat and fastening her seatbelt before John pulled out of the parking lot. "The whole vocabulary thing is quite fascinating," she said. "Do you know I actually embarrassed Aubrey the other day by telling him I liked his pants? He flushed beat red until Jade reminded me that pants are underwear here. So I told him I liked his trousers, but it didn't help much by that time. Poor guy!"

Looking over when John failed to respond, Caroline noted his white-knuckled grip on the steering wheel and his intense concentration on the rearview mirror.

"What's wrong?" she asked, the tension engulfing her.

"Since when do they collect the rubbish at night?" he replied. "Where is that security detail?" He pulled out his cell phone, presumably to contact them, but paused when the lorry drew nearer.

Accelerating, John made a quick right and then right again and the lorry disappeared from view. Caroline knew because her eyes were fixed on the side-view mirror.

A motorcycle suddenly appeared, speeding up. *If objects in this mirror are closer than they appear, we're in big trouble.*

"John!" she warned. Too late. *Smash!* The biker lobbed a small object through the shattered window and into the back seat of their brilliant blue Volvo. The object rolled and bounced around the bench seat.

Abruptly, John veered toward the motorcycle, sending it weaving toward the corner of the Shaw Theatre. It disappeared from view with a bump and crunch.

"What is it?!" he asked, his voice tense. "What did he toss in?"

Caroline released her seatbelt and looked over the head rest. "It's a cylinder or something. Made of metal. I don't know what it is!" she said.

"Get it and throw it out the window!" John commanded, dropping his cell phone into the cup holder and attaching both his hands to the steering wheel. He accelerated.

Reaching over the seat, she stretched and stretched, the headrest digging into her ribs. *Almost.* The object of doom brushed past her fingertips and she could almost reach … but the car bounced over a pothole and the cylinder slid beyond her grasp and under the seat. *Aughh!*

"I can't reach it! I can't get it!" she cried as she contorted her body over and around the seat, the item always out of reach. John slammed on the brakes, throwing her against the dash, her back colliding and head hitting the windshield. "Ouch!" she cried.

Fisting the front of her shirt, John dragged her across the gearshift and out onto the pavement. *Ow! Ow! Ow!* Not giving her time to gain her balance, he dragged her away to the corner and then around it. Pressing his body over hers, he flattened her into the asphalt. The explosion ripped up the street.

Caroline struggled to breathe. Grey pushed at the edges of her mind. *I'm going to pass out. Why is this happening?* Eyes shut tight and ears ringing, she felt her body thrust upright, slapping to protect herself. *Who is it? What do you want? John!*

"Caroline! It's me!" John yelled. "Are you all right?" Her eyes flew open and she nodded, shaky and unable to produce words to answer. "Come!" he commanded.

Taking her hand, he pulled her after him, clutching his ribs with his other arm. "Get your mobile!" he said. She reached into her pocket, but she was shaking so badly that she dropped it. He released her, shoving her forward. She assumed he retrieved it and dialled, because he was soon at her back again, forcing her forward, one hand holding the phone. Even through the buzzing in her head, she could hear his exclamations of pain and frustration, though she couldn't decode the words he spoke. *Why does everything smell like burnt marshmallows?*

Terror and shock driving her steps, she ran and ran, always his hand on her shoulder, her back, her hand, prodding her onward until finally they reached a grocery store. The bright ruby-red letters and familiar peaked roof called to her. *Thank you, God, for Tesco's.*

John pulled her into the store, slowing to a walk as he led her down one aisle and then the next, circling back and doing all the things that spies do to catch out their pursuers.

"They haven't followed. Caroline? They haven't followed us," he said, taking her firmly by the shoulders. Still gasping brokenly, she couldn't seem to capture enough oxygen for her lungs.

Wide-eyed, she looked around. They were back in the frozen-food section of a Tesco, the same one or a different one, she wasn't certain. People were giving them odd looks and making a wide arc around them.

"Caroline, look at me," John said. "We're safe now. Caroline?"

She gasped and then took a shuddering breath, finally filling her lungs. "I'm … okay."

John tipped her chin to meet his gaze, deep concern furrowing his brow. She fell against him, clinging, beginning to cry. He pulled back from her, gripping her shoulders again.

"Don't cry!" he ordered. "I can't let you cry yet, understand? Answer me!" His voice was firm and commanding.

"Bossy," she said, her voice quiet and quivering, sniffing to control her reaction.

Smiling at the accusation, he pulled her close again. She hugged him in return, lightening her grip when he grunted at the pain in his chest.

One arm around her, John reached into the freezer behind them and retrieved two bags of frozen peas, handing one to her and keeping one. She immediately held it to the back of her head where it had impacted the windshield. He released her and held his to his scraped and bleeding elbow, an injury she didn't even remember him acquiring.

"What now?" she asked tremulously.

"I'll try to contact Daffy and Bugs again." Caroline knew he was trying to keep her calm when he used her silly nicknames. "How did that bl … dam … motorcycle get so close?" He angrily punched the numbers into her cell phone. Following that, he called Aubrey to tell him what happened and instruct him to send backup, at least the plods, someone to get them home.

Ten minutes later, Caroline heard a siren outside the grocery store, and then there was an announcement.

"Could Mr. and Mrs. George Davis please report to the manager's office?" They recognized the names of their legends used in Burma—Aubrey's inspiration.

The police officers took in their shabby appearances and naturally assumed that they were the victims of attack.

"Do you need a doctor, sir?" the female constable asked.

John turned to survey Caroline's injuries. "No, I don't think so," he said. "Home will do."

"Very good, sir," the constable replied.

"How much backup did you bring?" John immediately took charge of the situation.

"There are two more cars waiting to escort you," she said.

John nodded. Taking Caroline's hand firmly in his, he followed the officers to the car and on to a third safe house that Aubrey had quickly arranged.

They drank about a gallon of water and then showered, carefully removing the grit and detritus and little pieces of their brilliant blue Volvo from their skin and hair. John checked every inch of Caroline clinically, tending each wound and muttering curses under his breath the entire time, finally concluding with, "Who is doing this? Who has enough money and influence to be this relentless?"

Caroline didn't bother responding. She knew he needed to vent. So, waiting patiently until he was finished ministering to her, she returned the favour. She knew that he would only stay still for a few minutes before his mind would require him to move to the next phase, which she suspected would involve several minutes of shouting at their security officers.

She was, in fact, correct. But he refused to take her out of the house again and refused to leave her alone. So he insisted the officers stand in the front hall while he harpooned them with sarcasm and disdain, finally dismissing them from his thoughts, insisting on a new security detail. He paced the upper room of the unfamiliar safe house with his Glock in his hand until the new detail arrived and he had double-checked their identities and qualifications by video-mail with Aubrey.

Once the house was tightly secured, John took her to bed, pulling her close and holding her tightly against him throughout the night.

John awoke feeling completely disoriented; the burnt-orange walls were strange, and the creaky bed was moving, the sound a disharmonious riot. Turning to Caroline, he saw that she was still asleep, thrashing at the covers, a look of intensity on her face.

"No! *No!*" she shouted. Hoping to calm her dreams, he reached over to touch her, and she swung at him, clipping him on the shoulder. "Henry!" she cried and came after him in earnest, flailing, kicking, punching.

"Caroline! It's me. It's John." He tried to grab at her hands, but she was wild, and he didn't want to hurt her. "Caroline!!"

Suddenly alert, she opened her eyes, frantically searching the unfamiliar room. She seemed to recognize him, and her eyes widened in relief. And then she burst into tears. Rolling into a ball, she covered her face with her hands. Sobs wracked her frame.

Moving cautiously closer, he tentatively touched her shoulder, still not certain she was really awake. "Caroline?" As soon as he touched her, she wrapped her arms around him, stroking her fingers along the scars on his back as though reassuring herself. "It's all right, my love, it's me. I'm here," he said.

"I don't know how much more of this I can take," she cried, shuddering in his arms.

Back in Thames House, their safety rumbled, John spent the next day storming through the Grid. Caroline spent the day acting as a shield between him and his officers and the registry clerks and the cleaning staff and anyone else who had the misfortune to walk across the Grid that day. Ryan came under fire so many times that he finally begged Hibb for an off-site mission. By evening, John had calmed to a very small degree.

They drove to another safe house, this one in Chelsea, past the row houses on Kings Road and onto a street of flats that could be best described as *grotty industrial*. John had insisted the service provide a pool car until they bought a new one to replace the exploded Volvo.

"I've finally coerced MI-6 into sending a team after Tor Grendahl," John said. "I had to threaten the Chairman of the JIC with—" He glanced aside at her and changed his mind. "Well, let's say I have evidence of a few choice secrets he'd rather no one discovered, particularly his mother."

Exhausted and dispirited, she leaned her head against the car window. She felt a perverse desire to laugh, but there was no humour in his voice. "They seem to find us wherever we go anyway," she said wearily. "Couldn't we just stay at home?"

"Not a chance!"

"You know, you don't have to speak to me in that tone of voice," she reminded him sharply.

Glancing aside, he rested a hand on her leg. "I'm sorry. I don't mean to take it out on you." Much gentler now, he continued, "We'll take a day to gather our things and then we'll need to get out of the city. It's one thing to be a target myself, but I won't leave us here where you're in danger as well. I've already started to make the arrangements with Aubrey. Day after tomorrow, we disappear for a while."

She nodded, replacing her head on the cool window. "Katie Hibbert sent a few books over for us to read."

"Hmmm. A book? What book?" he asked, clearly distracted.

"She said they really helped her and Hibb when they were dealing with his family," Caroline said. "If we do go away for a time, do you think we could read them together?"

Glancing over, he took her hand, pulling it to rest on his leg. "Do you think it would help?"

"I don't know, but I think it's worth a try," she replied.

"Very well," he said.

They concluded their drive in silence, parking around the back and entering through the rear.

"Could you please check our personal messages while I have a shower? In case someone who actually likes us has been trying to get in touch," she said, feeling *weary, weary … weary.*

"I like you, darling," he murmured, his hot mouth tracing a line from her collarbone to the crook of her jaw. She rested her head against his shoulder for a moment, giving him better access. "I like you a lot," he said.

Arching her neck, she kissed the spot just beneath his chin. "See you in a few minutes," she said.

"Hmmm," he murmured.

She wandered back out soon after. "I thought maybe a shower for two would be much more fun," she said. *And maybe, just maybe, it would help John relax.*

The telephone receiver cracked forcefully against the cradle. And John looked anything but relaxed sitting in the desk chair, his fingers stiffly covering his face.

"What's wrong?" Caroline asked, rushing over to wrap her arm around his shoulders. "John, what happened? What happened?" she repeated urgently. "Is it your father?"

Finally, he responded, blindly lifting the receiver to replay the voicemail message.

"Hello, Caroline. It's Simon, Simon Reldif. I've just arrived at Heathrow Airport and I was wondering if you knew of a good place to stay in London. Call me." Simon rhymed off a set of numbers and then concluded. "I'm really looking forward to seeing you again."

"He is not staying with us," John insisted, his tone hard and desperate, his face still hidden behind his hands.

"What? Why would he—" Pushing John back by the shoulder, she pressed her body between him and the desk. Brushing her fingers into his hair, she tilted his head up, carefully avoiding the nicks and bruises from the explosion. "John, tell me what you're thinking." He sighed, pulling her tightly against him, burying his face in her shirt. She waited but when he didn't respond, she insisted, "Tell me," becoming irritated by his persistent reluctance.

"What is he doing here?" John muttered. "How did he get our number? You are not—"

She pulled back abruptly and clapped her hand over his mouth. "Stop right there! We've settled this issue, haven't we? Mr. Bossyboots?"

"I'm not … don't call me that. I simply … oh, bloo … fine. Go to him." He dropped his hands to the edge of the desk and pushed away. Rising too quickly, he flinched at the pull on his ribs. Grunting at the discomfort, he strode toward the bedroom.

"Go to who … whom?" she called after him, bewildered, moving to follow him and uncover the mystery.

"S—"

Clapping her hand over his mouth again, she warned him, "If you say Simon, I am going to remove your chest hairs one by one. Understand?" She held him in a glare until his features began to relax. "I think I know what's running through that prattish mind of yours, but I'm not certain, so I'm willing to give you the benefit of the doubt. Tell me!" she insisted.

Caroline was annoyed that the arrival of Simon Reldif, the man John thought was in love with her, had triggered this response. *Oh Father, why now? Why now when we've only just clawed our way back into the vicinity of happy? When we have John's father to deal with? And an assassin?*

"Prattish? That is not a word." A smile ghosted across his lips.

"Pillocky? Boorish?" she said.

"Boorish could work." He tucked a lock of hair behind her ear. "Sorry."

"Because you're a—" She waited to let him fill in the blanks.

"Prat."

"And?" she said.

"A pillock."

"And?" she said.

"Hungry?"

Surprised, she laughed, and her anger dissipated for a moment. "Tell me," she said.

"No escape?" he said. And she shook her head at him. Visibly struggling, he finally dropped his chin in defeat. "Jealous," he muttered.

*Jealous? When I've faithfully stood by his side through this ugly mess of secrets and assassins?* Frustration exploded through her. "Why?" She was really angry now. "What cause have I ever given you to feel jealous?" He shrugged. "Arghh! You infuriating man!" she said. His shoulders slumped and suddenly she wanted to weep. *Will he ever trust me to stay?*

"John, would you ever leave me?" she asked.

He looked up, his eyes wide. "No. Never."

Exasperated, she inquired, "Then why do you always expect me to?"

"Everyone—" He stopped.

"What?" she urged him on impatiently.

"Everyone always leaves me. Eventually." His words were so quiet she had to strain to hear him.

How she could go from feeling such frustration to such pity in a millisecond, she would never understand. "Why do you feel that way? I understand that your mother betrayed you, and I know that when she died she left you alone to deal with your father's abuse, but surely by now you understand that that's not the same as intentionally abandoning you."

John went still, and Caroline could feel the menace coming off him in waves. "What do you mean, my mother betrayed me?" he said.

She sought to explain quickly as the warning bells began to clang. "She let your father beat the crap out of you. Why didn't she protect you?"

"She couldn't. She made an agreement with my father," he said.

His dark, inscrutable eyes were studying her very carefully, examining her. His jaw was clenching and unclenching. In a flash, his temper was strung as tight as a bow string. And, suddenly, she was afraid. She retreated, stepping back instinctively. Hand darting, he grabbed her arm to prevent her retreat.

"Tell me what you mean," he said. His voice was low and menacing, and she flinched at the heat there.

Bracing herself, she took a half step toward him. *I'm not running away from you.* "You let go of me now. This conversation is over until you calm down." His eyes widened marginally, but he didn't loosen his grip. "I mean it, John. Now!" Abruptly releasing her, he brushed past her and down the stairs. She heard the back door open and then close. That's when she began to shake. *Oh Father, why am I here? This is too hard for me.*

Her hands shaking, she texted Larry, their new security officer, informing him that John had gone out through the back door. Larry would follow John and protect him. Moe would stay behind to guard the house. Those weren't their real names, of course, but Caroline couldn't remember their names.

Glancing at the landline telephone that now seemed to loom large in the room, she remembered that she had Simon to thank for this current strife. *As if I don't have enough to worry and fret and cry and obsess about without jealousy to deal with. I need John on my side not—aaah! I can't believe this mess!*

However, if Simon was really in London for the first time, stranded at the airport, she really should call him back and give him directions to somewhere. The problem was, she didn't know where there was a good place to stay in London. The only hotel she'd been in was the Best Western where she and John had been debriefed by MI-5 upon their return from Burma.

Listening again to the message, Caroline jotted down the telephone number Simon recited and punched it into the phone. She activated the *record* button on the surveillance device that was meant to record suspicious calls, assuming that John was suspicious of any message from Simon.

"Hello?"

"Hi. Is this Simon?" she asked.

"Caroline? Is that you? Are you all right? You sound upset," Simon said.

Trying to calm her voice further, Caroline put on her most reassuring tone. "I'm fine. How are you? What are you doing in London? Are you still at the airport?"

"I'm fine," he said. "Much better now that I can hear your voice. Are you sure you're all right?"

"Yes," she said. "What are you doing here?"

"I wanted to see you," he said.

*Not a good answer, Simon.* "How did you get out? Burma's not exactly a country that promotes free and easy travel," she said.

"I got out through Thailand, went to Bangkok and got a new passport from the embassy there. It's so good to hear your voice. Do you have a spare bed or something?" he asked.

"I don't think it's a good idea for you to come here, Simon," she said.

"So you're still with John," he replied flatly.

"Yes. I'm still with John," she said, shaking her head in disgust. *Did he think it was all just a brief infatuation?* "If you're looking for a hotel, I'm not sure I can be of much help. I'm still really a newcomer myself, you may recall, and … John's out at the moment." *Storming jealously around Chelsea.*

"I'll just find a local YMCA. They have them here, don't they?" Simon said.

"Yes, of course. That's a good idea," she said.

"But you'll have dinner with me? Tomorrow night?" Simon asked.

"That should be fine. Why don't you call me tomorrow and let me know where you want to meet?" *And* we *will have dinner with you. There's no way I'm having supper with Simon unless John is there. Although … no. The only way to handle this is openly. If John punches Simon in the face again, then so be it. At the moment, I have far more important things to worry about, like surviving multiple assassination attempts without losing my mind … or my husband.*

"Okay. That's fantastic! It's really good to hear your voice," Simon said. He sounded so enthusiastic.

"See you tomorrow, Simon."

"Goodbye, Caroline."

She hung up the phone and turned the recorder off.

By this time, it was getting quite late. Checking her cell once more before bed, she saw a message received, having missed it while she was speaking to Simon. It read, *Can I come home?*

Sometimes he was just a little boy, and at those times, pity overwhelmed her. She replied, *Yes. Always.*

Deciding to get ready for bed while she waited for John, Caroline lay curled in the covers, waiting for what came next.

"Caroline? I'm sorry." Sitting up, she turned on the bedside lamp, and

John's face immediately came into view. He was leaning against the door frame, his face cloaked in misery. His breath caught on a sob. "I'm sorry. Can I … come over there?"

"Yes," she agreed, adding a warning, "That can't happen again."

He nodded as he approached and then knelt beside the bed. "It won't. I give you my word. I'm sorry. Please forgive me."

"You frightened me," she said.

Agony laced his every word. "I didn't mean to frighten you," he said. "I would never hurt you. Please believe me."

"Why, John? Why did you react like that?" she asked. "Is this about Simon? Your mother? Us? I don't understand where all that anger came from." With his head bowed over her lap, she couldn't see his face, so she waited.

When he spoke, his question surprised her. "Do you think I have the potential to become an abuser like my father?" he asked. Looking up, his eyes pleaded with her, and she took hope from the fact that he was openly displaying his emotions to her.

"No. I never would have married you if I saw that potential in you," she said. "Would you ever hurt me … physically, I mean?"

He flinched, probably at the implication that he regularly hurt her emotionally. And then he met her gaze. There, printed clearly in his eyes, was horror at the idea of doing violence against her. "Never, Caroline! I would never hurt you."

She relaxed just a little. *No, he would never hurt me.* "But tonight, you frightened me. You're supposed to be my knight in shining armour, but it's all rather dull and dented now."

He dropped his head into his hands, groaning with the emotion of it all. "Why do you stay with me?" His question was muffled behind his hands.

"You know why." Slipping to the edge of the bed, she put her arms around his shoulders.

He clutched her around the waist, burying his face in her lap. "All I ever seem to do is make you miserable."

"Stop it, John!" *Just stop it.* She held him tightly until she felt him begin to calm just a little bit. "I called Simon back. I didn't think it was fair to leave him standing at Heathrow just because we were … arguing. I recorded it so you can listen to it, since you clearly don't trust me."

"Don't say that! I trust you." He repeated more softly, "I trust you."

And suddenly, she was just so weary of it all, the conflict, the arguing and the anger. "I … I don't want to talk about it right now."

He nodded. "Anything you say. I'm sorry. Can … can I … ? I'll go sleep in the other room, shall I?"

"No." She pushed him back by the shoulders. "You have two choices, understand?" His eyes grew wide, and she could see the fear of what she was about to say plainly evident on his face. "Tell me what this is all about now or … but you probably can't do that, can you? Just promise to figure it out and explain. And don't expect me to patiently await your response," she concluded wearily.

"I can stay?" he asked, his voice quiet but full of hope.

"Of course you can stay," she said. "We are in this together." Disheartened, she rolled under the covers, turning her back on him.

"I'll do anything to make it up to you," he said, his voice full of promise.

Her voice muffled by the pillow, she told him, "All I truly want is an explanation."

"I give you my word."

# Chapter Eight
## Vivid Green Jealousy

John's usually controlled mind was a miasma of doubts, emotions and confusion. The JIC was receiving one channel of his mind: we know this-and-this about Tor Grendahl; yes, understandably, John should remove himself from London to prevent the loss of British lives; and, yes, it had become critical for MI-5 and MI-6 to locate Grendahl and the money behind the assassination contract in order to bring this threat to a satisfactory conclusion. *About time.*

The second channel of his mind was focussed on Section G and the safety of his officers. If he sent Caroline to a safe house far away and then slept on the third floor of Thames House, he could lead the investigation while minimizing the danger to his team. *Hmmm, perhaps that would be easier said than done. My wife is not likely to meekly walk away from this situation.*

The third channel of his mind was pain. He'd hurt Caroline … emotionally. *Groan.* And she felt betrayed by him. Add to that the fact that he'd put her in danger. And lastly, but worst of all, Simon was in town, his rival, or so he thought of him.

Pulling out his mobile, John pursued one avenue of potential relief: a way to enhance Caroline's safety.

"Duncan."

"Rory. It's John Brock."

"Ho John," Rory said, sounding pleased to hear from him.

"I … er …" John paused, releasing a sigh of frustration. "I need a favour."

"Anything, John," Rory assured him. "You know that."

"Caroline and I are meant to be meeting a … an acquaintance tonight for an early supper at La Roche," John said.

"Wasn't there another assassination attempt?" Rory asked.

"Yes. But she won't … there's no way I can ask her to … Blast it! She's about as upset with me as I can tolerate. The Chairman of the JIC has called me into a meeting, and I'm going to be late. Caroline should be safe. There's no way anyone can know about this supper arrangement, and Harry Blake is driving her there so there should be no chance of pursuit, but … well, I'd feel a lot better if I knew someone was watching over her until I get there," John said.

"I'll call Mick, and we'll be there," Rory said. "Tell me where and when."

"Mick? I thought he was spending a few days with his latest bit-of-stuff," John said.

"Nah. She threw him over," Rory said. "Personally, I believe when he gets bored, he simply puts on his most obnoxious and they're happy to give him the push."

"You're likely correct," John agreed. *Relief. If Mick and Rory watch over Caroline, she'll be safe. As long as …* Caution prompted a new thought. "Rory? Don't let Caroline see you, either of you."

"All right," were the words that Rory used, but the question was really, "Why on earth not?"

"If she decides I'm spying on her … don't let her see you." John rang off at Rory's confused chuckle.

Because of John's decision to completely divorce himself from his life pre-Burma and pre-marriage, Caroline hadn't yet met Rory and Mick. But there was no way John was going to underestimate his wife's abilities to see through him, to guess that these vaguely familiar men were actually connected to him. And if she decided that he didn't trust her … she already thought that … what was he going to tell her … how could he explain that it was simply too easy to believe that he, himself, could never be good enough for her …

Wearily, John sighed. This day, this entire week had simply been too long. The events he could process, the emotions he couldn't. It required Caroline-type empathy to sort out, and he simply wasn't ready to have the conversation necessary to solve things between them. The sanctity of his feelings for his mother was unbreachable. Supposed to be, anyway.

La Roche was *posh*. Caroline thought that was the right word. There were potted flowers scattered throughout the restaurant, filling the air with their subtle aroma. The waiters wore black vests and bow ties, and the maître d' wore a navy blue pinstriped suit with a brilliant green shirt and striped tie. *How on earth does Simon know about this place? What pull does he have to get us a table here?*

"Caroline."

Caroline turned to find Simon approaching her, his arms outstretched. "Hello, Simon," she said. "How are you?" She sidestepped his hug and shook his hand, allowing him to pull her in for a peck on the cheek. "This is a lovely restaurant. How did you hear about it?" Caroline asked.

"Oh, someone must have given me the name," Simon responded vaguely, waving away her question.

The maître d' attended promptly and led them across the room to a cozy corner. Two steps into their journey, Simon slipped his hand around Caroline's elbow. *O-kay.* As soon as they reached the table, she disengaged his grip, relieved when he seemed to accept that. Soon, however, he stepped behind her chair, leaning over to kiss her cheek very close to her ear as he tucked her into the table. *No. Not okay.*

When he sat, Caroline placed her hand on his arm, directing his attention to her. "Simon," she said firmly. "Don't do that again. I'm warning you, if you kiss me again, I'm leaving." *I wonder if Simon realizes that the only reason he's still alive is that John hasn't yet arrived. Otherwise, I can see Simon becoming another casualty of the Terrorist Act.*

"Sorry, Caroline," Simon said, though he didn't sound contrite. "It's just so good to see you. It feels like it's been years since I met you at the Katafygio."

*I wonder if I'd get away with putting my fingers in my ears and saying, "Nah nah nah"?* "What have you been up to? How have you been?" she asked, trying to distract him from his present topic.

"Not so good. I was pretty depressed after you left." He seemed to catch the warning in her eyes and quickly added, "The burning of the Katafygio was quite devastating. And, of course, the loss of Brother Phillip," he added, almost as an afterthought. "How are you, Caroline? Is Britain everything you thought it would be?"

"It's fine," she said. "I'm adjusting. I miss Canada, though—all the wide-open spaces and the abundance of wilderness. I can always see the border of the trees here. The Lake District is beautiful, and the Cotswolds, but there isn't really anywhere to go where you can feel lost amidst the woods."

"When I was a kid, my dad took my brother and me camping in Colorado. The mountains were awe-inspiring!" he said.

"Yes. The Rocky Mountains," she stated, wistfully remembering the majesty of the Canadian Rockies. "Once you've experienced the mountains, they get into your blood," she said, and then added, "John and I spent our honeymoon in Switzerland."

"Poor comparison," Simon replied with an edge in his voice, his not so subtle attack on John hinting to Caroline that all was not as it seemed here. *This is not simply a meeting of old friends.*

After the waiter came and took their orders—she ordered a meal for John as well, wishing he would get here sooner rather than later, although after Ruby Tuesday, he probably wouldn't eat it anyway—Caroline steered Simon back on track.

"Why did you choose to come to the UK?" Caroline asked.

"You know," Simon began. "After Brother Phillip died, I felt kind of free to pursue other interests in my life. So I came here."

"'Brother Phillip died'?" she quoted. "Wasn't he murdered?" *Something has definitely changed in Simon. A piece of him seems to be missing. He's creeping me out a bit.*

"He's in heaven now, anyway, with his wife. He's happy," Simon said. *How could he so blithely dismiss the unjust murder of a godly man? Maryn Dale shot Brother Phillip in cold blood! And Brother Phillip was John's mentor, the first positive paternal figure in his life, a fine Christian man.*

"How do you like working for John?" Simon asked, changing the topic.

*Excuse me?* "How did you know I work for John?" she asked, trying to keep her voice even.

A look of panic flitted across his features. "Oh, one of the others at the Katafygio must have told me," Simon said.

*That's not the first question he's evaded this evening. What is going on?* She replied cautiously to his earlier question. "I enjoy my job. It's quite challenging, and the people I work with, in general, are good people. What are you planning to do when you return to the States?"

"I haven't decided, yet. My decision is dependent on other factors in my life," he said and then smiled slyly. *What does he mean by that? What other factors?*

"I wonder what's keeping John," Caroline said, hoping to remind Simon of not only her husband's existence but the fact that his arrival was imminent.

Tension tightening his chest, John checked his watch again to see that he was now running an hour late. *Blimey! Any later and there won't be any point in going at all.*

Arriving and surveying the restaurant, he spotted Caroline in a corner table set into a half-walled alcove; he could spot her anywhere in any crowd. *There is nothing more striking than a woman who loves you.*

Given the height of the plants around Caroline and Simon, John thought he might be able to eavesdrop a little before making his presence known. *Not very gentlemanly, I know. But then, showing up without warning and inviting my wife out to dinner isn't exactly chivalrous behaviour either. All's fair … and all that.*

"Simon, why are you here?" That was Caroline. John's breath caught in his chest. Even when he knew she was upset with him, the sound of her voice could thrill him.

"Come away with me, Caroline," Simon said. "You're unhappy. It's so obvious. Come away with me to the States. That's why I came out of Burma, to get you and go home." Fury lit a fire in John's belly, and he pictured his hands around Simon's throat.

Clearly shocked by Simon's proposal, Caroline asked, "*How*, from what you know of me, did you get the idea that I would leave my husband?" The embers of John's ire cooled minutely.

"It's obvious he's made you unhappy," Simon said. "Why stay?"

"It's actually me who has made him unhappy," she said. Simon snorted, but she continued in spite of his derision. "I said something to him, something that hurt him, and he just can't seem to process it properly. I'm unhappy because he's hurting." John could plainly hear the sorrow in her voice. *Oh baby, none of this is your fault.*

"*Said* something?" Simon replied in a mocking tone. "What do words mean? I want you. I want to make you happy." John barely restrained the urge to reintroduce Simon's face to his fist, but the irritation in Caroline's voice stopped him.

"Simon, you're a Christian. How can you speak to me this way?" she said.

"So, because I'm a Christian, that means I don't deserve to be happy?" he asked. "That's absurd! God wants us to be happy."

"I don't think stealing other people's wives constitutes finding the 'joy of the Lord.' God wants to give us joy, Simon. We're not supposed to go out and grab whatever we think might give us a few moments of transitory happiness. Besides, God's rules on marriage are clear. Two shall become one," she said.

"Darling—" Simon said.

John clenched his fists indignantly. Caroline stood abruptly, her chair wobbling but managing to stay upright.

"Don't you ever call me that!" Her voice was low and threatening, gaining volume as she continued, "Do you hear me? I am not your 'darling' and never have been." John grinned at her response, relaxing his hands.

"Caroline, come away with me. Leave John. You don't have to divorce him. You don't have to marry me. Just come away from the unhappiness," Simon said.

"Simon, I will not leave John. He may make me unhappy at times—" Reminded of the misery he seemed to cause her regularly, John's chest clenched and he grimaced involuntarily. "But love isn't about happy-sappy feelings all the time," she said. "It's a commitment to love, even in the unlovely moments."

"Are you trying to tell me there's no way out of a marriage for a Christian?" Simon asked.

"No, I'm not saying that. The Bible is actually quite clear on the issue. But just being unhappy or not feeling fulfilled or wanting different things or not feeling in love anymore … they don't signal the end of love. Remember, Simon, I've been through this before. If a husband and wife stand by the commitment they've made, the romance returns, and then you can have the fairy tale. If you walk away, the opportunity's gone … and whether you're a Christian or not, the destruction to yourself and your family is the same. The rules are there for a good reason," she said.

"I'm surprised that such an intelligent person would have such outdated ideas," Simon said.

"Simon, your ideas surprise me," Caroline replied. "I thought that, as Christians, we held similar beliefs about life, the universe and everything. But it's clear to me that our ideas run in very different directions. I'm leaving. Take care, Simon."

"None of that matters, not to me. Come away with me. I want to be with you," Simon insisted, reaching to grasp her sleeve.

"Simon, that's enough," she said. "You want me. Do you love me?" John held his breath. "Or do you just love yourself?" she asked. "Don't even answer me. I don't want to know. I'm not leaving John, because I love him. But I am leaving this restaurant, now!"

John's chest expanded, the tightness leaving. But his relief had made him careless, and as Caroline turned to leave the table, she came face to face with him. He panicked, but she didn't. Rather than slap him as he probably deserved for spying on her, she simply shook her head at him, surprised and then clearly amused. Reaching up, she cupped his cheek, kissing him lightly. "You are a sweet idiot sometimes," she whispered, words only for his ears. He could feel the flush of embarrassment rising up his neck, but she simply took his hand and pulled him along behind her. John had an urge to thumb his nose at Simon … *She's mine, not yours.*

"Caroline! Wait!" Simon called, but the maître d' intercepted him, suggesting rather strongly that the gentleman would be well-advised to settle his bill before exiting the restaurant.

Stopping at the door, John observed the rain outside and pulled Caroline back into the restaurant. Slipping off his suit jacket, he placed it around her shoulders. Leaning down to her as he straightened the fabric, he whispered, "I owe you an explanation."

Smiling brightly at him over her shoulder, she rested a hand on top of his, and his heart lightened. Why did he ever think that there should be topics of discussion sacrosanct from his wife? If Caroline thought his mother had betrayed him, then as much as the idea hurt him, she was probably correct. In the confusing morass of emotions and memories he'd unsuccessfully tried to ignore all day, he thought he'd finally discovered the explanation for his anger last night. He wanted to get her away to himself to explain.

His arm around her shoulder, he led her toward the door.

"Caroline?" John began, and when she nodded, he continued quietly, "I'm very sorry for being such an insecure prat. Please allow me an opportunity to explain. I love you."

Surprising him, she stopped to turn in his arms, thrusting him against the wall. "I'm looking for—"

Her smile shattered a split second after the plate glass window of the restaurant. Pulling her down beneath him, John drew his Glock, aiming out into the street. They were surrounded by the silence of shock. Bullets sprayed into the building again, and soon they were engulfed in a screaming chaos of terror.

Lifting his head minutely to see over the ledge of the window, John scanned the street, spotting two rifles on the second floor of the building across from them. Harry Blake was crouched behind a blue Ford Focus to the right of the entrance.

"Caroline?" John said. He heard an "hmph" from beneath him and assumed that was her acknowledgment muffled against his shirt. "Text Harry and tell him ten o'clock and two o'clock. Up two." He heard the "mhmph" and felt her shifting position slightly, moving her head to the space between his arm and his side. He watched as Harry pulled out his mobile, checked it, and then looked over his shoulder. He met John's gaze with a single nod. John rose a little higher to communicate with Harry, but a barrage of bullets sent him back to the floor to cover his wife. Well, there was no mystery for who the bullets were launched. *I've got to do something.* If he waited too long to act, the assassins would come in after him.

Once the gunfire paused, John rose to a crouch and pulled Caroline after him back around a wall inside the restaurant. "Stay here," he said. "Text Harry and tell him to come in. I'm going after them, but I need a better vantage point." John kissed her on the head, leaving before she could protest.

A hand gripped John's arm. A fresh surge of adrenaline flooded him. He reacted immediately, spinning, raising his elbow to take down his attacker.

"John. It's me."

John froze. "Rory. You nearly—" His heart pounding, John slowed his breathing to hide the fact that Rory had almost ended his life by heart attack. "Never mind. Stay with her," John said, and Rory nodded in agreement.

"Mick's by the kitchen," Rory said. "Take them out, John."

John nodded. *That's exactly what I'm planning to do.* Crawling through the restaurant, John searched for an access to the third floor. In control this time, he didn't flatten Simon when the man clutched his shirt. But he wanted to.

"John. What's going on?" Simon asked.

"Simon? Get down, you pillock. Let go of me," John said.

"What's happening?" Simon asked again.

"There are gunmen outside shooting people. What do you think is happening?" Sarcasm and impatience wove a braid of disgust in John's mind.

"What about Caroline?" Simon asked.

"She's safe." John nodded over his shoulder. "Over there."

"You have to protect her," Simon insisted.

"I can do that better by stopping the bloke who keeps shooting at her," John said.

Simon drew in a deep breath as though bracing himself for action. "I'll protect her." And then Simon stood to run toward her.

"Simon! Get down!" John called. "Blast!" John changed direction to chase Simon down. "You'll get yourself shot! Get down!" John said. People scattered around them.

"Simon, get down!" John heard Caroline shout. Reaching forward, John grabbed Simon's belt, dragging him down, irritated by the pull that put on his ribs. Caroline moved forward to flatten Simon.

"Caroline, get back!" John ordered, sending her back behind the wall. John watched, relieved, as Rory pulled her back the last few inches. Then John released Simon.

Movement by the front door caught John's attention. Ryan was moving in their direction, his handgun at the ready. *Ryan? What is Ryan doing here? Armed?* Suddenly, Simon broke away, stepping to cross the distance to Caroline. She stood to push him back.

"Ryan, don't shoot!" John called out, glancing back and forth between his wife and man with the gun. *No no no!*

Grabbing Simon around the shoulders and simultaneously pushing Caroline back into Rory's grip, John lurched as a gunshot exploded from Ryan's gun, slamming into Simon's chest. The force threw John back, his ribs exploding in agony at the hard impact with the floor. Fresh shrieks filled the air.

"John!" He heard Caroline shout his name as a grey mist pushed at the edges of his vision, friction burning his side as Rory dragged him behind the wall. And then her cool hand was on his face. "John. Darling. Stay with me," she said.

Struggling against unconsciousness, he shook his head to clear the mist. "All right. I'm all right." John reassured her. He heard her gasp in relief when he responded. "Simon?" he asked.

"Can you grab him?" Caroline asked … Rory. She was speaking to Rory. Rory crawled back out of cover to haul Simon behind the wall.

Caroline took hold of Simon's shoulder and belt and turned him onto his back. Shocked, her face drew John's attention to the growing crimson stain across Simon's shirt.

Caroline crouched beside Simon, slapping his cheeks to awaken him. "Simon. Simon! Stay with me, Simon." John reached over to grab a tablecloth, dishes and cutlery scattering everywhere, revealing a family of four hiding beneath the table. John balled a corner of the cloth and pressed it against the seeping hole in the centre of Simon's chest.

"I didn't know. She said—" Simon drew a rasping breath. "Caroline. Help me. I didn't know. She said you needed me. She said you'd be mine."

"Who, Simon? Who told you that?" Caroline asked.

"She did," Simon gasped. "She was so beautiful, but not as lovely as you. I gave it up … I gave it all up for you, Caroline." Simon grasped her shirt in his bloody fist.

"Simon. Don't give it up. It's not too late," Caroline said.

"My chest hurts." Simon reached into his coat pocket, but his hand fell limply to his side. "It's too late."

"It's not too late," she insisted. "You had your faith once, I know you did. Don't die without it."

John studied her, trying to process this bizarre conversation.

"Caroline? John, forgive me." Simon sighed, a gurgle escaping as he lost consciousness.

"John, he needs an ambulance. John!" Caroline clutched John's sleeve. John nodded brusquely, searching around to see Harry close by. Ryan Carstairs had disappeared from view.

John bunched her hands onto the balled-up tablecloth on Simon's chest. "Caroline, hold this. I can hear the sirens, but we need to take down those gunmen before the paramedics will come in. Stay here." John's eyes met Harry's and then Rory's. "Protect her. I'm going up."

"Yes, sir," Harry said, acknowledging John's orders. "We'll keep her safe."

Crawling to the kitchen, John opened the door a crack and then a little further. Wrenched from his grip, the door slammed back against his temple. Hands dragged him upward, bringing him face to face with a gunman dressed all in black. John landed one punch.

"Armed Response Unit! Back away! Now!"

John froze and realized that the caliginous man was ally, not foe. Raising his arms first, John allowed himself to be restrained, impatiently waiting for the officers to realize that *he* was an ally not a foe. John began a patter of identification, using every keyword and term he could think of. The force pressing his body into the wall did not lessen, and his ribs burned fiercely in his chest. John's mind spun during the interminable wait. *Is Caroline safe? How did Ryan get so close to the restaurant without being shot by the assassins? Why did Ryan shoot Simon? Is Caroline safe back there? I've got to end this quickly. What is taking so long?*

Finally, John was released when Mick Adair arrived.

"Ho, Freddy. How's your new wee babe?" Mick asked.

"Fine, Adair. She's a real beauty. Sleeps like an angel," Freddy replied.

"I see you've got my man, Brock, here," Mick said.

"You know this bloke?" Freddy asked.

"Undoubtedly. We served together," Mick said. "My guess is he's after the gunman, and just between you and me, he might prove useful."

John waited for Freddy's response. *Come on. Come on.* Finally, Freddy decided. "All right. Release him," Freddy said to the officers confining John.

John turned, greeting Mick and introducing himself properly to Officer Fred Jones, who then introduced John to his immediate superior. The four men conferred on a plan, but John couldn't get permission to fire on the gunmen, the assassins. He chose to concede the point rather than allow the argument to prolong any further inactivity. *As long as those assassins are still in the same position, this should work.*

Donning the Kevlar vest, whisper mic and earpiece handed him by one of the officers, John ascended to the SFO, Specialist Firearms Officer, already in position on the third floor of the restaurant building. Mick ascended to the position of the SFO sniper targeting the second assassin.

Coming up behind the SFO sniper, John identified himself, presenting his badge. Making contact with Mick first, learning that he was in position, John turned his attention to the specialist beside him.

"Update," John ordered.

"I've got this one dead-to-rights. Second shooter is sighted," the sniper reported, hesitating and then continuing, "But we have no orders to shoot, sir."

"I'll take the responsibility." Pressing the whisper mic, John made contact. "Mick?"

"Yes, sir," Mick replied, and John heard him speaking to the sniper at his position.

"On my mark—" John began, speaking now to the sniper beside him. "Be ready, Mick."

"Yes, sir, but—" the sniper interrupted.

"On my mark, constable. Now. Fire!"

The two shots rang out so perfectly timed that the acoustics blended into one. John watched as one assassin disappeared from the window. The second assassin pitched forward and into the street, where he remained motionless.

Switching channels on the communicator, John contacted Officer Jones. "One gunman down. Get your men out there and find the second gunman." He removed the earpiece so he wouldn't have to listen to Freddy's profanity. And then, patting the sniper's shoulder as a *well done,* John descended the stairs to the dining room in record time.

As John moved across the room toward Caroline and Simon, he heard, "Armed Response Unit! Put down your weapon!" coming from the front of the restaurant. Putting his body firmly between any possible gunfire and his wife, John pulled his Glock and spun toward the front of the restaurant, setting his stance, ready to fire. One glimpse of the assassin was all that was afforded before the man disappeared beneath an avalanche of armed officers. John relaxed his stance, stepping out to see that the two assassins were well in hand.

Stepping back, John observed Ryan stealthily advancing along the wall of the restaurant toward … Simon? His instincts fired an alert.

"Ryan!" John called. Ryan turned in his direction, and John could see the fury in the young man's face. Ryan's gun slowly revolved with his body, coming to point directly at John's chest. John planted his body firmly between the muzzle of the young man's handgun and anything or anyone in the vicinity of his wife, praying that either Ryan's bullet was not meant for him or if it was, the bulletproof vest would stop it. *And isn't it odd that I would even entertain the possibility that my own officer would fire on me?*

"Ryan!" Harry Blake called, distracting the young man, and then John was standing in front of him, taking possession of Ryan's handgun.

"Watch him. And find out what is going on," John ordered Harry.

John stepped around the wall to find Caroline still kneeling beside Simon, holding the blood-soaked fabric to his chest. Rory crouched beside her.

"John," Rory said quietly, and then he simply shook his head. All was not well.

Crouching beside Caroline, John tipped her chin gently to get her attention. "Are you all right?" he asked.

She didn't respond, but he could see her tears falling silently, splashing against the puddle of blood between her hands on the tablecloth she held tightly to Simon's chest, trying to prevent his life from spilling onto the floor of La Roche.

# Chapter Nine
# *Please Don't Leave Me*

JOHN WAS FRIGHTENED. CLEARLY in a state of shock, Caroline hadn't uttered a word since the paramedics had wheeled Simon away. With Caroline in this state, there was no way John was leaving her side, so he'd left Harry in charge at the restaurant and instructed him to call in Hibb.

In the bustling A&E department, John accosted a nurse and insisted she provide him with bandages. Then, pulling Caroline into an empty examination room, he carefully washed away the blood from her face and arms, discovering beneath Simon's blood some of her own. *Oh, baby.* Cleaning the glass fragments from her skin and hair, he covered the larger wounds with bandages. He checked her head for bumps and found none. Her pupils were equal and reactive. *No concussion.* But she still hadn't spoken or looked him directly in the eyes, leaving him anything but certain about the mental state of his wife.

He bought her a cup of sweet, creamy coffee from the hospital café and ordered her to drink it, and was more concerned when she passively obeyed. Silently, they sat side by side waiting for news of Simon.

After she handed him her empty cup, he tried to get her attention, pulling her hand onto his leg, brushing his thumb across her knuckles. When that didn't work, he sang to her.

At his voice, her gaze moved to stare at their conjoined hands. "Larry Norman and Steve Camp. 'If I Were a Singer,'" she said, her voice husky with exhausted emotion.

"Yes," he replied, so relieved to hear her speaking again.

"What do you think he meant?" she asked.

"About what?" he asked mildly, not certain whether she was discussing the song or the attack.

"He said, 'I gave it all up for you.'"

*Simon.* "I don't know, baby. What do you think?" He studied her carefully.

"I think he came for me." Caroline turned to study John's face. "Who told him I'd leave?"

"I simply don't know," John said.

She moved her free hand to trace a line from the bruise on his temple to his jaw and around to his lips, lightly tapping a wound he wasn't even aware he had. "I have no intention of ever leaving you. You realize you're stuck with me forever," she said.

His heart beat happily at her assurance. "I can live with that."

"Good," she said, slumping against him. He slipped his arm around her shoulder, pulling her close. "Who was the man who stayed with me?" she asked.

"Er, Rory Duncan. A friend." He waited for more questions, but she remained silent. "Why don't you lie down on the chairs and get a little sleep?" he said. "You can use my leg for a pillow."

He felt her shaking her head. "Uh uh. I want my explanation first."

Confused at first, he sought to clarify her meaning. "Explanation?" And then he remembered his promise to her. "Are you certain? It can wait."

As she spoke, her tone and manner began to approach normal. "I want to know. I understand, at least at some level, why you're jealous of Simon, though I find it quite insulting that you don't know me better than that by now. I even understand why you were eavesdropping on our conversation. But I simply can't understand why my comment about your mother made you so angry that you would grab me."

*Because what you said hurt.* "Do you truly believe that my mother betrayed me?" he asked.

"I shouldn't have said that to you. It's not really that she betrayed you, but she failed to protect you. I know you loved your mother, and I know she's been the one ray of goodness in your life, but I think she let you down. I've thought that for a long time, but I didn't want to hurt you by saying it. I guess I just didn't think before I spoke," Caroline said.

He sighed heavily. "I think I've finally sifted it through in my mind." She turned her face into his shoulder. Her fingertips slipped between the buttons on his shirt, their tender touch giving him the courage he needed to continue. "When I was about nine years old, one evening, after my father had thrashed me yet again, my parents had a huge row, an argument. I stepped out into the hall from my bedroom to find my mother dressed in her coat with a suitcase in hand. My father grabbed her by the arm and hauled her around. He told her that she was free to leave, but she was not taking me with her. She walked out the door. She came back the next day, very tearful, apologizing to me and saying she'd made a mistake, that she wouldn't leave again, but I never truly felt safe after that. I realized that mothers do leave their children. I realized that if things got bad enough, I might be left alone with my father. Then she did leave me—she died, and everything I'd feared for three years happened." Caroline remained silent, and strangely, he couldn't read her expression. "I've never trusted anyone since, and I've been right," he said. "Everyone has always left me, even those who promised to stay."

John continued speaking, trailing his fingers through her hair as he spoke, discarding the tiny fragments of glass he'd missed earlier. "I've always known that it's too good to be true. And when things are rough between us, I panic. Unfortunately, my panic usually expresses itself as anger." He faltered into his confession, each word costing him dearly. "I know that Henry was a better husband than I am." Haltingly, he continued. "But I truly am doing my best."

Caroline gaped at him. "Uh, John? What makes you think that Henry was a better husband than you are?"

"You once told me that you and he rarely fought—" John admitted.

Caroline laughed, adding to his confusion. "I have really messed this up, haven't I?" she said. "After fifteen years of marriage, we rarely fought. Henry and I fought on a regular basis in our first year of marriage. Henry ..." She paused, and John wondered what she would say. "Henry used to hog the bedspread. Henry snored. Henry never put his dishes away. He would set them two inches from the dishwasher but never put them in. Henry drove me crazy, dragging me to every railway right-of-way in Alberta, British Columbia and Saskatchewan. I mean, really, they're just lumps of dirt covered in grass." John laughed softly, some of the tension easing from him. Caroline continued, "Henry was not perfect. Yes, we were happy. But John, *you* make me happy."

Caroline popped a button on his shirt and stroked her hand along his chest, skirting the line of his collarbone, stroking the smooth triangle of his shoulder. His mind buzzed with the sensation, and he knew he should stop such intimate contact in such a public place, but he was afraid to do anything to tip the balance of her mood. Her next words pulled him back to the conversation. "I just wish I could get my hands on your parents and shake the bejeebers out of them. You have never been unlovable. I can see how their issues would make it hard for you to trust. But I love you," she said. Extracting her hand, she slipped off her chair, kneeling beside him, hands resting on his leg. His gaze locked on to hers. "You are a wonderful man," she began. "And I am lucky to have you. I love you. So much so that sometimes I don't think I can contain the joy of it. And when things are tough between us, I pull that joy out of my memory and smooth it over my hurt and it helps to heal it." She planted her hand over his heart. "I want you to trust that my love is forever, but I don't know how to make you believe it."

"Don't give up on me," he said. "You're not responsible for my childhood, and neither am I. But I am responsible to you." He stood, pulling her up and into his arms. "I don't know why you love me, but I'm so very glad you do. And I've always known that I am exceptionally lucky to have you."

He kissed her deeply, ignoring the sting from the wound on his lip. Pulling back to reposition himself closer, he kissed her again, tasting her familiar flavour, losing himself in his beloved wife. Breaking off, she rested her head against his chest, their bodies shifting until every hill and valley fit perfectly together. After a time, she looked up at him, and he couldn't resist the urge to kiss her again, keeping his kiss light, just sampling the cupid's bow of her top lip.

"I'm sorry about Simon," he said.

"I know. He was a friend, but something happened inside him. I don't know what that whole episode was about. I feel horrible that he was shot because of us, though," she said.

John smiled that she included herself in the "us," even though the assassin had only targeted him. *Two shall become one.* She was truly remarkable.

"Was he just in the wrong place at the wrong time?" she asked.

"Ryan shot him," John said.

Clearly confused, she clarified, "Ryan? Why would he shoot Simon?"

"Claims he thought that Simon was attacking you," John said.

"Wh—" she began, but a man in a white lab coat interrupted them.

"Er, hello, I'm Dr. Dennis. Are you Caroline?"

"Yes," she replied, a question in her voice.

"Mr. Reldif had this on his person, and when I was informed that there was a man and a woman waiting for news, I took a chance." Dr. Dennis handed over an envelope to Caroline. It read, *My Dearest Caroline.*

"How is Simon, doctor?" John asked.

"I'm afraid he didn't make it. I'm sorry." The doctor patted Caroline's shoulder sympathetically and walked away.

"I'm so sorry, Caroline," John said. *Oh no. What does this mean for us?*

Studying the envelope, Caroline finally tucked it into John's pocket. "I don't want this. I was never his." Wrapping her arms around him, she held him tightly as she cried. "Take me home."

Ignoring the pain in his ribs, he pulled her closer. "We'll have to go to another safe house until I get this sorted."

"I don't care, but John, please don't leave me alone tonight. I don't think I could stand it."

"I won't. I'll stay with you," he said. As much as he wanted to untangle the mess, he wanted more for Caroline to feel safe.

"I don't ever want to move from this spot," Caroline remarked. She curled into John's side, slipping her hand beneath his T-shirt and stroking her fingers through the ebony curls hidden there.

"That's a good idea. Why don't you stay here today?" John suggested. Immediately, he felt the tension in her body.

"I … no."

Tipping her chin, he witnessed the panic dart across her expression. "You're not yourself, sweetheart," he said. "Stay here and get some sleep. Give yourself time to recover."

"It's not that," she said. "I don't want to be apart from you today. Please don't leave me behind here. It won't be safe without you." He heard the panic rising in her voice. "Couldn't I come and stay in one of the medical suites on the third floor of Thames House?" she asked. "Then you could just text me to let me know where you're going."

She sounded so like a frightened child that pity tugged on his heart. "I could arrange that," he said. "I don't want you working today, though," he said, holding his breath as he awaited her response. *Hang tough and wait for explosion.*

"Okay," she agreed, surprising him. "I don't think I could really concentrate on anything anyway. You will text me when you go out, won't you?" Her limpid eyes met his, begging for reassurance.

"Oh yes. I know the rules," he said. "I'm not to leave the country, the city or even the building without letting you know … ever." He smiled warmly, reminding her of her words to him when he'd returned from India.

She blushed lightly, burying her face against his chest and then pushing up his T-shirt and kissing him from his navel to his chin, setting off an unexpected round of passion.

Finally ready to face the day, they rode together in the back of a pool car as Lawrence drove them to Thames House with the other watchers providing surveillance and support. John delivered Caroline to a third-floor suite and then sighed into his office chair.

"John," Aubrey interrupted immediately, leaning in through the office doorway. John looked up, motioning him inside. Aubrey continued. "Something dodgy's come up in the vetting on that American from Burma. Simon Reldif?"

John nodded, steeling his expression. *Will I never be free of that man?* As far as his team knew, Simon was merely an unfortunate victim of the shooting at the restaurant. Although Harry probably realized there was more going on.

"He travelled in China during Uni."

John snapped back to the present. "What did you say, Aubrey?"

"Simon Reldif spent some time in China during university. And he's been in the UK before," Aubrey said.

"When?" John asked, his instincts flashing a warning.

"A year ago February, about two months after you and Caroline returned to London," Aubrey replied. "It was all done on the QT. I had to dig deep to find the trail." Aubrey was studying him strangely. "I'll need more time to trawl through CCTV, but as near as I can suss it, he spent three days in London and then flew to Beijing," he said.

"Beijing?" John muttered. "What did he do while he was in London?"

Aubrey hesitated. "I believe he was searching for Caroline."

The blood draining from his face, John inquired hoarsely, "What makes you say that?"

"I've got him on CCTV at an Internet café," Aubrey replied. "There were several searches conducted on that computer for every possible spelling of her Christian name and surnames. The same computer was also used to check on news coverage of Myanmar, sorry, Burma." Aubrey hesitated, drawing a bracing breath before continuing, "And it was used to check an e-mail account that contained one message only … from Ryan Carstairs."

"Another connection to Ryan," John muttered.

"John. Simon Reldif was not a random civilian, was he?" Aubrey asked.

"No."

"If I've discovered this connection, someone else will as well," Aubrey warned. "Wouldn't it be better to, as the Americans say, 'come clean'?"

John laughed without humour. "Come clean," he repeated tonelessly. "I need to speak to Caroline. Can you assemble the team for a briefing in half an hour? Except Ryan. Find him an errand."

"You suspect him of something," Aubrey said, a statement rather than a question.

Not answering, John asked, "Is Hibb around?" Aubrey nodded, and John instructed him to send Hibb in.

John dialled his phone. "Janice? It's John Brock. Would Sir William have a few moments to spare me?"

"He will be available for three minutes at ten-fifteen," she said. "Would that suit you, Mr. Brock?"

"Yes, thank you," he said.

"Very good, Mr. Brock."

He rang off, looking up to see Hibb standing in the doorway. "Come in. Close the door."

Hibb complied, coming to rest across the desk from John. "Trouble?" Hibb asked.

John sighed, praying for guidance, *Father, help me.* "Two nights ago … no, I need to go further back." John sighed again, looking up to meet Hibb's gaze. "When Caroline and I were in Burma, staying at the hidden village, the Katafygio, before we were married, Caroline struck up a relationship, a friendship with Simon Reldif." He sighed again, not wanting to discuss something so personal with anyone but Caroline.

"Is that the fellow you socked in the gob?" Hibb asked.

Shocked, John met the big man's gaze. "How did you—"

"Caroline told Katie all about it," Hibb explained blandly. "Katie told me the story last night when she saw the name of the victim on the telly."

Completely deflated, John didn't know what to do. "His name was mentioned on the news? My officer shot him dead." John repeated the important details, his voice thick and slow, reflecting the rhythm of his heart.

"That's a lot of history to explain. Was Caroline meeting him there?" Hibb asked.

*It's not what you think.* "We were supposed to be meeting him together, but I was held up by the Chairman of the JIC, Trevena," John said.

"Unfortunately, we weren't able to keep a lid on it," Hibb apologized. "The story's all over the news."

"There's no connection to me, is there?" John asked. *Please don't let there be a connection to me.*

"Beth recognized you coming out of the restaurant on the news," Hibb said. "I swear that child could spot you at a thousand paces."

Beth was Hibb's next-to-youngest daughter who, for some reason John couldn't fathom, had taken a liking to him, making him paper cards and sending them home with Caroline whenever she visited with Katie.

"What are you going to do?" Hibb asked, drawing John back to the present situation.

*Good question. Resign? Fade away before this all comes out?* John sighed morosely. "I've got a meeting with the DG in fifteen minutes. But I need to speak with Caroline first."

Hibb's eyes widened. "You'll be hard put to make it to the safe house and back in that time."

"She's upstairs in one of the medical suites. She's on the edge, Hibb, completely wrung out," John said. "I don't know how she's going to deal with this."

"Maybe we should send her over to my house. Katie would love to see her. They are the best of friends," Hibb said.

"No, it's too risky." John immediately declined. "The assassins seem to have only targeted me, but with this connection between Simon, Ryan and Caroline … well, we couldn't put your family at risk."

"You suspect Ryan of summat? You've never been too taken with that young man," Hibb said.

"No. There's something about him that sets my teeth on edge. I'd like to know who was responsible for bringing him on board while I was away," John said.

"I'll check into it. And him, if you like," Hibb said.

"Yes. Thanks, Hibb. I'd better nip upstairs before I see Sir William," John said. Hibb nodded and rose, exiting the office.

Mounting the steps to the third floor, which had taken on the incline of the Himalayas, John made his way upstairs feeling like he was dragging a burden of regret behind him. Checking in with the guard outside the door, John learned that the room had been silent since Mrs. Brock had arrived, and no one had sought entrance.

Locking the door behind him, John slipped into the dimly lit bedroom, noting that she'd left the bedside lamp on. She truly was round-the-twist. At home, she always demanded complete darkness. And then, suddenly, he was overwhelmed with the need to wrap his body around her and protect her for all time, never leaving her side for any reason.

Prying off his shoes and shedding his suit jacket and tie, John slid onto the bed over the covers, wrapping his arm around her middle and burying his face against her neck, inhaling the scent of her.

Groaning, she shifted, wiggling her backside closer against him. "John."

"Hi. How are you feeling?" he asked.

"Sleepy," she replied. "Everything okay?"

"I need to speak with you, and I have to meet with the DG in fifteen minutes," he said.

Drawing in a deep breath, she rolled over to face him, burrowing into his chest. "What's going on?" she asked soporifically.

John struggled with himself, wanting to interrogate her about Simon to test whether she knew of his earlier visit to the UK. He perceived, however, that she would quickly react to the distrust his questions would imply. He had told her he trusted her. The question was, did he when it came to Simon Reldif?

Propping herself on her elbow, she came more alert, clearly sensing the gravity of the situation even without knowing what was going on. He studied her eyes, reading their depths, and all he saw was love and concern … for him. And then he knew. He would trust her until the end of time.

"Darling? What's going on?" she prompted him.

"Aubrey turned up some information about Simon," John said. "He was in London last February." Pausing, he studied her response. "He was searching for you."

"For me? Why?" Her eyes fell, and his heart rate increased in panic as to the meaning of her response. She continued wearily, "No, don't bother. Who got to him, John? I really don't think that Simon was in love with me when we were in Burma. What shifted? I mean, I married you right in front of him. Not many people require a bigger hint than that. I haven't responded to a single letter from him since we left Burma. I've written to the others, but not Simon. I always passed those letters on to you. I just don't understand."

He was silent for a moment. "Did you …" He screwed his courage to the sticking place. "Did you want to see the letter …" Biting back a deep groan, he continued. "The letter Simon left for you?" And then he simply couldn't seem to breathe, and his chest tightened painfully. *Please say no. Please say no.*

"Sure," she replied tonelessly. "You can read it to me."

Retrieving the page from his suit jacket, he opened it and read, "My dearest Caroline, when I received word that you were unhappy with John, I knew that we were meant to be togeth—"

"Stop!" Caroline commanded, covering John's mouth with her hand. "Just read it to yourself and destroy it! I don't want to hear any more." Her voice was hard, but John could hear the brittleness beneath the edge.

Hesitating, John folded the letter and then cleared his throat. "There's more." Her gaze lifted to meet his, and the hardness vanished into a pit of sorrow as he continued, "Simon received an e-mail message from Ryan Carstairs."

Groaning, she asked, "What is going on? Ryan and Simon? Tor Grendahl? What connects all these people?"

"I don't know, Beauty."

Burying her face in his shirt, she clung to him for a long time and then pulled away with another gut-wrenching moan. "Why are you seeing Sir William?" she asked.

"Evidently, I'm visible in one of the news reports about the shooting. That makes a public connection between me and Simon," John explained.

"So it's become public?" She released a guttural noise halfway between a groan and a growl. "Heaven forbid. We know what the Security Services think of publicity," she continued bitterly.

"That coupled with the bomb attempt …" He left the thought hanging.

"What's going to happen?" she asked.

"I'm not certain, but I think they're going to try and build a case against me because of the connection with Simon and the fact that he was shot by one of my officers," John said.

John's mobile interrupted them, and he rose to take the call in the other room. Uncharacteristically, Caroline didn't follow.

"John," Sir William proceeded without a greeting. "I'm going to need you to bring Caroline in for questioning. The Home Secretary is furious about the publicity, and somehow he's learned of the connection between you and the now-dead civilian, Reldif. Evidently the fact that one of your officers shot him at point-blank range is felt to look rather suspicious."

"Is Caroline under suspicion?" John asked.

"Of course not," Sir William responded, clearly disgusted at the mere thought.

"Sir, she's been through so much," John said. "Couldn't it wait? I'd like to take her away for a few days, give her some time to recover."

"I'm sorry, John," Sir William replied. "You must know that I would never put her in this position if it weren't critical. I will watch over her. Once this is settled, perhaps you could take her away for a time. Did you have something in mind?"

"I was thinking we'd disappear into Wales. We can find a remote spot without leaving the country. No borders. No passports. No trace," he said.

"That's a very good idea," Sir William replied.

"Thank you, sir. Am I still able to meet with you?" John asked.

"I think you'd better. I've scheduled Mrs. Brock's debriefing to commence in one hour."

"Very well."

Caroline couldn't believe she was seated in the dungeons of Thames House. John and Hibb had accompanied her, and John had given her a reassuring squeeze and a sealed bottle of water before she entered the room—sealed so she could trust it.

Smelling faintly of bleach, the interrogation cell was a square room with dark grey cinder-block walls and a light grey concrete floor with a drain in the middle. The bare room housed one square metal table and two fold-up metal chairs on opposite sides of the table. There were three visible cameras mounted high up on the walls and one entrance through a coded door.

Caroline had been allowed to forego a strip search, and so she was sitting impatiently in her own clothes on her metal chair waiting for her interrogator. She gripped the water bottle firmly in her hands, hearing the plastic crinkle.

It felt like hours but was likely only about fifteen minutes that she had to wait, her nerves building with every passing minute, the grief and confusion of the past few days weighing heavily on her heart.

Without warning, the door flew open and a mid-thirties blond-haired man pushed his husky frame through the doorway and walked directly up to the table. He slapped his beefy hands down and leaned his piercing green eyes into her face. Caroline flinched.

"What do you know of Simon Reldif's mission in the UK?" the man asked.

"Well, um, I don't really know anything about his mission, I guess," Caroline replied unevenly. *Jeepers creepers! Did they really have to choose this guy to interrogate me?*

"You guess!" He mocked her through his petulant lips. "I'll make it simpler for you. Where did you first meet Simon Reldif?"

"In Burma," Caroline replied, remembering John's advice to give the information requested, no more.

"Burma? Isn't that more properly referred to as Myanmar?" the man asked in derision.

Narrowing her eyes, Caroline responded hotly, "Myanmar is the name assigned by the military junta. Burma is the name used by its people."

"Where in *Burma*?" The man rolled his sarcastic green eyes at her, openly mocking her.

"At the … um …" She stopped.

"At the 'um'? Caroline, do I take it that you are being uncooperative?" he asked.

"Look, Brian—" she began, but he interrupted her.

He slapped the table again. "How do you know my name?" he asked. He was a very angry man. "I haven't told you."

"I know your name because I typed the review vetting for your promotion," she snapped back, anger strengthening her withering nerves. Bullies were simply infuriating! "You know the promotion which my husband refused to give you." Understanding dawned. *Uh oh.*

Flushing crimson, he stepped toward her. *Has anyone noticed that this guy is overreacting?* In one smooth movement, the door slid open and Brian Simms found his forward progress halted by the appearance of Harry and Hibb.

"What do you think you're doing?!" Brian's protest was cut off when an agent who Caroline didn't know entered the interrogation room carrying a sheaf of papers. She was petite, not a hair above five feet, grey-haired, slim and very confident.

The new agent walked over to Brian. "You're relieved. DG's orders." And then she turned her back to him and approached the table where Caroline still sat. Pulling out the second chair, she perched on it, sitting forward so her toes could touch the floor. Over the shoulder of the new agent, Caroline watched Brian yank his arms free and march out of the room. Hibb smiled reassuringly at Caroline, and then he and Harry exited the room.

"Now, Mrs. Brock, what was the nature of your relationship with Simon Reldif?"

Caroline slid her eyes from the door, which was now shut, to the officer across from her. The confidence in the woman's manner and her absolute calm helped Caroline begin to order her own seriously unsettled emotions. *Father, help me do this. Help me not to make things worse for John.* "Simon Reldif?" the interrogator repeated kindly.

Caroline shook herself to return her focus. "Um, we were friends." *What just happened?* "Um, who are you?" Caroline asked.

"Mabel Dodds," the agent replied, reaching across to offer Caroline her hand. "When did you last see Simon?" Mabel asked.

"At La Roche. He called from Heathrow three nights ago and said he was in London and wanted to get together," Caroline said.

"Another man invited you to dinner? How did your husband react to that?" Mabel asked.

"He was …" Caroline paused. "Uncomfortable."

"Uncomfortable as in angry?" Mabel asked.

"Look," Caroline began. "A marriage is a precious thing. It should be nurtured and protected. One way I protect my marriage is not going to dinner alone with other men. And, just for the record, my husband doesn't go to dinner with other women, either. I was planning to have dinner with Simon *and* John, but John was late."

The interrogator nodded. "What did you discuss with Mr. Reldif?"

Caroline thought for a moment. "We discussed some of the people we knew in common. We discussed his reasons for coming to London."

"Did Mr. Reldif broach any topics that made you uncomfortable?" Mabel asked.

"Uncomfortable? Not really. Annoyed? Yes, definitely. He tried to persuade me to leave John and travel to the States with him," Caroline said. *Honesty. No lies.*

"What was your answer?" Mabel asked.

"I told him that I had no intention of leaving my husband," Caroline replied.

"Did your husband fire on Mr. Reldif at La Roche?" Mabel asked.

"No. It was Ryan Carstairs who shot Simon. John was being fired upon by two gunmen. And for some reason, Simon felt he had to get to my side." She paused, shaking her head in disbelief. *Moron. As if he could protect me better than John.* "But it was Ryan who shot him, not one of the assassins."

"Is your husband capable of using his authority to compel Mr. Carstairs to fire his weapon on Mr. Reldif?"

"No. If John had wanted to shoot Simon, he wouldn't have asked someone else to do the deed," Caroline said, trying to keep the wryness from her voice. "But there was no need to shoot Simon, certainly not to kill him. I'd already refused Simon's advances. And now, with Simon dead, we have no way to find out what he was doing in the UK, now or before. And why did Ryan shoot him? It makes no sense."

Looking satisfied, Mabel stood and extended her hand. "Thank you, Mrs. Brock. You're free to go. It's been interesting meeting you."

Caroline stood and shook the proffered hand. "Thank you, Ms. Dodds."

Caroline exited the room hoping to see John, but he wasn't there. Hibb greeted her, clapping her warmly on the shoulder and congratulating her. He must have noted her disappointment, because he explained.

"He was here, but it's his turn next." She nodded sadly at his words. "You did well, Caroline. I particularly enjoyed the part where you shouted at Brian Simms. Very entertaining. By the by, our man Simms has been sent for anger management training," Hibb said with wry humour, keeping his voice gentle. "Er, Caroline?" She nodded, looking up at him. "The DG wants you to head over to Employee Services for a PiffDee."

"A what?" she asked.

"A psychological assessment to determine your fitness to perform your duties," Hibb said.

"Oh for goodness sakes!" she exclaimed. "How did John react to that?"

"Derision," Hibb said. "Said you were the only truly well-balanced person here. He has to undergo one as well."

A slow smile spread across her face. "Really? Hibb, I've got to have a copy of it. Any ideas?"

He grinned. "One or two. Come on. I'll escort you to the psych tank."

"Thanks."

# Chapter Ten
# The Unlovely Moments

"What do you think you're doing sneaking out at this time of the morning?"

John froze, glancing back at the irate figure of his wife. *Blooming heck!* She was angry. Again. Caroline had handled the interrogation brilliantly. He was so proud of her. But ever since, she had been angry with him. Everything he did was wrong, insensitive and selfish. She seemed to blame him. *But what for? The interrogation? Simon's death? Having a Y chromosome? What?*

Forcing himself to sound calm, he replied, "I thought I'd get a leg-up on the day."

"And what about me?" she asked, hands on hips. "Am I supposed to walk to Thames House?"

"You told me you weren't going in to work today," John replied. He realized his fists were clenched and shoved them into his pockets to camouflage the obvious evidence of his frustration. In the last seventy-two hours, his anger had only made things worse.

"When?" she demanded to know.

"Yesterday," he replied.

"No. No way." She stepped up to him. "You said—" She poked him in the chest. "You thought—" *Poke.* "I should take today off." *Poke.*

John gritted his teeth to hold back the words he wanted to say. "I still think—"

But she wouldn't let him finish, whirling about and slamming into the master bedroom of their current residence, MI-5 safe house Delta Upsilon. It sounded like a fraternity.

*All right. She's angry but not furious. I could leave now, and then the argument would be over.* John deflated. *Nope. She'd simply call a taxi and follow me in. Public displays of antagonism I can do without.*

Sounds of weeping filtered out from the bedroom. *Blast! Now she's crying.* John hung his head in defeat. Opening the door to the ugly brown bedroom, John saw Caroline lying on the lumpy safe-house mattress, her face tucked into her elbow. Sobs wracked her shoulders. *Oh, heck!*

Sitting beside her on the bed, he brushed her hair aside, trying to get a glimpse of her face. "Caroline," he said, speaking softly. "I'm sorry. I didn't mean to hurt your feelings."

"You just don't want me there," she said through her sobs. "You think I'm incompetent, that I can't do my job."

Swallowing a groan of frustration, he searched for a way to handle this situation. *Father, any inspiration here would be most welcome.* "I think you're competent," he said.

"Gee, thanks," she replied sarcastically. When she glanced up at him, he caught a glimpse of her tear-stained face. *Oh baby.*

"You're more than competent, Caroline. But I still think you need a few days off," he said.

"Fine." She bolted upright in bed, clearly furious with him. "Go away. I don't want to see you."

"All right," he agreed. *Blimey, what happened to my sweet and wonderful wife?* John moved to stand, but she grabbed him desperately by the sleeve.

"You're leaving?" she asked in the smallest, highest voice he'd ever heard from her.

"Simply to go to work," he reassured her.

"Without me," she said tonelessly.

*Blast ... ruddy ... crap.* Sometimes John really missed profanity.

"Well, fine!" she said and flopped back onto the bed, pulling a pillow over her head. Now she was angry again.

"Aargh!" he growled. "Caroline, you're driving me round-the-bend!"

Rolling off the bed, she pointed at him. "You're not exactly my favourite person at the moment either," she declared, stomping into the loo and slamming the door.

John's mobile rang. "Brock here," he said. His voice was still harsh.

"Mr. Brock, sir?" a familiar voice began tentatively. "The Chairman of the JIC was hoping to meet with you as soon as possible."

"Of course," John replied. "Thank you." *And thank you and thank you, Mr. Trevena.*

John tapped on the door to the loo. "Caroline. Louis Trevena's assistant called. The Chairman of the JIC? He wants to meet with me. Before the meeting with the Joint Intelligence Committee."

John flinched back when the door swung open. "I know who Trevena is," she replied hotly. Glaring at him, she stiffly crossed her arms. "I guess you'll have to go then."

He reached for her, but she pulled back. A myriad of emotions floated across her face. She was so transparent. There was absolutely not a modicum of guile in her. So why was she acting like she hated him?

"Caroline—" he began.

She cut him off. "Work. Go. Bye." And then she slammed the door in his face. *Maybe she does hate me.*

Three hours later, John sat in his office with the blinds drawn. He couldn't seem to concentrate on anything. He'd cancelled the morning briefing because … he simply didn't want to hear about it.

*Knock!*

"Come," John said.

Hibb entered carrying a cup of coffee, which he set down beside John. "You okay, mate?" Hibb asked.

*Mate.* Hibb had never called him that before. "Fine," John replied automatically, feeling anything but fine. "What have you got for me?"

Hibb studied him a moment and then handed over a stack of documents he pulled from his back pocket. "Ryan Carstairs' personnel file. He was recruited by MI-6 for a drugs op; apparently, they needed a football player to participate in an amateur international tournament in Delhi. Ryan was promised a place on the team in exchange for certain information."

"How did he end up in Section G?" John asked impatiently.

"After the op, there was apparently talk of returning him to sport, but somehow he was transferred to us instead," Hibb said.

"Somehow? Not very useful information," John said grimly.

Hibb frowned. "Don't you think it's suspicious that his path isn't clear to us? Why would a junior officer rate this kind of secrecy?"

"Why indeed? He's not even a good officer," John muttered. "Keep checking."

"Right." Hibb remained seated. "John, is summat wrong?"

John shrugged noncommittally.

Hibb shifted in his seat. "Is Caroline coming in today?" he asked.

"No. Maybe. I don't know," John replied morosely.

"This nonsense has been going on for three days, John. Go home and sort it out," Hibb demanded, rising abruptly and walking out.

*Blast and crap!*

John braced himself with a cleansing breath and a prayer as he entered the safe house. Rufus didn't greet him, and he honestly couldn't remember whether the dog was supposed to be here or whether he was somewhere else. *The Hibberts', that's where the dog is.*

"Caroline," John called.

"I'm upstairs," she replied.

*Step one, find my wife. Step two, gauge her mood ... calm, from the sound of her voice. Step three, find out what the heck is going on.*

*So far, so good.* She was reading a book, curled up on the most hideous-looking couch he'd ever seen. Where did they get the furniture they used in MI-5 safe houses?

"How are you feeling?" he asked.

She looked up from her book, meeting his gaze. "Are you trying to start a fight?"

Panic. "What? No. Of course not," he said, taking a step back.

She looked back down at her book. "There's a pot of coffee on if you want a cup. Or should I say a cuppa." She tilted her head as if pondering the mysteries of the universe. "No, wait, that's for tea." She shook her head. "Never mind."

He rolled his eyes. "Caroline," he said, waiting until she looked up again. "Something is seriously wrong here."

"Where?" she asked, glancing around the room.

*Give me strength.* He chose to ignore her question. "Is this about Simon?" he asked.

"Simon? What?" She finally put down her book.

"This … discord … between us," John said, watching her very closely as he spoke. *I have no clue what I'm doing here. Emotions! Bah!*

"Of course it's about Simon," she said, her gaze darkening.

"Do you … did you really miss him so much?" he asked.

"Miss him? I didn't miss him. Is this some insecure prattle about him again? Don't you trust me at all?" she said. Her mood was definitely escalating quickly … but to which emotion? Fury? Fear? Hysteria?

"I don't understand," John replied, confused. "You're either sizzling with anger or sobbing or laughing hysterically. Scratch that, I haven't heard you laugh in days. What is going on?"

She sprang to her feet, and red wrath flashed in her eyes. "It's about seeing someone I know shot before my very eyes. It's about watching him slowly bleed to death beneath my hands. Yeah, I found that a little upsetting. Duh!"

"Caroline …" he began, but his voice faded out.

"What?" she said, but the word sprang forth as though launched from a catapult. And then she began to cry. "It's not just about him. It's about Curly and Ziggy. They were killed protecting us. Did you know that Curly has a new baby daughter?" She hugged her arms to her chest. "It's about the fact that I can't sleep in my own bed, walk my own dog … And you! You just … oh, I don't know … You're just a ginormous jerk. I'm outta here!" Stomping down the stairs, she slammed out of the house without a second thought for a sweater or jacket.

John immediately contacted the security team to ensure that they were following her, and then he paced the upper hall. *A jerk!* That was one Canadian insult he understood. *She hasn't called me a jerk since the prison in Burma. Father in heaven, what do I do? I am completely out of my depth here. It's usually Caroline who sorts out all the emotional-relational stuff. I don't know how to help her … or me … or us.*

John called the only person he could think of who could be of assistance.

"Hello?"

"Hello, it's … John … Brock."

"Yes, I did recognize your voice," Caroline's mother said, clearly amused by his formality.

"I … I need your help," John said.

Immediately on alert, Caroline's mother responded, "Is it Caroline? What's wrong?"

"It is Caroline, but she's fine," he said. "She's not hurt or sick. At least I don't think so."

"What is it, son?" she asked, clearly confused.

*Son.* She always made him feel a part of the family. "I think maybe Caroline hates me," he said in his smallest voice.

"Hates you? What have you done?" she asked.

Immediately defensive, John replied, "Nothing. At least I don't think so. I haven't broken any of the rules."

"Rules? What rules?" she asked.

"Caroline has three rules," he explained. "Absolute fidelity; no abuse of any type or description; and—oh, what does she always say?—it's not enough to stay together, you also have to be happy, even if it kills you." Caroline's mother chuckled. "I haven't stepped out on her," he said. "I haven't—"

"Stepped out? What do you mean? Wait," she said. "John?"

"Yes, ma'am?" he said.

"Son. Let me speak to Caroline," she said.

"Yes. That's probably best. I'll see if I can find her," he said.

"Find her? Son, what is going on there?" she asked.

"We're in the middle of some trouble and … Give me a minute. I'll find her." He put the telephone on hold and then contacted the security team and ordered them to bring Caroline home, PDQ. What difference did it make? She was going to be angry with him no matter how he handled this situation.

Moments later, Caroline came stomping up the stairs. "I was just around the corner. Why did you—"

"Your mother is on the phone for you," he said, interrupting her, holding out the receiver.

She blithely approached and snatched it from his hand. "Hello? Mom?"

John slipped away, torn between wanting to eavesdrop and simply not being brave enough to listen to all the things his wife could be telling his mother-in-law about him. He paced the foyer at the bottom of the stairs. Half an hour later, Caroline called him up.

"John, sweetheart, my mother wants to speak to you," she said.

*Sweetheart?* He took the phone with trepidation. "Hi, it's John. Again."

"Are you in danger, John?" Caroline's mother asked. She knew enough about John's job to understand the implications.

"Er, yes," he admitted.

"Danger enough to frighten Caroline?"

"I would say so," he said.

"Then what you're experiencing is normal. After Henry and the children died, Caroline spent three months in emotional flux, happy-sad-angry. Give her time and patience, and she'll come around," she said.

"So she's not angry with me?" John asked, subdued.

"No, son," she said.

"Truly?" he asked, feeling very dubious.

"Yes," she said. "She's just been thrown for a loop. She loves you, John. Very much. In fact, you could say that, because she trusts you, she's able to let loose. She knows you'll stand by her."

"I will. Without a doubt. She still loves me?" he asked, still uncertain.

"Yes." He could hear his mother-in-law smile down the phone.

"What do I do?" he asked.

"Just love her back. And be patient," she said.

"I can do that," he said, confidently.

"Goodbye, son. Good luck."

"Thank you. Thank you very much." He rang off and turned to find Caroline watching him.

She opened her arms to him. "I'm so sorry, darling. Everything's just built up inside me until I feel like I'm going to explode. Please be patient with me. I love you." And John's world was suddenly set right. Yes, there was a group of assassins targeting him and conspiracies all around him. But Caroline loved him. All was well with the world.

The direct route to Wales would have been the M4, almost a straight line west from Twickenham. However, in order to throw off pursuit, they took the long way to paradise. At least that's what John told her. So rather than driving for just over two hours, they spent four hours doubling back and changing cars. Finally, they crossed the Severn Bridge just at dusk, the pink hue of the clear sky beautiful above the blue waters of the River Severn, the border between England and Wales.

They and four of their security officers stopped at Chepstow Castle, the oldest surviving stone fortification in Britain, situated on a narrow ridge between the limestone cliffs of the river and the Dell Valley. John and Caroline walked the battlements hand in hand and climbed St. Marten's Tower to gaze out over the River Wye.

They drove on through the lush greenery of Wales past the ruins of Tintern Castle and on to the Wye Valley, reaching Rose Cottage in the dark of night.

"Oh, John. It's lovely!" Caroline said as she stepped out of the car and approached the cottage.

Set on a hill above the River Wye, Rose Cottage was a two-storey stone structure surrounded by five acres of fields. In the dark, Caroline couldn't see the bluebell fields or the terraces, but the pictures in the brochure John had shown her looked lush and beautiful.

John unlocked the door with a brass key and, taking her hand, led her in, lighting each room as they went. Caroline ignored the fact that the security team moved ahead of them, clearing each room before they entered. She explored the prettily decorated sitting room with the wood-burning stove and the television room fit with a fairly powerful stereo system. The back of the house had a fully stocked kitchen and a breakfast nook with patio doors that she presumed exited to the terrace and gardens.

Upstairs, they found two bedrooms, one containing two twin beds and one containing a queen-sized bed.

"Where do you want to sleep?" asked John.

"Very funny," Caroline replied wryly.

Her nerves were still on edge, but she was no longer using John as her battering ram. Well, not as often as before. And since his conversation with her mother, he had been patient and loving. It seemed as long as he knew that he wasn't truly in the doghouse, he could handle anything she threw at him. And wasn't that an irritating thought? Why? *Who knows?*

"Why did we come to Wales?" she demanded to know, not even close to being able to conceal the irritation in her voice.

"You said you'd always wanted to come here," John calmly replied.

"Don't be obtuse! I mean if the bad guys are after us, why don't we go somewhere far away?" she replied warmly, but not in the warm embrace kind of way, more like working your way up to angry.

"Grendahl's network is international. Here we can disappear without leaving the country," he said.

"Why don't we just go to Canada? We could stay in the house in Grand Prairie," she said.

"You still own that?" he asked.

Finally, here was something that surprised him. *But that wasn't fair, was it?* "Yes," she said, calming somewhat. "The housing market isn't exactly booming in northern Alberta."

"Sorry. I just didn't realize. You don't think I might stand out a smidge in Canada? Though I could probably manage a 'G'day, eh' if necessary," he said, putting on his best Canadian accent.

Her mood broke, and she laughed once and then again, sliding her arm around his waist beneath his suit jacket. Picking up their bag, he wrapped an arm around her shoulder and led her to the master bedroom.

"Ooh, it's very elegant," she exclaimed.

"You like it?" he asked, clearly very pleased by her response … until she started to cry. And then he simply kicked the door shut behind them and pulled her close, sighing and shaking his head. "How long did your mother say this would last?" he muttered.

Her tears bubbled into laughter. "I'm sorry. I know I'm acting like a loon. It's as bad as being pregnant." She rested against him. "Would you mind if we started the evening with a nap?"

"Not at all." He grinned lasciviously. "I'm always happy to sleep with you."

She laughed again. "Not that. Just sleep."

"As you please," he replied, sliding her jacket off her arms and running his warm hands up her sides, lowering his head to a breath from her mouth.

"Well," she murmured breathily. "Maybe that first and then sleep." He chuckled happily. But suddenly, her fears were back, and she clutched at his arms. "John, are we safe?"

"I've brought a case of Aubrey's gadgets, and Hibb has hired four private security officers to watch over us in addition to the protection Special Branch has provided. And," he emphasized the conjunction, "we are not leaving until you feel safe again."

She settled again, intending to hold him to his promise.

Caroline was at loose ends the first few days, wandering the fields, beginning to tidy, beginning to bake, beginning to read, until the cottage was littered with half-finished projects.

"What about the books that Katie Hibbert sent?" John asked, clearly trying to interest her in something that would last longer than fifteen minutes before leading to tears.

She wiped her current puddle of tears on the tissue in her hand. "They're all about families and dysfunction and such. Are you sure you're ready for that?"

"Would it help you to have something important to focus on?" he asked.

"Yes. I think so. I would really like to understand who you are," she replied, blowing her nose.

"Then I'm ready. It can't possibly be worse than watching you suffer this emotional roller coaster you're on," he said.

She laughed wetly. "Okay. Bring it on." Jumping up from her chair, she retrieved the books and descended the stairs to drop them on the desk in the sitting room. John pulled the top book from the pile, opened it and sat in the chair behind the desk.

Caroline pulled one of the soft chairs over and propped her feet on John's leg. As they read, his hand dropped from time to time to massage her bare toes or stroke the top of her foot.

"John, listen to this. 'Shame conditions every other relationship in our lives. Shame destroys self-esteem.'"

"Shame?" he said.

"Yes," she said. "The parent imposes shame on their child by a variety of types of abandonment."

"Such as—" he said.

"Such as physically leaving, emotionally abusing them, using children to take care of their marriages, by hiding or denying their so-called 'shame secrets' so children have to cover them up to keep the family balance. Whoa!" She lifted her head. "Were you expected to hide your father's alcoholism?"

"Oh, my sweet innocent, of course; one doesn't speak of such things." He adopted a very imperious tone for the last part.

"I don't know how you survived!" she said. Her heart squeezed within her at the thought of John as a boy in a home without a haven of peace.

But John just shrugged. "What is that one from?"

She flipped the book over to view the cover. "John Bradshaw's book. *Bradshaw On: The Family: A New Way of Creating Solid Self-esteem.*" She flipped it back again. "He says that once shame damages self-esteem, the child is forced to develop a false self as a defence mechanism to protect them from pain and loneliness."

"Can I see that?" he asked, holding out his hand. She leaned forward to pass the book.

"You already figured out that your mother leaving when you were nine, even though she came back, damaged your ability to trust. Do you think it would have caused this 'shame effect'?"

"Hmmm, I suppose. The feeling that I wasn't worth staying for," he said.

"John?" she said.

"Hmmm," he continued perusing the pages.

"John love." He looked up at her. "I think you're worth staying for," she said.

Love shining from his eyes, he replied, "Thank you."

She smiled softly. "No thanks necessary."

John pulled her up and over to the couch, where she snuggled against him. They continued reading.

"This exactly describes what was done to me," John said, pointing at the page. "That the parents decide right and wrong and the child is held responsible for the parent's anger."

"I read there too that if the child seeks to change his role within the family, the parents are completely threatened. They punish the child, even after the child is an adult, for forcing the parents to see that they themselves may be in the wrong," she said.

"So when I left home, I damaged the system?" he said.

"No, I think when you realized that you weren't who your father and mother allowed you to believe you were, you destabilized the system," she said.

"When I realized that I was intelligent and capable; when I decided to live by a different set of rules. When I stood up to my father," he said.

She nodded. "I especially enjoy that story. Not many children get to stand up to the emotional abuse of their parents in that way. I'm proud of you."

"Thank you."

She straddled his lap, linking her arms around his neck. "The PiffDee was right."

Quirking an eyebrow, he questioned her, "What in Wellington's trousers are you on about?"

She chuckled at his turn of phrase. "Hibb got me the results of your psychological fitness assessment."

"You know that was highly inappropriate?" John scowled at her.

"Conclusion," she quoted, unperturbed. "'Subject has unresolved issues from his childhood.' Do you know what the recommendation was?"

"Hmmm?" he replied, frowning.

"'Subject should find a leisure activity,'" she said.

Cradling her face tenderly in his hands, he kissed her, languidly exploring the shape of her mouth. "Mmmm. My favourite leisure activity," he murmured against her lips.

She chuckled breathily. "Yes. Not suggesting you should replace this with any other activity." She lost herself in the warmth of his touch for a time. "Hmmm, rugby," she murmured.

"What?" he asked, pulling back to look at her.

"You could play rugby again," she suggested.

"I'm fine, darling. I only want to make you happy."

"It would make me happy to watch you play rugby," she said.

He smiled. "As you wish." He shifted her closer to him. "Caroline? I've been thinking … these books we're reading …" He trailed off for a moment. "You were right about my mother. She should have protected me. You would have protected me."

"I'm sorry she didn't protect you. She loved you. I don't know what your father had over her, we may never know, but I'm sure she loved you," she said.

"Do you love me?" he asked.

"Yes. Forever always," she said.

"That's all that matters," he said. "I'm very grateful—"

"You don't need to be grateful, darling. Just be you, the real you, the 'you' that exists as the man God created you to be," she said.

"How do I find him? Who is he?" John wondered aloud.

"Silly man. I know him well," she said. "He's the man who laughs and jokes with me. He's the one who thinks I'm beautiful and wonderful and tells me so. He's the one who holds me when the nightmares come and never ever complains when the laundry's not finished or the dog is suffocating in dust bunnies. He's the one who is fascinated by God's love and what the Bible says. He doesn't demand anything except that I love him. And I do. I love him with my whole heart."

John sighed the happy sigh that she loved to hear.

Maryn was awakened by those same blue eyes again, piercing through her flesh to rend her heart in two. Sonam Narayan groaned in irritation at her, and she resisted the urge to kick him. There was still a glass beside her bed, and she took it out to the kitchen to fill it with Scotch and water, hoping to tranquilize the burn of her panic. *If Tor can't succeed, perhaps I'll need to do it myself.* The morning light was peeking through the blinds and so, rather than heading back to bed, she dressed for a jog, trying to outrun her despair.

Caroline awoke later the next morning, but not nearly as late as she would have liked. The bedroom light was on, and John was singing loudly about waking, the King and eternity. The faintly muffled, joyous sound rang out from the bathroom.

She groaned when she looked at the clock. "John?!"

He walked into the bedroom still brushing his teeth, pausing to greet her with a bright smile. "Good morning, lovely," he said.

"Why?" she asked, covering her eyes with her hands.

"Since you're up, I wondered if you'd like to come into Cardiff to see the Royal Maritime Reserves demonstration of amphibious landings," he said.

"Since I'm up?" She groaned. "I'm up because … because you're a pest."

"A pest? Me?" He pulled a face of mock outrage.

She laughed. "Incorrigible. That's the word for it, isn't it?"

He pounced on the bed over her. "Want to come?" He leaned down and kissed her, trailing his lips along her cheek, leaving behind a residue of toothpaste that she quickly removed with her hand. "If you are coming, however, we need to leave soon," he said.

She hooked her right leg around his left knee, braced both hands on his right shoulder, and shoved him over, perfectly exchanging positions with him.

"I wanna come," she said, blowing gently across his ear. "Now?" she asked, lazily nibbling his ear.

Shuddering, he automatically lifted his shoulder to fend off the tickle. "Yes, now. Kiss later. Boats now." Tickling her once, he flipped her onto her side before he jumped off the bed. "Now come on. You can't laze around here all day. I'll make you some toast with peanut butter … Blah." He stuck out his tongue to show what he thought of her food preferences.

Heartily, she laughed at the expression on his face. "One question," she said. "Where are Batman and Robin?"

"Who?" he asked. He was clearly confounded by her superhero reference.

"The security team. You know, Ryan and Benny, or Bernard or something."

"Bowen Banyard? I don't know, and frankly, I don't give a toss." John paused and his brow furrowed in concentration. "Ryan? Ryan Carstairs?" She confirmed with a nod. "Why would Hibb have placed Ryan on the detail?" John asked, puzzling over the mystery.

"Sir William said that Ryan requested assignment to my security detail. Didn't you know?" she asked.

"No," John replied thoughtfully. "Why would he do that?"

"Hmmm." She tapped the corner of her mouth with her finger in a humorous gesture. "Maybe he thought that if he was on *my* security detail, you wouldn't be able to boss him around for a while."

Diving onto the bed, John grabbed for her, nibbling her neck as she struggled in his arms, laughing. "Bossy? Why do you always accuse me of being bossy?"

"Stop! Stop and I'll tell you." She shrieked with laughter as he renewed his assault, kissing across the base of her throat. "Stop!"

"All right. I've stopped," he said.

"Let go," she said, still releasing light giggles. When he did, she slipped off the bed and took a few steps away toward the bathroom. "I tell you you're bossy … because you are!" And she took off into the bathroom, shutting the door and locking it.

The room was silent on the other side. "Hmmm, perhaps not such a clever idea," she muttered to herself. Peeking under the bathroom door, she tried to see if John was still standing there, but she couldn't tell. Her stomach growled, and she realized just how hungry she was.

Finally, she called out, "John?" But he didn't respond. "Truce?" Still no response. "Hmmm. Surely he's not that patient. I could just slip down the back stairs and get to the kitchen first." *He won't tickle me if I'm cooking him bacon.*

Abruptly, she flung the bathroom door open, but he was waiting. Both hands were braced against the door frame, and he was blocking her way, sporting an enormous grin. "Not only are you bossy," she accused. "You cheat!"

"You going to kiss me so we can have breakfast?" he asked, raising his brows in question.

"No, but I may let you kiss me," she responded, winking coyly.

He leaned in slowly, just lightly touching her mouth. Licking his lips, he brushed across hers. She moaned, stepping closer to increase the pressure of his mouth on hers.

"Caroline?" he asked, breathily. She moaned in response. "I'm hungry," he said.

She stopped, looking up in surprise and then breaking into a bright smile.

"I love you," she exclaimed, wrapping her arms around his neck. He smiled in return, hugging her tightly against him.

After breakfast, Caroline slipped into the car beside John and the parade began: their car followed by a variety of vehicles conveying Jimmy Storm, Ben Grimes, Suzette LeBlanc and Rhys Dixon, aka the Fantastic Four, and Batman and Robin, aka Bowen Banyard and Ryan Carstairs.

Abruptly, John pulled to the side of the narrow road and turned to her. "Come here," he commanded. "Those yawns of yours are the most erotic gesture I've seen in a long time."

"John!" she exclaimed. Blushing at the thought of six security officers watching them snogging in the front seat of the car, Caroline still moved toward her husband, winding her fingers into his thick brown hair as he possessed her mouth. Moaning at the sensation, she took over the kiss and he gave up possession to her.

The blaring horn of an oncoming car forced them back to the present, and they continued on to Cardiff. Down by the Queen Alexandria Dock, Caroline submitted to two hours of amphibious landing assault demonstrations until she truly felt she'd peaked on the experience.

"John," she said, pulling on his sleeve.

"Hmmm? Look at that, sweetheart. Can you believe they have the technology for that now?" he said.

"Outstanding," she murmured. *How much longer can this possibly go on? My father always told me it was good to be bored, but I have to admit that I'm sceptical. I wish I had long hair. Then I could braid it. I wonder if John's hair is long enough to braid.* She finished pulling all the blades of grass from the stone wall beside them and braided them instead. *Groan, this is boring.* When she looked up, John was watching her.

"You're bored, aren't you?" he asked.

She blushed lightly. "It's okay. It's not so bad."

He smiled at her. "We can leave now."

"But isn't there some aqua-boat thingy or something big still to come?" she said.

"It's nought, sweetheart," he said. "You've been more than patient. Thank you for joining me."

Suddenly, she felt bad for dragging him away from something that he clearly enjoyed. "Maybe you don't need to go yet. I could walk back into town and have a coffee or a pop or something while you finish here," she suggested. "By the time I walk downtown, you'd be able to see the boat thingy and drive to meet me."

John's smile fell away. "I don't want you off alone," he said.

"The assassins are after you, not me," she said.

"Nevertheless," he said.

"Excuse me, *syr*," Batman said. "The Côte Brasserie lies *gerllaw*, close by. I would be happy to accompany Mrs. Brock."

"That's not necessary," John replied.

"John, I really would like to sit and have a cold drink," Caroline said. "I'll be fine."

"It is a mere few steps from the Millennium Centre," said Bowen. "I know these streets, *syr*. I will keep a close watch."

"It'll be fine, darling," Caroline said. *Come on, John. Don't make me admit just how bored I am.* "I'll meet you there in an hour. Okay?"

"Very well. Watch her closely, Banyard," John said, and there was no mistaking these orders for a suggestion.

"Of course, *syr,*" Batman said.

Banyard/Batman walked half a step behind Caroline, his eyes in perpetual motion, scanning their environment.

"So what do they call pop here?" Caroline asked.

"Pardon, ma'am?" Batman said.

"Pop. Um, it's soda in the States, well, many of them. They call it soda pop as well, and fountain drinks depending on where you're travelling. The English call it fizzy drinks. What do the Welsh call it?" she asked.

"Fizzy drinks would be *byrlymog diod,* ma'am," Batman replied.

"I never realized how much I'd have to adjust to living in the UK," she said. "There are more cultural differences than I expected, and the vocabulary gap has been a challenge."

"Yes, ma'am. What have you learned?" Batman asked. Caroline knew he was just being polite, but it was still nice of him to ask.

"I've learned not to comment on people's pants," she began, and Batman chuckled. "I've learned that I need to find a Chemist if I want more paracetamol. I've learned to stop for Elevenses and have a cuppa and a biccy, and that I need my torch to locate the fuse box."

"You have done well, ma'am," Batman replied, scanning the environment, his hand ever close to his chest. As he walked, she occasionally saw the leather of his shoulder holster beneath his jacket. Knowing that her companion carried a handgun was not alarming. She knew that in English culture, only specific law-enforcement officers carried guns. John had been very concerned about her reaction the first time he'd pulled out his Glock. For Caroline, though, it was not a problem; too much James Bond, perhaps.

Batman received a call on his cell phone. "*Ie.* Of course. *Dim.* No. I'll be right there." He turned to Caroline. "Mrs. Brock. Something has come to Ryan's attention that he would like me to see."

Caroline scanned the environment. They were standing on a street between two large warehouse-style buildings. One of the buildings had a door that led into what looked like a small nameless eatery. Batman led her to that door. "If you could wait in here for a moment, I'll return shortly," he said.

"Okay. Should I call John?" she asked.

"No need, ma'am. I will return shortly," Batman assured her.

"Okay," Caroline agreed, perfectly willing to relax and wait.

Before long, Caroline noticed a woman clad in black leather slacks and a red leather jacket. She had frizzy blonde hair and the oddest expression on her face. She was leaning against the building directly across from Caroline's position, and she was definitely watching her. A few minutes later a burly man, tattooed and hairy, wearing black trousers and a white cable-knit sweater, entered through the rear of the eatery and sat two tables away from Caroline. He kept glancing in her direction.

*She is definitely watching me. And so is that big, scary guy over there. Father, please keep me safe.* Standing abruptly, Caroline walked toward the back of the eatery to hide in the bathroom until Batman returned but, after two steps, the big, scary guy stood as well, moving to intercept her trajectory. Caroline heeled about and exited the eatery. Now she was scared. She pulled out her cell phone, continuing to walk as she watched the strangers around her. The weird lady and the hairy, scary guy were walking behind her.

John answered on the first ring. "We're almost finished here, darling. I'll just nip down and fetch you and we can—"

"John, I'm scared," she said.

Immediately on the alert, John asked, "What's happening? Where's Banyard?"

"He … got a call from Ryan … went off but he hasn't returned … and there's this red-jacket lady and a hairy, scary guy, and I think maybe they're following me." Panting, she increased her pace. "I'm scared."

"Where are you?" John asked, and she could hear the deep concern in his voice and the uneven tempo that indicated that he was on the move.

She sobbed once. "I don't know. I don't know. John, they're getting closer."

"I'm on my way, Caroline. Tell me where you are," he said, and she could hear him calling orders to those around him.

She sobbed again, walking faster. "I don't know. I just don't know."

"Describe what you see," he said, keeping his voice calm for her.

"I'm between two big buildings, like warehouses. I was sitting in some kind of eatery and … and … and—John, they're getting closer! John, help me!" She screamed.

"Caroline! I will find you. Caroline—"

She ran, clutching the phone in her fist. John's voice came through the speaker but she couldn't process his words. She simply ran. Mister Hairy-Scary and Mizz Weird were converging on her position and then, over to the right, she saw Ryan. Relief flooded through her. Slowing, she put the phone back to her ear.

"It's okay, John," she said, panting heavily. "Ryan's here."

"Don't hang up," John said, and she could hear the urgency in his voice as well as a car starting. "Stay with me."

She headed forward directly to intersect Ryan's path. He had his eyes fixed on her … and he nodded … once … to Hairy-Scary.

Abruptly, Caroline stopped, her instincts flashing a warning. "No! Not him!" she exclaimed to the air. Fear enveloped her. "John!"

"Run! Baby, run! I'll find you," he yelled through the phone. "I give you my—"

Caroline ran. Ryan and the assassins sped toward her. Suddenly on the left, Caroline saw a café. She darted for the door, running through, knocking over chairs as she went, ignoring the angry remarks of staff and customers. *Back door. Back door. Back door. There's got to be a back door to this place.* Caroline ran past the men's and ladies' straight toward a grey steel door. She slammed through, suddenly inside a well-lit room stacked with crates. She searched to the right. Nothing. To the left there was another grey door, and she pushed through it, hearing the alarm sound as the fire door opened into a parking lot. Caroline jogged past the variety of pickup trucks and out into the street, almost colliding with a yellow Opel. Stumbling back first, she continued on, racing across the street. She made a quick left into an alley and ran, dodging the rubbish bins and other refuse, spinning past two men sharing a reefer beneath a fire escape. She turned right out of the alley, through another parking lot, her legs burning and her lungs bursting for breath. Turning right again, she dodged through the group of toughs on the sidewalk.

Caroline's cell phone rang. She hadn't realized she'd disengaged. As she lifted it to her ear, a massive torpedo of flesh knocked her into a wall. She bounced and landed on the sidewalk. The cell phone went spinning from her grasp. Glancing about her, she saw that she was alone except for the nefarious trio of pursuers. Before she could gasp in a fresh breath, she felt her arm grasped and an inexorable pull toward a darker alley behind them and away from the safety of witnesses. A beefy hand covered her scream. Eyes wide, she stared around her. Ryan, Mizz Weird, and Hairy-Scary surrounded her.

Caroline struggled and resisted, trying to breathe around the meaty hand covering her airway. Slammed against the wall, she bounced off and fell to the asphalt, gasping to catch her breath. Rough hands hauled her up, shaking and shaking her. A fist connected with her face, and her eyes exploded in light. She struggled up again, but halfway to a crouch something harder than a fist connected with her face, and she felt her flesh tear. Stunned, she was unable to draw breath to scream. Hauled up and pinned to the wall, she couldn't focus as waves of nausea coursed through her.

"Enough! That's enough." Ryan's voice. Was he her ally?

"Get the needle," the woman commanded, and Caroline watched as Ryan drew a hypodermic from his jacket pocket, loaded and ready to—what?

"Ryan," Caroline gasped. "Why?"

"They're only going to hold you as bait for John. He'll pay for humiliating me," Ryan ground out.

"Don't," she gasped.

A meaty fist slammed into her belly, and she collapsed forward. Pulled up again, she struggled to breathe. Weird Woman ripped aside Caroline's shirt—no female solidarity here—revealing Caroline's shoulder as the needle drew closer, but she couldn't see it, couldn't focus on anything but the misty grey washing across her vision. And then blackness.

Caroline woke to the reek of garbage. Wondering who was groaning so loudly, she realized it was her own voice she heard. Lying on asphalt, slimy black asphalt, her head was pillowed on a black plastic bag, which she was convinced contained the effluence of an all-night student rave. Her vision was bobbing and bouncing and throbbing to the rhythm of the pain in her neck.

She flinched back as hands reached for her. "No," she protested, weeping openly. "Enough."

"Ma'am, y'awright?" Caroline looked up into the eyes … of a complete stranger.

"Who are you?" was what she meant to say, but it came out as a groan. She wept, curled into a ball beside the garbage. "I want John," she moaned.

"John? Who's John?" the stranger asked, and she could hear the mutter of several voices around her.

"My phone," she managed to utter.

"No phone on ye'. Use mine," he said.

Nodding slowly, she uncurled herself enough to accept his phone. But her hands shook so badly that she couldn't dial. Still on her side, she handed the phone up to the man where he crouched beside her. But then she paused. She couldn't give out John's number to a stranger. What if this supposed Good Samaritan was really an enemy? Other allies had turned out to be villains.

She opened her eyes properly to view the men who had quite probably saved her life. Except that they weren't men, they were boys—teenagers really, a gang of shaved-head, tattooed adolescents wearing sleeveless jean jackets and grubby jeans. Many of them had chains, hoops and rings protruding from various pockets in their clothes and holes in their bodies.

The youth who'd clearly been speaking to her held out a plastic water bottle. He was not as tall as some of the others but massively built—a definite linebacker if he'd been born in a different time and place. His muscled arms were decorated in a pattern of crosses, fish and anchors.

Caroline let him help her sit to drink. As she came fully vertical, her head exploded with pain. Clutching at his jacket, she gripped the filthy denim tightly until she could see again. Sipping the water once, twice, she pushed the youth away abruptly.

"I'm gonna throw up," she warned him. And then she did. She vomited violently, retching out the contamination of the situation. *Ryan! The entire time it was Ryan!*

"Get your hands off her!" John roared, running into the alley as though prepared to take on the entire gang of armed youths if necessary. "Baby," John exclaimed, rushing to kneel beside her. His face gradually came into focus, her knight in shining armour.

The hiss and click of drawn weapons filled the eerie silence that followed. John spun, disarming two in seconds and preparing to do worse to the leader.

"John. Stop," she said, gasping out his name. "They saved me … helped me."

John unclenched his fist from the young man's shirt. "Are you certain?" he said, his eyes never leaving the tattooed youth.

"Yes, John. He and the others, they saved me," she said, holding her head as she spoke to try and contain the pounding that threatened to detonate her brain.

"What happened?" John addressed the gang leader.

The gang leader, however, first addressed Caroline. "Dis 'ere yer bloke?"

"Yes," she said. John was nearing apoplexy in his concern for her.

"Ye' trust 'im?"

"Yes," she replied. John managed to stay quiet a moment longer.

The gang leader nodded once and then turned to John. "Dese blokes. Dere were free of 'em. Free of 'em agin' dis 'ere lady. We whupped 'em. Sent 'um packin'."

John seemed to follow the rough-speak with ease. He checked in with her to ensure that he'd been told the truth. When she nodded slowly, she watched him temporarily reign in his anger. He turned back to the young man who had spoken.

"Thank you," John said. "I'm truly grateful." And then her husband did something she'd rarely seen. He took out his business card and handed it to the young gang leader. "If I can ever return the favour, let me know."

"Ta," the young fellow replied, gesturing to his mates. They faded away.

"What happened, darling?" John asked her just as the Fantastic Four thundered into the alley, guns drawn.

"What happened here?" Grimes demanded to know.

"I don't know, do I?" John said, nearly shouting the words at the man.

Intimidated, Grimes immediately backed down. "I'm sorry, sir. What would you have us do?"

"Nothing," John said. "Wait. Find Carstairs and Banyard. Now." Every syllable John spoke was imbued with barely leashed fury.

"Yes, sir." Grimes turned to the other men, giving orders and then turning back to John. "Jimmy will stay and take your lady to the hospital."

John crouched down beside Caroline. His hands gently brushed her hair back from her face, rounding her jaw line and lifting her chin. She watched his jaw clench in anger as he saw the bleeding cut on her cheek and the bruises on her jaw. "Where are Bowen and Ryan?" he muttered, obviously trying to keep his anger from touching her.

"It was Ryan," she said, a giant sob wracking her body, chased by another and another. John held her firmly around the shoulders, murmuring soothing words of comfort as she sobbed the tragedy of betrayal.

Even when she finally began to calm, he kept her firmly tucked against his body. "Where are Batman and Robin?" he asked again, very softly.

She released one chuckle at her silly nickname from his lips. "It was Ryan." She began to weep again, more gently this time. "All along, it's been Ryan giving away our positions, letting them know our schedule."

"Oh, baby, I'm so sorry. Darling, you're safe now. Don't cry," John said. He held her and soothed her.

Jimmy Storm interrupted them. "Excuse me, sir. We've been unable to contact Carstairs or Banyard. But, sir, the plods are on their way. Do you want this reported?"

"No," John said, shaking his head. "Is the car here?"

"Yes, sir. Grimes left it at the end of the street," Jimmy said.

"Help me get her there. We'll go back to the cottage—no, blimey! We need to get her to a hospital." John said, clenching his fist, looking like he desperately wanted to punch something—or, more likely, someone. "Call in the others. Task someone to get our things from the cottage and send the rest to escort us to the hospital."

"John—" Caroline began, and then her own retching interrupted her.

"Take deep breaths, sweetheart," he said. "Slow, deep breaths, in through the mouth and out through the nose."

Gently, John helped her stand. She leaned heavily on his shoulder.

"John, I want to go home," Caroline said, only just holding back from whimpering in piteous sorrow.

"We're going to the hospital first. Then I'll take you home," he responded tenderly, helping her into the car. Jimmy took the wheel.

"Where are the rest of the Fantastic Four?" she asked.

"They're here, sweetheart. We're well-protected," he said.

"No, not so well," she said, and a gentle weeping took over again.

Wrapping his jacket around her, he pulled her tight against him. "I should have sent them with you," he murmured guiltily.

She wasn't certain whether she should reassure him that she was okay, because she didn't really feel okay. Her lip and the inside of her cheek were raw and swollen. Her cheek felt lain open, and even the air moving across it burned like acid. Like, well, what she imagined acid would feel like. Well, okay, it probably wasn't that bad. Caroline suddenly realized that she was saying these things aloud, and that probably had more to do with John's concern than the wound on her face.

"I'm sorry, sir," Jimmy called back over his shoulder. "We can't figure out which hospital in Cardiff has an A&E department."

"Of course," John replied, his voice laced with irony. "Banyard was the Welshman. Never mind. Just take us to London. West Middlesex will do," John said.

Caroline felt very sorry for the receptionist of the Accident and Emergency ward of West Middlesex University Hospital.

"What do you mean, there's a three-hour wait?" John said, storming up to the poor woman.

The receptionist tried her very best soothe-the-wild-beast voice. *Big mistake.* "Now, sir, we have—"

John cut her off with a gesture. Turning to Caroline, his manner became gentle. "Come with me, sweetheart." He led her into the waiting room and found her a chair against the wall, rolling his jacket for her to use as a pillow. "I'll be right back," he said once she was settled.

"John, I can wait three hours. I'll be okay," she said. He returned her gaze with a blank look, and she was pretty sure there was a grizzly bear hiding just behind his façade of calm. She sighed wearily. "Okay. Just promise me one thing," she said, conceding the battle.

"Yes?" he replied.

"Don't have anyone arrested."

"All right," he replied calmly, and her eyes widened. *Had he really been considering doing just that?*

Ten minutes later, John returned with a wheelchair and an orderly who escorted Caroline to X-ray and then provided her with a painkiller and anti-nausea medication. Within fifteen minutes, she was ensconced in an examination room, having seven stitches inserted along her cheekbone. John stood by, holding her hand the entire time.

Once the stitches were inserted and a bandage applied, the doctor disposed of his non-latex gloves and returned from a cupboard over the sink with a prescription pad. He inscribed the Latin and finished with an illegible signature.

"You have a concussion," the doctor began. "You may experience headache, dizziness, nausea, anxiety and blurred vision. You need to take it easy for at least the next twenty-four hours and certainly refrain from strenuous activity for several weeks. You should follow up with your own doctor." Caroline couldn't figure out why he kept glancing at John as he spoke.

"These are painkillers to help ease your discomfort." The doctor handed over the prescription. "You can take one every four hours."

John took the page from the doctor, studied the script and then pocketed it. The doctor watched John, his mouth open as though waiting before continuing. John scrutinized his every movement with a keen eye.

*O-kay. What is going on here?* Caroline reached over and tugged on John's sleeve to get his attention. "John sweetheart? Could you please fill the prescription downstairs for me?"

John narrowed his eyes at the doctor and then looked back at her again. "Are you certain?" he inquired.

"Yes, please. Then I don't have to stand around waiting," she said.

He nodded and left, but she felt like she could see the warning arrows he shot at the doctor on his way out.

"Doctor?" she asked. "Is there something else you need to tell me?"

"Is your husband a gangster, ma'am?" the doctor said.

Caroline laughed and then groaned at the pounding it set off in her head. "No, he's just very protective of me."

"Are you certain that it is protection he provides?" And Caroline realized that because of the fierce fire in John's eyes, the doctor suspected him of being the cause of her injury. The doctor continued, "He threatened the duty physician, actually threatened him to get me here. I'm a plastic surgeon. I don't normally do A&E coverage."

Caroline smiled in spite of herself. "I'm sorry about that. But he is protective." She reached out a hand to rest it on the doctor's arm in order to hold his attention on what she was saying. "My husband would never hurt me. And I would never hide it if he did." Tears began to prickle in the corners of her eyes. "Will the scar be very visible?"

"Of course not." The doctor responded as though she had insulted him. "In time, it will be a fine silver thread, only enhancing your beauty."

"Thank you, doctor. Thank you so much. Could you please see if my husband is back? I don't think I'm steady enough to go looking for him," she said.

"Of course. Be sure to get plenty of rest for the next few days. The brain is a delicate organ and must be guarded," he said.

"Thank you," she replied.

Panting lightly, John soon returned, carrying a single red rose and pills rattling in his pocket, clearly having run up the stairs to return to her quickly. Immediately, he offered her his arm to steady her.

The pounding in her neck had lessened, and the world had stopped spinning whenever she moved her head. However, the freezing on her cheek made her feel like her skin was slowly sliding off her skull, a sensation that made her feel slightly nauseous.

"Please take me home," she whispered. He kissed her temple and agreed, leading her out to the car. Jimmy Storm drove them home.

Once home, John grouched at Rufus so vehemently to stop him from jumping on Caroline that the poor beast shrunk away with his tail between his legs.

"Don't be so hard on him, John. He's just happy to see us," she said, reprimanding him lightly. "How did he get here anyway? I thought the Hibberts had him."

"I thought it might make you feel more at home," John said.

"Hibb's fed up with him, isn't he?" she asked, knowing only too well how Hibb felt about Rufus.

"The girls have gotten rather attached, I understand," John said.

"I don't know why Hibb won't just buy a puppy. Katie's happy to do it," she said.

John shrugged. "Something about 'over,' 'dead' and 'body,' I believe," he said.

After helping her change into her favourite blue flannel pyjamas, John tucked Caroline into bed and brought her a glass of water to go with the prescribed painkillers.

"Do you think you could tell me what happened?" John asked tenderly, drawing a chair close to the bed, holding her hand in both of his.

"Yes, I think so." She recounted the events, beginning to cry again as she concluded. "I can't believe it, John. It was one of the team. Why does he hate me so much?"

"The contract is not on you, my love," he stated plainly.

Her wet gaze tilted to meet his. "You think he was telling the truth? They were only going to hold me as bait? He wasn't trying to kill me?" she asked.

"Most likely," he replied evenly.

She groaned. "That doesn't make me feel any better. Who is *doing* this?"

"I don't know, Beauty, I wish I did," he said. His voice sounded so calm, but she knew that he was furious. She could read it in his eyes.

"Maybe we should leave the country like Hibb suggested," she said.

"Yes. I think you should. I'll miss you, but it's for the—"

"John?" she interrupted softly, waiting for him to meet her gaze. "We go together or not at all. 'Where you go, I will go. Where you die, I will die, and there will I be buried,'" she paraphrased from the Book of Ruth, her voice soft and gentle.

"No," he gasped, his eyes filling with moisture.

"Yes," she replied softly. "You promised you would never leave me."

"That was … this is … this is completely different!"

"Not to me," she concluded firmly, her eyebrows knitting together as she decisively nodded once.

He stood abruptly and paced the room. "I … This is my fault. Why did I ever open my heart to you? All it's brought you is danger and misery!" He sobbed once.

"John? Please come here, because otherwise I'm going to have to get out of this bed and come and get you, and I think if I stand up, my head is going to fall off," she said.

He looked up at her, his eyes full of moisture but his cheeks still dry. Shaking his head at her in wonderful exasperation, he stripped to his boxers and crawled into bed, moving to spoon against her, very careful of her injuries.

"Why do you stay with me?" he asked, kissing her leopard-scarred shoulder.

"The sex," she replied.

A laugh burst forth unexpectedly. "So that's it!" he replied, chuckling.

"Well, the other stuff, too," she said, humour in her voice. "None of this is your fault, my love. Let it go. Just love me. That's all I need right now. Oh, and the happy sigh."

"What happy sigh?" he asked, bewildered.

"You always release a happy sigh when you pull me close." Her eyes began to droop and her breathing deepened.

"I don't think I could honestly sigh happily, Caroline, but I can love you. I always love you. I wish it had been me they hurt," he said.

"I don't."

As she fell asleep in the warmth and protection of his arms, she knew that he would stay awake reviewing everything he knew about the situation, trying to discover the source of such hatred against him.

# Chapter Eleven
## *Unraveling the Broken Cord*

"What do we know?" John asked the next morning in the Grid's meeting room.

No one seemed willing to answer him or meet his gaze. Eyes were averted all around the table.

Finally, Hibb acquiesced. "Ryan Carstairs has disappeared. No trace."

"No trace," John repeated, keeping the deep fury he felt out of his voice but unable to keep it from his eyes and his tightly clenched jaw.

"I can't believe it!" Alexa slapped the table, rattling the teaspoons. "It was one of us!"

"He was never one of us, Lex," Harry replied.

"There's no way Ryan had the skills to plan something this complex. I'll wager he didn't even plan the attack on Caroline," Hibb said.

John flinched at his words. *Attack ... Caroline ... Failure to protect ...* The ideas tormented John's heart.

Just then, Aubrey burst into the room. "Stone the crows, I've sussed it! They are all connected." Excitedly, Aubrey glanced around the room, but the others just hung their heads.

"This is no chin-wag, Aubrey, it's not the time," Hibb suggested tersely.

"Stone the crows, I say! What is wrong with you people?" Aubrey's voice grew fierce. "Don't you want to catch the blaggards who did this to our Caroline? She is the gentlest, sweetest, most intelligent woman I've ever met.

Well, maybe not the most intelligent, but she is very intelligent and very sweet—"

John replied, his frown lightening minutely. "Who's connected, Aubrey?"

"Ryan Carstairs and Simon Reldif and … Colonel Shing, formerly of Chinese intelligence." He sat proudly beside John in Caroline's empty chair.

Hibb slapped his palms against the table top, a smack resounding from the walls. "What are you on about?" he asked sharply.

Aubrey had everyone's attention now. "Ryan is adopted. We knew that, of course, because it was in his records. His father was a factory worker in the Midlands. His mother was from Suffolk. His biological mother was also from Suffolk, the victim of a violent assault in her teens. Her father—Ryan's biological grandfather—is Chinese, a low-level functionary attached to the military in the office where our infamous colonel had his first posting."

"Did we know he had made contact with his biological mother? Don't they usually track that sort of thing?" Alexa asked.

"My guess is that someone approached him through his grandfather, and the connection was never made official," Aubrey replied.

"Simon Reldif?" John prompted. The momentum of his interest was increasing.

"We know already that Simon Reldif traveled to China during his university days and then again recently," Aubrey began. He turned aside to John. "I was mistaken, John. Reldif wasn't trying to make contact with Caroline." John's eyes flitted around the room, an embarrassed flush lightly warming his cheeks. "He was making contact with Ryan Carstairs."

"Proof?" Harry asked.

"Indeed," Aubrey replied. "I've got them on CCTV on three separate occasions, all three locations that are not generally known to have coverage. But I like to keep my eye on things." Aubrey looked smug, leaning back in his chair to rest his arms across his fifty-year-old paunch, barely containing his desire to spin in a circle.

"Aubrey, have you been conducting unauthorized surveillance?" Hibb asked seriously.

"Not technically," Aubrey replied evasively. Hibb rolled his eyes.

Harry interrupted the exchange, "Okay. We know the connections. What do they mean? Neither Ryan nor Reldif could have arranged this. Shing?"

John shook his head. "He's never come after me here before."

"There must be a connection we're not seeing," Harry suggested. "Ryan, Simon, Shing, Akram—"

"Wait!" John slapped his hand on the table, surprising everyone. "Of course! I couldn't see it because I was missing that last connection." He looked up, hope and realization growing.

"Who?" Hibb urged him to share the information.

"Maryn Dale," John said.

"Got it in one," Aubrey affirmed with a satisfied air.

"I need to see the DG," John stated, starting to rise.

"I've done that already," Aubrey told him. "He has tasked a unit from MI-6. They are to pursue and acquire Maryn Dale with haste and enthusiasm until caught." Aubrey remained confident.

"How can we be certain they're not her men if they're from '6'?" Alexa asked sceptically.

"The unit was chosen with great care," Aubrey said. "There are two women who were cuckolded by Maryn and two men who were thrown over by Maryn for each other. They lost everything because of Maryn, their homes, their families. None have any love for Maryn Dale, not an ounce of support lingering in any corner of their minds."

John sighed, great relief in his voice. "Thank you, old man." Aubrey nodded once, rising and returning to his lair.

"Hi," Caroline greeted, poking her head in the door of the meeting room.

John bolted from his chair, leading her to a seat. "You're supposed to be in bed," he said, reprimanding her lightly.

"I got lonely," she pouted, trailing a finger across his chest. He blushed lightly while the others glanced at the ceiling, wall or carpet to provide an illusion of privacy.

"What have you taken?" John asked suspiciously.

"Oh, a bit of this and that," she said. "I'm feeling very nice at the moment."

"You didn't drive, did you?" John asked. His eyebrows rose in concern.

"No, course not. You people all drive on the wrong side of the road," she replied, one giggle sneaking out. "Huey … or Dewey … or Louie … anyway, one of them drove me in." She giggled again.

John chuckled. "You're high."

"Well, yes, a bit. Can I stay, oh lord and master?" she asked unevenly.

John laughed outright. "I suppose, but as soon as you feel ill you tell me, all right?"

"Yes," she replied, batting her eyelashes at him, except that with her current state of brain-fog, it came out as a slow blink.

John made eye contact with Hibb, who murmured sympathetically, "Women!"

"Watch it, Hibbert!" Alexa said.

John brought them back on track. "Okay. Akram and Shing, what do we know?"

"Maryn Dale passed secrets to Colonel Shing and General Akram," Caroline replied in a slow, drowsy voice. Her comment surprised everyone at the table. "The couple we met at the Katafygio had to flee China because they witnessed it. That's how we knew to be suspicious of Maryn Dale."

"Right," John said, at a loss for words. *How am I meant to keep this information from her if she's already this close to guessing it? Mind you, hiding information was what got me into so much trouble before.*

"Colonel Shing has been after you for years, John," Alexa said. "What exactly did you do to him?"

"I've interrupted a number of his nasty plans," John replied. *And rescued a number of his victims.*

"Plans to interfere in government and industry, correct?" Aubrey added, reappearing at the door.

"Yes. But interference in Southeast Asia, not the UK," John said.

"Indeed," Aubrey said, taking his place at the table.

"It makes sense," said Harry. "We have an Indian Communist and a Chinese Communist in league together, both men known to be involved in industrial espionage."

"We have a bomb at the Chinese Embassy conveniently eliminating five MI-5 assets, all of whom were helping to monitor Chinese-owned interests in the UK," Jade added.

John stood to pace the room. *What's this all about, though?*

"We also have an assassin who has targeted the one individual at the hub of these disparate factions," Hibb said.

John paused. *The Summit.* "All of this is taking place mere months before the Summit in Vancouver," he said.

"Natural gas," Harry said. They turned to look at him. "Think about it. What is the one commodity giving the Cabinet sleepless nights?"

"Natural gas," Alexa replied. "Of course. Her Majesty's Government is looking into any option that prevents the necessity of climbing into bed with the Russians for future resources."

Caroline raised a hand, lowering it again to prop up her drooping chin. "Haven't the generals in Burma made a deal with the Chinese government about natural gas?"

"Yes," John replied, and he wanted to swing her into his arms in gratitude for her insight. Instead, he took his place beside her, giving her arm a two-pattern squeeze, *love you.* "With the generals playing president, they're looking for new recognition on the world stage, an end to sanctions."

"They conducted a democratic election, didn't they?" Harry asked.

"By making it illegal for any party to run that had a member who had been jailed. Aung San Suu Kyi, who had been elected *democratically* in the eighties and then held under house arrest, was disqualified, and therefore her party either had to run without her or be disenfranchised. The generals themselves held her under house arrest for years. No, there's not even a hint of democracy in Burma," John said.

"But if pressure was brought to bear by the Chinese just before the Summit, and HM's government was highly motivated to ignore the paltry issue of human-rights abuses, could Burma become the UK's source for natural gas?" Alexa asked.

"Certainly worth killing for," Aubrey added.

"Aubrey!" Caroline protested. John took her hand and continued to hold it.

"All right," John began, but Hibb interrupted him.

"What about Louis Trevena?" Hibb said, altering the course of the conversation … or so John thought.

"What do you mean?" asked John.

Hibb explained. "He has twice blocked our apprehension of assassins."

"Has he? The dirty, rotten blaggard," Caroline muttered.

"Easy," John whispered.

"He really does have a hate-on for you, sweetheart," Caroline murmured and then seemed to gain her voice. "Has it always been that way?"

John thought for a moment. "No. In fact, we had an easy relationship before Burma." *But* ... "But investigating him will not be an easy task. Not if any of us choose to remain employed."

Aubrey cleared his throat. "I would suggest sending Caroline over for tea. When she's quite recovered, that is."

"Why?" John asked suspiciously.

"Ten minutes in his presence, and I'll wager that she's sussed him," Aubrey said.

"I can do that," Caroline said, stifling a giggle. "But perhaps after I have a nap. I'm feeling a little bit naff."

"Knackered, dear," John corrected her.

She grinned at him. "He's so rad, isn't he?" Caroline announced, nodding at John.

Alexa and Harry laughed at the uncharacteristic slang coming from their usually proper but clearly high-on-painkillers intelligence analyst. Caroline smiled in return, only a small smile though, to protect her aching face.

"Time to take you home?" John said, a small grin playing at the corners of his mouth.

"Yes, please."

John and the parade of security officers escorted Caroline home. It wasn't really fair to call it a parade, since they were largely good at being invisible.

"John?" she said. Her voice was sleepy as she walked up the stairs, her hand on his shoulder.

"Mmhmm," he replied, tightening his grip around her waist as she wobbled on the steps.

"I was a little high on painkillers, wasn't I?"

"Yes," he chuckled lightly, love in his eyes.

"Can I have more now?" she asked. "My face hurts."

"You can have anything you desire," he said.

She sighed happily. "John?"

"Yes?"

"Thank you for bringing me home. Can you stay?"

"I'm afraid not. It's still early in the day. I'll ensure you're settled and then head back in. Call me if you need me," he said.

"I always need you," she said, and he kissed her on the ear, smiling against her. She let him lead her into the bedroom. "What happened to Batman?" she asked.

Pausing first, he replied, "He's dead, I'm afraid. They killed him."

She sighed sadly. "So much pain. So much death. Did you figure out who's behind it?"

"Yes."

"Are you gonna get him?" she inquired.

"MI-6 has sent a team."

"You know what I want?" she asked.

"What?"

"I'd like to give them a piece of my mind, though, perhaps, at the moment, I can't spare it," and she began to giggle, stopping as the laugh set off a fresh headache.

"Have I told you lately that I love you?" he said huskily, kissing her on the temple.

"Once or twice," she responded, offering a lopsided grin.

He kissed her once more and then put her to bed.

"Sing to me, John?" she murmured against her pillow.

"Of course."

"Caroline," John called through the semi-open door of his office.

"Yes," she called back, teasing him.

"Caroline?" John called again. The Grid was virtually empty, everyone off following the trail of espionage. There were just a few of Aubrey's apprentices floating around on his errands.

"Yes?" she called back, grinning when his face appeared at the door looking slightly confused. "You see, it didn't take much more effort to actually come and get me," she said. He completed the journey to her desk, his eyes narrowing at her obvious grin while a smile pulled at his own mouth.

"I take it you're feeling better after your little vacation?" he asked.

"Indeed," she replied.

"Could you please accompany me to my office, if you're not too busy, that is?" he asked, making a great show of humility.

"Well, what exactly would be in it for me?" she asked, keeping her voice low and sexy.

He patted at his pockets, finally retrieving a mint and holding it out to her. She laughed aloud, drawing some attention. Smothering her humour, she shook her head. He paused, thinking. Then he reached into his inner jacket pocket and pulled out a pen, handing it to her. She quirked a brow and took the pen, writing on a corner of her notepad. Nothing. She looked up quizzically.

"Invisible ink," he said. "You can read it under ultraviolet light."

She gave him a half-grin and a shake of her head.

"Don't have anything else." He held his hands out, open, palms up. Suddenly, he snapped his fingers and pulled a sticky note and pencil from her desk, scribbling a message hurriedly on it and handing it to her. She blushed deeply.

"Right behind you, sir," she replied, grinning through her blush.

Closing the door behind him, John joined Caroline on the couch in his office.

"Um," he began and then stopped.

"Yes?"

"Er … Aubrey said you took tea with Trevena," he said, but she could tell that he was stalling.

"Yes. I don't think he really hates you, John," she said.

"Do you think he's involved in the plot?" he asked.

"No. I'm not positive or anything, but I think he's just jealous of you," she said. His eyes widened as though she'd taken him by surprise. "I don't know if you knew this, but his wife left him three years ago. She seemed to feel that he was a heartless automaton who thought only of his job."

"He told you that?" John asked, clearly surprised.

"Not him, no. His admin assistant, however, was only too happy to fill me in on the details while I waited in the outer office. Solidarity amongst AAs, I suppose. Anyway, I think that Louis Trevena saw you as a … well, a kindred spirit of sorts, and when you returned with a wife and a new outlook on life that included the substance of things hoped for and the evidence of things not seen … well, he was jealous. If there is such a thing as God and salvation and love that lasts and overcomes, then he's forced to see that he's been mistaken in the way he's chosen to live his life."

John shook his head at her. "You are a wonder to me." He was silent for a time, and Caroline tried to maintain her patience waiting for him. "Do you really think I've changed?" he asked.

"For me, sweetheart, it's more like you've been revealed. The longer I know you, the better you become. But the others, they all say that you've changed—that you have a peace that's new and a sense of compassion. They see that you try to live by a set of rules now that never used to hinder you in the past. You're the same man, but new," she replied.

"Born again," he said.

"Second Corinthians 5:17 says, 'Therefore if any man be in Christ, he is a new creature: old things are passed away; behold, all things are become new.'"

"Indeed," he replied.

Finally, she didn't want to wait any longer. "But you asked me in here to tell me something, didn't you? Something you think I don't want to hear," she observed.

He rose and began to pace the office. "It's been so busy since we returned from Wales that I haven't had an opportunity to fill you in."

She watched him sceptically. "We sleep in the same bed. That provides plenty of opportunity."

Sitting beside her, he sighed heavily, tapping his fingers on his knee.

"You're tapping," she observed. He stilled his hands, jamming them into his trouser pockets. "I take it this is going to make me angry." She waited, finally demanding, "John, just tell me!"

"We've discovered who is behind the assassination contract," he said.

"And you didn't think I needed to know that? Is that why we're living back at home again? How long have you kept this from me?"

His gaze flat, he watched her. "We figured it out … well, Aubrey gets most of the credit … the day after the attack when you were … er … rather high on pain medication."

She studied him carefully, seeing the blank look on his face, the façade of calm betrayed by the nervous movements of his hands. A new thought occurred to her because of his hesitancy. "You're not concerned about making me angry, are you? You don't want to frighten me." Drawing a deep breath, she calmed herself. "Okay, I'm ready."

Pausing, he gathered himself. "It was Maryn Dale."

Flabbergasted, Caroline's mind swirled in a cyclone of confusion and then went blank before slowly rebooting. "Her! She! She stood in this office and—Ryan, of course—Simon—She! 'She told me you'd be mine.' It was Maryn! She got to Simon and convinced him I'd leave you. She used Ryan's resentment against you. She did this. Of course! She was witnessed passing secrets to Colonel Shing of China and General Akram of India. India. Akram. That's why you were sent to India." Heat and cold passed through her body, and she rose abruptly to pace the room, her fists clenching and unclenching. John watched her carefully and quietly, waiting, but she didn't know what for. "What an idiot!"

"Me?" he asked as though he fully accepted the charge.

She stopped and turned to face him. "Simon," she clarified. "He watched her shoot Brother Phillip." A spasm of pain crossed John's features. "I'm sorry, sweetheart. I know that you feel Brother Phillip's loss deeply. I don't mean to be blasé. But Simon was there. How could he see that and then trust that woman, that vixen?!" The heat of her anger and disgust torpedoed through her gut and then spiralled down as the implications took hold. Stepping back to the couch, she sat very close to John, and he wrapped an arm around her. "She really hates you, John."

"Yes."

"She's very jealous of me." Caroline turned to face John. "With everything she has, with the many, many men she's conquered and cast aside, she wants you. But you're mine."

"Yes."

"And she can't have you." Wrapping her arms tightly around his waist, Caroline spoke the phrase with clear determination. "She will not have you or harm you."

"I belong to you." Tipping her chin, he kissed her deeply and thoroughly, leaving her with no question as to his loyalty. Brushing her hand up his chest, she hooked her fingers between his shirt buttons.

"It's not nearly so scary when you know who's after you," she observed.

"No."

She rested against him for a time and he stayed with her, ignoring the ringing of his telephone and the fact that the walls of his office were made of transparent glass.

"Are you going to be all right?" he asked.

"Yes. We're in this together."

Smiling, he bent to kiss her again, reminding her of the taste of love.

"There's more," he said. "The team from MI-6 still hasn't apprehended Maryn. No one can find Grendahl, but he seems to be back in business. I've contacted every agent and asset in Mumbai, Hyderabad and Delhi in an effort to find Akram. This morning, I got a call from the director of CSIS with a name."

"What did he say?" she asked apprehensively.

"He has a contact who may be able to locate Akram. Chandrakala, my contact in the Devangari, seems to feel that Akram is one Qasim Akshan, an Indian Communist. Chandrakala really wants Akshan, lusts after his capture, I would say."

His voice deepened as he spoke of the Indian intelligence agent, and Caroline shuddered at the violence that John implied to be a part of Chandrakala's character.

"What will you do?" she asked, though she really didn't want the answer.

"I'm going to India to apprehend General Akram. Chandrakala has accepted my assertion that I have a source who can lead us to him. If we can get Akram back here, we can question him about Maryn."

"I can see why you'd need to do that," she acknowledged sadly. "I don't suppose there's any way I could go with you?"

"Not a chance!" Her brows rose at his tone of voice, and he modulated his tone. "Sorry, sweetheart. It would be far too dangerous for you to accompany me. I don't trust Chandrakala, and if Maryn resents you as you suspect, then it would paint a target on your back. Please don't ask to come. I can try to make contact with you. I'll have Aubrey look into it. All right?"

In spite of the transparency of his office, Caroline flung her arms around her husband, her voice tight with apprehension. "Okay. Please be careful, John. Don't leave me alone again," she pleaded, speaking of the rest of her life rather than the next few days.

With one arm around her waist, he held her tightly against him. He drew a gentle fingertip in a line from her temple, along the pink line of her scar and down her neck to rest on her shoulder. His thumb tenderly stroked the scars hidden beneath the fabric.

"I'll be back. I give you my word."

## Chapter Twelve
# My Enemy's Enemy

A wave of humidity hit John as he stepped out of the Rajiv Gandhi International Airport in Hyderabad, India. He had become Ugo Ducley again. As Ugo, John met Colonel Chandrakala in the parking lot of the Secunderabad Railway Station, a British colonial-style building with clean stucco lines.

"*Namaste*," John greeted Chandrakala as he joined him in the rusting green Fiat.

Within minutes, John spotted the tail: a familiar blue Vespa motor scooter three cars behind them. *Back again, are you?* John touched Chandrakala briefly on the elbow and then nodded at the rearview mirror. Chandrakala seemed to understand John's message, but rather than take evasive action, he began a tour guide's monologue.

"Hyderabad, the financial, economic and political capital of the state of Andhra Pradesh, is the largest contributor to the state's Gross Domestic Product, state tax and excise revenues. Also known as the City of Pearls, it was once the seat of Nizam, the ruler of the largest and the most opulent of the princely states." *Bloomin' heck, what is he on about?*

Chandrakala spun the wheel without warning and accelerated into the Old City. *Now what?* John decided that despite local custom, a fastened seatbelt would be a wise precaution, clicking it closed across his middle.

Speeding around the slow crush of traffic, dodging bicycles, carts and cows, the Fiat gradually managed to pull away from the Vespa. Quickly taking the next left turn past the British-colonial hotel and then the next right, the Fiat finally outdistanced the Vespa.

"Golconda Fort, certainly the most magnificent structure in all of India, lies ahead," Chandrakala's lesson continued. *Blimey! Have I entered the Twilight Zone?* Abruptly, Chandrakala reached between John's knees, feeling around beneath the edge of the dashboard. *Blast it!* Disconcerted by the move, John pressed himself back into his seat to give the man space to explore. *Whew!* When Chandrakala retrieved a listening device from the nook beneath the AM/FM radio, John finally understood. "Built on a granite hill, it lies surrounded by massive crenellated ramparts. In 1143, on the rocky hill called 'Mangalavaram,' a shepherd boy, in his wanderings, discovered an idol, a find which he conveyed to the ruler of the time."

Abruptly, Chandrakala pulled to the curb, exiting, his voice continuing his travelogue. "The king ordered the construction of a mud fort around the holy spot, and nearly two hundred years later, Bahamini rulers took possession of the fort, constructing from those humble beginnings the 'Golla Konda' or Shepherds Hill ..."

Confidently approaching an Indian tour guide and his Japanese tour group, Chandrakala engaged the man in a short conversation while he slipped the listening device surreptitiously into the guide's *peshwi*. He then returned to the Fiat.

"Very interesting, Colonel," John replied wryly when the other man settled behind the steering wheel again and pulled out into traffic. "I take it you're under surveillance?"

"Hmmm," Chandrakala replied noncommittally as he chewed his moustache for a moment—the only hint of unease John had detected in the man—before turning toward the motorway and resuming their journey to Orissa. *That was an impressive way to throw off pursuit. Maybe I could learn a thing or two from this man.*

"What do you know of Akram?" John inquired.

Chandrakala glanced in his direction and then continued looking forward, dodging through the traffic with one hand on the steering wheel. "A communist. Risen through the ranks after a dishonourable discharge from the army. Coward. Keeps bodyguards for protection. Have yet to find his hideout. Rumours of a mistress."

"Not much to go on," John replied tonelessly, subsiding into silence when no more information was forthcoming.

"*Konark!*" Chandrakala rent the air with his exclamation.

John furiously searched his mind for the Hindi word while he scanned the environment to find a clue to the man's comment. *Konark?* A magnificent structure rose before him, unusual in architecture, reminding John of the temples of Bagan in Burma.

"The Black Pagoda." Chandrakala the tour guide had returned, for no reason that John could detect, further adding to the mystery of the man beside him. "Considered the culmination of temple architecture, the Sun Temple of Konark once sat upon the shores of the sea, a navigational point for European sailors. Built in the thirteenth century, the temple was designed in the shape of a colossal chariot, carrying the sun god, Surya, across the heavens." Chandrakala's voice altered as he quoted, "'Aloft his beams now bring the good, who knows all creatures that are born, that all may look upon the sun. The seven bay mares that draw thy car bring thee to us, far-seeing good, O Surya of the gleaming hair. Athwart in darkness gazing up, to him the higher light, we now have soared to Surya, the god among gods, the highest light.'"

"Striking imagery," John replied cautiously. He was certain that the mentioned sun of light could not compare to the Son who was the light of the world.

"*Mūrkhatā!*" Chandrakala spat. "Foolishness! The only path to light is the annihilation of one's enemies."

"So endeth the lesson," John muttered ironically. This man truly was an enigma.

Chandrakala abruptly stopped the Fiat, inertia thrusting John against his seatbelt. "The lesson you will learn from me, Mr. Ducley, is that I will not be crossed." Horns bleating around them, Chandrakala remained still, the depths of his black eyes conveying menace and determination.

Keeping his face blank of emotion and his voice steady, John met the colonel's gaze across the space. "I believe, sir, that we have a common goal, the apprehension of Akram."

Chandrakala's death-stare held for a long moment, and then he reached across John to open his door, gesturing for him to disembark. John was careful not to flinch at the proximity of the man or the pungent scent of sour yoghurt that wafted across from him.

"Konark," Chandrakala said again.

Pacing between the two giant lions at the entrance to Konark, each crushing a war elephant, John found the CSIS contact, a man whose wife was cousin to a Naxalite flunky. Dark and thin, short and bent, he gave the appearance of a man who bore the weight of the world. John noted easily during a handshake greeting that the man was missing the last three fingers of his right hand.

John led him back to the Fiat and Chandrakala, introducing them both.

"*Namaste*, Manny," Chandrakala greeted the young man. "You have what we need?"

"Yes, Sahib," Manny replied.

In a flash, Chandrakala spun in his seat, planting his revolver in the young man's crotch. "You had better."

Manny's head nodded rapidly in the affirmative as he shrank backwards as far away from the gun as his gluteal muscles would pull him. Chandrakala studied him long and hard and then nodded once, turning back to the steering wheel, reversing the car out and onto the highway.

Northeast up Highway Seven the green Fiat raced, jostling for position on the motorway, heading northeast and then east toward the Bay of Bengal, the geography changing from foothill to mountain to plain, humanity fading from city clusters to villages.

Pulling off the road, the Fiat came to a stop amongst a stand of trees. Chandrakala turned in his seat again. "The penalty, Manny?"

"I want this as badly as you do, Colonel," Manny stated, his body straightening, tall and resilient.

"Why?" John asked, suddenly seeing so much more to this situation.

"General Akram murdered my wife," Manny said.

John fixed him with a stare, long and hard, praying for insight into the man's motives, insight that he finally found behind the aged young man's eyes. John nodded once, putting his life in the hands of the man behind him.

"*Calō calatē hai*," John said. "Let's go."

Exiting the vehicle, they moved stealthily, remaining along the edges of the trees, up and over the rocky hills and down into a sheltered cave.

"Now, we wait," Manny informed them. "After dark, General Akram comes with his bodyguards to see his mistress."

"Security?" John inquired.

"The house is normally policed by two security guards, but when Akram is in residence, he brings his three personal bodyguards, and the security guards return to their homes for the night."

"Why does Akram keep the lady this far away from civilization?" John asked.

"She is Pakistani," explained Manny.

"Ah." The two men nodded their understanding of the political implications of such a relationship—Indian communist and Pakistani Muslim.

"How do you know of this place, Manny?" John asked.

"After my wife was murdered, I came here seeking revenge. My wife's cousin had mentioned once that Akram kept a mysterious woman on the edge of the Bay of Bengal. I searched and searched, thereby giving purpose to my purposeless life, until I found it. I tried to do as we plan to do tonight, but on my own." Manny held up his right hand. "This was my punishment."

"And if you're caught again?" John asked.

The young man returned a dark look that answered John's question clearly. *Certain death.* The men settled in to wait.

The plan was simple. Manny would create a diversion with some firecrackers, John would crawl through the bedroom window, and Chandrakala would cover him. Manny had planned the time well. Forty-five minutes later, the house was lit by floodlights, and a large black Chevy, rocking on its shocks like a boat on the ocean swells, drove into view. A massive Indian man stepped out, moving around the front of the vehicle and opening the rear passenger door for a uniformed, moustachioed Indian man, tall with skin the colour of oak. His grizzled features sat naturally around his cruel eyes.

Haughtily, the uniformed man adjusted his jacket, reinserting the gold buttons and stopping to run his fingers along his thick black moustache, very Fidel Castro in cut and trim. This was Qasim Akshan, better known as General Akram.

Akram made his way to the house, greeted by a very shapely young woman clad in a black negligee. Her lithe stocking-clad legs traveled all the way up. Two more Indian men exited the car and took up places around the perimeter of the building.

John waited patiently to give Akram time to become involved in his intended evening activity, and then they began. Manny faded into the darkness to the west, and John and Chandrakala made their way to the perimeter of the light, lying flat on their bellies and waiting. John fingered the syringe in his pocket and saw Chandrakala check his revolver, keeping it in his hand.

*Crack-cr-crack-crack!* The first set of firecrackers got everyone's attention; the second, third and fourth urged the bodyguards into motion. Two made their way into the darkness. The third took up his position at the front door. *Excellent!*

John counted to ten to allow the bodyguard a few seconds to settle into his new location and then leapt to his feet, sprinting to the bedroom window at the rear of the building. He slid his knife along the catch, unlocking the window and raising the pane slowly and silently. Pushing his knife tip through the slit in the curtains, John could see through the opening what he assumed to be Akram's back glistening with sweat, sliding back and forth along the bed.

Once certain of the positions of the people in the room, John pocketed his knife and pushed himself up and over the windowsill. He slid down as quietly as possible between the wall and the floor-length curtain and then across the floor, staying just behind Akram's line of vision.

The woman had her head turned away and her eyes closed. *Poor girl!* Just as the pace began to intensify, John sprang from a crouch, punching Akram in the side of the head, knocking him off the woman and onto the floor. Eyes widened, she sat bolt upright. John clamped his hand over her mouth to keep her silent, motioning for her to remain that way. She nodded, and her relief was plain in her eyes.

Stepping around the foot of the bed, John came face to face with the dazed self-appointed general, the ally of Maryn Dale. Punching again, John's knuckles met Akram's shoulder. With his left this time, John punched again, an uppercut that snapped Akram's head back. Akram crumpled as though in slow motion, bouncing off the wall behind him and sliding to the floor. John injected the side of his neck with a sedative.

Turning back, John noted the woman sitting on the bed with the sheet pulled to her chin. Her wide, fearful eyes stared at Chandrakala where he stood at the foot of the bed.

"Whore!" Chandrakala declared, spitting on the sheet where it covered her legs.

"There's no need," John whispered tersely. "She hasn't made any noise. Leave her be."

Grabbing a pillow that had fallen from the bed, Chandrakala replied, "We can't leave her conscious." Quickly, he moved over, covering her face with the pillow, pushing his revolver at her head and firing, the discharge muffled by the pillow's fluff. She barely had time to struggle before her lifeblood oozed into the down stuffing.

*Blast it all!* John exploded across the bed, fisting the lapels of Chandrakala's jacket and shoving him up against the wall. "That was not necessary!" he whispered tersely into the man's face.

Chandrakala shrugged nonchalantly. "She was the enemy of my people."

"That is no reason!" John insisted, disgusted by the violence in the man.

"Perhaps not," Chandrakala replied smoothly, meeting John's eyes levelly. And John suddenly understood that he was going to need a backup plan, or he would shortly meet a similar fate.

Releasing the other man with a jerk, John insisted, "Help me with him." He jerked his thumb over his shoulder to indicate Akram.

Carrying Akram hand and foot, they moved to the front of the house, catching the bodyguard unawares. Chandrakala rendered him helpless with a blow to the head.

"Him?" John asked forcefully, indicating the bodyguard.

"He is my political opponent, but a countryman."

Disgusted by the man's perfidy, John locked down his emotions, helping to load Akram into the trunk of the Chevy. Aware of the imminent return of the bodyguards, John worked quickly to hotwire the boat-like car. *Manny must have set them a merry chase to keep them distracted this long.* Reminded of the man, John inquired about Chandrakala's plans for him as they drove away from the mini-compound.

Chandrakala shrugged. "The key is in the ignition." He was referring to the Fiat.

John was torn. He didn't want to abandon the young man who had helped them, who had lost so much in his search for revenge. But he didn't trust Chandrakala, and he needed Akram in London in order to obtain the evidence against Maryn Dale that would send her to prison. So John stayed in the driver's seat, maintaining enough speed on the dark circuitous roads to make it too dangerous to kill him while he was behind the wheel.

Back in Hyderabad, Chandrakala directed John to the nearest police station. Together, they dragged Akram inside. Flashing his badge, Chandrakala received every convenience: an interrogation room, a telephone, a cup of tea.

"What are your plans, Colonel?" John asked, trying to sound very calm and reasonable, not agitated and angry as he actually felt.

"We will encourage him to tell us everything he knows about the Naxalite terrorists' plots." Chandrakala turned to John, meeting his gaze directly. "Any concerns?"

"For this man?" John replied, trying to sound disgusted. "None at all."

Chandrakala studied him for a moment and then turned away, obviously content with what he saw printed in John's well-camouflaged eyes.

Soon, three uniformed police officers entered the cell, two of them carrying pails of water. Each leg of the table was placed in a pail. The water intensified the effects of a Taser on a human body, the metal table essentially acting as an amplified electrical conductor. First stripping Akram, they lifted him onto the metal table in the middle of the room and fastened his arms and legs, immobilizing him. The police officers retreated to the wall, pulling out their rubber billy clubs, awaiting their next orders.

John felt nauseous. *Blast!* He knew that the first step was to beat on the man's chest with the billy clubs. John had experienced that particular torture in Serbia. It was painful. After a series of beatings, the taser was so much more effective because it contracted and battered the already abused muscles, amplifying the pain.

John was at a loss. He had never actively participated in the torture of an individual. He'd done his fair share of smacking people about, but not this. He had been on the receiving end of torture often enough to understand what it did to your mind to be held helpless before the violence of your enemies.

His legend, Ugo Ducley, was employed by the Devangari, which made Colonel Chandrakala his superior officer. But getting the information he needed from General Akram required him to become John Brock. That would destroy his legend. If Chandrakala discovered that he was a British officer, he would kill him, of that John was certain. But John needed to interrogate Akram … properly. *God, I don't know if you're interested in this dilemma, given that it must be a long way from where you want me to be, but I need your help. Please help me!*

John turned as the cell door opened and a battered Manny was dragged into the room and tied to a metal chair. Chandrakala paced over to him slowly, leaning menacingly into the man's face.

"Manny. You escaped, my friend." Chandrakala punched him in the stomach quickly before John realized the colonel's intention, following up with two hard slaps across the face. John grabbed Chandrakala's hand to stop the third.

"He helped us," John asserted. *This is how you treat your allies?*

Chandrakala straightened slowly. "He has information that I wish to obtain."

"Then simply ask him," John advised hotly.

"I thought you understood our ways, Ugo. Perhaps you wish to join our friends here." John maintained the colonel's vicious stare, not willing to back down to this despicable man. Chandrakala dropped his gaze first, shrugging casually. "Perhaps you should occupy yourself elsewhere while I get down to the business of Intelligence."

John nodded tersely, leaving the room, sparing one last glance at the weeping Manny and the awakening Akram. Any intervention he attempted would lead to the death of the men in the interrogation room … or his own. He didn't want to make it to heaven before Caroline, and he certainly couldn't abandon her to widowhood a second time. *God, I need your help.*

Suddenly, an explosion rocked the walls around him. *What is going on?* John dropped to the floor, rolling under a desk as the plaster dropped from the ceiling.

When the dust began to settle, John emerged, grasping the arm of a fleeing police officer. "Is it an attack?"

"No, sahib, the boiler blew up. Half of the station is in ruins."

"Give me your sidearm," John insisted. The constable complied, much to John's relief.

John had hope. He sprinted back to the interrogation room, stepping over the rubble and finding the door blocked by a beam. Struggling beneath it, he forced his way into the room to find two of the police officers unconscious beneath a fallen section of roof and two clearly dead. A man-sized hole had been blasted in the wall of the interrogation room, leading in a direct line to the alley behind the station and the idling police car behind it. *Thank you, God.*

Chandrakala was staggering, dazed. John could see that the beatings had progressed in his absence, but both prisoners were still alive and conscious.

"What has happened?" Chandrakala demanded to know.

"Bomb," John replied. "We need to get out of here immediately." Chandrakala nodded, but rather than moving to release Akram, he drew his revolver, holding it against Manny's head and cocking the trigger. Manny's eyes pleaded with John.

Believing completely that Chandrakala would murder a bound man in cold blood, John still asked the question, "What are you doing?"

"We've all we can get from him," Chandrakala said. "Release Akram and we'll depart."

John reached behind him in a flash to engage the pistol he'd obtained from the young police officer. "There's no need to kill him. Step back."

Without pause, Chandrakala's gun was raised to the centre of John's chest, but John fired first, the bullet driving into Chandrakala's chest cavity, burrowing through to his spine. The man's eyes registered shock just before their light extinguished.

Stepping over cautiously, John checked for a pulse, finding none. Pulling out his knife, he released Manny from his bonds and instructed him to help carry General Akram. Releasing the ersatz general, John ordered him to put on one of the dead policeman's trousers and then handcuffed his wrists behind his back. Prodding him into the alley, John ordered Akram into the trunk of the police car. Manny, he demanded to take the wheel, occupying the passenger seat himself. He held the pistol pointed directly at Manny's belly.

"Drive," John ordered Manny. "Out of Hyderabad. West to Pune."

Manny nodded, following John's orders. John knew that there was an MI-6 safe house in Pune. If they could get there unmolested, John could get help to extract himself and Akram to the UK. Then Akram could be interrogated properly. Manny—well, he would need to decide what to do about Manny. John prayed. *I never thought that I could ask for your help, Father, not like this. But I need a little more.*

John had Manny circle the block twice before parking in the driveway of the safe house. He pushed Manny before him, keeping the pistol in the small of his back as they advanced to the front door. John lifted his face to the hidden security camera, knowing that they would have his picture on file. Then he raised the gun above his head, quickly replacing it in the small of Manny's back to show that he was the one in control of the situation, not the other way around. The door buzzed, and an elderly Indian lady greeted them.

"*Namaste.*"

"*Namaste, memsahib.* I have need of assistance. My companion in the car—" He watched her eyes flit to the seemingly empty vehicle. "—has need of transport, as do I." She flicked a glance behind the door to someone hiding there and then nodded. John pushed Manny through the door and then retrieved the handcuffed Akram from the boot.

"You're John Brock, aren't you?" an MI-6 agent asked. John recognized him as Sandy MacTavish.

"I need this one kept …" John indicated Akram. "And I need extraction PDQ for the two of us. This one …" He pointed at Manny. "I need privacy to speak with."

John retained his gun as he stood across the kitchen table where Manny was nervously sipping a cup of tea.

"I work for the British Security Services. I can offer you employment, here or there," John said.

Manny's mind seemed far away. "When my wife was murdered," he began. "I felt that my life had lost all meaning. Do you know that she was a Christian? My grandmother was furious when I brought her home, having raised me to be a faithful Hindu. But I loved her. I never understood her beliefs, but I knew that I had found someone special. Her father was a greedy man, and he willingly gave his daughter to me when I agreed to forego a dowry—very happy, I think, to be rid of his daughter and her different beliefs." Manny stopped speaking, examining the tea in his cup. "I sought revenge, but in the end, suffered the same fate as the man I sought to cause to suffer, my enemy. Why did you save me?"

"I happen to agree with your wife," John stated plainly, allowing the man to make his own connections.

Abruptly, Manny seemed to come to a decision, setting his cup firmly on the table. "I would come with you and see if my life can find a different path."

Nodding once, John left the man to his thoughts and conferred with the MI-6 officers, Sandy and another man named Hunter.

John made a request. "Can you keep an eye on these fellows? I need to go out for a few minutes."

"Of course," Sandy said. "We've called into London for an extraction. They're sending a Sea King, ETA three hours."

"Thank you. I won't be longer than an hour. Don't let either of them out of your sight. The older one probably needs some water," John said.

"Very good," Hunter replied.

John walked three blocks to the Pune Internet café, logging on to a computer, finding the blog that Aubrey had set up for him and Caroline. There in the drafts folder was her message, "Gd d. Lv. YFA." He smiled, interpreting, "I had a good day. I love you. Yours forever always." He replied, "Bd d. Sf. Lv2." Then he added a second line. "Linus. Pune. 6. Help." Hopefully, Caroline would understand who the message was for. He couldn't risk any other form of communication, because he didn't know who was under Maryn's influence and who wasn't. John logged off and returned to the safe house, checking that his prisoner and his recruit were still safely held. He ate whatever leftovers he could find in the house and waited for the Sea King.

"Aubrey? Come and look at this." Caroline said.

"I'm definitely not interested in romantic messages from your husband," Aubrey said.

"Aubrey," she replied indignantly. "For goodness sakes. I wouldn't ask you to read that. This message doesn't make sense to me." Aubrey pushed off with his toes and rolled his chair over to Caroline's side, bumping her shoulder lightly. "Look," she said, pointing at the screen. "I understand this: 'Bad day. Safe. Love you too.' But what does this mean? 'Linus. Pune. 6. Help.'"

Aubrey tapped his lower lip with his pencil thoughtfully. "Well, stone the crows! A trip down memory lane. Many years ago, on an undercover operation, my codename was Linus, you know, the young philosopher in some children's cartoon?" he said. Caroline nodded at his explanation. "Well, I would say that he's in an MI-6 safe house in Pune, but he's concerned that he may not be extracted safely. I'll check into the arrangements." He turned to her. "You go home, my dear. I'll ensure he's out safely," Aubrey said.

She rested her hand on his arm, warmth filling her heart at this kind-hearted man. "No, thank you. I'll stay until you know the details."

"Very well." Aubrey spent the next half hour on the telephone to the DG, the head of MI-6 and the commander of the Sea King, which was being employed to extract John.

Caroline didn't breathe easily again until John was back in her arms—filthy, exhausted and absolutely wonderful. She held his hand in the back of the pool car that drove them home. Once home, she pulled him into the house, stripping him and pushing him into the shower, moving away to make him some coffee and the scrambled eggs he requested. She massaged his shoulders as he ate, repeatedly bending down to kiss his ear, his head, his neck until he stuffed the last three mouthfuls in, drained his cup and dragged her willingly into the bedroom.

Pulling her onto the bed and into his arms, he sighed the happy sigh she loved to hear.

"Tell me," she said.

"I met a sad man who'd lost his wife," John began. Nudging him onto his back, she straddled his hips so that she could watch his face. He continued, "I met a hateful man whom I thought I could trust."

Concerned, she leaned forward to study his eyes. "Are you okay?"

He shook his head. "I'm not sure I'll ever be quite the same again." She frowned. "But in a good way," he said. "Come down here—" He tugged her gently to lie against him. "And I'll tell you all about it." She rested her head on his shoulder and her knee possessively across his leg. Taking her hand, he placed it against his chest, holding it there. And then he told her everything.

"John Brock's office," Caroline said.

"Mrs. Brock? It's Janice Goldbloom calling for Sir William Jacen. Is Mr. Brock available for the DG?"

"Yes. I'll put you through." This was the last time she would need to interpret the complicated assortment of codes that determined who the call was from and where it was meant to be sent. The new secretary was due to begin later today. *Hurray!*

Returning to her task of packing the last of her things, Caroline shifted them to her new desk, which sat directly across from John's middle window where she could keep an eye on him, she had teased. How was he ever going to get any work done, he'd complained, teasing her back.

"Caroline. Could you come in for a moment, please?" John called, pulling her from her thoughts. She trooped in with a happy smile.

Before continuing, he closed the door behind her, alerting her to the potential gravity of his news. "That was the DG. They've broken him … General Akram."

"What does that mean?" she inquired cautiously, hearing the fierceness in his voice.

His face was grim, his eyes bright without even the hint of laughter. "He's given them the evidence they need to arrest Maryn Dale. They've located her in Prague. We've got her!" He clenched his fist, his fingers as tight as his voice.

"Are you okay?" she asked, deeply concerned by his manner. There was a deep fury, tightly controlled, simmering in his eyes.

"Okay?" His eyes narrowed dangerously, but she wasn't afraid. She knew that she had nothing to fear from him. "How can you ask me that?" he said. "We've got her. I've been pursuing her for—"

Caroline interrupted, attempting to apply a cold wash to his volcanic mood. "John. John!" She insisted he pay attention to her. "Why are you so enthusiastic about capturing her?"

"You ask me that? How can you not understand?" he said, ire lacing his voice.

"John. Tell me why," she insisted sternly.

"She was responsible for my imprisonment in Burma, for the contract on my life, for Simon's murder. That, at least, should matter to you," he said.

Initially irritated by his comment about Simon, she leaned back and watched him sceptically for a moment, ignoring the attempt to get her off-topic. "Shall I tell you what I think?" she said, attempting to convey her calmness to him.

John leaned against his desk, tension coming off him in waves. "Yes. I think you'd better," he said, and there was no mistaking the challenge in his voice.

"I think that you want to avenge the murder of Brother Phillip. I think that he was the first positive father figure you had met in your life, and you are very angry to have lost him so soon after meeting him. As long as he was alive somewhere in the world, even if you didn't see him again, you knew that there was a man who thought lovingly of you as his son." John's eyes grew wide. "In addition, I believe that you feel you owe the people of the Katafygio justice because their secret village, their haven of safety, was burned to the ground. I believe you feel you owe them that justice because you feel they suffered for protecting you." She watched the emotions flit across his face. "Am I right?" she asked.

John dropped his head, and she thought he might be ashamed. But when he raised his eyes to hers, there was a soft smile on his face. "Yes. You are a wonder to me," he said, his voice gentle and his manner tender.

Relaxing, she smiled at him. "I too would like Maryn to stand trial for the murder of Brother Phillip. I understand that that can't happen because it occurred in Burma. Standing trial for treason will have to do. After all, she did betray you to Colonel Shing, and she would have handed you over to him again if she'd caught you. I yearn to make the people pay who tortured you in Burma," she said, her eyes growing dark. Pensive for a moment, she continued, "Dolly said that it really bothered Maryn when Brother Phillip forgave her—that Maryn seemed to go into shock at those three words."

"Come here. Please," he said gently, pulling Caroline into his arms, and she could feel the fury dissipating. "Now, we wait to see if the DG's plan will work. He's sending a team into Prague tonight to pick her up. He's using SAS officers rather than '5' or '6,' hoping to avoid anyone who might warn her."

Caroline spent the day orienting the new secretary, Evie Horton, to her responsibilities, finding her to be kind-hearted, bright and willing to learn. Evie absorbed more about the telephone system in one afternoon than Caroline had in a month on the job. John reassured her that it was because her bright mind was made for analysis. She laughed at the idea but accepted the compliment.

Heading home at the usual time, avoiding the crush of traffic around Twickenham Stadium, John and Caroline made supper together and then went jogging through Rosecroft Gardens, along Chertsey and over to Moor Mead Gardens. Caroline rode her bike for the first half of the journey accompanied by her security officer and then gave up and returned home. John was out for another hour, telling her clearly by his actions that he was very agitated waiting to hear of the success of the Maryn Dale operation.

They went to bed as usual, but Caroline woke to an empty room at one in the morning. She pulled on a sweatshirt to ward off the chilly damp of the late-summer London night and padded out to the great room, only to find it empty as well. Soon she realized that there was music coming from downstairs. Following it, she found John on the bench press in his workout room. His T-shirt and pyjama bottoms were damp with perspiration.

When he noticed her, he propped the weights onto their T-bar and sat up, wiping his face with a towel.

"Did I wake you?" he asked.

"Just missed you. When will the unit reach Prague?" she asked, and he shrugged in response. "Why don't you have a shower, and I'll make some hot chocolate," she said. "I have some cookie batter left from Saturday. Would you like me to make some fresh chocolate-chip cookies?"

"You don't need to do any of that, sweetheart. But if you're determined, then yes, I'd love some of your cookies." He grinned and she laughed.

Three cookies in, the telephone rang.

"Brock." John answered the phone and then said not one other word. After a few minutes, he silently replaced the phone on the receiver. Suddenly, he slammed both fists down onto the desk top, kicking the back and leaving a dent in the wood. "Aargh!" he yelled, slamming the desk again. "I'm going for a run."

"No you're not! I know you're angry, John, but it's the middle of the night and there are still assassins on your tail." She moved closer to him. "Tell me what happened."

"She got away! Someone tipped her off and she got away! She, and the Tibetan, Sonam Narayan, and Augustus Doon."

"Crap!" *Oh no! Father, how will John cope with this?*

"I need to do something, Caroline." His voice was intense as he spoke to her.

She thought for a while. "I know! Let's go to the Richmond Y. They're open twenty-four hours, and you can run on the indoor track. Run your brains out if you want to."

Breathing heavily, he flopped down onto a soft chair and bowed his head into his hands. "I can't believe it! Where is the justice in this?"

"I'm afraid that I don't think life is about justice. Do you want justice for everything you've done?" she asked. "I know I don't. Life is about grace."

She walked over to the stereo, finding the song she wanted. Soon the words of John Newton, the redeemed slaver, "Amazing Grace," began to fill the room.

"We don't always get the justice we're seeking in this life," she said. "But God's grace is amazing." Stepping closer, she rested her hand on the top of his head. "Let Maryn go for now. There's nothing we can do anyway."

John spent a long time in silence with his head bowed, and she guessed that he was struggling in prayer. Finally, sighing deeply, he seemed to release the tension in his chest. "How did you get to be so wise?" he asked.

"I'm not wise."

"You are wise," he said and then pulled her onto his lap and kissed her.

"Do we have to go into hiding?" she asked.

"No," he said. "She's on the run. She won't risk returning to the UK. Her allies have all turned against her."

"No more security?" she inquired hopefully. "Life back to normal? Church, rugby, Bible study and walks in the park?"

"Soon, darling."

She sighed. *Soon, but not yet.* "I do love you, John."

"Good thing, because I have no intention of ever losing you," he said, surprising her with the intensity of his speech.

# Chapter Thirteen
## *The Summit*

Three weeks later, Tor Grendahl was apprehended … briefly. Exploding the stun grenade hidden in his bread box, he fled through the window and down the fire escape of his flat, hotly pursued by MI-6 agents. He tossed a concussion grenade behind him, leaving one agent screaming with his hands over his bleeding ears. Out to the front of the building, he turned back to launch a fixed blade knife … and didn't see the bus that ended it all. End of fixer. End of "hit contract." And Maryn Dale was on the run.

Mid-September found Caroline in the largest meeting room in the awe-inspiring glass-encased Vancouver Sheraton. She stood beside John in the formal welcome and briefing of the Security Services for the tenth G20 Summit. The first speech was presented by Aldrich Maracle, Chief Superintendent and Divisional Operations Commander of the Integrated Security Unit.

"I am pleased to welcome you to the G20 Integrated Security Unit. The eyes of the world are upon us as we seek to establish and maintain the safest and most secure environment possible for the leaders and dignitaries involved in the Summit as well as visitors to and residents of Whistler, Vancouver and surrounding areas.

"At the heart of this operation is the partnership involving the Royal Canadian Mounted Police, visiting Security Services, allies and partners. Together we form the team that will represent the largest deployment of security personnel for a major event in Canadian history. I thank you all in advance for your professionalism and commitment to our shared goal of a safe and secure Summit. I am confident that we will exceed expectations."

Next, they were required to listen patiently to the protocol advisor, Elliot Rice, reviewing the rules of etiquette for peace officers at the Summit. *La-di-da-dee-da. I am so bored.*

"… Prime Minister of Canada and other heads of state are entitled to a salute. By saluting these dignitaries, you formally acknowledge the position they hold. If you are engaged in your duties, do not interrupt to salute …"

John rolled his eyes at Caroline surreptitiously as if to say, *Did we really need to be told that?*

The RCMP Incident Commander, James Yang, took over next. Caroline's back was beginning to ache.

"The Con Ops—" Caroline began to flip pages in the security handbook she'd been given as she listened. Con Ops was the Command and Control Concept of Operations. "—will outline decision-making procedures and will provide guidance for the exercise of authority by the ISU." She flipped again to Integrated Security Unit. "The UCC—" Flipping again, she found the Unified Command Centre. "—located at the PNE Grounds, will be the highest level of command and control for the Summit. It will be made up of commanders from all participating agencies, departments, services and forces. The RCMP Incident Commander will assume the role of overall Commander. Two Area Command Centres will be operating as the next level of command and control, one at the Vancouver Airport and one at the Cristal Lodge at Whistler led by Commanders from the RCMP. The ISU has unique jurisdiction and control operated by the Vancouver Police Service …"

Caroline's attention began to wander around the room, trying to discern the legitimate security officers from the spies sent to observe events, though where the line crossed from one to the other was definitely blurry. This was more boring than the preparatory speech back home. *Wait a minute! When did there become home and here become—what?*

The speech at Vauxhall Cross, the headquarters for MI-6, the UK's foreign intelligence service, had launched the Summit Operation, as it was named. That speech had gone on for an hour, repeating the phrases "Queen and Country" and "duty to defend" more times than Caroline could count.

John nudged her, and she snapped back to the present. She had been humming. "… Controlled Access Zone, the CAZ, is defined as the immediate area surrounding the event and is assigned the highest level of security. The Restricted Access Zone is assigned the second level of security along the outer perimeter of the CAZ. The Secure Area that occurs along the perimeter of the RAZ is assigned a lower level of security. Escort may be required. The Interdiction Zone …"

Caroline's eyes began to glaze over in boredom. She jerked back to the present when John's hand reached for her own. He leaned down to speak to her.

"Why don't you go back to the room and set up the computers?" he whispered. She raised an eyebrow at him. "I'm obligated to stay, but you aren't. I'll catch you up later." She squeezed his fingers twice and slipped out of the room.

MI-5 had been assigned two hotel rooms and two suites at the Vancouver Sheraton. Hibb had taken one room, she and John had another, and Harry and Alexa had decided to share one of the suites. The second suite they had set up as Mission Control. They had been assigned one computer work station at the UCC, the Pacific National Exhibition building, but had arrived with lots of Aubrey's toys as well. Each security service would have done the same, John told her, but he was banking on the fact that Aubrey was brighter and more skilled than any other individual he had ever met.

Sliding her pass through the card-key slot on their room door, Caroline went inside and changed from her black skirt and red blouse into jeans and a navy blue Oxford U sweatshirt and then made her way down the hall to Mission Control. The first thing she noticed was the layer of white powder on the floor around the stack of cases in the centre of the lounge. *Hmmm, someone definitely tried to open the top case, triggering the booby trap. I wonder who would do that.* Sending a quick text to Aubrey and Jade, who would be on duty at Thames House throughout the Summit, she requested assistance.

*PHT&SND.* Caroline chuckled at Aubrey's garbled response, replying, *What?* Minutes later, she received a response: *Photograph case and powder and send to me.* Seconds later, a second message arrived: *Please.* John was clearly giving etiquette lessons to his officers.

After sending the photos as requested, Caroline followed the procedure for opening the cases properly and setting up the computer systems just as Aubrey had taught her. She scanned the room for listening devices and disabled them.

Just as she pulled out the little coffeemaker provided by the hotel, John and the others returned from their briefing—not that there was anything *brief* about it.

"We're set up and ready to go. I was just going to make some coffee; anyone else interested in a cup?" Caroline asked.

Harry and Alexa exchanged a glance. "We were going to find the nearest coffee shop and then scope out some local sights," Alexa said.

"I was going to head over to the big bookstore on the corner and buy summat for my sprogs before we get busy," Hibb said.

Once the others departed, John walked over and took Caroline by the hands.

"I guess that just leaves the two of us," he said, and she could hear the invitation in his voice.

"Any ideas what we could do to fill the afternoon?" she asked, grinning at him, suspecting she could read his mind.

"I can think of one or two things," he said before leaning down to kiss her languidly on the mouth.

As soon as they crossed the threshold of their hotel room, John's pocket beeped. *So close!* She groaned. He pulled out a mobile phone and flipped it over so she could read it. "I'm being paged," he said. "It's time for me to meet with the RCMP liaison officer."

"Where did you get that phone? It's not the one Aubrey gave you," she said.

"Each team leader was assigned a mobile when we registered." He quoted, "'To improve ease of communication.'"

"To increase surveillance, you mean," she said.

"You're learning." He smiled, and she couldn't help feeling a little pride that she'd impressed him. "Would you care to accompany me, or would you prefer to stay here?"

"I wanna come, baby. Do I need to change my clothes?" she asked.

"Please," he said and then leered at her. "Everything, if you want." She smiled and gave him a nudge just for good measure. Changing her top, she replaced the Oxford U sweatshirt with a pale green blouse covered in daisies.

Caroline followed John to the Burrard Room, where they were introduced to the security liaison officers from Brazil, Turkey and South Korea who were also meeting their RCMP liaison officers. Led to the corner of the room, John and Caroline were introduced to an officer in his early thirties, dressed in his red serge tunic, blue breeches and shiny brown leather boots. He was a couple of inches shorter than John, very blond, with blue eyes and a sturdy frame, not skinny but never to be mistaken for heavy.

"Welcome. My name is Sergeant Clarke Milles of the RCMP." Clarke offered his hand to John, who shook it.

"John Brock, UK. This is Caroline—" John began.

"Caroline Wells, isn't it?" Clarke interrupted. His smile of welcome sobered into something more serious that looked remarkably like sympathy. *But why?* "You don't remember me," he continued. "That's not surprising under the circumstances."

"You do look familiar." Caroline glanced at Clarke again and then at John, noting his frown.

"I was the investigating officer on the Hay River crash, the flight out of Grand Prairie to Great Bear Lake. Again, I'm so sorry for your loss," Clarke said.

*No, it can't be.* Caroline paled, and she suddenly felt cold. *Say something,* she urged herself. "Um, thank you." She took his proffered hand with her shaky one.

"What brings you here?" Clarke asked guilelessly.

"Um." She looked up at John, seeking guidance, but he seemed stunned into silence. "Well," she said. And then she cleared her throat. "I've married again. This is my husband, John … Brock." *How can this be happening?* "I … well … I work fo—"

John cut her off. "For Her Majesty's government."

She glanced up at him, but his face was blank. *I forgot, I'm not supposed to let on that I work for MI-5. We're civil servants or security or secretaries. I can't remember.*

"I'm sorry," Clarke said, obviously picking up on the tension he'd created. "Your husband," Clarke repeated the words, glancing at John's face. "I didn't realize." Clarke's jaw clenched, probably to keep it from dropping to the floor in astonishment.

Caroline floundered, reaching for John's hand. It was unresponsive to her touch, and she felt tears burn at the back of her eyes. *John, please help me. Father. Please.*

Abruptly, his fingers closed about hers, and he seemed to snap out of his shock all at once, finally absorbing her need.

"Caroline," he said, calling her name softly. She couldn't seem to meet his eye, but it was okay because he tenderly lifted her chin so he could meet her gaze. "Caroline. Why don't you head back to the room, and I'll deal with this?" His eyes were flitting across her face, likely noting her paleness and tremor. "Caroline?"

She finally met his eyes, nodding once. *Okay.*

"Uh … excuse me … thank you … later," she murmured and then made her way to the elevators and finally into their hotel room, where she flopped onto the bed and curled in on herself.

"I'm sorry," Clarke said. "I shouldn't have—"

"It's all right," John interrupted through clenched teeth. "Let's crack on."

Clarke didn't respond right away, and he seemed to study John a moment. And then he seemed to decide. "I have a list of protocols for you, and my pager and cell-phone numbers so that you can contact me at any time. I am fully at your disposal throughout the talks. If there's anything you need, please let me know." He handed a package of materials and a business card over to John. "Perhaps we should leave the tour for another time?"

"Yes," John responded clearly, moving to exit.

"Mr. Brock?" Clarke reached out to touch him on the arm.

John turned back impatiently. "Yes, Sergeant."

"Your wife … well, it was remarkable how she coped. I'm sorry to have reminded her of her pain," Clarke said.

John studied him up and down, seeking a reassurance of his intent. Satisfied, he finally replied, "I'll let her know. And you're correct, she is remarkable."

John immediately made his way back to their hotel room, finding his wife curled away from the door in a foetal position on the bed. He pried off his shoes and slipped off his suit jacket, coming to curl his body around hers, holding her tightly to him and pressing a kiss to her neck. All he really wanted to do was remove her pain, but since he had no idea how to accomplish that, he waited.

"I remember him now," she said, speaking so softly that he had to strain to hear her. "He was very kind in spite of being very young and inexperienced. There was a lot of pressure on him to wrap the case up quickly, but he insisted it remain open until all of the bodies were found."

"It's okay to cry," John assured her.

She rolled over to face him, tucking her knees between his legs. "I'm okay, surprisingly. It was a shock, to be sure, but I'm all right." She buried her face against his chest, and he could feel her fingers tracing the fabric of his shirt, searching for the pattern of scars hidden beneath. Somehow, those marks always seemed to reassure her. He held her tightly to him.

"Life is so weird!" she finally exclaimed.

"Indeed," he agreed. *That's my girl.*

She took another deep breath and pulled back. He brushed the hair from her face and met her gaze. "Thank you for taking care of me," she said. *Got it right!* He smiled, and she sat up. "All right. Enough moping," she said. "Let's go have some fun. I want to go to the Vancouver Aquarium in Stanley Park before we get too busy, and while we're there, I want you to buy me a present."

He laughed. "What kind of present would you like?"

"Hmmm," she replied thoughtfully, tapping her chin. "I want one of those slug mugs."

John's eyes widened. "What in Wellington's trousers is a slug mug?"

She smiled. "They have the hugest yellow and black slugs here, as big as your thumb." She held up his right thumb between her thumb and forefinger. "When I was doing my Master's degree at UBC, they had them in the gift shop, but I never bought one." She looked up at him coquettishly. "I'll buy you one too if you want one."

*A slug mug?* Raising the eyebrow of scepticism, he said, "There might be something I'd prefer to an artificial gastropod." Nuzzling her neck, he tickled her until she squealed and then he kissed her on the cheek. "Let's go."

"Oh, darn," she said. "What about the gear and the computers? We can't just leave them unguarded. Someone already tried to break into the cases."

"Did you load the encryption programs?" he asked. She nodded. "Did you set up the transmitters and receivers?" She nodded again. "We're peachy.

Anyone who can get through Aubrey's firewalls deserves to get in. Aside from that fact, we haven't done anything yet that needs to be protected," he said.

For the next three hours, John followed Caroline through the Vancouver Aquarium. He was captivated by her as she exclaimed over the tropical fish in the humid rainforest room. He brushed the hair back from her face so he could watch her eyes sparkle in humour at the pair of teens feeding the sea otters. She told him about the times she and Henry had brought the boys here and what each child's favourite animal had been. She smiled as she spoke about the children and John watched her, seeing the transformation of her grief into a memory of joy. And for the first time in their married life, he didn't feel jealous of Henry when she spoke about him. *She loved Henry. She loves me, too.*

It was a gloriously sunny day, and they wandered hand in hand through Stanley Park, seeing the hollow tree, the miniature train and, most of all, the hugest slugs. Caroline bought him a Beluga whale neck tie and a native-design killer-whale travel mug. He bought her a jade and mother of pearl necklace and ... a slug mug. Afterward, they took a taxi back to the Vancouver Sheraton to change for the formal reception to be held amongst the totems at UBC's Museum of Anthropology.

Kitted out in her calf-length burgundy velour dress accented with the jade necklace John had bought her in the afternoon, Caroline felt conspicuously uncomfortable amongst the various dignitaries in their finest formal attire. John, of course, looked as natural in a black tuxedo as in jeans and a T-shirt. He was wandering the rooms amidst the elaborately carved feast dishes and Bill Haida's *Raven and the First Men*, which depicted the raven coaxing the small humans out into the world. While John was busy chatting-up the guests, Caroline stood in a corner, watching the others and trying to spot the spies, just for fun.

"Excuse me, Mrs. Brock." She turned at the gentle tap on her elbow to see Sergeant Clarke Milles in full dress uniform, red serge jacket adorned with insignia and medals, blue breeches, brown riding boots, belts and spurs. The uniform was definitely eye-catching and made Caroline proud to be identified as a Canadian. "I wanted to apologize for earlier," he said. "I'm so very sorry." He looked positively despondent. If this was an act, he was very good at playing a part ... like Sidney Poitier good.

"It's okay, Mister… Officer … Detect—" she began. *What the heck am I supposed to call him?*

He smiled. "Clarke."

"Clarke. I'm all right. It was just a shock." She wanted to console him. *You really have been healing me all this time, Father. It no longer feels like shards of glass ripping through me every time I'm reminded of my family.*

Clarke seemed to have more to say. "Excuse me, ma'am, but … how on earth did you wind up here, at an international conference representing the British government?"

*You cannot begin to imagine, young man.* "It's a long, strange story," she replied.

"Your husband … your first husband was a geography teacher, wasn't he?" he asked.

"Yes, he specialized in Environmental Studies," she said.

"You had children?" he said, tentatively speaking the words.

"Yes. Five boys. They were all killed in the crash." He probably already knew that, but Caroline felt the need to say it anyway. Perhaps someday she'd be able to say it without the gut-wrenching grief that always accompanied the memory. "After that, as you can imagine, I had difficulty finding a way forward in life. I'd lost everything I'd hoped for and worked for. So I decided to travel to Singapore."

"Singapore?!" he repeated, clearly astonished.

"To work in a school for missionaries' children," she explained. "Well, I never made it there. The plane was grounded in Burma. I was arrested and, effectively, disappeared."

"Burma? Is that Myanmar?" he asked in his innocence.

Caroline's eyes narrowed. "Myanmar is the name assigned by the military junta. It's still called Burma by its people."

"Excuse me." Clarke had obviously noticed the change in her demeanour and was probably confused as to why the name held such importance for Caroline. "But I still don't see the connection with Britain."

Caroline softened her expression. "I met John in Burma."

"John," Clarke repeated thoughtfully. "John Brock of MI-5. I've been asking around. I heard that he escaped—" Slowly, Clarke nodded at her, wonder in his eyes. "You are the two intelligence officers who escaped from

Burma! That escape is legendary. Your husband, Mrs. Brock, is known throughout the intelligence community. They call him—"

"Ironheart, I know." She smiled warmly.

Clarke lapsed into silence for a moment. Finally, he bowed a simple nod in her direction. "I'm at your service."

She shone him a friendly smile and he moved away, soon replaced by John, who handed her a wine glass of ice-cold water.

"What did you get for yourself?" she asked.

"Water. From this moment on, we can't relax our guard," he said. "Too much at risk."

"Aye aye, Cap'n," she replied, grinning at him.

"Hmmm." He frowned at her. "Are you being insubordinate?"

"Definitely, if it gets me out of this stuffed-shirt festival." He grinned at her. He almost always appreciated her humour. What more could you ask of a man? Handsome, brave, kind ... and he always laughed at her jokes.

Spontaneously, Caroline tiptoed up and kissed him on the cheek. He smiled in return, taking her by the hand and pulling her out of the corner and into the festivities. They spent the evening chatting, eating, chatting, dancing and chatting until Caroline was finally more bored than she could tolerate. She went back to the hotel and then to bed, leaving John, Harry, Alexa and Hibb to make connections and glean intelligence from the various delegates and spies within the room, who were all trying to do the same.

The next morning, Caroline was up and out by seven, meeting Clarke and the others for breakfast, where they reflected upon the previous evening's entertainment. After that, Caroline and Harry made their way to Mission Control while Hibb, Alexa and John were on the road, escorting the British Prime Minister and the Chancellor of the Exchequer to various meetings, briefings and events. Both dignitaries had teams on close protection as well, but it was John's responsibility to ensure that security was coordinated and effective, at the same time rooting out the real intentions of certain key dignitaries in attendance.

Caroline and Harry were monitoring all communications to and from the British delegates and, although a fact not to be known, the Chinese, American and French delegates as well. *Boring!* Harry and Caroline amused themselves by listening to the police-radio frequencies.

One man was detained for driving through Vancouver with a chainsaw, gas cans and a crossbow in his trunk. He was to be charged with possession of "weapons dangerous."

"Seriously, Caroline, if he didn't want to be arrested, perhaps he should have let someone else bring the chainsaw to the party," Harry said.

She joined his laughter. "He must be from Canmore," she quipped. "Just making a trip into the big city for a little light … what? Hunting? I mean really, who hunts with a crossbow and a chainsaw?"

Another man was detained for driving a Suburban down Cambie Street with an improvised rooftop carrier that, it turned out, contained ammonium nitrate.

"Harry, what's the deal with having ammonium nitrate? Isn't that just fertilizer?" she asked.

"Fertilizer …" Harry paused for effect. "And a crucial component in explosives."

"Ah," she replied. "Will he join the chainsaw dude in the Special Summit Detention Centre?"

"Indeed."

"From this transcript," she said, "he seems completely oblivious to the implications of his situation. He's more concerned that someone's going to look after his dog than the fact that he's being detained at an international summit on suspicion of terrorist activities."

Harry laughed, shaking his head at the irony of the situation.

Caroline's favourite, though, were the four men who were arrested coming out of a manhole beyond the fence into the RAZ, the Restricted Access Zone.

"Okay, Harry. You might forget that you put your chainsaw in the back of the car. You might even forget that you picked up the fertilizer at the Co-op last week and didn't unload it, but seriously, who takes a wrong turn down a manhole cover?"

"Who indeed?' he replied. "Have a look at these blokes, Caroline."

She glanced over at his screen to witness three young men dressed in combat fatigues, storming the restricted zone with some sort of—"Harry, what are they holding in their hands?" she asked. *Please don't let it be grenades. John is near there, organizing security.*

"Watch and see," Harry said, and before long it was evident that the youths were lobbing paintball grenades at the surrounding buildings.

"Wait a minute." *Who is that?* One of the young men pushed up his balaclava which had slipped over his eyes. "Harry." She reached out and grabbed his arm. "Isn't that Warren Yang, son of the RCMP Incident Commander, James Yang?"

"I believe so. Call John," Harry said.

"John?" She called him on his MI-5 Aubrey-encrypted mobile phone. "Can you see the kerfuffle over at the RAZ? The three young men about to be arrested?" He acknowledged that he could. "One of them is James Yang's son. What should we do?"

"I'll take care of it." And he did. She watched him through the monitor. First, he flashed his badge and bullied his way into the situation, stating that this young man was a person of interest to HM's government. Then he replaced the young man's balaclava and dragged him away quickly before the police officers thought to stop him. Evidently, because he wasn't leaving the Restricted Zone, he was allowed to pass unhindered.

"Caroline. Contact Hibb, Alexa and Clarke and have them meet me at the Summit Detention Centre," John said.

Caroline flipped between the surveillance channels until John finally called her back.

"John. What happened?" she said.

"Clarke called Yang, and I passed the subdued young hooligan over to his father," John said.

"What did his father do?" she asked, almost feeling sorry for the attention-seeking young man.

"Nothing in front of me. Commander Yang did, however, hand me his private contact information and his eternal gratitude. That, I think, may come in handy one day," John replied.

"I suppose the embarrassment to his career would have been devastating," she said.

"Indeed," Harry replied from beside her.

The next three days passed in much the same manner, with many professional protesters and unthinking or foolish citizens detained. Caroline found it alternately mysterious, aggravating and entertaining. Every move, initiative and idea was closely monitored, using every known tool of surveillance available—half of which Caroline could neither operate nor understand.

Alexa rooted out the MSS officers in place at the Summit, and Harry and Caroline uncovered evidence of three Chinese plots to exert influence over the British PM. Each plot was meant to reduce the UK's voice against human-rights abuses in China and/or to maximize the influence of policymakers favourable toward the Chinese government.

John spent three hours in a private meeting with the beleaguered director of CSIS discussing the Chinese, returning discouraged.

"If only we could unite to stand against China until they reversed their human-rights policies," John said.

"What about Burma?" Caroline asked.

"The director knew nothing about China's current plans in Burma aside from their keen desire to have sanctions lifted," John said.

"Was anything accomplished in the Summit that might help Burma?" Caroline asked.

"Doubtful, sweetheart. At the moment, China wields a great deal of power economically, and the West is prone to ignore the inconvenient unless forced to acknowledge it. You can definitely keep Burma on your prayer list," he said, folding the paper in his hand and tucking it into his inner jacket pocket.

"What's this?" Caroline asked, reaching in and pulling out the page, examining it. "An invitation?"

"The American cousins, your northern countrymen, and we from '5' are cordially invited to an evening of celebration and relaxation at the Vancouver Art Gallery tonight after the closing ceremonies in order to strengthen relationships," he said. "Interested?"

"Not in the teeniest tiniest least. But you go ahead and have fun," she replied.

His face fell and then tightened into a blank look. "We don't have to go."

"John. Don't be silly. I don't mind if you go out with the other spooks and spies," she said.

"I don't feel right going out without you," he said quietly. "What will you do all evening?"

"I'll curl up in bed and watch a movie. I really don't mind," she said. He seemed so unsure. "However," she began, and he watched her carefully, "if you are going to be out partying, then I need some new pyjamas to keep me warm." He began to smile. "And … some flowers."

"As you wish, my lady." He pulled her into his arms and kissed her. And then he kissed her again.

Later that evening, accompanied by his three companions, who were noisily shushing each other, John walked down the corridor to his hotel room. He hadn't been drunk, not even a little drunk, since he'd married Caroline, and he didn't plan on getting drunk tonight. Since his companions weren't ready to call it a night, John wanted to let Caroline know that he would be sleeping on a cot in Hibb's room, thereby allowing her an undisturbed night.

Dragging out his card-key, John steadily inserted it and opened the door. Entering the room, he was surprised to find the light on. As he moved forward, he could see that Caroline was not in the bed and the loo was empty. The flowers he'd bought for her were still on top of the television, but they looked like they'd been trampled by a bison.

Confused, John sat on the bed, paper crunching beneath his hip. Pulling it out to see what it was, he read the typewritten sheet:

Dear John,

I am leaving you.

I can't make this work anymore.

I'm too scared to talk to you face to face.

Don't look for me.

"John, hurry up, mate. Let's go," a hoarse whisper came from the hallway, interrupting his thoughts.

"Leaving you," John repeated. *I certainly deserve to be left, but …* Floods of memories assaulted him, memories of his stupidity and selfishness. But these memories were followed by images of Caroline's love and steadfastness. *No.*

"*No!*" John declared, rising to his feet. "No! I don't believe it."

Hibb entered the bedroom, glancing around. "What's going on? Where's Caroline?" John handed him the piece of paper. "She's run off?" Hibb said, sounding truly astonished.

"No, no way! Look at it," John said. "It's not signed. It's typewritten. I don't believe it."

Harry and Alexa entered the room. "What's going on?" Alexa inquired. Hibb handed over the paper. "Oh. Sorry, John," she said, handing the note off to Harry.

"No. I don't believe it," insisted John.

"Are you certain, John? The two of you have had a rough year," Harry added.

"But that's it, don't you see? We've been through the rough times. Why would she leave me now if she didn't leave me then?" John pleaded for some reassurance.

"Perhaps being in Canada—" Harry began.

"We spent three days with her family. Why not simply stay behind? Why wait until we're three thousand miles away?" John snatched the note back from Harry. "It's typewritten," he said, pointing at the page. "There's no signature. And look at this. This isn't the way Caroline writes. It's like somebody doing a bad impression of a third-form pupil. And look at this … 'scared.' Since when has Caroline ever been afraid of me? Hibb?" *Except that one time … but …* John turned to his second-in-command, his friend.

Slowly, Hibb took the page and studied it again. "It certainly doesn't sound like Caroline."

"Would she leave me?" John asked in a quiet voice, desperate to be told that his instincts were true. Caroline would not leave him.

Hibb returned his plaintive look and then glanced to both Alexa and Harry. "No. I agree with you. She's simply not the type."

"I agree." Surprised, John turned to Alexa, who continued, "Harry, remember Kolkata? After what she and John went through in Burma, I don't believe she'd leave him. They've been through hell together. Why leave now, when they're so happy?"

Harry took over. "All right, John. What do you want us to do?"

"Help me find my wife."

"Agreed."

First, John called in his favour with Commander James Yang. Hibb called the Vancouver police. Harry called Clarke Milles, RCMP. Within twenty-five minutes, the Scene of Crime Officer had arrived to photograph the bedroom, and Aneta Bohdan, the attending detective, had delivered a speech … *the disappearance of an MI-5 officer immediately following an international summit on Canadian soil was an unprecedented crime …*

John's distracted mind could barely even pretend to listen to the platitudes. *Blah blah blah. Just find my wife.* Bohdan finally moved away to call in the Forensic Science Unit.

"Sir," one of the investigators called. Approaching John, he handed him the cap from a hypodermic needle. John took it carefully in his gloved hand. *What does this mean?* His knees gave way, and he found himself sitting on the edge of the bed—the bed he had shared with his wife not twenty-four hours ago. *Don't think about that. It will only drive you round-the-bend.* He pressed his hand against his face, trying to still the convulsions that threatened to overtake his body.

John flinched when he felt a broad hand on his back. "John? Mate?" Hibb said with deep concern in his voice. Without raising his head, John reached up his right hand, showing Hibb the cap. "She *was* taken!" Hibb exclaimed.

John's tumultuous thoughts began to settle. *She didn't leave me! Now I know she didn't leave me.* He didn't know what Hibb saw in his manner that concerned him, but he followed numbly when the big man hauled him up and led him out onto the balcony, closing the glass door behind them. John leaned heavily on the railing, looking out over Stanley Park to Grouse Mountain.

"You weren't certain, were you, mate?" Hibb asked gently.

John shook his head. "She has every right to leave me, Hibb. She deserves so much more than I have to offer."

"She loves you, John."

"I know," he said, acknowledging the wonderful truth of Hibb's words. "I've got to find her."

Harry interrupted them. "John, come and see this."

John followed Harry to the mirror in the loo. One of the investigators was projecting black light using a wood's lamp onto the surface of the mirror.

"You can see here, sir, there's some writing. Someone attempted to wipe it off, but you can still see a portion of it." The technician pointed.

John could see the smudged residue of the letters -A-R-Y-.

"Mary? Harry?" Harry questioned. "Switch off the light," he instructed the investigator. The writing immediately disappeared. "How did she get fluorescent ink?" The black light was reinstated.

"I gave her an invisible-ink pen as a joke a while back." John bent forward toward the mirror, studying the letters. He straightened. "Not Mary, *Maryn*! Maryn Dale. Hibb, Maryn Dale snatched her!"

Caroline gradually became aware that the pounding bass of the tuneless melody was coming from inside her head rather than the noisy neighbours. As that awareness took hold, flashes of memory came back: a call informing her that John was hurt; men in uniforms arriving at the door; Caroline's insistence on contacting John before allowing them in, followed by the sounds on the balcony that forced her to realize that she was in danger. Grabbing her cell phone, she'd run into the bathroom, locking the door behind her.

Whimpering in fear, hands shaking, Caroline had rifled through the toiletries bag, trying to find anything that could help her: a pocketknife, the invisible-ink pen that John had given her, deodorant, shampoo, acetaminophen—nothing useful. Her thoughts were interrupted by pounding on the bathroom door. *Grendahl is dead. No more assassins. Right? Oh, Father, what is happening?*

"Mrs. John Brock. I feel that you have misunderstood our intention here." Caroline heard a familiar voice, a woman's voice. *Who is it?* "We've come to take you to John. He's been badly hurt. If you'll come out of the loo, we will take you to him." The voice paused a moment, but Caroline remained still and silent. "He's asking for you."

*The loo, not the bathroom? English accent. Who is it?* Caroline called John. Her cell phone engaged, and Caroline's panic was interrupted by John's voice. "John Brock. Leave a message." It was his voicemail. *Oh no!* The tone sounded, ending the recording before she left a message.

Caroline redialled and reached his voicemail again. "John, help me. Someone's here. There are at least three men and one woman. I think two of them came in from the balcony. I recognize the woman's voice but I can't place it—" A sob interrupted her words. "Help me, John." Her whispered words halted as the banging resumed.

"Mrs. Brock, you remember me? We had a lovely conversation at Thames House not long ago."

Again, the voicemail on John's phone ended. The home answering machine would continue to record as long as there was noise. Caroline called John's phone once more. "Call home. John, I love you. Help me!" She used the phone to call home, and once the message engaged, she hid the phone under the lip of the bathroom counter. *God, help me. Send John.*

Maryn Dale! That was the voice! She pulled out the pen and wrote a message on the mirror.

MARYN DALE

HELP ME

I LOVE YOU

The door burst open. Caroline grabbed the pocketknife and extended the blade. She tried to remember everything she knew about self-defence, but nothing was effective enough to prevent the two men from dragging her into the bedroom. As they held her shoulders down on the bed, the third man held her legs, and Maryn Dale popped the top off a hypodermic needle and plunged it into her shoulder. Darkness descended in wobbly waves. The last thing she heard was, "Sanitize the room!"

"Sir, we found this hidden under the bathroom counter." The investigator who had found the cap brought a bright red flip-top mobile phone over to John.

"That's Caroline's mobile." John hit number redial and realized the number was his own. Reaching into his pocket, he brought it out, turning it on to find that he had three messages. The first message sounded like static. He proceeded to the second message.

"John, help me! Someone's here—" John's hands began to shake, and all the blood drained from his face. Unresisting, he allowed Hibb to snatch the phone from his grasp and close it, cutting off the message.

Hibb immediately took charge. "Harry, you and Alexa carry on here. We're going to my room. Call my mobile if you find anything else." Harry nodded at Hibb's instructions.

Hibb kept a strong hold on John's arm, forcing him to stay upright and continue moving forward until they entered Hibb's room. He pulled John over to the couch and then allowed him to sit. John slumped forward, elbows braced on his knees, his head sinking low between his shoulders.

Shoving him back by the shoulder, Hibb thrust a glass beneath his nose. John automatically raised it to his mouth and then stopped when he smelled the Scotch within it.

"No," John said. His voice was raspy and alien. "Caroline doesn't like me to drink." He placed the glass on the floor, the liquid sloshing around as his hand shook. "Give me the phone."

Hibb handed him the phone, and John listened to the messages. Phoning home, he retrieved the message, listening step by step to the abduction of his wife, her screams and struggles and then the efforts of Maryn Dale's henchmen to cleanse the room. *Oh God!*

John's hands were shaking, and his breath wheezed in his lungs. "I'm going to be sick," he announced.

Hibb dragged him into the toilets and placed him over the bowl. He emptied his stomach into the basin, though nothing could purge him of his grief and guilt. When the heaving subsided, John leaned back against the cool wall, burying his face in his hands.

"John, are you all right?" Hibb was beside him, shaking his shoulder. "John!"

"I'm all right. I'll never be all right again." John groaned unevenly. He looked up at Hibb, his eyes revealing the agony of his rending heart. "Why did I turn off my phone? To have a little fun? If I had kept my phone on, I might have been able to get there in time." His body convulsed, but he felt too guilty to cry. Instead, he began to shake again.

Hibb crouched beside him and firmly gave his shoulder one shake. "John! Mate! You canna help Caroline if you fall apart." John looked up at him with what was likely the most pathetic gaze. "Pull yourself together, John. Right now!" Hibb commanded.

John stiffened at being spoken to in that manner. He pulled out his mobile again and replayed the messages, this time listening to every word she said; then again, listening to every sound in the background; then again, listening to every voice; then again …

Caroline realized that she was seated in a chair, a hard chair. Weakly, she opened her eyes to gaze down, seeing her hands on her lap bound in zip cuffs for the second time in her life. She was grateful she'd worn proper pyjamas to bed, red silk with bursts of dusty blue blossoms falling in patterns of teardrops across the fabric. She was always cold when John wasn't in bed with her, so she had worn the silk pyjamas he had bought for her rather than her nightie.

"Mrs. Brock." Maryn Dale pronounced each syllable distinctly. "Caroline. May I call you Caroline?"

Caroline lifted her heavy head, eyes blinking to adjust to the lighting. The room was dark and dank, paint peeling from the once cream-coloured walls. It was a large room divided by a wall, with an open doorway at either end. Off to Caroline's left, there was a third doorway and a large window that led into a smaller room which appeared to have been recently painted.

"I'm thirsty," Caroline said. One of the men who had grabbed her in the bathroom brought her a plastic water bottle, generic brand. Well, now she knew that Maryn was cheap. A small chuckle played across her mind. *Careful! Humour and hysteria are probably not too far apart.*

Caroline tried to remove the lid, but whatever drug they had given her was making it difficult to coordinate her hands and mind. She heard a disgusted sound from Maryn, who waved at the burly red-haired henchman. As he came over and undid the lid, pushing the bottle back into Caroline's hands, she noticed the vivid scar vertically bisecting his right eye. *I wonder if that was a present from Maryn.* Drinking deeply, she listened to the cheap plastic crinkle as the contents spilled into her mouth.

Maryn's voice again. "Well, you're obviously not a field agent." Caroline looked up with a question in her bleary eyes. Maryn explained. "A field agent would never accept a drink from an enemy."

"Are you my enemy?" Caroline asked simply.

"Oh yes!" Maryn replied gleefully.

Caroline took another drink and handed back the bottle. Maryn gave her a quizzical look.

"What do you want from me?" Caroline asked blearily.

"I—"

"Wait!" Caroline interjected, and Maryn was visibly astonished by the interruption. "That day at Thames House," Caroline said. "Did you know who I was?"

"Of course. As soon as I returned to the UK and heard that John had taken up with a bint, I had you fully investigated." Maryn smirked, clearly enjoying the thrill of secret plans.

"What's a bint?" Caroline murmured.

"Spare me your ignorance," Maryn said in obvious disgust.

"How did you know—" Caroline began.

Maryn waved away Caroline's questions impatiently. "My wee mole kept me well informed."

"Ryan. How did you convince him to betray his colleagues?" Caroline asked. Ryan himself walked out of the shadows, looking forlorn and more than a little guilty. "Why, Ryan?" Caroline asked him.

"Enough!" Maryn said, the word bursting forth from her lips. Abruptly, her manner changed from fury to appeasement, assuming a sultry gaze as she sauntered over to Ryan. She caressed his cheek with her fingertips and then ran her fingers across his chest. "Are you my very own special bloke? Are you my creature?"

Ryan seemed mesmerized by her grey eyes, which had taken on an ebony hue in her anger. Stopping in front of him, her hand flat against his chest, Maryn licked her lips, and Caroline watched Ryan's eyes follow the woman's tongue from corner to corner. His breathing ceased for a moment as Maryn leaned in and kissed him sensually on the mouth.

As Maryn pulled back, Ryan lowered his gaze, responding in a husky voice, "Of course."

Maryn lifted his chin, "Now, I want you to take her into that room, and when she comes out, I want her to be willing to tell me anything that I want to know." Maryn held his gaze through his look of horror until a look of sorrowful resignation replaced it.

Caroline shook at Maryn's bloodless words. After all the times she'd been in danger in her life, it would be a colleague, a boy who was barely a man … *Father, give me strength. "God is our refuge and strength, a very present help in trouble …"*

The two men—the henchmen, as Caroline thought of them, the burly, red-haired man and the equally burly but much shorter Tibetan man, Sonam Narayan—moved over to stand on either side of Caroline's chair. But Caroline had one more question to ask Maryn.

"Wait!" Caroline said, her voice carrying enough authority to stop Maryn.

Maryn turned as though she expected Caroline to beg and was anticipating the pleasure of refusing her.

"How did you get to Simon?" Caroline asked. "I understand how you got to Ryan. He's young, and he would want revenge on John for belittling him. But Simon? How did you convince him?"

Waving her hand in the air as though swatting away a gnat, Maryn replied, "Simon was easy. I simply sent him a message stating that I could help him meet with you, that you needed him." Maryn snapped her fingers. "Piece of cake. It was effortless to convince Simon that John had made you unhappy and that you needed rescuing. And then I sent him off for a wee holiday to China so our illustrious Colonel could show him what kind of man John truly was."

Caroline was struggling to put it all together as she inquired, "But Simon wasn't in love with me when I left the Katafygio. I know he was attracted to me beyond what I felt for him, but I'm sure he wasn't in love."

Maryn snorted in disgust. "Love. What a pitiful fantasy! It was easy to convince Simon that he couldn't live without you." Maryn seemed to derive some sort of perverse pleasure from boasting.

"How did you get back into the Katafygio again?" Caroline asked. "I mean, after what you did to Brother Phillip, I can't imagine them welcoming you with open arms."

Maryn's body went dangerously still for a moment. Sonam Narayan coughed, and Maryn seemed to jerk back into the moment. "Pfft. There was no need. I simply obtained a photograph of you walking your animal in Moor Mead Gardens and then used it to entice Simon away to meet with me. Simple!"

*Animal? Rufus or John? Careful,* Caroline admonished herself. *You can't afford to lose it before John comes for you. Oh, John. Where are you?* "Simon was just a tool for revenge on John, wasn't he? Revenge for choosing someone else?" Caroline said.

Maryn's face lit with red wrath. "Don't ever think that you have something I want!" Flicking her crimson gaze to her henchmen, she seethed through clenched teeth, "Augustus. Sonam. Take her away!"

Augustus and Sonam each grabbed an arm and immediately pulled Caroline from the chair and forced her into the smaller room. This room was decorated in a combination of prison-cell grey and pre-war medical. It looked like an ancient doctor's examining room, with a sink to the left overlooked by a mirror and several shelves containing hypodermic needles and vials of multi-coloured liquids. Straight ahead was an iron bed with leather straps at the head and foot. On the right were a stainless-steel toilet and an empty toilet-paper holder with, positioned directly above, a series of pegs holding a variety of leather straps and whips. *Oh, Father. Not me.* Looking up, she saw, hanging from the centre of the room directly over the drain in the grey concrete floor, a large wrought-iron hook. Caroline began to shake.

The door behind her clicked, and she flinched at the sound, turning to see that Ryan had followed her in. The henchmen left, closing and locking the door behind them.

A voice crackled over the speaker in the corner of the room. "Don't take too long to begin, my poppet!" Maryn said, the threat carrying easily through the metal box.

Caroline's knees were shaking so badly that she decided sitting on the bed, in spite of the buckles and straps, was preferable to collapsing on the concrete floor. *I thought when I escaped from Burma that I left this sort of danger behind.*

"Ryan," Caroline said, her voice quivering. "Why are you doing this? You were willing to drug me and kidnap me in Wales, but you never hurt me. Are you really willing to torture me now? What have I ever done to you?"

"Caroline." Ryan spoke softly, probably aware that everything they said was being overheard. "I'm sorry. You've always been very kind to me."

"How did she convince you to do this?" Caroline asked.

"She told me that I would be able to get revenge on John. I didn't know, Caroline. I'm sorry," he said.

"That's what Simon said after you shot him."

"I'm sorry. I don't have a choice. If I don't do this, they'll kill me," he said, and Caroline could hear the agony he felt.

She held his gaze. "If you do this, Ryan, you'll never be the same. And they will kill you anyway."

"I don't have a choice." His voice now bore resignation in its depths.

"We always have a choice," Caroline insisted.

Maryn's voice crackled through again. "Get on with it!"

The two henchmen burst through the door, grabbing Caroline and lifting her arms above her head, placing the zip cuffs over the hook in the ceiling. *Don't beg! Don't beg!* Caroline ordered herself. *It never helps anyway. Oh God, help me! "I will lift up mine eyes unto the hills—from whence comes my help? My help comes from the Lord, which made heaven and earth …"*

Maryn walked in and circled Caroline once, coming to stand in front of her. Caroline's shoulders were already starting to burn, and her fingers were tingling. *How did John survive this kind of treatment?*

"You're afraid now, aren't you?" Maryn inquired.

"Yes, I'm afraid," Caroline replied unevenly.

Maryn was thoughtful for a moment. "I'll make a bargain with you. Take young Ryan to bed here ... now ... and I'll release you ... relatively unharmed. We'll send a few pictures to John, but you'll be free."

Caroline was shaking, and her stomach threatened to empty itself onto the immaculate concrete and away into the drain in the floor. "I can't," she replied, her voice husky, tears forming in her eyes.

Maryn was puzzled again. "What do you mean 'can't'?"

"Absolute fidelity. 'Keep yourself only unto him.' I promised." Silent tears began to fall from Caroline's eyes.

"But I'm offering you an exchange." Maryn was clearly confused by Caroline's response.

"I know, and I'm very afraid of what you're going to do to me, Maryn. But I won't betray John. I promised." Caroline's shoulders were shaking with the force of her tears.

Abruptly, Maryn turned her back on Caroline. "Get on with it!" she ordered Ryan. "I want to hear her scream. Or you'll take her place!"

Caroline began to pray the words she had just been sent: "I lift up my eyes to the hills ... where does my help come from—"

Ryan interrupted, the strain sounding in his voice. "What are you doing?"

"Praying," Caroline said.

"I'm sorry," Ryan moaned softly.

Then Caroline spoke the three hardest words: "I forgive you." A strange peace descended on her—not fearlessness or resistance to pain, just peace ... enough peace to keep from losing control. *'My help comes from the Lord.'*

"Enough! Beat her! Beat her now!" Maryn screeched, and then she slapped Ryan hard across the face.

"*No!*" the young man yelled, agony seizing his spirit. Sonam Narayan grabbed him, holding him firmly.

"You will pay for your disobedience! Get this failure, this spotty youth, out of my sight." At Maryn's direction, Sonam hauled the unresisting Ryan from the room.

Maryn spun on Caroline, slapping her with a resounding smack. Caroline's head recoiled from the force, her eye immediately swelling as trickles of blood oozed from the furrows dug by Maryn's fingernails.

Ripping a leather strap from the hook on the wall, Maryn stomped up to Augustus.

"I want to hear her scream."

# Chapter Fourteen
## Ask According to His Will

John sat on the grey-tiled floor of the loo. Again and again, he played his wife's messages, gleaning every bit of data available. Hibb's mobile rang, and John watched him walk away into the bedroom to answer it.

"Hibbert." John heard his voice. "We'll be right there. Where should we meet you?" Silence. "Aye. Five minutes."

John was up and waiting when Hibb stepped back. "Where to now?" John asked, frantic to move toward a resolution, anything … anything at all to save his wife.

"Security room. Alexa's going through the CCTV, but she needs the information on your mobile to pinpoint the times we're looking for," Hibb said.

John nodded and followed Hibb. After twenty minutes of staring at fuzzy black-and-white images of tourists moving in and out of their cars and rooms and back again, John felt like he was being driven slowly insane. There had to be something more valuable he could be doing. He had already snapped at the security officer twice for being too slow.

"John." Hibb pronounced his name calmly. "Why don't we—"

"Sorry," John apologized again tonelessly. His body was in perpetual motion, pacing the tiny room already overfull with the Security Officer, an RCMP officer, Alexa, Hibb and himself. But he just couldn't be still. His hands were constantly moving, pushing through his hair, flipping Caroline's phone open and closed, open and closed, flicking buttons, adjusting shades.

"Hibb! Will you get him out of here? Please!" Alexa growled.

Hibb nodded, grasping John by the arm and firmly leading him from the room. How had he not noticed the strength of the man before?

Once outside, John pleaded with him. "I've got to do something, Hibb. I can't stand it. If Maryn has her … Maryn is capable of anything."

"I know, mate. Come with me," Hibb said. John followed him out the front doors of the Vancouver Sheraton, right on Burrard, past Yuk-Yuk's, and right on Nelson. Hibb pushed John before him into a small door in the side of a very large building. The door was, surprisingly, unlocked.

John looked around, continuing to step forward, realization dawning. "A church?" he said. *A church.* John stared at his friend. *Of course, a church.*

"Yes," Hibb replied, grabbing a Bible from a pew and flipping quickly to the back of the book, finding the verses he wanted and thrusting them in front of John.

Pointing, he instructed John, "Read this."

**1 John 5:14-15**

And this is the confidence that we have in him,

That, if we ask any thing according to his will, he hears us.

And if we know that he hear us

—Whatsoever we ask—

We know that we have the petitions that we desired of him.

"Now get on your knees and pray for your wife!"

John stumbled forward, finding the altar and collapsing there. *God! Oh God!* John began to weep until sobs shook his shoulders, convulsing his body. As he began to quiet, he heard the still, small voice. *"The Lord shall preserve thee from all evil—The Lord shall preserve thy going out and thy coming in from this time forth, and even for evermore." God, please watch over Caroline. Protect her and bring her back to me. Forgive me for causing all this trouble; for the bad life I led. Please don't let Caroline pay for my sins. Bring her back to me, please! But if you let them take her life, then take my life too. If she goes—I don't want to live without her. Please. "And this is the confidence that we have in him, that, if we ask any thing according to his will, he hears us…" If He hears me, then I knowHe'll act according to His will.*

Caroline gradually drifted out of her nightmare only to realize her nightmare was simply a replay of real life. She lay on her left side facing the grey wall, curled in a foetal position on the bed in the small room. The zip cuffs had been removed. She could see that her left wrist was swollen and rather an odd shape, the realization bringing a surge of nausea to the back of her throat. Every part of her body ached and throbbed, and she couldn't see through her left eye. Her shoulders were burning. Her head felt like someone was beating on it with a cement block. Her mouth was as dry as Henry's coffee cake, but she had to pee. Seeking to relieve the pressure on her bladder, she shifted position. Now she wished she hadn't taken the water offered by Maryn. Her mind held a debate on whether it was worse to try to move or just lie here and wet the bed.

Hibb's mobile rang. "John! They've got summat! Clarke pulled in a favour from the Vancouver Police and accessed the extra cameras they put in place for the Summit. They think they've found her, John."

John was off, up and out the door, running back to the hotel with Hibb hot on his heels. John was still desperate to find Caroline, but he now found a modicum of peace within him—enough peace to help him think and plan and rescue, enough peace to keep him from losing his mind.

Harry met them in the lobby with Clarke. "Look here, John. Look at these pictures. Could that be Caroline?"

John studied the pictures carefully. He definitely did not want to waste time chasing down a false lead. Then, there in the third picture, he saw them: the silk pyjamas he'd bought for her in Chinatown. She'd insisted that if he was going to be out all night partying with his mates, she needed pyjamas to keep her warm. So he'd bought them for her, leaving them on her pillow for her to find. She definitely would have worn them. Caroline always used his gifts right away, even if she never used them again.

"It's her. I bought her those pyjamas. They're a very unique pattern. I didn't see anything else like them on the street. It's her." John was confident.

"Come with me," Clarke commanded. They entered the waiting RCMP vehicle, racing through the streets to the headquarters of the Vancouver Police. Clarke pointed at the screen of the GPS. "You can see here, they turn onto Marine Drive and then out toward … Langley? Then we lose them. Commander? Are we able to contact the Langley Police to start a search for this vehicle?"

"Of course."

Caroline gradually realized that she needed to move if she was ever going to move again. Because if the henchman moved her, it was going to hurt a heck of a lot more if she didn't first stretch out her tormented muscles. Unfolding herself inch by inch, she moved up and to the edge of the bed. Taking a deep breath to still the spinning room, she braced her hands on the edge of the cot, but her left hand wouldn't grip properly. Thinking about it made her nauseous, but she definitely didn't want to throw up. The agony that would cause was beyond considering.

For the first time, she noticed that the door to the room was open, and through it she could hear the buzz of conversation outside. *I'll just make a run for it.* Caroline chuckled then groaned as she braced her good arm across her ribs. *How did John survive this? They haven't even begun to approach the torments he endured. Oh God, please let me see him again. I love him so much.*

Bracing herself again, leaning primarily on her right arm, she pushed off the edge of the bed and shuffled over to the toilet in the corner. The relief she expected at emptying her bladder was halted by the muscle spasms that wracked her back because of the beating. She breathed deeply, trying to calm her body enough to void. *This is as bad as labour.* She groaned aloud, not really caring if anyone heard.

Finishing, she stood to inch up her pyjama bottoms with one hand, noticing Maryn lounging against the doorway.

"Hurts, does it?" Maryn grinned maliciously.

Caroline couldn't be bothered responding. She continued her task and shuffled back to the bed, gingerly folding herself back into the least painful position she could find that still allowed her to keep her eye on Maryn.

"I thought you might like to know that when we snatched you from under your husband's nose, we left behind a note telling how you were leaving him and that he shouldn't look for you." Maryn pushed off the doorway and exited.

*Will John believe it? He's still so insecure. Does he still believe I would leave? Is he coming for me, Father?* Caroline began to weep. Each gasp and shudder sending barbs of pain through her body. Would he believe in her? Would he come for her?

Sometime later, Caroline's ears perked up at the sounds coming from outside her room. Had she been here long enough to think of it as "her room"? Maryn was angry, very angry. The men were trying to explain. Oh, she hit Augustus. *Yes, hit him again. I'll never forget his ugly face as long as I live, nor the sound a leather strap makes when it hits you on the legs, the back and the stomach.* Caroline shuddered, whimpering at the memories.

Maryn appeared at the doorway.

"Well, it seems that your *husband* ..." She said the word with a bilious sneer. "... has located you more quickly than I expected. It appears that Ryan's reports of your marital discord were greatly exaggerated. Well, he will pay for his folly. I'm going to send him to John ... with pictures of you."

Sonam entered the room, and with the help of Augustus, they stretched Caroline out on the bed, attaching her right wrist and both ankles to the bedrails and then opening her pyjama shirt to reveal the worst of the damage. Her left wrist was too swollen to be contained in the leather cuff, so the red-haired brute kept her arm firmly trapped in his meaty hand. *Ouch! No!*

She struggled weakly against her captors. *No! Not that! Please, God.* When the camera appeared in Sonam's hands, she finally understood; the sight of her bound and disrobed would do more to unsettle John than anything else. *Oh no. John is going to kill someone.*

"Very good," said Maryn. "You may as well untie her. She's not going anywhere, and we may need to move her quickly. Now, get Ryan. He's going to deliver my message to John."

The pitiful young man was dragged into the room. He had been beaten or worse. His head hung low between his shoulders.

Pausing as she weakly fastened the buttons on her pyjama top, Caroline pleaded with Maryn. "No, Maryn! Don't send Ryan. John will kill him," she said, her breathy voice coming in gasps.

Ryan looked up briefly at her pity.

"Oh no, he won't. If Ryan doesn't return ..." Maryn paused. "*I* will kill *you*." Maryn grinned and was gone.

"This is taking too long," John complained for the umpteenth time, pacing the halls of the Langley police station.

"Wait! We've got it! An approximate location," Clarke reported eagerly.

"John, wait." It was Alexa. "Maryn Dale sent a message to the Sheraton. We've had it forwarded here."

She stepped aside, allowing Ryan Carstairs to enter the room.

John straightened and advanced on the young man, grasping his shirt in his hands. "Where—is—my—wife?" The words seethed past his clenched teeth.

"He was carrying this," Alexa responded, handing a large envelope to John. Releasing Ryan, John took it in his hands, opening it and looking at the pictures contained within. His hands began to shake and his face went white, though not in grief; this white was pale fury. Dropping the pictures, he grabbed Ryan's shirt in one hand, simultaneously slamming his right fist into the young man's face. Blood exploded from Ryan's nose, spraying onto John's shirt and flowing down the young man's chin. John punched again; his ears were deaf, his eyes were blind, all he saw and heard was fury. His third punch connected with empty air. He was being pulled away. *No, I want it back!* He was going to kill this man—this man who had betrayed his wife, this man who was responsible for the pictures in that envelope. His darling wife stripped, beaten and bound. *No, I won't stop!* The voices could say whatever they wanted. He was going to kill this man. John landed another punch.

"John. Think of Caroline! She would not want you to kill him! John! Stop!" Nothing they said could stop him. He struggled and twisted and fought. John was mad with wrath. It took Hibb, Clarke and Harry to pull him back from Ryan.

"If I don't return in time, they'll kill Caroline!" Ryan's pitiful pleas exploded out of his battered body.

John went perfectly still, his eyes fixed on Ryan's face. "Don't you ever say her name again!" His voice was low, frigid and terrifying, a dragon's frozen bane. Ryan paled more than it seemed possible, the red from his nose contrasting vividly with his pallor.

"I have to deliver … uh … you … a message and return, or they'll kill … her," Ryan stuttered, his voice uneven as he shook visibly.

"What's the message?" The heat of John's ire was palpable.

"You're to—" John's growl interrupted the young man, and tears formed in Ryan's eyes. "Be at the centre of the boardwalk at Lake Sasamat tonight at midnight. Take Ioco past the abandoned school. You mustn't pass there before 11:45 p.m.," Ryan said. "Someone will be watching," he warned, but there was no heat in his voice. "Have the police keep the northern gates open and park in lot C. Descend to the beach and take the trail around the eastern edge of the lake. Come alone. If anyone follows you or if there is anyone else in the vicinity, Maryn will know and she will ki—" Ryan cleared his throat wretchedly. "Kill—come alone and bring one million Canadian dollars and Ca—" John's eyes ignited. "Uh, your wife will be returned to you. Wha … what is your answer?"

"I'll be there. Of course I'll be there!" John took one menacing step toward Ryan, who scuttled back a step. "But Ryan, don't ever come back to work. Don't even think of trying to enter the country again. You're finished! And if I ever have the opportunity, I *will* kill you."

John crouched down, retrieved the pictures from the floor and walked out of the room.

In the chief's office at the Langley police station, John finalized his plan with Sergeant Clarke Milles, Commander James Yang, Hibb, Harry and Alexa.

Clarke looked up from studying the map. "Okay, John. My people are in place. Are you sure this is a good idea?"

"Maryn won't be easily fooled. This is the only solution. I'll take Ioco. If she has someone in those boarded-up buildings, she'll know whether or not I've been followed. After parking in the upper lot, she's only given me a short time to reach the boardwalk," John said.

"Even with the moon tonight," Clarke said, "it's going to be nearly impossible to see once you're in the trees on the path. You'll be vulnerable to anyone with line of sight or … or a flashlight."

John nodded, not caring about any details but the rescue of his wife, his sweet and wonderful wife, tortured by his foe. None of the violence John had endured in his life had ever made him feel as sick and gutted as the thought of Caroline suffering.

"Maryn will meet me in the middle of the footbridge. She will have secreted her men all over the area, and I'll wager she'll have Caroline with her, even if only to taunt me. I need you all to stay well back until Maryn reveals Caroline." John turned to the others. "I don't care what she does to me, you all stay back until Caroline is safe. Promise me! Clarke? Hibb? You'll get Caroline out alive?" Desperately, he held the men's gazes until they each nodded in agreement. There was no way back now.

"The million dollars?" Alexa asked.

"A bluff," John responded confidently. "Maryn doesn't care about the money."

Taking his place behind the wheel of Yang's Jeep Cherokee, John reviewed the route once more, blowing out a breath to try and calm his raging emotions. Following the confusing maze of streets, John desperately searched for those that would take him closer to Caroline.

Chugging up the steep mountain roads, John swerved abruptly as a horn blared, reminding him that he was not the only occupant of the narrow streets. He suffered a moment of doubt that he'd forgotten which side of the road to drive on. Wouldn't Caroline find that amusing? He groaned. *Father, help me get this right. Please.*

The tree-lined road pressed in on both sides, the tall evergreens crowding him, the narrow ribbon of sky visible above. Soon, even that ribbon was crowded out by the overhanging branches of the deciduous joining their coniferous guardians. *Where is it? Where is it?* And then John found the parking lot.

Praying constantly for courage and wisdom—and most of all, that Hibb and Clarke would keep their words—John jogged down the steps of the parking lot, scattering the Canada geese who had settled in for the evening. *Move move move.* Accelerating, he descended quickly to the narrow beach normally covered in an international assortment of families fit with barbecues, umbrellas and beach balls. Tonight, however, it was empty but for John, the geese and a vicious kidnapper.

The dusky green of the lake was deepened to ebony in the night. Walking quickly, John checked the time to see that he only had seven minutes to get to the centre of the footbridge. Accelerating to a jog, he finally made it to the edge of the forest, pressing the signal device in his pocket to the let the others know that he had arrived at the path.

The light of the moon winked out as John stepped into the trees. *Blast! It's as dark as a tomb.* The ground to his left sloped steeply up and, a few feet to the right, dropped into the lake. Unable to check his watch in the grim darkness, John jogged onward, negotiating the gravelled walkway, slipping off the edge of the path more than once. Catching his toes on the unexpected stairs, he lurched forward, scraping his hands on the metal screens put in place to provide traction, certainly not meant for a midnight run. *Augh!*

Emerging briefly from the trees, John caught sight of the footbridge across the opaque waters of the lake. Back into the trees he ran, sliding on the gravel, dodging the broad cedar trunks, the ferns lightly slapping his legs. Accelerating to make up for lost time, he slid off the edge and his foot splashed into the abyss of the lake, wetting his shoe and sock, his heart drumming at the fear and need he felt. *Hurry hurry hurry!*

At last, he'd made it! One more step and John would be out in the open, ready to take his first step onto the footbridge. Heaving in a few deep breaths, John sought to calm the raging beat of his heart, resting with his hands on his knees. After one final deep, deep breath, John stepped onto the footbridge ... out into the open. It was always possible that Maryn's intent was to kill him, but John was fairly certain that she preferred to torment him first.

Sending one last plea heavenward, John commenced the evening's events, shouting west across the southern tip of Lake Sasamat. "I know you're here, Maryn. Come on out. You win."

The stunning brunette sauntered down onto the central bridge across the water, black-handled flick knife in hand. She met John in the middle of the walkway. Circling him once, she came to stand in front of him.

"Hello, John. How are you?" Maryn greeted him with the customary words.

"I'll be much better when you return my wife," he said, not fooled by her calm manner.

"You've lost your wife? How careless of you, John!" Maryn mocked him. "Well, you never were made for marriage, anyway."

"People change," he said.

Maryn's eyes flashed at those words, as though bringing back the memory of a grey-haired man with bright blue eyes and tranquility in his gaze.

"Hands up!" she ordered.

John complied. Clearly agitated, she rested her knife against his side. When he instinctively lowered his hands, she pushed the point of the dagger into his flesh, drawing just a pinprick of blood.

"Keep your hands up, John," she reminded him, leaning in close to his face. "My men are very close at hand. They've got you in their sights and all approaches covered." He felt the knife pressed harder against his side and then dragged slowly across his belly to a button on his shirt. He winced as the air traveled through the tear in the cotton to the newly made slice in his side. It wasn't very deep, but it stung.

Maryn flicked her knife between the cut halves of the fabric. "Hmmm. You always did have the most delicious skin. Let's have a look at you." She stepped a few paces away. "Remove your clothes."

*O-kay.* John studied her for a few moments and then complied, slowly unbuttoning his shirt and sliding it off his arms, setting it neatly on the boardwalk. He had to draw this out as long as possible to give Hibb and Clarke time to get into position.

"Shoes and socks," Maryn purred.

John pried off his shoes and bent down to thumb his socks off.

"Trousers," she said. Maryn licked her lips as though in anticipation of a feast. In disgust, John felt like shuddering at the thought of her mouth. But he kept himself still, lowering his hands to his belt, releasing the buckle and sliding his trousers down and off, piling them neatly with his shirt.

"Mmmm," she moaned. "That will do." She shifted her knife to her other hand and grazed her fingertips along his chest, creating a triangle down to his belly button. "Hands up," she said. He raised his arms. "Lace your fingertips behind your head and turn," she said. "Very slowly."

John complied, feeling her fingernails brush lightly across his chest and shoulders almost like a caress. She dragged a single nail along the whip scars Vlad had imparted in Burma.

"Tch tch. That must have hurt." She moved around to stand in front of him again, stroking the back of her hand down along his ribs and further still, clearly enjoying the sharp inhale he involuntarily released. "You're still a very handsome man, John; a little grey at the temples and a little pudgy in the middle, but still in fine shape." She stroked along him, seeming to be disappointed when his body didn't react. "I'll tell you what. Take me right here, right now, and I'll let your tart go."

*Tart?* John buried the emotion of the insult, focusing instead on Maryn's intent …which *was* very interesting. She still wanted him. Just as Caroline suspected, Maryn was jealous. This could be very useful or very dangerous. But to betray Caroline?

"I can't," he replied.

"What do you mean? Have you lost the ability?" Her voice became mocking or slightly agitated, he wasn't certain.

"Absolute fidelity. My wife has very strict rules about these things," he said.

"Hah! You? Faithful? To one woman? I don't believe it." Maryn sneered at him. John remained silent. "Right here, right now, John, and I'll release her," she said.

"I can't do that to Caroline," he said.

"Just a one-off. You know you want to." Maryn's voice took on a persuasive quality. But he was long past being persuaded by anything that Maryn had to offer. "If nothing else, John, we were always great in the bedroom," she reminded him.

"Were we? I honestly can't remember." John replied before he realized the implication of what he'd said.

Maryn lowered her knife to where her hand had been. *Yikes! Think before you speak, Brock.*

"Perhaps we should remove these. Then what will your tart think of you?" Maryn asked.

"My *wife* will still love me. She'll still want me," he replied confidently.

"What? For decoration?" Maryn mocked.

"There's more to love than the bedroom, Maryn. I'm sorry you haven't experienced that yet," John replied, and he did indeed feel a brief moment of pity for the woman before him.

But that was a miscalculation. An ember glow ignited in Maryn's ebony eyes, and her jaw clenched to contain the fury shuddering through her frame. John could see her visibly calming her angry response, but there was something dangerous in her eyes now. *God, grant me wisdom. Please.*

"I have everything I need, Brock. Don't think there's something you have that I want." She was angry now, and anger made Maryn Dale unpredictable … and vicious.

John remained silent, waiting for a clue as to what would come next. Maryn stepped away from him and seemed to shake the anger off like pond from a soaked dog.

"Oh well. It would have been fun," she said. Her voice was easy and calm again.

Maryn turned and gestured to someone hidden across the footbridge within the dense trees on the opposite shore. Two men appeared, dragging someone behind them … *Caroline!* Bound and gagged, she stared straight at him, terror in her eyes.

Fury surged through his frame, and John took a step in her direction.

Abruptly, the men lifted Caroline up and over the railing. She disappeared immediately into the murky depths of Lake Sasamat.

"No!" John kicked out, swiping Maryn's feet from under her. He grabbed the knife from her hand and took off at a run down the footbridge, stepping up the railing and diving head first into the water.

With her hands and feet bound, she would plunge to the bottom of the deep waters. John kicked out to drive himself further down, frantic, desperate to reach her before she ran out of air. *Shalom! Peace!* The voice drove John to the surface for air. *Calm down, Brock, or your wife will surely die.* Inhaling deeply, John forced himself again toward the bottom of the lake. It was difficult to keep his lungs full of air in the cold shock of the water. But nothing would stop him.

Up to the surface and then down again, he searched. His toes felt the soft embrace of seaweed … except softer. John dove deeper, his lungs burning in his chest, his arms fanning through the opaque water, feeling once again the tickle. He grasped it, pulling up … and the body rose with it. Sliding his hands along her wrists, he found the straps and sliced through, freeing her hands and feet so she could help him haul her to the surface, stroke by stroke. *Faster faster.* Chest on fire, he finally broke through, gasping and heaving to fill his tortured lungs.

John flipped over, still grasping Caroline's shirt, and pulled her to shore. Exhaustion threatened to suck him down, but he refused to submit. Hands were suddenly helping him lift her limp body as well as his own onto dry ground—hands from the men and women who had remained hidden in the bush, approaching only after Maryn had met John on the bridge.

John fell to his knees at his wife's side, feeling for a pulse. It was there, thready, but there. Someone had removed the gag. *Good.* John slapped her gently and then a little more forcefully.

"Caroline! Caroline, wake up!" John started chest compressions, stopping every thirty to give two breaths. "Caroline! Wake up!" He continued, desperate. *Breathe! Please breathe!* The air wasn't entering her lungs. "Caroline, please! I beg you. Wake up! God, help me! I need her!"

Caroline spluttered awake, coughing water onto John and the ground around him. He turned her onto her side so she could empty her mouth.

"Hurry!" she gasped.

Laughing and crying, John pulled her to his chest, repeating "yes yes" as he kissed her again and again. Hibb arrived with a blanket to cover her and another to cover John. Soon the paramedics arrived and were tending to Caroline. John complied when Hibb pulled him away a short distance.

"Let them have at it," Hibb said as he kept his arm firmly around John's shoulder, keeping him in place and out of the way. John's eyes were fixed on Caroline. Harry brought John's clothes over, and he dressed with shaking hands.

The paramedics gave a thumbs-up to John, who pushed back to Caroline's side. *Move move move.* He never left her side again as they bundled her into the ambulance and departed for the hospital. They didn't even bother to explain the rules, that he wasn't allowed to ride in the ambulance. No one wanted to argue with the fierce protectiveness in his eyes. He gripped her hand, his eyes feasting on her face for the entire ride to Vancouver General Hospital. Once there, he was led away to a waiting room where he found Hibb and Clarke already pacing.

"Maryn?" John asked.

"She … er … she escaped past the paramedics while everyone's attention was on Caroline. I'm sorry, John," Hibb and Clarke replied, hopeless echoes of each other.

After a marathon of pacing, a doctor entered the waiting room. "Mr. Brock, your wife is stable. She sustained a variety of injuries: a broken wrist, a cracked rib, and various abrasions and contusions. Essentially, she is bruised from her shoulders to her knees. We've given her something to help her sleep. But she's going to be fine. You can see her now, if you like," the doctor said.

Nodding once, John followed the doctor out of the waiting area and to Caroline's room, finally alone with her. He stood at the door for a time, watching her sleep. He knew he should go to her, but he didn't have the courage to see her wounds up close. Not yet. She looked so peaceful and relaxed, but he knew that, turned away from him as she was, he couldn't see the left side of her face, which he knew had an eye almost swollen shut and three scratches on her cheek. Her left arm was hidden beside her body, encased in plaster or whatever they made casts out of nowadays. And beneath the crisp white sheet and powder-blue blanket lay the battered body of his wife.

Rage built up within him at the thought, the pictures he had seen flashing through his mind. John let the fury wash over him, and then he shaped it into a cube and forced it into a box. He wouldn't let his wrath touch his wife, but he wouldn't let it go either. He would save it and bring it out when he needed it. Someone was going to pay for her suffering.

Next, he was assaulted by a wave of guilt that crashed against his senses. This he allowed to stay, though he pushed it to the edge of his mind. He had opened the door for this to happen. The guilt would always remind him of that. He would never let her be hurt again. He would protect her from everything.

Taking a deep breath to gather his courage, John walked quietly over to the bed, gazing down at Caroline, the single best thing that had ever happened to him. Seeming to sense his presence, she groaned and turned her head toward him. The swelling had gone down a little and the scratches on her cheek were dressed. As he tentatively took her hand, her eyes fluttered open. She smiled weakly when she saw him.

"John," she whispered. "You came for me. You believed in me." Tears streamed from her eyes and a deep sadness sucked at his senses.

"I will always come for you!" he assured her, passion filling his voice.

Reaching up, she hooked the fingers of her right hand in his shirt and drew him down. "Kiss me then. Now," she commanded, smiling slightly. He bent to her and kissed her, but she wouldn't let him off with a simple peck. She wanted him; she wanted to taste and feel and know him. She wanted there to be no doubt that he belonged to her. Opening himself to her, he let her kiss him until she'd had her fill, and then he held her until she drifted back into a drugged sleep, tossing and turning with the memories of what had happened. John sat on the chair next to her holding her hand throughout the night.

Caroline was awakened by the beeping. *Where am I?* She rolled to see if John was beside her and was assaulted by agony—pain ripping through her trunk. Gasping, she squeezed her eyes shut, trying to block out the pain, and then opened them to try to locate the source of the noise that had awakened her. There were tubes rising above her to a clear plastic sac hanging from a metal hook. And when she carefully bent her neck to survey her body, she saw her left arm lying across her, encased in a cast. The rest of her body was covered by a powder-blue hospital blanket. *Hospital?* Of course! *Maryn Dale.*

The last thing she remembered was falling into the water, her hands and feet bound, unable to swim, to escape. *Wait!* Hadn't she seen John? *Oh, I don't know. Boy, Maryn knows how to inflict pain. Every time I breathe, it feels like a giant is squeezing my ribs while wearing wooden gloves. How did John survive this kind of treatment? John. He was here. He came for me. He kissed me. Where is John?*

Turning her head, she could see a tall Styrofoam cup with a straw sticking out of it on the nightstand beside her. *That must contain water. Why does it feel so absurd to want a drink of water after someone has tried to drown you?* As she reached for the cup, a sharp pain stabbed her in the side and she groaned, curling into a ball on her right side.

"Caroline!" John approached her quickly, coming from the direction of the bathroom, still holding the tiny white towel he was using to dry his hands. "Darling, what do you need?"

She groaned in response, "Water."

Brushing the hair tenderly from her face, he offered her the straw. She took several short sips, each breath in between causing a gasp of pain to escape her lips. "Don't they have morphine-laced water in here?"

John suppressed a surprised expression. "I'll ask," he said as he returned the cup to the nightstand and then pulled over a chair to sit beside her.

"You been here the whole time?" she asked, eyes still closed to keep the pain at bay.

"Yes. Why? Could you smell me?" At his familiar words, she opened her eyes to see his soft and tormented gaze.

Trying to reach across to pull him close, she knocked him on the head with her cast. When he flinched at the impact, she began to cry again, each sob chased by a groan. *I'm sorry.* John rubbed the emerging bruise with one hand and slipped his other arm around her. Tenderly, he kissed her, murmuring reassurances as she wept.

"It's all right, baby. It's all over now. Shhh," he said.

"How did you survive this … this treatment? I hurt everywhere!" She groaned. "Oh John, it was horrible!"

John held her while she cried, until a tentative knock interrupted her grief and relief.

Alexa poked her head around the door. "Hi, um … I don't mean to disturb you," she said.

"Then come back later," John grouched.

"John," Caroline reprimanded him softly, eyebrows raised in consternation, sniffing back her tears. "Come in, Alexa. Let me just blow my nose." John held the tissue box while she pulled one out and used it. He perched on the edge of the bed as though acting as a shield between her and the world at large.

Alexa moved tentatively closer to the bed, her eyes flitting back and forth between John and Caroline.

"How are you feeling?" Alexa asked.

"How do you think she's feeling?" John snapped hotly.

Caroline wanted to force him to stop, but the pain made it too difficult to argue, so she sent him on an errand. But he was having none of it.

"I can get you a coffee later. You can't even drink more than a few sips at a time." His words carried ire, but his eyes carried a gentle entreaty: *Don't urge me to go!*

Caroline sighed, a sound interrupted by a gasp. She pulled John nearer and whispered in his ear. "Please calm down. It's harder for me to cope when you're angry." The words did the trick. John visibly calmed and became silent.

Caroline prompted Alexa. "How goes the battle?"

"We're doing everything in our power to apprehend them," Alexa said. "Do you have everything you need?"

"Of cour—" John began, but Caroline squeezed his arm to stop him.

"Yes. John is taking good care of me," Caroline said. "Thank you, Alexa. And thank Harry and Hibb and the others for all they did to save me. We're very grateful." Here, she squeezed John's arm again.

Alexa replied earnestly, "We're glad you made it." She seemed about to say more, but changed her mind when she looked at John, likely because of his stormy gaze. "Well, take care." Alexa gave a small wave and departed.

Caroline turned on John. "You were very rude and ungrateful." His gaze went blank and his face remained impassive. She sighed, shaking her head slightly. "Come here," she commanded, and he leaned down to wrap her in a gentle hug. "Thank you for saving me." He held her until she fell asleep.

She woke three hours later craving a good cup of coffee, and John finally agreed to leave her side and purchase one. Hibb's face appeared at the door, accompanied by a soft knock.

"Hello," Hibb greeted cheerily. "Has our man gone to the hotel to get some sleep?"

"No. I've sent him off to get me a cup of coffee that was not institutionally brewed through a dirty sock," she replied, sticking out her tongue at the thought of the hospital's version of coffee.

"You and John and coffee," Hibb mused, chuckling and then asking kindly, "How are you feeling?"

"I feel pretty awful, to be honest," she said.

"You will for a while. How's our man? Alexa returned looking rather pallid this morning," Hibb said.

"Yes, I'm sure. I'm really worried about him, Hibb. I can't decide if he's wracked with guilt or riddled with rage. On the surface, with me, he's calm and sweet, but he won't tell me anything that happened. He keeps putting me off and saying we'll discuss it when I've recovered. But then, these emotions just leak out—well, lash out—all over Alexa and the doctor and the nurses. I've never seen him like this before. He's not closed or open. I—" Caroline shrugged, wincing at the sensation.

Hibb sat on the chair beside the bed. "He fell apart, Caroline. When he found the phone messages you left for him, he crumbled inside. I thought he was going to completely lose his grip. I think he believes that this is his fault." Hibb patted her hand. "You know that you are his world."

She sighed sadly. "He hasn't slept. I'm really worried."

"Aye, I'm aware." Hibb's gaze never left her face.

"Tell me what happened," she said.

Hibb paused a few moments, and Caroline knew that he was praying. "John wanted to let you know that he would be sleeping in my room so that you wouldn't wait for him, but when we got to your room, you weren't there."

"Hibb? Was he drunk?" she asked.

"John? Drunk? No. He spent the evening drinking coffee. He loosened up and was actually enjoying himself, enjoying the camaraderie. It was good to see. He didn't need alcohol to have a good time, unlike Harry and Clarke and Alexa and the others." Hibb shifted position. "He didn't believe the note." Caroline quirked an eyebrow at him. "Not even for a minute. He insisted you would never leave him until he convinced the rest of us. If he hadn't responded so quickly, we never would have found you in time."

"Maryn told me essentially that," she said, relieved nonetheless to know for sure that John had believed in her.

"When Ryan showed up … I thought John was going to kill him. It took me, Harry and Clarke to pull him off the lad." Hibb shook his head sadly at the memory.

"I was afraid of that. That was Maryn's cruellest joke, I think. Sending the man John blamed within his reach but denying him revenge," she said. "How did you find me?"

"The pyjamas," Hibb said. "Alexa found a CCTV image of a woman wearing red pyjamas being carried from the building, and John identified the pattern on the material. We used the extra surveillance that had been put in place for the Summit to follow the vehicle. Once we located—"

"What are you doing?" John's angry voice interrupted the tale. "What is wrong with you? Can't you see that she's been through enough?!"

Caroline wanted to defend Hibb, but she knew it would only make the situation worse. Hibb sighed loudly, standing and approaching the door.

"Katie wanted me to tell you that she's praying for you," Hibb said, directing his statement to Caroline.

"Thank you, Hibb. Ask her to pray for John too, okay?" Caroline requested. Hibb nodded, said goodbye and left.

"Why do you want her to pray for me?" John inquired gently, mystified.

"Don't you think you could use some prayer?" she asked.

"Yes, of course," he agreed. "But—"

"Sweetheart, I'm worried abou—"

John's gaze shifted. "I'm fine. You're the one who was injured."

Instead of responding, she just stared at him for a long time. *What is going on inside that mind of yours, my darling?* John eventually ducked his head, she supposed to avoid her gaze. Instead, he began to prepare the coffees he'd acquired, adding the cream and sugar in appropriate amounts, and then setting them unsampled on the bedside table.

*Father, what can I do for him?* "Bear? Would you hold me?" she asked.

His gaze gentled. "Of course." He moved to sit on the chair beside the bed and wrap his arms around her.

"No. I mean really hold me. Please, lie down with me," she said.

His eyes widened a fraction. "Caroline, I can't. The nurses will think—"

"Didn't you once say we shouldn't care what others think?" She pulled a small smile, holding his gaze. He seemed to struggle with himself for a brief moment and then capitulated, giving in, she hoped, to what he truly wanted to do.

"All right. Shift over," he said. Prying off his shoes, he stretched his body alongside hers, excruciatingly careful of her injuries. She saw some of the tension ebb from his frame. Rolling onto her side, she pulled herself as close to his body as she could manage on the hospital bed, entwining their legs and resting against his chest, ruffling his shirt with her breathing.

"Sing to me," she said. He complied, and she hoped that the music of love and fidelity he offered her would begin to soothe his own tightened and tortured heart.

Caroline woke gradually to the feelings of comfort and love and a full bladder. John was leaning on her, breathing heavily into her hair. She didn't want to wake him by leaving the bed, but she needed to find the toilet. Soon. *Why didn't they leave the catheter in? It was so lovely to pee without having to struggle to the bathroom.* She chuckled lightly at her own humour.

Extricating herself as gently as possible, she lowered the side rail and slipped out from beneath John's arm, limping away. Returning to the bed, she slid a chair closer and watched him sleep. Much of the worry and pain was extinguished in repose.

As she sat there, she noticed a new bouquet of flowers on the dinner tray. *Where did those come from?*

"Stop watching me and come back to bed," he said, humour in his voice, his eyes still closed.

"What will the nurses think?" she teased.

John growled lightly. "Woman. Get in this bed!"

Caroline laughed, as hard as her aching muscles would allow. "Oh yes, m'lord. Anything you say, m'lord." He pulled her carefully against him as she slid gingerly onto the bed. She popped the buttons on his shirt, sliding her hand along his chest.

Pressing his hand against hers to still its movement, he remarked, "If you keep that up, we truly will be compromised."

She chuckled lightly, continuing to lightly trace his ribs. "John?"

"Mmhmm."

"Did you buy those flowers?"

"Yes."

"When?" she asked.

"While you were sleeping?"

She smiled. *How on earth did he manage that?* "Thank you. I don't know why it is, but getting flowers always make me feel beautiful."

"You are beautiful," he said, and she believed that he believed it with all his heart.

She kissed him on the chest. "You're very nice. You know that, don't you?"

He chuckled wryly. "Nice. Just what I strive for."

She laughed softly. "I love you."

"I love you, too. So much." He pulled her hand to his lips and kissed each finger. Soon, she drifted off to sleep.

When Caroline woke again, John was sitting on the chair beside her with two fresh cups of coffee and a newspaper, his feet propped on the edge of the hospital bed.

"Feeling any better?" he asked from behind the wall of newsprint.

"Oh, not really. Well, maybe a little. Is one of those coffees for me?" she asked, pushing to sit on the edge of the bed. He put aside the paper and handed her a cup. "John?" she began.

"Yes," he responded, watching her face.

"Tell me what happened. Tell me what's going on inside your head," she said.

His brow furrowed, but whatever he was going to say was interrupted by a knock on the door and Hibb's face appearing inside the room.

"Come in," Caroline called, sighing in frustration.

"I'm sorry to disturb you, but I have news," Hibb apologized, obviously seeing the look on her face.

"What news?" John's voice came out tense, anger flirting around the edges.

"Maryn Dale has been apprehended," Hibb said, watching John.

"How?" John asked, teeth clenched.

"The RCMP located her when she tried to cross the border. She used an identity known to the CIA. She was furious, I guess, almost intimidated the officers into releasing her, but fortunately some junior Customs official had the foresight to contact the RCMP, and they instructed Customs to hold her," Hibb said.

"Did they get her henchmen?" asked Caroline.

"They arrested the big ginger-headed blighter with the scar across his eye," Hibb said.

Caroline cheered. "Oh yes! That's the fellow who beat me. Did they have to subdue him with force or anything?"

A small chuckle escaped Hibb's lips. John sent him a missile of warning that clearly said, *Nothing about this is funny!*

Hibb sobered immediately. "No, unfortunately. He was quite a coward when it came down to it; gave himself up," Hibb replied.

"He was only able to assault a helpless woman," John muttered, heat seething through his teeth. Caroline watched him intently, her brow furrowing. Oblivious to her observation, he asked, "What about Ryan Carstairs?"

"He escaped with the Tibetan," Hibb said. "I guess they had split up at the border, and those two traveled further east, heading into the Kootenays toward Alberta. Maryn seemed quite willing to give them up, but she doesn't actually know where they are."

"They've got to find him. He can't get away with this," John asserted darkly.

"Hibb, thank you for the news, but could you excuse us, please?" Caroline said.

Once Hibb had departed, Caroline took John's hand and urged him to sit on the side of the bed.

"John—" she began.

"Don't start," he said, interrupting her. "He's got to pay. He betrayed you, me, the entire team. He betrayed his country. I can't let him get away with this."

"How did he betray me? When did he betray me?" she asked softly.

"When he crawled into bed with that traitorous whore!" John said, and she was shocked by the vehemence in his voice.

Caroline took a deep breath, bracing herself for what she felt she needed to do. "Then you betrayed me as well," she asserted simply.

A look of shock broke John's anger. "What do you mean?" he asked breathlessly.

"You crawled into bed with 'the whore' as well. If you hadn't slept with her all those years ago, would this have happened?" she asked. Grief flooded John's face as the truth assailed him. "And what about all the other women you've been with?" she said.

"I … I … " He faltered quickly, and Caroline could see the deep sorrow in his eyes.

"John, the deeds of our lives are written in a book, and after we die, on Judgment Day, we are each going to have to stand before God and hear those deeds read out. Heaven or hell depends on that book." She paused to let him consider that. The agony etched across his features tore at her heart, but she knew he needed to hear this. "What if hell isn't about burning and fire? What if hell is replaying the worst moments of our lives again and again? How would that make you feel?"

"Hopeless. Is that what you think? I can't face that. Caroline?" he beseeched her.

"When you became a Christian, Jesus took the book of your life and tore out all the pages. He threw them into the deepest sea and they will never … *never* … be looked at again. Jesus, who lived as a human on this earth but was perfect, the perfect Son of God, replaced your imperfect record, the record of your wrong deeds that he had destroyed, with his perfect record. When you stand before God at the end of time, He will open your book and see Jesus's perfect record, and He will declare you perfect. You do not have to pay the consequences for your sins, because Jesus already did on the cross. When we willingly accept His sacrifice, we become perfect in God's eyes."

John's eyes became hopeful … until a new thought occurred to him and his gaze fell. "What about the things I've done wrong since then? You, of all people, know the mess I've made of my life, of our life together."

"God doesn't ask us to become perfect when we accept Jesus Christ into our hearts. He asks us to be willing to let Him lead our lives. He knows we'll still mess it up, but He forgives. One time, in Burma, you asked me about King David, about why he was called 'a man after God's own heart' when he had made so many mistakes. Do you remember what I told you?"

John nodded once. "It wasn't that he was perfect, it was because he was willing to follow God's will, and when he messed up, he was truly sorry."

"Yes. You're God's now, aren't you?" she asked, taking his hand and playing with his wedding ring.

"Yes. I do want to follow Him, even though sometimes I don't really know how to do what He says. But I wouldn't give up the peace He's brought me for anything," he said.

"There's a verse in the Bible that says, 'I believe; help thou mine unbelief.' I love that verse because it says that I can be willing to follow God but still need His help to do it."

"What are you trying to tell me?" John asked.

"Think about this," she said. "If all your misdeeds were placed on one side of a scale and all Ryan's were placed on the other, which way would the scale tip? Yet you don't have to pay the eternal consequences of your sins, because you handed your life over to Jesus and let Him replace your imperfect record with His perfect one. Do you really want to send Ryan to hell now, with all of his deeds still written in his book?"

"He has to pay." John's words were the same, but his tone was completely different.

"Before the law, he has to pay. Will you send him before God … like this … when you've been freed yourself?" she asked.

He took her hand and played with her fingertips for a long time. "Do you hold my past against me? Do you blame me for Maryn Dale?" John asked.

She brushed her hand up his arm and stroked her fingertips along his jaw until he looked at her. "Romans 8:1 and 2 says, 'There is therefore now no condemnation to them which are in Christ Jesus who walk not after the flesh, but after the Spirit. For the law of the Spirit of life in Christ Jesus has made me free from the law of sin and death.' No. I don't hold Maryn Dale against you. Nor do I hold Ryan against you, or any of the mistakes you've made in your past. I love you, John." She offered a small smile. "I'm not naïve. I know who you are, who you really are. You don't seem to know, though, that you are a wonderful man." She smiled at him. "Maryn and Ryan, they are desperately in need of a Saviour. You, however, you are my knight in shining armour. You believed in me. You came for me, and I will always treasure that gift from you. I love you."

"Forgive me? Please," he begged her earnestly.

"I forgive you."

# Chapter Fifteen
## *Take Me Home*

The doctor stopped by after supper to examine Caroline and answer any questions about her care.

"Mrs. Brock," he began. "You are doing much better, and I don't see why you can't go home tomorrow."

"She is clearly not well enough to be released!" John protested vehemently.

"Mr. Brock, I understand that your wife is still in a great deal of discomfort, but there is nothing that requires the presence of a physician. Take her home and let her rest."

"Of course I'll let her rest, but she's hardly in a position to sit for a six-hour flight home," John protested.

"No, that's true," the doctor admitted. "Do you have somewhere local that you could stay for a few days until she's well enough to fly?"

"We're—"

"John!" Caroline interrupted, using her *mommy* voice, something she'd never done with him before. "Stop giving the doctor a hard time!"

John fixed her with a hard stare, but she made sure that her tone left no room for argument. "Fine!" he conceded ungallantly.

She turned to the doctor, "Thank you for everything."

The doctor nodded and then shook his head as he exited.

Turning back to John, she felt pity at his driving need to protect her. "Sweetheart? Bear?" The endearment drew his eyes to her. "Come here, please." He walked over to her where she sat on the edge of the hospital bed. Reaching for him, she drew him closer to stand between her pyjamaed legs, resting her head against his chest and holding him tightly around the waist. She sighed deeply, and the expansion of her rib cage caused her breath to catch for a moment. When he moved to look down at her in concern, she pulled him back against her. He complied, holding her until she moved to release him.

"I want to go back to London," Caroline said.

"We are not flying all the way to the UK when you're in this condition," John asserted hotly, likely still annoyed that she had contradicted him in front of the doctor.

"I want to go home," she pouted.

"That sounds more sensible to me. Can you stay at the house in Grand Prairie?" he asked in obvious relief.

"Grand Prairie?" she said, querying his intention in mentioning it.

"Do you want me to call your mother to come stay?" he asked gently.

"My mo—I want to go home!" Caroline raised her voice. She was tired and sore and quickly losing her patience with this stubborn man. "I don't want to go to Grand Prairie or Iqaluit or Smiths Falls or anywhere else! I want to go home!" She groaned from the extra breath it took to yell at her husband.

"I don't think you're ready to travel that distance yet," he replied firmly.

"I want to go home," she insisted more quietly, still pouting.

His voice left no room for argument. "Caroline. I let you have your way about being released from hospital, but I am not putting you on an airplane when you're in this condition." He stood with his hands on hips, letting her know that no matter what she said, she wasn't going to get her way.

"Fine! Want to be a Nazi prison guard? Go ahead!" She reclined on the bed, folding her arms angrily across her chest and rolling away from him.

"Very mature," he quipped, obviously annoyed. She turned a blazing glare at him, taking in his angry stance and the red flush of his cheeks.

"Oh, go boil your head! Stop glaring at me and come to bed! Impossible man!" She released her arms, rolled to face him and lifted the sheet to invite him into the bed.

His body relaxed, and he smiled. "How could any man resist such a sweetly phrased invitation?"

She chuckled then and sighed. "Love you, you grizzly bear."

"Love you too, you stubborn—"

"Hey!" She reached out to lightly smack him on the hip, but he intercepted her hand, kissing the palm and resting it against his chest as he reached his other arm around to gather her close.

Caroline was released from hospital the next day in spite of John's misgivings. Clarke arranged a safe house for them to occupy until Caroline was well enough to travel. Well, until John decided that she was well enough. *Grrr!*

The apartment was too small, she decided, and not in a very nice neighbourhood, being a little too near Quebec and East 13th for Caroline's comfort. The dog doo in the hallway and the water dripping through the ceiling into the kitchen sink only increased her annoyance at being forced to remain away from home. Her exhaustion, however, kept her angst at bay as John tucked her into bed. Soon, she drifted into a fitful slumber.

A screech on the street, either human or automotive, woke Caroline in the middle of the night, alone in an unfamiliar bedroom. The sound had thrust her out of a nightmare where a group of anonymous faces were lined up, each holding a leather strap. As the first arm was poised to strike, she awoke, panting and shivering in fear. *John. Where's John? Did he leave me alone? Oh, man, I need to pee.*

Struggling out of the too-soft mattress, Caroline went in search of the bathroom, knowing that if she didn't find the tiny puce-green room soon, she would need towels and not toilet paper. *Where's John? He wouldn't leave me alone, would he?* Emerging from the bathroom with dripping hands because there was, in fact, no towel to be found, Caroline stopped short when she saw the six-foot frame curled up on the couch.

Frustration surged through her. "John! What are you doing out here?!" she yelled.

He leapt to his feet, drawing a Glock pistol from under the couch cushion he'd been resting on. "What is it? What's wrong?" His eyes searched the room as he stood in a battle stance. "Caroline! Are you all right?"

"Yes, I'm all right. What on earth are you doing on the couch? Come to bed! No wonder I was cold. I—"

He straightened and advanced on her. "You scared the crap out of me! Don't ever do that again! Caroline—"

"Why are you sleeping out here?" she demanded hotly.

"Caroline! For—" He cut himself off and swallowed the profanity that wanted to leap across the room and throttle her for scaring him like that. "Go back to bed!" he ordered and then changed his mind. "Wait! Come here." He engaged the safety and tucked the pistol into the back of his waistband. He extended his arms toward her. "Please. Come here. You nearly scared the life out of me."

His gentle order quelled her anger. She walked over, her right arm braced across her battered ribs, and walked into his embrace, melting against him. "I'm sorry," she said. "I didn't mean to startle you. I was having a nightmare and I woke alone, and then there you were out here on the couch and I just—" She stopped, pressing her body against his. She inhaled deeply, breathing in the scent of him. "I just wanted you."

His arms tightened around her. "Go back to bed. Get some rest," he murmured gently, leading her into the bedroom. He retrieved an extra blanket from the closet to cover her.

"Please come to bed with me, John. Please," she begged him.

Slowly, he shook his head. "You need to rest."

Grasping his sleeve, she tugged him toward the mattress. "Please." Her eyes filled with tears. "Why don't you want to be with me? John?"

Clearly tormented, he replied, "I … I want you … but I don't want to hurt you."

"You won't hurt me," she reassured him. "I want you." She looked up into his face, beseeching him. "I need to have you with me."

"I would always rather be with you, my love," he murmured, relenting. Placing the gun safely on the bedside table and sliding out of his jeans, he slipped in beside her. She instantly wrapped her body around him, nuzzling into his side. He sighed. It wasn't the happy sigh, but it was close enough for the moment.

It was the drugs shooting at the Three Lions on East 9th that finally convinced John to take Caroline home. With Ryan Carstairs and Sonam Narayan still at large, the RCMP insisted that John and Caroline were at risk and needed their protection.

"I can protect her better myself," John insisted grumpily.

"Look," Clarke began. "I'm only the bearer of this news, not the manufacturer."

“What about Maryn Dale?” John asked, feeling the urge to spit.

“The British government has allowed us to keep her until she stands trial for kidnapping. Following that, she will be extradited to Britain to stand trial for treason.” Clarke paused to think for a moment, scratching his cheek absentmindedly. “I can try to locate a different safe house for you. It shouldn’t be difficult getting permission after last night’s shooting.”

John shook his head. “No. No, thank you.” He turned to Caroline. “You still want to go home?”

“If by home you mean our house in Twickenham, then yes,” she said.

John nodded at her and then turned back to Clarke. “Can you get us on a secure flight to the UK?”

“That shouldn’t be a problem,” Clarke said.

Caroline was so excited to board the Bombardier for home. Vancouver, Grand Prairie, Smiths Falls—these would always be places of familiarity and warmth for Caroline. She would always, in her heart, be a Canadian, but her life with John was in London, and she anticipated her return with eagerness.

The first hour was pleasant, seated beside John, holding his hand and reminiscing. The second to the sixth hours were uncomfortable; her chest ached, her head pounded, she couldn’t find comfort in any position. She told John thirty-five times that he had been right about her not being well enough to travel. She told him sixty-two times that she was sorry for being grumpy. And she told him off three hundred and twenty-one times for everything from bumping her with his elbow to drinking from her bottle of water.

She heard him singing, low and quiet. “That sounds surprisingly like ’N Sync’s song, ‘U Drive Me Crazy’,” she said.

He stopped and turned to her. “Sorry,” he murmured, looking acutely chagrined.

“John? Can you please see if there are any sleeping pills in the med-kit?” she asked.

“Of course,” he said, and he looked relieved that she wasn’t scolding him.

He brought her the bottle of medicine, and she chuckled at the expressive sigh he released when she swallowed the pills. “I’m sorry, Bear. You really are wonderful, you know,” she said.

"Anything for you, my love," he sang to a tune of his own making.

She smiled brightly at him.

"Now go to sleep," he said.

She laughed.

Two weeks later, Caroline made her way out of the computer lab and onto the Grid, wondering at the sight of Hibb, Harry and Alexa staring at the security pods.

"What's wrong?" she asked, puzzled by their manner. She tapped Hibb on the elbow. "What is wrong?"

First exchanging a glance with Harry and Alexa, Hibb took a long breath and then responded, "Maryn Dale has escaped."

Caroline blanched. "Where's John?" Harry shrugged, and Alexa shook her head. "Where is John?" Caroline said. "Where's John? Where is he? If Maryn's escaped, he could—" She rounded on Hibb, raising her voice. "Where is John?!"

Hibb took her by the shoulders. "We don't know. He went still, turned and walked away. What do you think he'll do?"

"I think—" she began.

John appeared at the pods, waiting as the bulletproof doors closed and then opened again. Caroline was struck by the frigid blue rage in his eyes as he grabbed her by the elbow and pulled her into the pods. Not a sound escaped him as she walked with him down to their car, his hand still firmly on her elbow. *O-kay. What is going on?*

Once he pulled the car out of the Thames House parking garage, she put her hand on his leg, hoping that her touch would get his attention where her mere presence hadn't.

"John. Where are we going?" she asked very softly.

"Maryn Dale escaped," he responded, studying the traffic.

"I know," she said.

He abruptly pulled to the curb, screeching to a stop in a yellow no-parking zone. "How did you find out? When did you find out?" His voice was intense as he leaned into her to obtain his answers.

"Two minutes after you did!" she exclaimed. "The others were staring at the pods, so I asked what happened." He sighed heavily and slumped back in his seat. "You're really beginning to concern me, John," she said.

"Don't be concerned." He straightened in his seat, sliding his emotions behind his blank gaze.

"You don't seriously believe that's going to work, do you?" She grasped his sleeve as he reached to put the car into gear. "Please tell me what's going on."

Suddenly subdued, he cast a tentative glance in her direction. "I'm taking you to a safe house."

She turned sharply to face him, wincing at the pull on her ribs. "Oh, no, you're not! I am not being shut away from you in some safe house for an undetermined length of time. No! No way!"

His eyes pleaded with her. "Caroline, I need you to be safe."

"Then keep me safe," she retorted.

He sighed, resting his forehead against the steering wheel until Caroline warned him to pull away from the curb, as they were being advanced upon by a Rita the Meter Maid. She waited until he moved the car back into traffic.

"When I'm at work, I'm safe, correct?" she asked, and he nodded in response to her statement. "At home, you're with me. Safe?" she asked. He nodded again. "When Tor and his assassins were after you—"

"Who were hired by Maryn."

"Yes. When they were after you, we were only in danger when we were away from home or work. Right?" She relaxed into the car seat.

"Wrong. Bombs," he replied.

"True. But they were set by Grendahl's men, not by Maryn. You know that Maryn prefers the personal touch," she said. "You could teach me self-defence and how to fire a weapon so that I can better protect myself."

He glanced aside at her, glanced again and then chuckled. "Like you would get in field training, perchance? Do you always get your way in the end? Did Henry ever notice?"

She smiled, pleased that he could talk about Henry in such a casual manner. "Possibly," she replied mysteriously. "Fortunately, the two of you can't compare notes. And don't think I'm going to fill you in on the ways he got his own way," she warned.

They drove in silence for a time, and Caroline knew that he was considering all possibilities. Finally, he pulled the car into the parking lot of the London Library.

"All right. I'll concede the argument on one condition." As he turned his look of intensity toward her she sobered, seeing the fierce love and protectiveness in his eyes.

"As long as I don't have to agree to leave you, I'll do whatever you ask," she told him.

He studied her and finally nodded. "During the time that Maryn is at large, in any safety considerations, you do exactly as I say without question or argument. Agreed?"

Her eyes widened. "You're going to be bossier than usual?" She grinned, but her smile soon faded.

His voice was gentle as he said, "I'm serious, Caroline. I understand now that I cannot keep you safe, that your life is in God's hands. However, I can do my best to keep you as safe as possible while still loving you enough, giving you what you need, to make you happy. In this matter, I need your submission to my needs to be rather traditional. But in exchange, I vow to be your obedient servant in all things not pertaining to your safety … without question. I'll cook. I'll clean the house, do the laundry and watch any romantic movie you desire. I'll even talk about my feelings." His face took on a pained expression. "Anything."

She chuckled lightly at his version of sacrifice. But what won her over was the love in his eyes. "Okay, John. I promise," she said.

He nodded. "I'll teach you to shoot. We'll get you a handgun that you will carry with you at all times. You won't go anywhere off the Grid without me. I will also be carrying my Glock as I did during the active threat from Grendahl. You will carry a panic button and two mobile phones, one of which will be directly linked to the Grid." He turned to study her face for a moment. "Agreed?"

"Agreed." She nodded in confirmation.

"You and I will practice hand-to-hand every night at home. Agreed?"

"Yes. You're beginning to frighten me," she said.

"Better a little frightened than in the clutches of Maryn Dale. Don't you agree?" he said, a bland look on his face.

"Do I have to agree with everything you say as well?" she asked, hiding her mischievous grin.

Deadpan, he replied, "I thought I was the incorrigible one."

She smiled softly at him. "I will do as you ask."

John nodded and drove them back to Thames House, escorting her onto the Grid before making his way to the DG's office.

"John, do you believe that Maryn Dale will come after Caroline?" Sir William asked.

"Yes. I believe that she will retreat for a time to re-consolidate her power and then come after her. Maryn wants revenge. That evidence you showed the courts is conclusive. Maryn passed state secrets to General Akram and Colonel Shing. She has lost everything. MI-6 has hung her out to dry. She'll stand trial and go to prison either here for treason or in Canada for kidnapping."

"Why would she not simply take this opportunity to disappear?" Sir William asked.

"Maryn is conceited. She believes that she can attack Caroline, and thereby me, and then disappear. She doesn't for a moment consider losing," John said.

"Very well. Are we placing Caroline under close protection?" Sir William asked.

John cleared his throat. "No. She … er … won't allow it." John blushed. "We've come up with a plan."

"Well, Mr. Brock, that wife of yours has certainly set your life spinning on its axis," Sir William said.

Suppressing a fond smile, John agreed. "Yes, sir. She certainly has."

"You're a lucky man, John. I envy you. Though I would appreciate it if you never let my wife know I said that," Sir William said wryly and then continued. "I'll pull in all our assets and resources and see if we can find Ms. Dale," Sir William said.

"And Ryan Carstairs," John said. A black look crossed his face before he brought his expression back under control.

"Yes," Sir William agreed reluctantly, clearly concerned by the new darkness in John's gaze.

# Chapter Sixteen
# Aid From My Enemies

Caroline flung open the door to the workout room. "Hyah!" she shouted, releasing a steady stream of water onto … an empty weight bench? Stepping further into the room, she scanned the furniture. "John?" she called. His name was quickly chased by a squeal as he popped up from behind the hideously ugly soft chair and squirted her with his water gun.

Ducking back into the hall, Caroline dodged around a curious Rufus and into the spare room, secreting herself behind the door. Waiting, she tried to quiet her breathing. *This is hopeless. He's always far more patient than I am,* she mused affectionately. *For a man with such a serious job and such a horrible childhood, he really is the greatest playmate. I get it now when the Bible talks about becoming like a child. There's a depth of joy and hope and faith that becomes so difficult to attain once the responsibilities of life begin to weigh upon you. I thought that when the children died, I would never again experience the pleasure of play.*

As important as speculation could be to personal growth, it wasn't a substitute for diligence. Three rapid streams of water hit Caroline in the belly.

"Hey! That's cheating!" she complained, barrelling out of the spare room, guns blazing, only to find a completely empty foyer. Even Rufus had disappeared.

*Upstairs or downstairs?* Deliberating quickly, Caroline chose *up* and stealthily ascended the stairs to the great room, scanning the environment for any indication of John's whereabouts. *Maybe instead of tae kwon do and weapons training, I should have enrolled in a counter-surveillance class.* Slowly, she popped her head above the top step and quickly surveyed the upper room. She spotted the tip of a water gun peeking out from behind the desk. *Hah, got him!* Crawling across the space, she circled to the other side of the desk planning to come up behind her husband.

"Hello," John said, greeting her cheerily before expressing the oxygenated hydrogen from a turkey baster. Spluttering, she spun to fire on his retreating form, chasing him directly into the bathroom, where she was greeted again with a cheery "hello" and the shower nozzle. She squealed.

Finally, their laughter simply hurt too much to continue the battle, and Caroline conceded the victory to John, who claimed his spoils in a languid kiss. After wiping off all the wet surfaces, they tossed the towels into the dryer, and John offered to make hot cocoa.

Caroline moved to answer the ring of the front doorbell at, of course, the same moment that the telephone rang. She called up the stairs, "I'll get the door. You get the phone." And then she stepped outside.

"Cheers," John acknowledged Caroline's instruction, greeting the caller with a "Yes?"

"John, it's Sharon. Dad's had a heart attack. You need to come and make your peace with him," Sharon said.

"Is he asking or are you?" John said.

"I am. You need to get over this, John," she said, clearly angry.

John's reply was immediate, his voice emotionless. "Not really. No, I don't."

Suddenly, he realized that the front door of the house was open and he couldn't see Caroline. Panicking, he dropped the phone onto its cradle without a goodbye and launched himself down the steps.

None other than Ryan Carstairs stood on the path to John's own front door, the man who had betrayed his wife to Maryn Dale's abuse. In two steps, John came face to face with his foe, fisting his hands in Ryan's coat and pulling him close. Holding Ryan's gaze with his fiery heat, John knocked him onto his back with a ferocious blow. Ryan's eye immediately began to swell.

"John!" Caroline shouted from the front stoop. "Please listen. He's come to help."

"*In. Now!* Get in the house *right now!*" When she hesitated, he glanced at her. "You gave me your word."

"Yes. Just listen, please, before you do anything. For me." She turned and walked into the house, closing the door behind her.

"Lock it!" he called and heard the click when she complied. His instructions exploded from his chest like bullets. "Gun!" He imagined her furrowed brow as she heard his command but knew she would comply. She'd given her word.

After a moment, he heard her knock twice on the door, signalling her return. Backing to the door, he fixed his eyes on Ryan, who remained on the ground, propped on his elbows. Caroline passed John his Glock through the letterbox, and then he heard her race upstairs to retrieve her own. John disengaged the safety, loaded the first bullet into the chamber, and took aim at Ryan's chest. Immediately, a flash of pictures assaulted his mind, but he pushed it aside, returning his focus to his enemy.

"What did I tell you, Ryan?" John inquired, his voice as chilling as the misty evening air.

Ryan bore a look of terror blended with despair on his face. "You said you would kill me if you ever saw me again. Go ahead. I've already told Caro—uh, your wife what I came to tell you. Go ahead. I can't live with myself anymore." Ryan burst into tears. "Kill me quickly. I find I'm not as brave as I used to think," he said through his sobs.

John's voice was hard. "Do you honestly think that there is pity in my heart?" John said. Ryan shook his head as an answer, and John watched him carefully. "Tell me what you told Caroline. Now!" John demanded.

"Maryn Dale has escaped. She's going to come after Caroline again. She's … she's …" Ryan's pitiful gaze rose to John's face. "She's going to hurt her this time, John. Worse than anything you can imagine."

*Father, please no!* John swallowed the bile in his throat. "Why are you here?"

"What do you mean?" Ryan asked desperately, his sobs subsiding. "I came to warn you."

"Why?" John said.

"Caroline has only ever been kind to me," Ryan replied piteously.

"Let me be clearer," John said. "Why would Maryn let you out of her sight when you already refused an order from her with respect to Caroline?"

"She doesn't realize that I know her plans," Ryan said.

"Strip!" John ordered, motioning with his gun for Ryan to stand. "To the skin." John followed Ryan's panicked gaze to the tall evergreens running out diagonally from the front corners of the house, perfectly concealing them from the neighbours. Across the street there was nothing but an empty field.

Ryan did as ordered, revealing that he possessed no weapon of any kind or any tracking device that didn't have to be swallowed, inhaled or inserted. "Leave your clothes there. Cover yourself and walk ahead of me." John ordered Ryan to stop at the front door. The young man had already started to shiver in the cold night air. "Caroline?"

"Yes?" she replied through the door.

"Unlock the door. Fetch my dressing gown and the handcuffs and stand with them at the side of the stairs in the great room. Remain armed. Yes?" John said.

"Yes," she said. He heard the click of the lock followed by her footsteps on the stairs.

His Glock pressed against the base of the young man's spine, John reached around Ryan, turned the doorknob and pushed the door open. Caroline was not visible anywhere. John forced Ryan up against the wall beside the stairs—moving the handgun to press against the base of Ryan's skull, a sure death if the gun went off—and ordered him to link his fingers behind his head.

"Toss me the handcuffs." They landed squarely in John's waiting hand. He pushed the handgun into the back of his jeans and roughly trapped the young man's wrists in the cuffs, tightly closing them around flesh and bone. "Dressing gown." It landed, hooked across John's arm. John pulled it tightly around Ryan's body, covering him and then using the tie to bind his arms securely to his sides.

John pushed Ryan up the stairs, instructing him to kneel on the hardwood floor at the top. John kept his Glock pointed at the young man's chest, moving to sit on the edge of the couch back. He instructed Caroline to shut and lock the front door and engage the security alarm, which she did. Then he instructed her to contact Aubrey at once and leave the phone on speaker so that he could record everything.

John's attention never wavered from Ryan. "Now, you tell me everything I want to know, and we won't need to investigate your threshold of pain."

"John—" Caroline said with reprimand in her voice.

"Your word, if you recall. Yes?" John said.

"Yes," she agreed.

"If I tell you to shoot him—" John left the sentence hanging, awaiting her response.

"I shoot him," she agreed.

John nodded, satisfied. "Ryan, it's your turn to speak."

Ryan's voice quivered as he spoke. "After Lake Sasamat, I escaped with Sonam Narayan. He's a cruel man with unusual tastes." Ryan shuddered. "Perfect for Maryn. We traveled around quite a bit, sleeping rough, spending nights in dark alleys or forests, depending on which country we were in at the time. Finally, when we reached Dresden in Germany, I thought we'd settle in and lay low, but there was a package waiting at the dingy motel, a package from Maryn. It contained money, false passports and two plans. One plan was how to facilitate her escape, and the second was a backup plan on how to kidnap Caroline." Ryan's tormented gaze flitted to Caroline and back to John, and a sob caught in his throat. "I was in agony, you must believe me. I didn't want any part of it!"

Ryan subsided into silence until John's terse instruction to carry on. "I got my hands on some schnapps and got Sonam drunk. It took a while, believe me. He has a great capacity for alcohol consumption. I kept at it until he told me what they planned for Caroline. Once he passed out drunk, I made my escape. I took my false passport and fled east to the Czech Republic and then to France. I used my contacts there to establish a new identity, but while I was awaiting the money transfer from my emergency fund, I heard that Maryn had escaped."

"You immediately departed, I imagine," John added sarcastically.

Ryan's outlook fell. "I was afraid. I boarded the airplane to Santa Cruz, but I couldn't do it; I couldn't sit back and let this happen. Once I knew what they were planning to do … to Caroline, of all people." He looked at John, pleading in his eyes. "She is the kindest person I've ever known. I couldn't let her be hurt, not like that." The look of pleading in his eyes intensified. "John, I didn't hurt her … in Vancouver. You know that, don't you?" He turned his pleading eyes to Caroline. "You told him, didn't you? Caro—"

Abruptly, John lurched from his perch on the edge of the couch. "You speak to me!" he insisted. Once Ryan nodded, hanging his head, John asked, "Does Maryn know you've come to London?"

"No. When I left the Tibetan, I went to France, adopted a new identity and traveled to South America. There's no way she could have known about the new identity," Ryan said.

"Are you certain?" John asked.

"Yes, it's the only information I kept from her, some dormant spook instinct perhaps. I told her everything else." Ryan slumped back on his heels.

John was thoughtful for a moment and then agreed. "All right. If you're telling the truth, then I will give you the opportunity to help us stop Maryn. You will accompany my officers—" Ryan seemed to flinch at the implication that he was no longer one of *them*. "—to Thames House, where you will cooperate in all ways in the apprehension of Maryn Dale. If you cooperate, I will speak for you at your hearing, but as far as I can see it, you will spend time in prison. What say you?"

"Yes. I'll help," Ryan said. "I give you my—"

John's voice was glacial cold. "Your word means nothing to me, Ryan. You are nothing to me. Do you understand? You will go to prison for what you did."

"I understand," Ryan responded, resigned.

John was visibly surprised by Ryan's answer, having expected pleading or more sobs.

"Aubrey?" John called toward the telephone.

"I've got it all, John," Aubrey replied through the speakerphone.

"Send Jade and Alexa to pick him up and escort him to the dungeons," John said.

"Very good," Aubrey replied. "They're already on their way."

Caroline disengaged the phone when Aubrey hung up. They waited, Ryan still on his knees and John's handgun still pointed at the young man's chest. Caroline sat in the chair behind the desk until the doorbell rang. John left the handgun with Caroline, instructing her to keep it trained on Ryan.

John let Jade in, informing Alexa that Ryan's clothes were on the front lawn.

"You're lucky no one called the police if you had him strip on the front lawn," Alexa mused aloud.

"I keep my hedgerows poorly groomed to avoid such complications." John nodded at his shrubbery. "Take Ryan to Thames House and confine him. Securely. He has admitted to being in league with Maryn Dale." Jade's eyes darkened. "He has also agreed to help us capture Maryn; that we will allow him to do."

Jade and Alexa lifted Ryan bodily from the floor and led him out the door and away. John immediately relocked the door and re-engaged the security alarm.

He could feel Caroline's eyes on him as he returned to sit on the corner of the couch. His mind ricocheted between fury, terror and a desperate need for comfort that he knew he didn't deserve.

Slowly, Caroline's soft and gentle voice reached him. "I've never seen Ironheart before," she said.

"Haven't you?" he replied brusquely. *Don't be kind to me. I don't deserve it.* "In Bourey Prison in Burma, he was there. He was the one who took your every kindness and threw it back in your face. After the attack by those muggers in Sinde, he was the one who shut you out of his heart … tried, at least. You've seen the worst of me."

"I've also seen the best of you," she said. His eyes downcast, he saw only her feet as she moved closer to him. "Why didn't you kill Ryan?" she asked. Her voice was quiet and sad.

His gaze remained on the floor. He simply couldn't meet her eyes, too afraid of what he'd read there. "I couldn't. When it came right down to it, I couldn't. What you said to me in the hospital in Vancouver about the book of my life and standing before God on Judgment Day kept running through my head. Every time my hand began to squeeze the trigger, I saw another replay of the actions of my life." She brushed the hair back from his forehead, kissing him there. *I don't deserve this.* But he couldn't resist what she offered him and leaned into her as he continued, "I don't have to face eternity with the burden of my guilt. Why should Ryan have to? If he had raised a hand to you, I would have killed him, but—"

"He didn't."

"No." John raised his face to his wife. "Do you still think of me as Ironheart?"

"I have never thought of you that way," she said, and he read the truth in her eyes. "I was afraid that you would shoot him before you listened, but you didn't. I'm proud of you. I love you."

*You love me.* Dropping his handgun onto the couch behind him, he wrapped his arms around her waist, drawing a deep breath of relief into his lungs, a breath that was full of her essence … forgiveness, love and lavender-scented soap. He smiled. "Too bossy, though, eh?" he mimicked her accent.

"Utterly!" she exclaimed, mocking his.

He laughed once. "Thank you for listening to me. I'm sorry for being so bossy."

Slipping her arms around his neck, she nestled his head against her chest. He breathed deeply, relaxing into her embrace. "Can we go back to normal now?" she asked.

"Once Maryn's in custody."

"Will you kill her?"

"I don't know."

John was awakened by the stillness surrounding him. Something was bothering Caroline, he was certain. Rather than sleeping sprawled across him, grumbling whenever he moved, she was curled into a tight ball on the furthest edge of the bed. He could wait here for her to tell him what was wrong, or he could uncharacteristically take the initiative and ask.

She sighed heavily. *Oh, baby.* Sliding over, he wrapped his arm around her waist and then kissed her on the neck. She didn't move closer, a sure sign that something was indeed bothering her, and it had to do with him.

"What's wrong, baby?" he said.

She sighed again, releasing a long breath rather than answer.

"I know you're awake," he said. "You're not snoring in my ear."

She chuckled breathily. "I do not snore!"

"And how would you know?" he protested.

She flipped to face him and shoved his shoulder. "Doofus!"

"I cannot even begin to guess what that is," he said. Brushing her hair aside, he tucked it behind her ear. "Caroline, what's wrong?"

"Would you really have tortured Ryan?" she asked in her smallest voice, her eyes downcast.

"Tortured? What do you mean?" He knew she was bothered by the encounter earlier, but he hadn't expected that question.

"You told him that he needed to cooperate or you would explore his threshold of pain," she said.

Brushing his fingertips along her jaw line, he traced the shape of her face. "It was only a threat … to frighten him."

"Are you sure?" She looked him directly in the eyes, pleading with him for something he couldn't identify. "Would you ever do the things that were done to you by Vlad in Burma?" she asked as though fearful of his response.

"I can't tell you what I would have done to Ryan, because I don't know myself, but I do know what I would not have done. I would never torture nor participate in the torture of another individual. I know what it does to a person to be held helpless before the violence of your enemies," he said.

She sighed again, beginning to look relieved. "Why did you make Ryan kneel in front of you?"

John replied slowly, careful of his words. "I knew that the reduced circulation to his feet and the pressure on his knees would work together to make it difficult for him to try anything."

"What did you think he would do?" she wondered.

"I wanted to be prepared for any contingency." Tipping her chin, he studied her gaze. "Why did you think I kept him on the floor?"

She shrugged, and he could feel that she was relaxing, leaning into him. "I didn't understand, and what kept occurring to me just didn't make sense with what I know of you."

"Hence my reprieve from the nightly serenade?" he asked, humour in his voice.

She gaped at him, giving his shoulder a shove. "I do not snore!" She hesitated. "Do I?"

He rolled on top of her, balancing his weight on his forearms. "How would I know? I'm sleeping!"

Laughing lightly, she reached up and kissed him deeply, taking his breath away. "Thank you for being the man I thought you were."

"Thank you for giving me the opportunity to be."

Eight days later, the DG called John into his office. Finally, with Ryan's assistance, Sir William told him, they had located Maryn Dale. She and Sonam Narayan were in P'yŏngyang, North Korea.

"Let's get her. There's a warrant for her arrest in the UK and Canada. Put a team together and let's go," John demanded, his desire for resolution driving him to his feet.

"John, sit down," Sir William said. "I'm afraid it's not that simple." John sat heavily in his chair as the DG continued. "I'm not certain that you heard me correctly. Ms. Dale is currently residing in *North* Korea."

"So? We move in from the Chinese side. Dandong is very close to P'yŏngyang. Tour groups run between the two cities on a regular basis," John replied.

"She must have connections within the North Korean government, because they have pronounced her unjustly persecuted. The Democratic People's Republic of Korea has offered her asylum. The Embassy of North Korea in London has issued a statement to Her Majesty's government stating that any attack upon a person of value to the Korean people will be seen as an attack on North Korea itself," Sir William said.

John's hands fisted, and red wrath rose up within his chest. "No!" he whispered tersely. "It's not possible. After everything she's done, she can't get away with this."

"I'm afraid that there is nothing we can do. At least we know where she is. John." The DG leaned forward, trying to catch John's eye. "John! As long as Maryn Dale is in North Korea, she is of no danger to Caroline."

"Now. She's no danger now. But when?" John's dark eyes finally met the DG's gaze. "For how long?" He rose. His fists were tapping a rhythm against his thighs.

"John, I cannot sanction any move against Maryn Dale at this time. I—"

John turned abruptly and strode from the office, oblivious to the words that Sir William spoke.

"Yes?" Caroline answered her telephone.

"Mrs. Brock, this is Sir William. I need you to locate your husband PDQ."

Immediately coming alert, she asked, "Why? What's happened?"

Caroline stood, fiddling with the phone cord as she listened to his explanation, praying throughout the DG's words that John would be well. Slamming down the receiver without saying goodbye, she searched the Grid with her eyes, moving quickly into the computer lab.

"Aubrey. Locate John, please. Immediately!" she said.

Aubrey studied her for only a split second before complying. Before long, Aubrey responded. "Tickety-boo, Caroline. He's in his office."

Running to John's office, she looked inside. "He's not here, Aubrey!"

"Wait! No, of course ... Rome?" Caroline walked up behind Aubrey as he spoke. "Now he's in Albuquerque, New Mexico ... Sioux Falls ... Timbuktu ... Yangon. Why did I ever teach him how to do that?" Aubrey mused. He was obviously proud of John's skills of obfuscation.

"Aubrey, what's happening?" Caroline wrung her hands as she awaited his explanation.

Aubrey cleared the room of his apprentices, sending them off on errands. "John is routing the tracer in his phone around the world, hiding his location."

Hibb leaned through the doorway into the computer lab. "I need to speak with John. Have you seen him?"

"Try Albuquerque," Aubrey retorted.

"With Bugs Bunny?" Hibb chuckled.

"Anyone seen John?" Harry entered the room.

"What is wrong with you people?!" Caroline exclaimed. They all stopped to stare at their usually calm and happy analyst. "Maryn Dale is in North Korea. The government won't let us pursue her," she said as though that explained everything.

Hibb reached out a gentle hand to lightly touch her shoulder. "Caroline, we didn't know."

"But I know." She pulled her arms tightly across her chest, trying to quell her apprehension. "I've got to find him," she said.

"If he's chosen to disappear, you won't find him." Jade joined the discussion, and they were shortly thereafter joined by Alexa.

"I've got to get home," Caroline insisted. "I'll take a taxi."

"Caroline, I'll drive you," offered Harry.

"No. No, thank you. It's kind of you, but if John is there, I'll need to meet him alone."

"What is he going to do?" Alexa asked.

"I don't know." Caroline hesitated. "That's a lie. I'm sorry. I do know." She turned and walked from the room, leaving her colleagues to watch her exeunt.

Caroline moved into the house. As she was about to flip on the light in the entryway, a voice called out from the darkness.

"Don't. Leave it off," it ordered.

"John, is that you?" She moved tentatively closer to the source of the voice. The foyer was dark as night, and she couldn't hear Rufus anywhere. "John, you're frightening me."

"Don't be afraid, sweetheart. Come into the spare room, but don't turn on the light," he said.

She complied and soon found herself wrapped in John's arms, resting her cheek against the smooth coolness of his leather jacket. Her hands began to roam, studying his attire: jeans, a denim shirt and the leather bomber jacket. She reached down his arms to finger his wedding ring.

"So you're not going on a mission," she said.

"No."

"You're going after Maryn Dale."

"Yes."

"I thought you might leave without telling me. Just disappear," she said.

"I intended to, but in the end, I couldn't. That extra voice in my head, you know the one you say is the Holy Spirit, not schizophrenia?"

"Yes," she said, smiling lightly.

"It wouldn't let me leave without seeing you, explaining to you," he said.

"Thank you." She hugged him tightly as she asked, "What will happen if you go? The DG told me that we can't pursue her."

"He called you directly?" She nodded to confirm his words. "Interesting." He mused a moment and then returned his attention to her. "Simply put, if I go, I become deniable. MI-5, MI-6, HM's government, no one will come to my rescue. They'll declare me a rogue agent and hang me out to dry."

"Oh, John! So if something goes wrong, you'll be left to the mercy of the North Korean government. How could I—"

They were interrupted by a persistent knocking that increased in intensity until it sounded like there were five elephants stamping on the door in cadence.

"You'd better see who it is," John said as he drew his Glock from its holster. "You have your gun?"

"Yes," she confirmed as she moved out of the spare room and toward the front door. "Who is it?" she called through the door.

"It's Hibb, Harry and Alexa, Jade and Aubrey. We're not leaving, so you might as well let us in."

John's hoarse whisper followed her. "Don't, Caroline."

*This is one command I can't obey, my love.* She cast her eyes heavenward. *Grant me wisdom, Lord.* Caroline opened the door and let them all into the house.

"We know you're here, John, and we're not letting you do this on your own," Alexa announced.

Moments passed before they heard a long sigh from the spare room. John stepped out, his Glock held limply in his hand. "I can't let you do that," he said.

Ignoring his words, Aubrey began to pull a turbo-netbook from the pouch he was carrying. "Now, where can we meet discreetly? I have a plan."

He looked over at Caroline, who nodded at the workout room. "This room is built like a fortress. There's only one small window in there, which we can cover. It smells a little, but it's private," she said.

The five spooks walked past John and into the workout room, greeted by a very subdued Rufus, who seemed unable to decide whether to wag his tail or sit on it. Taking John's hand, Caroline kissed it once and then his cheek and pulled him after her to follow the others.

"Here's the plan," Aubrey began. "Caroline—"

"No!" John interrupted tersely. "She is not getting involved!"

"Hush!" Caroline ordered him. "Aubrey, continue."

John looked back and forth between them, trying to interject, but everyone ignored him.

"Caroline is going on holiday to Seoul, South Korea. Alexa and Jade are being sent undercover ... somewhere ... I'll find a location. John, you, I'm afraid, will have to disappear. No one will believe that Caroline went on vacation without you."

John straightened abruptly. "What kind of plan is this?! We put Caroline in—" He stopped. "What are you doing? This makes no sense. I'm going after Maryn on my own wherever I need to."

"John! Hush!" Caroline put her hand firmly on his arm and a finger to her lips.

Aubrey nodded once decisively, as if to confirm her instruction. "All we need now is a messenger to tell Maryn where Caroline is. She will guess that John is with her and—" Aubrey turned to John. "Will Maryn be able to resist the temptation? When her prey is so close?" John shook his head, conceding the fact. "In order to get to Caroline, she will have to leave the protection of the North Korean government," Aubrey explained. "South Korea is currently looking for any reason to annoy the North because of the North's warmongering. Therefore, there is a good chance that the South Korean government will turn a blind eye to the capture of an ally of the North. In fact, they themselves might see her as an enemy of the state."

"A messenger," Alexa repeated thoughtfully.

"I know someone who would do that," John offered quietly. They all looked at him. "Ryan Carstairs."

Caroline glanced at John. The man he had mistrusted and despised since his first day in the section would now be the man he relied upon to bring him his enemy?

"How will we get Ryan out of protective custody without being charged with a crime?" Harry asked.

Aubrey tapped his lower lip three times and then proudly snapped his fingers. "Piece of cake! A clerical error calling his morning guards away one hour before his afternoon guards arrive. We organize a terrorist incident of some sort to divert everyone's attention, and Bob's your uncle … Ryan disappears."

"We can't participate in terrorist activities to release a guilty man from custody!" John protested.

"We respond to all bombs and bomb *threats*, do we not?" Aubrey reminded him.

Caroline watched John's tension finally begin to ease. "Indeed," he replied. His gaze faltered, and Caroline slipped her arms around him.

"What is it?" she asked gently.

He wrapped her in a warm hug and kissed her on the forehead. "I … uh, only … thank you … my friends." They all smiled in return. "Aubrey, I don't want her flying alone."

"You can fly with her, but under a legend. You, I'm afraid, are going to have to blatantly disobey orders for this to work. Are you prepared for that?"

"Without a doubt."

At half past six the next evening, Sir William Jacen made his way onto the Grid.

"Horace," the DG called to Hibb where he spotted him just exiting John's office. Hibb paced over to Sir William.

"Yes, sir. It's not often we see you here, sir."

"Where is John Brock?"

"We're not certain, sir."

"Caroline Brock?"

"She's decided to take a holiday."

"A holiday?"

"Yes, sir. She still had plenty of time coming. I checked," Hibb said.

"Why are so many desks empty?"

"Jade Kovic and Alexa Donnehy are on assignment."

Sir William's expression made his scepticism abundantly apparent. "I understand that Ryan Carstairs has gone missing."

"Really, sir? That is a surprise," Hibb said.

"Has he left me anyone?" the DG asked, flabbergasted.

"I don't know what you mean, sir. Harry is getting coffees from the canteen, and there's Evie and me."

"Mr. Davies as well?!" Sir William exclaimed, exasperated.

"Aubrey had some holiday allowance owed. Three years' worth, I believe, if you add up all the missed vacation time."

The DG slapped his hand against his forehead in the most comical gesture.

"Let's just hope Al Qaeda don't come to hear of this." The DG looked up to meet Hibb's gaze directly. "John understands the consequences?"

"Aye, sir." That was the first question that Hibb had answered directly.

Sir William turned and exited, muttering and shaking his head.

Seventeen hours and forty-five minutes later, after a three-hour stop in Dubai, Caroline stepped off the Airbus A380 with her husband, who was now occupying the legend of one Michael Edward Bramwell, businessman and world traveler. "Mr. Bramwell" was an identity that Aubrey had prepared for his own retirement should he find himself in the unenviable position of needing to disappear into the mists for one reason or another. The world of espionage was politically fickle, so one never knew what the future in the service could hold. Aubrey had happily sacrificed this retirement plan in order to help bring down Maryn Dale, traitor and kidnapper. In any case, he had three other fully prepared identities in reserve.

Caroline rode in silence to the Hotel Benhur—chosen because John loved the movie—on Yeoido-dong, Seoul, South Korea. Entering singly, they checked into separate rooms, with Michael Edward Bramwell paying cash and Caroline Brock using her own personal credit card. No need to make things too difficult for Maryn. John was supposed to drop off Michael's belongings and make his way to Caroline's room.

As soon as she heard his first knock, she flung open the door and pulled him inside.

"I'm afraid," she admitted.

John drew her into his arms, holding her securely. "Don't be afraid. I'm here."

"When are the others due to arrive?" she asked into his shirt.

"Two or three hours."

As Caroline relaxed into his embrace, she became aware that his hands and mouth were roaming in a manner that did not evoke comfort as much as desire. His lips skimmed across her collarbone, and she realized that he'd already opened her blouse, one hand warmly possessive against her breast while the other skimmed down to her waistband, his fingertips just slipping beneath the fabric. Smiling, she returned the favour, pushing his shirt buttons free of their confinement, kissing each patch of skin newly revealed. And when the job was completed, she opened his shirt and rubbed her face across his chest, enjoying the rasp of hair against her cheeks while inhaling the scent of him. How, after that interminable flight, could he still smell so good?

"Mmmm," he moaned, finding the skin of her back and smoothing his hands up to her shoulders and down again. "You feel good."

Lifting her face to him, she coaxed a kiss, opening herself to his exploration, so distracted by the sensations that it took her three tries to undo his cuffs and slip his shirt off. Pulling back, she ducked under his right arm, running her hands down his chest as she paused to kiss each scar he'd received from the whip in Burma. A moan escaped him, and he reached for her wrist to tug her back in front of him, but she resisted, instead sliding her hands down his belly to the buckle on his belt, releasing it first and then pausing on the waistband of his trousers. Pushing his hands away as they tried to hasten her, she dealt with the button and zip painstakingly, millimetre by millimetre, feeling his breathing deepen with desire and anticipation. As she worked, she drew his body backwards, tiny step by tiny step.

Twisting to reach her, he found himself hampered by his trousers and, growling low in his throat, he complained, "I want to touch you."

Without warning, she hooked her arm around his waist and pushed him back onto the bed. He laughed in surprise as he bounced. She smiled down at him while she removed his shoes, socks and trousers. Then she stood back and crossed her arms, teasing him.

"You do have a wicked streak. You know that, don't you?" he said. He reclined, propped on his elbows, looking up at her. "Come here, my beautiful wife."

She shook her head. "What did you say your name was, sir? Michael what?"

"Are you coming, or am I chasing you?" he asked. "Because one way or another, I mean to taste your luscious lips."

Caroline laughed aloud, enjoying the play. As he began to count, she shrugged at him, feigning indifference. He sat up very slowly as he got to eight, then nine. At ten, she was prepared to flee, but he didn't move any further than the near corner of the bed as he continued on to eleven and twelve.

"How high are you going to count?" she asked as he got to fourteen and fifteen. He continued on to twenty-one and twenty-two. She took a step toward him and poked his shoulder. "Are you—" That was as far as she got before she found herself trapped between his knees, his hands on her bottom, holding her there. Rather than removing the rest of her clothing as she expected him to, he merely placed one sucking kiss on her belly button as his hands slipped down the backs of her legs and then back up. And then he stopped, resting his chin against her belly.

She looked down to see his eyes closed. "Are you okay?" she asked. He nodded and smiled. "Is that it? Are we finished?" she asked. He shrugged. She groaned in frustration, slipping off her shirt and bra and pushing him back onto the bed, straddling him. "More," she demanded.

Languidly, he opened his eyes, reaching up to cover her breasts. "You're not the only one who knows how to get their way." She laughed as she leaned down to kiss him. His hands found a familiar and then a new pattern to drive her wild as she let him have his way with her. Who ever said that marriage killed passion?

Three hours later, Aubrey arrived at the door disguised in wig and beard and dressed in white coveralls, carrying an electrician's bag.

"There was a complaint filed in the computer about the cable reception in this room," he said.

"Yes. Please come in," Caroline replied, stepping back to allow him to enter. Once the door was closed and locked, Caroline turned back to see Aubrey unloading his set of state-of-the-art cameras and listening devices. "Sorry, Aubrey, I forgot to make the call to complain about the cable. I was … uh … distracted." John winked at her, and she couldn't resist the blush that rose up her cheeks.

Aubrey frowned. "I took care of it." He pulled out the last of the little devices and a tiny set of screwdrivers and other unidentifiable mini-tools on a tray. "I assume it is now safe to plant these devices? From now, you'll carry on your … er … marital business in Mr. Bramwell's room?" Aubrey looked back and forth between them. Caroline's blush deepened, but John looked rather pleased with himself.

"Aub … can't really tell … I mean … tidied up … how?" Caroline muttered, clearly flustered.

John put an end to the discussion, still smiling in satisfaction. "That's none of your business, old man. You simply carry on and do your job."

Once the devices were in place, John, Caroline and Aubrey made their ways separately to the room directly above Caroline's. Inside, Jade and Alexa were waiting.

John greeted them. "Any trouble getting past the CCTV?" he asked.

"No," Jade replied. "Our man Aubrey took care of that. No one knows we're here at this hotel. No one knows we're in Korea."

"Very good," John said, satisfied. "Ryan?"

"He's on his way to Maryn," Alexa replied. "He's much braver as a redeemed criminal than he ever was as a spook."

"Aubrey, do you have a plan in place for him if he succeeds?" Caroline asked.

Aubrey nodded. "I told him that I had found his Bolivian identity in twelve minutes. That frightened him. Then I told him that you had asked me to supply a foolproof new identity for him. He'll be safe … if he survives this."

Soon Caroline felt John's hand warm around hers. She smiled her thanks at him. *Poor Ryan. What will become of you?*

"All right. Everyone knows their jobs?" John asked, bringing them back on track. They all nodded. "We begin."

Ryan stepped out of the stairwell with its peeling nondescript beige paint and pushed open the creaking door onto the second floor of the P'yŏngyang Yeoinsug. Really just an oversized three-storey wooden structure, it had once been a stopover for invading armies to water and rest their horses. It had clearly been added to and modified several times over the past century, resulting in staircases that ended in stone walls and pentagonal rooms with no exterior windows.

Ryan made his way to the room at the end of the hallway to the right, knocking twice when he got there … quickly, before he lost his nerve.

"*Neujge wassguna*!" a voice accused from the interior and then continued in English. "I can't get any service in this one-horse village." The door swung open to reveal Maryn Dale in all her simmering beauty. "Ryan," she said, only the subtle darkening of her grey eyes reflecting her surprise. "I didn't expect you. Sonam will be so disappointed that he wasn't here to greet you." Maryn could use the sweetest words to threaten you.

"I suppose I will need to apologize to him for leaving before he awoke," Ryan said.

"You might want to take a step back before you speak to him. I had to punish him for letting you escape." Maryn blew on her long, sharp fingernails as though to emphasize her point.

"I didn't escape. Is that what you think?" Ryan said. He tried to sound shocked that she would think such a thing. Quelling the fear rising within him, he took a step closer to her, knowing that retreating would be viewed as fear, and cowardice meant death in Maryn's company. "Maryn, why would I escape? I have nowhere else to go. John Brock will see me dead. He has contacts around the world. Where could I hope to go?" Trying to adopt a more relaxed bearing, Ryan leaned against the door frame.

"Would you care to explain, then, why you left?" She trailed her nails down his chest.

"I left in order to gather information," Ryan said.

"Was that what your little jaunt to Bolivia was in aid of?" Maryn asked.

*Uh oh!* Trying to hide the blush rising up his cheeks, Ryan rubbed his hand across his face as though to clear his head. Had it really been so simple to uncover his flight? "I have contacts there. Sometimes I think you forget that I am a spook."

"Stop waffling and tell me, what did these *contacts* tell you?" Maryn asked.

"John Brock is setting a trap for you," Ryan said.

Maryn stiffened in astonishment, her eyes wide. "What do you mean?"

"He's bringing Caroline to Seoul to draw you south out of the protection of the North Korean government," he replied.

"The Home Secretary would never have sanctioned that. John must be working against orders," she mused aloud, finally moving aside so that Ryan could enter the room. He closed the door behind him, startling as it slammed open just before it clicked closed.

Defensively, Ryan spun at the sound, seeing an enraged Sonam Narayan in the doorway, fists clenched, menace in his stance. In one step, he gathered Ryan into a bear hug and began to squeeze.

"Sonam, pet, put him down," Maryn said. Her voice was soft and sultry. In defiance, Sonam shook his head. "I don't want to have to punish you again, darling," she said, her voice still calm and even. Sonam's gaze flickered, and he flung Ryan away from himself to land against the coffee table.

Gasping to refill his lungs, Ryan looked up to see Sonam's purple face and the three healing gouges on his cheek. Ryan knew Maryn well enough to understand that those were the visible reminders. The others would be hidden. Maryn could be vicious.

"He has actually come to us with useful information," she said to Sonam. She turned back to Ryan. "I think it's time now to make up with Sonam."

A leer formed in Sonam's eyes, and Ryan paled.

Waking the next morning, Ryan pushed his battered body off the couch and made his way to the hotplate next to the sink, filling and putting on the kettle for tea. Sonam entered the kitchenette, elbowing Ryan out of the way as he pulled the teapot out of the cupboard and scooped in the green tea.

"Ah, my two favourite gentlemen, it's so sweet to see you making breakfast together. I'll have eggs." Maryn sauntered back into the bedroom, her thin silk dressing gown fluttering around her legs, revealing glimpses of curves and softness. Ryan looked away in disgust. All that beauty, so deeply flawed by hatred, simply a trap for the witless and gullible. *How could I have ever thought her beautiful?*

Before long, Maryn returned, freshly dressed in lavender silks and black leather boots. Ryan was surprised to see the stains on her skirt—she was normally so careful to appear immaculately attired.

"So, John has set a trap for us." She tapped her ruby-painted nails against her teeth in a syncopated rhythm. "Without the support of MI-5, he will have few resources." She turned to Ryan. "He is with her?"

"Yes. He's traveling under a legend," Ryan said.

"Excellent!" She was becoming excited. "I know all of his identities. At last, he's made a stonking great gaff! The tart, now, she is probably travelling under her own name. Where is she staying in Seoul?"

"If I had computer access, I could easily track her," Ryan offered, remembering to chew on the right side to avoid his swollen gums on the left.

Maryn waved at him in disgust. "So could I." She tapped her teeth again—ta-de-dup. "What is he planning?" Standing, she paced the room. "I know him. What will he do?"

"He's not the same man you knew," Ryan stated.

"Pish tosh. He's had a little fling with a housewife. Lots of spies have the spook and Mrs. Fling fascination. It will never last. Really, we simply need to snatch her and bring her here. Then we will have her at our leisure—No! That was my mistake last time. We need to kill her." Turning to Sonam, she apologized. "I'm sorry, my pet." She stroked her fingertips through the big man's jet-black hair. His eyes flickered shut, a look of exquisite pleasure on his face. "We won't be able to let you have your wicked way with her." Sonam's eyes blinked open at that, and a definite pout appeared on his mouth. "Well, perhaps a little fun," she said, giving in. He smiled slowly, a smile that held only peril, no mirth. Ryan shuddered, as he knew only too well the perverse *pleasures* of Maryn's man.

Maryn continued, "Even if he had his entire team with him, he couldn't protect her all the time. We simply formulate a plan, spring the trap, play a while and kill her. Then we return here. The English would never dare defy the North Koreans."

"But Maryn, as soon as we enter South Korea, we're at risk," Ryan protested.

Heat in her gaze, she rounded on him. "You, you spotty youth, are at risk everywhere. I and Sonam have been offered protection here." Pointing to the ground beneath her first, she then hugged herself and did a little twirl. "Once she's dead, I'll finally be free of that man. Then John will be the one with night terrors." Her voice changed, the shrill of hysteria entering it. "Those blue eyes. That white hair. That strength. That *forgiveness—*" She spat out the word. "—will no longer haunt my nights! I will be free!" Snapping her fingers like they were castanets, she danced around some more, the lavender fabric twisting around her legs. "Once John and that woman have been made to suffer, that old man's face will disappear from my dreams. I will be free!" Abruptly, her hands fisted and her jaw clenched. "Free!" she gritted out. "Free. I don't need some Christian's forgiveness. I am free of all constraints." She began to laugh, the pitch rising to approach hysteria until, abruptly, Sonam slapped her once.

"Brother Phillip is dead!" her man yelled at her.

Maryn went very still, her eyes flitting around the room until they came to rest on Ryan's confused face and then passed back to Sonam.

"Yes. Of course you're correct." A shiver passed through her body. She continued, her usual tone returning to her voice. "We will fly tomorrow to Incheon where we can obtain what we need to kill Caroline Brock."

# Chapter Seventeen
## *Assassin's Trap*

Caroline ate supper with "Michael Bramwell" once again in the hotel dining room. They had been in Seoul for four days, and so far, nothing had happened.

Caroline poked her Gim again with her fork. "Do you trust Ryan?"

"No," John replied. "He could as easily betray us."

Pausing as she wrapped seaweed around a portion of sticky rice, she commented, "You've never liked him. Why?" She popped the bolus into her mouth.

He shrugged noncommittally but answered when she pressed. "There was something needy about him that I despised from the beginning. He was always trying to impress me, to 'suck up to me,' as you would say. I never got the sense that he was in the job for the good he could do but rather for the women he could do."

Her mouth dropped at his unexpected words. "That's pretty harsh."

Shrugging one shoulder, he replied tersely, "You asked me. I answered."

Turning her head toward the window, she attempted to hide the burgeoning hurt in her eyes. Soon, she felt his hand, warm on her arm.

"I'm sorry," he said, remorse in his eyes. "I'm on edge. I wish we could get this over and done with."

Brushing her fingertips along his palm, she inserted her fingers between his to hold his hand across the table. "Me too," she said. "Some of these tracking devices Aubrey has on me are very irritating." They sipped at their water for a time in silence. "Are you sure she'll fall for the trap? Will she come?" Caroline asked.

"She'll come," he assured her.

Caroline poked at her food a bit more. "What brought her to this, John?"

He shrugged. "Bitterness, greed, envy, jealousy, spite. They're all traps that lead us further from God until we're bound in hopelessness."

Her eyes widened in surprise at his insight. *Wow! Deep!*

"What?" he said indignantly. "You don't have to look so surprised. I am capable of critical thinking."

She laughed at the expression on his face. "I just didn't expect …that."

He chuckled wryly. "I understand it because I've experienced it. Doesn't Larry Norman have a song that talks about the fact that nothing really changes; history repeats itself?" He leaned toward her and began to sing softly.

"Yes." She smiled thoughtfully. "But you have to finish the song. Nothing really changes unless you let Jesus set you free."

"Indeed," he replied. "We're caught in the traps of life until we choose freedom."

"'You shall know the truth, and the truth shall make you free,'" she said.

John furrowed his brow, thinking. "Jesus said, 'I am the way, the truth and…and the life'." He paused, struggling to remember the rest of the verse, paraphrasing instead. "No one…comes to the Father—wait a moment—except…except through me?"

She nodded, smiling at his attempts. "'If the Son shall make you free, you shall be free indeed.'"

He smiled tenderly. "I love you, you know."

"I know, and I'm very glad," she replied sweetly. Leaning back in her chair, she maintained her hold on him a moment longer. "However, I do need the *hwajangsil*."

John chuckled. "Your Korean is improving."

"Yeah, now I can say toilet in three languages, four if you count British."

He chuckled again. "Colonial."

"Prig."

His chuckle followed her as she walked away to the ladies' room. She had been forbidden to use any bathroom stall that had a window or had been recently occupied. That let out numbers two and three. Number one and number four were locked. *Irritating. Okay, number five it is.* She pushed it open, surprised at the prick on her hand. *Must be a sharp edge of plastic or something.*

As she spun to drop her drawers and take her seat, the world continued spinning. Grasping for support, her hand slipped off the toilet-roll holder, and she fell against the door, sliding down to the floor. Her chest tightened, and she struggled to draw breath. Her eyes began to burn and itch and her tongue swelled, constricting her airway. Black crept in around the edges as she lost the ability to breathe.

Gasping, struggling, she watched the hazy stall door swing over her body, revealing a man filling the doorway, broad but not too tall. She felt him take her by the arms and pull her out of the confined space, and for a moment the impending sense of doom lifted as she imagined him her rescuer—until she watched him kneel between her legs. She recognized him just before she slipped into unconsciousness. Sonam Narayan.

John checked his watch again. He'd give her one more minute and then he was going in. *I would rather embarrass her than know that I waited at the table sipping water while she was in danger.*

Then he saw Aubrey running toward the ladies' toilets. His heart in his throat, John leapt from his chair, knocking it over as he raced toward the loo. Arriving, he pushed the door open to see Aubrey injecting Caroline where she lay on the floor of the ladies' toilets.

"What happened?" John demanded to know, dropping onto his knees beside Caroline. "Aubrey, what happened?!"

"Schtum up!" Aubrey commanded, checking Caroline's pulse again and lifting her eyelids to check her pupils.

"He's rousing. Help me!" Jade demanded. John noticed her for the first time, seeing her sitting on Sonam Narayan's back, her knees pinning his shoulders, riding his back like a buffalo. John took two steps over, kicking the big man in the face once and then again. Jade caught his leg, as he wound up for a third. "John, she's not dead."

"The swelling's lessening," Aubrey said, and John heard the relief in his voice. He gave her a second injection as John returned to her side.

"What is that?" John could hear the fear in his own voice.

"Epinephrine," Aubrey replied.

"Will she be all right?" John asked desperately.

"She should be fine. I think they've used that new experimental histamine-releasing drug. They're using it on animals to study anaphylaxis, trying to find a cure. The epinephrine reverses the effects," Aubrey said. "Simple cure, but if we hadn't arrived, she would have died of cardiovascular collapse."

John held her hand tightly as Caroline began to rouse slowly. "What happened? Please tell me," John begged, his pleading eyes searching Aubrey's, Jade's and the newly arrived Alexa's.

Jade replied first. "I was on duty. I followed her to the toilets, called Aubrey who said the space was clear so I waited outside."

Aubrey took over the explanation. "Three of the trackers on her give positional indices, so when I saw that she had fallen in the loo, I knew that she had either been attacked or drugged. Since there was no one else in the toilets, I assumed it had to be drugs. I grabbed the med-kit on my way down. Much longer though, and she would have been beyond help."

John pointed at the big man unconscious on the floor. "Him?"

Jade responded, "As I said, I was outside the toilets. Then I saw him—" She smacked the unconscious Sonam on the side of the head. "Stride right into the ladies' toilets, a very unusual sight. When I entered, the Tibetan was kneeling over her. John, he was preparing to—"

Abruptly, John held up a shaky hand to stop her next words.

Caroline's eyes fluttered, and Aubrey loaded the syringe again.

"Don' wan' a needle," she mumbled, her speech thick and awkward.

"How are you feeling?" John asked gently.

"Blaah! Wha' happen? John?" Caroline looked to John, who was now watching Aubrey examine each of the stall doors, stopping at the furthest to pry something off.

"Look at this," Aubrey said. "True spy gear. You simply place this on the point of most likely contact, and the pressure of your touch releases the drug held within this little sac. Bob's your uncle. Drug delivered."

"Someone drugged me?" Caroline asked.

"They might have killed you without an antidote quickly applied," Aubrey said.

She pushed herself up a bit, and John supported her with his arm. "It happened so fast," she said. "I couldn't reach the panic button."

"I was already on the way when Jade red-flashed me. Alexa went back to check the CCTV feeds," Aubrey said.

"How did you know to bring … whatever you shot me full of?" Caroline asked, pushing up to lean on her elbows.

"I brought it all as a precaution," Aubrey replied.

Alexa interrupted. "I recognized Ryan on the hotel CCTV. He was dressed as a janitor and coming out of this room fifteen minutes ago."

"So we can't trust him?" Caroline observed, and her question was laced with disappointment.

Setting Caroline gently on the floor first, John stood abruptly. "Aubrey, is she out of danger?"

"Yes. She'll be fine now," he said.

"Jade?" John said, nodding at her prisoner.

"I've already called the South Korean police. We'll leave him here, and they'll find him," Jade said.

John dropped to his knees again, kissing Caroline on the forehead. "I have to go."

She nodded. "Go."

"Thank you, Aubrey, Jade." John strode to the door. "Let's go," he said to Alexa, and they were gone.

Aubrey lifted Caroline by the shoulders. "Jade, help me. We need to get her upstairs before the police arrive."

Jade gave Sonam one more kick in the ribs for good measure and joined Aubrey at Caroline's side, taking her up the back stairs to Michael Bramwell's room.

John's mobile rang just as he and Alexa reached the street.

"Green Elantra." *Ryan's voice.* "Follow my signal."

John spotted the Elantra just pulling away from the curb. Sprinting across the street to the hotel parking garage, he ascended the stairs, pressing the key remote as soon as he came in view of the Hyundai Accent they'd rented upon arriving in Seoul. Alexa slipped into the passenger seat and John took the wheel, reversing out of the parking spot and then descending the steep, narrow ramps to exit the structure.

"Find him on the tracker," John said. His voice was grave and commanding. Minutes passed as John drove the car toward the Han River, hoping this was the right direction.

"Got him. Turn right. He just crossed the Mapo Bridge," said Alexa.

Turning right, John accelerated, weaving in and out of the crush of traffic to turn left onto the Mapo Bridge across the Han River, formerly a major trade route with China. Now the absence of shipping only pointed yet again to the continuing hostilities between North and South.

"He's slowing near the base of Namsan," Alexa said.

Turning right, John drove parallel to the river, curving through the city to a warehouse on the southeastern edge of the city, right up against Namsan Mountain. The warehouse was dwarfed by the verdant shape of the hulking rock.

"John, can we trust him?" Alexa asked, stopping John's exit from the car.

"Caroline asked me the same question. There's no way to know except to move forward. Are you with me?" John asked.

"Of course," Alexa replied, pulling out her handgun and chambering the first bullet. "Ready."

John nodded, exiting the vehicle and moving stealthily toward the building. The old shoe warehouse was cavernous, every shuffle and step echoing wildly. John motioned to Alexa to circle around the back to a second entrance, instructing her to silence. He checked his locally obtained TT-30 semiautomatic pistol just one more time, secreted his extra clips of armour-piercing shells around his body, secured his commando knife, and entered the building. As soon as he slipped through the door, he heard their voices arguing about something. John listened carefully.

"It's done, Maryn." *Ryan's voice. Is he friend or foe?*

"That is simply smashing! A pukka triumph! Excellent! Did she suffer? Did she scream? Did she recognize her doom before she blacked out?" *Maryn.*

"You didn't expect me to wait around and find out. John was only a few feet away in the dining room!" Ryan exclaimed.

"You're on our team now, wazzock. You'll do whatever I ask." That was definitely Maryn. John recognized the demeaning tone in her voice. "You'll stay with us because you know that John will kill you if he finds you alone."

"I *have* done what you asked, Maryn. Why are you so desperate to hurt Caroline this way?" Ryan asked.

"You berk!" *Maryn seems to be raining down every insult she's ever learned on Ryan.* "This is not about her. Do you think I haven't reasoned this out carefully? The only way to hurt John is through his slut of a wife." John clenched his fists. *How dare she?* "He needs to suffer as I have suffered. That blue-eyed duffer, I have to exorcise him from my mind." *She must be talking about Brother Phillip.*

"Maryn—" Ryan began, but Maryn obviously wasn't listening.

John could see her more clearly now. Her eyes had a feverish, faraway look. Her hair was wildly unkempt. She looked like a one-woman security force, clad in a flak jacket—which would not stop John—two fixed-blade knives at her belt and a 30-caliber carbine assault rifle in her hands, restored from the Korean War from the looks of it. She kept fiddling with it in her hands; a few times it looked like she'd taken aim at Ryan, but then she would move the muzzle aside.

"Sonam will take her. He will have his dirty little way with her, and John will know that this was all his fault." Her voice had become icy, and John shuddered at the chill.

"Maryn!" Sharply, Ryan insisted that he be heard this time, enunciating each syllable carefully. "It's over."

That was the cue—if Ryan were truly working with them. John made his way around the stacks of boxes and crates and up the stilled conveyor belt to ascend to the level of the conspirators. He hesitated for a moment, waiting to see if Alexa was in position, and then returned her nod and gestured his instructions for her to keep Maryn in her sights.

Blowing out a breath, John climbed to the top of the stack, almost level with the walkway where Ryan and Maryn stood.

"It's over, Maryn. We're taking you in," John stated calmly, pointing his pistol squarely at Maryn's chest.

Her eyes widened in shock and then narrowed at Ryan. "You betrayed me?" she whispered, sounding truly puzzled.

Ryan backed away from her. "You're a cruel and wicked woman, Maryn. Caroline is good and kind. There was no contest."

Maryn's blood-curdling scream surprised them all. She fired at John, forcing him to jump down to a lower level to avoid being shot. Ryan leapt from the walkway across five feet of space for the stack of crates, bouncing off and hitting the floor, screaming as he landed. He lay unmoving at the bottom, his leg bent at an awkward angle. Alexa was nowhere to be seen.

"Give it up, Maryn! There's no way out of this. The North Koreans can't protect you here," John warned.

"*No! No! No!*" she screamed, incensed.

Bullets pinged off the crates all around John's head. He dove to the side, smashing his elbow against a corner, his pistol falling from his grip.

"I saw that, John! You're unarmed," Maryn screeched, and then from near-hysteria, her voice changed, ringing lower, smoother. "Come out and maybe I'll let you live."

John pulled his knife out of the sheath strapped to his ankle and slid it into his jeans pocket, pulling his shirt out to cover it. And then raising his arms, he stood slowly.

"Climb on up here, Johnny lad," Maryn gestured with her rifle, and John began to climb up the crates until he was level with the walkway.

"Freeze!" Alexa yelled, looking across from the top of the conveyor belt. In that blurred moment, three things happened: Maryn fired; pulling out his knife, John dove for Maryn; and Ryan shot Maryn Dale in the chest with John Brock's gun. His task completed, the trap sprung, Ryan slumped to the ground, perspiring heavily from the pain in his knee.

Rising slowly, John stood over Maryn, her chest heaving, blood bubbling from the corner of her mouth. She tried to raise the rifle but he kicked it away.

"Alexa, are you all right?" John called, keeping his eyes on Maryn.

"Fine."

"See to Ryan."

"Yes, sir."

"Why, Maryn? What did I ever do to you? What did my wife ever do to you?" John demanded to know.

"I ... I couldn't let her win. I couldn't ... let ... him win. It should have been me. It ... should ... have ... been ... m—" And Maryn Dale breathed her last. The look of peace in Brother Phillip's eyes on the day at the Katafygio in Burma when Maryn murdered him in cold blood was not reflected in her eyes.

John gazed down at Maryn, a woman the world had judged as beautiful and successful, and he felt only pity and disgust. The assassin's trap had closed on her heart long ago. But Caroline was free.

# Chapter Eighteen
## Freedom

"It's done," John said.

"We're safe?" Caroline replied, confirming his message. "We're safe! We can go home and finally live a normal life—well, some spooky James Bond version of normal, anyway!" She flung herself into his arms and kissed him loudly on the cheek right in front of Aubrey, Jade and Alexa, who seemed to enjoy the spectacle.

"You'd better pack so we can get out of here," John suggested, his voice quiet, his eyes soft and warm. He watched her thank Jade, Alexa and Aubrey and practically skip from the room. She was free; free from fear and oppression. Free from the mistakes of his past. *Thank you, God.*

Grinning, clearly enjoying Caroline's enthusiasm, Aubrey stepped over to John.

"You've made her smile, John," Aubrey said.

"I have, haven't I?" John replied, pleased by the thought. "How's Ryan?"

"The clinic gave him a splint. He's torn the ligaments in his knee. He'll never again be a football star, but he should make a good recovery," Aubrey said.

"He'll never be a spy again either. But he'll be safe now? He did earn it, in the end," John said.

"Yes. I've used one of my retirement alternatives to set him up nicely.

He has a lot of personal daemons to sort through, but he'll be safe to do it," Aubrey said.

"Thank you, Aubrey." John turned to the others in the room. "Thank you, Jade. Alexa. I don't know how I'll ever repay your kindness."

Jade stepped forward and gave John a quick peck on the cheek. "That's what friends are for," she said.

Astonished by the gesture of affection, John felt a blush rise up his neck.

"Why, I do believe you've made our man show his emotions clearly and openly," Alexa said to Jade, obviously amused.

Aubrey chuckled, and John soon joined the laughter. "I will see you all at Thames House tomorrow," John said. "And now I'm going to find my wife."

John made his way to Caroline's room, knocking only once before she opened the door and dragged him inside. She couldn't seem to stop kissing him, and he laughed aloud as he held on to her. That was one of the things he loved so much about her, her capacity to find joy in life.

"You did it, darling! You saved me," she said, wrapping her arms around him. "I could never have asked for a better Christmas present than my own life."

"You're glad you were left behind?" he asked softly.

Suddenly serious, she replied, "Yes. I believe I am. Thank you, John. You make me very happy … and glad to be alive." Her eyes filled with tears.

He groaned. "You're not going to cry, are you?" he asked, and she laughed.

"It's my life, and I'll cry if I want to," she said.

He pulled her close, swinging her up and dropping her onto the bed, following her down. "I love you," he said.

"Yeah?" she said. "How much?"

*What's this about?* "More than the air I breathe."

"And?"

He raised an eyebrow at her. "More than my very body?"

"That doesn't count, because your body already belongs to me," she said, grinning mischievously.

"Indeed. And the corollary?" he said.

"Oh yes."

*Give me a clue, sweetheart. What game are we playing?* He watched her for a moment but she was silent and still … smiling, but still. "Caroline? My love? I need a hint. What are you asking me?"

Her smile grew wider. "How much you love me," she replied simply. "Enough to invite my family to our home for Christmas?"

He groaned dramatically. "All of them?"

She laughed. "All of them. Next year. For no more than one week."

"Next year?" he asked, hopeful, eyebrows raised.

"This year I want you all to myself. Christmas Eve and Christmas morn," she said.

"Anything you desire," he said warmly.

"Really?" she said. "Because I was watching this show on Korean television and … well … lean down. I don't think I can tell you and look you in the eye."

Puzzled, he complied, bending his ear to her mouth … and then blushing to the roots of his formerly liberal lifestyle. "Are you serious?"

She pulled back to meet his eyes. "Sure. You game?"

He laughed. "Who ever said that marriage killed passion?"

"I don't know. It wasn't me!" she said.

"You are a wild woman," he observed happily. "Shall we begin?"

"Oh yes," she replied, her voice husky and deep.

He kissed her … and didn't stop.

"It's finally Christmas Eve. Well, Christmas Eve morning," Caroline said, emerging from the bedroom in time to see John preparing scrambled eggs and toast. It seemed to be his favourite meal. She smiled as she watched him dish up their breakfast and pour the coffee.

"Come eat," John said, inviting her to the table with a bright smile. He was so handsome with his hair still tousled from sleep, clad in only his boxers and a Pink Floyd T-shirt.

"With pleasure," she replied, stepping forward and then changing trajectory as the telephone rang. "I'll get it." But she couldn't resist one kiss before she did.

"Hello?"

"Yes. Er, it's Charles Brock, er, John's father."

"Hello," Caroline replied, astonished. "Uh, how are you?"

"Not well. I seem to have had a heart attack."

"I'm sorry to hear that," she said.

"I … hmmm." Charles subsided into silence, and Caroline watched John walk slowly toward her, munching a piece of toast, concern on his face.

"You okay?" John mouthed at her, but she shook her head, not really providing any comfort, she could tell by his now furrowed brow.

Charles began again. "I was … thinking … perhaps you and I should speak. Here. At the hospital. St. Mary's. Please."

"O-kay." When he was close enough, Caroline grabbed the front of John's T-shirt, pulling him closer until he reached his arms around her.

"What is going on, Caer?" John asked in a whisper directly against her ear.

Shaking off the tickle, she responded to Charles, "I'll need to speak with John."

"Perhaps that would not be best—" Charles began.

"Look, Charles." Caroline paused as she felt John stiffen. "I—"

Abruptly, John cut off her words, pressing the mute button on the telephone. "Is that my father? You are not—"

She pushed his arm away and activated the speaker, pinning John to the spot with a glare. "As I was trying to say, I won't come without John. You're not exactly a reliable person, so I'm bringing him with me … if he'll come. If he refuses, then I won't be there."

"Er … you … John. I have … very well," Charles finished in a rush, ringing off.

She turned on John with a cold stare. "You don't ever really trust me, do you?"

He pulled her close, holding her tightly to him, speaking into her hair. "Don't say that. I only want to protect you."

She softened into his arms. "You silly man, I wouldn't have gone without you." She held him for a time, waiting for him to release her, but he didn't seem to have any intention of letting her go. "John?" She pulled back to meet his eyes, seeing the pain there. "I'm so sorry, John, sorry for all you've suffered."

"Don't be sorry. Simply love me," he said.

Holding his face tenderly, she told him, "I will always love you." She waited patiently. "John? Are we going to the hospital to see your father? Are you ready to do this?"

Sighing deeply, he murmured, "What are we doing?"

"We're giving your father the opportunity to apologize to you. If he doesn't, he doesn't. We don't need him in our life. As long as you're at peace about your father, I'm good. He can be in our life or out of it. It makes no nevermind to me. If he won't follow the rules and behave, he can just make do without us. Can you live with that?"

John finally pulled back to meet her gaze. "You are a wonder to me. Yes, I can live with that. It's exactly what I desire to live with. I don't have to humiliate myself and kowtow to him?"

"Certainly not! Definitely not! He messed up. You've dealt with it. Can you forgive him and release the pain even if you don't hear the apology?" she said.

"Yes. I don't think I could have even a month ago, but now I can. He follows the rules or he doesn't," he said.

"Precisely."

"Let's go and get this over with," John said.

Entering St. Mary's Hospital, they were given the appropriate room number in the Cardiology Unit and instructions on which painted lines to follow.

"I need the loo," John said as they approached his father's room.

"Okay. I'll meet you at the room," she responded.

He reached for her arm. "No. Wait here."

"I don't want to wait outside the men's bathroom. But I won't go into your father's room without you," she said.

"Please wait," he beseeched her.

"Fine," she conceded, crossing her arms and leaning against the wall. When he re-entered the corridor, she was waiting. "What exactly are you afraid he'll do to me? He's hardly going to come after me with a belt," she said.

"I know."

"I'm not afraid of what he thinks of me. I couldn't care less. Unless …" She paused as she finally understood. "You're afraid of what he'll tell me about *you*, aren't you?"

Ducking his head, he blushed lightly. "I was a rotten kid."

"If you're afraid of me finding out from him, then tell me yourself," she said.

Pain seemed to take up residence in his eyes. "I'm not exactly proud of my youth."

"John. Kids do dumb things. It's a fact of life. You can't hold youth against a person. It's simply not fair. Whatever you did—well, for one thing, I can probably guess what you did—for another, blackmail only works if you want to prevent a person from hearing something. If you tell me, there's no more apprehension." She reached out and pulled him close to her as she stood against the wall. "Nothing you can tell me about your past will change who you are now, who we are together."

"Are you certain?" he asked, his hands on her hips, doubt in his eyes.

She tiptoed up to kiss his cheek. "Yes." He breathed a deep sigh of relief. "Now, come on," she said. Grabbing his hand, she walked down the corridor to Room 603.

Caroline turned into the doorway, surveying the stark white space. John's father was sitting up in bed, pillows propped behind him, a drip attached to his right hand and wires protruding through the left sleeve of his hospital gown. Two of the other three beds in the room were unoccupied, with the one roommate snoring softly across the room.

John's father began to fidget with the covers as John and Caroline entered the room.

"Hello, Charles," Caroline greeted, keeping her voice even.

"Uh, hello, er, Caroline. John," Charles said. His eyes darted around the room. He reached over and took a sip of water and then fussed with his blanket again.

Caroline could feel the tension in John's body behind her. She glanced back at him. His hands were still and his face was blank. He was closed.

Sighing, she turned back to Charles. "Well, I'm here. What's next?" Caroline said, feeling it was better to get down to business than allow the tension to continue.

"I was … hoping … to speak with you alone," Charles said and then ducked his head.

She turned to John. "Do you—"

"No!" John asserted strongly.

She studied him for a moment before turning back to his father. "I don't think he plans on leaving. Can you just give me an idea of what you'd like to discuss?"

The older man seemed completely flummoxed by the situation. Caroline watched anger, frustration, envy and, perhaps, grief flit across his visage. Finally, he released a huge sigh, studying his own fidgeting fingers as though they contained the cure for heart disease of all kinds. "I merely wanted to ask how John is doing."

Caroline moved to sit by her father-in-law's bedside, but John grasped her sleeve. She sighed again, taking him by the hand, turning and wrapping him in a big hug. When she turned back to the bed, John's father was sitting, his fidgeting stilled, an expression of shock on his face. Perplexed, Caroline shook her head at being caught in the middle of this bizarre situation. One hand in John's, she reached her other hand to pull a chair closer so that it sat approximately halfway between the two Mr. Brocks, one standing and one reclined in a hospital bed. Releasing John's hand, she sat.

"If you want to ask John how he is, then ask him. He's here," she said.

John's father kept his eyes at the level of John's knees. "Ho … how are you … John?"

"Fine," John responded tersely.

"Good. That's good." Charles stopped for a time, and Caroline waited.

Charles sighed loudly. "Being ill … I've been thinking … regret …" His voice trailed off.

Caroline stood abruptly, drawing the two men's gazes to her, heat rising in her face. "This is stupid! Charles Brock, if you have something to say to your son, say it now, clearly and plainly, because if you die tomorrow, you will not have another opportunity! Contrary to what you may believe, your son has moved on. He's dealt with your abuse, his mother's failure to protect him—everything. If you want an opportunity to be a part of his life, then you need to earn it. You need to fix this situation."

Charles's bleak gaze filled with moisture, flitting to his son and then away. He turned his eyes to Caroline, asking quietly, "What do I do?"

"Apologize. But only if you mean it," she warned, waggling her finger at him.

Charles sat quietly for a long time, fidgeting with the blanket, adjusting his covers, moving objects about on his bedside table. The silence stretched out for three and then five minutes.

"Enough, Caroline! He's not sorry. Let's go," John said.

She nodded, rising to leave with her husband.

"Wait. Son. I am sorry. I was a bad father. I treated you very badly. I'm sorry," Charles said.

John turned back, a look of plain shock on his face, and then his features morphed. "Why?" he asked fiercely, stepping closer. "Why?"

"Your mother loved you," Charles said. "She always loved you better. Always."

Surprised by the revelation, John's voice grew softer. "Why, Dad?"

"You were her son. The apple of her eye and … I was jealous. How pathetic is that? I was jealous of my own son." His bleary eyes looked up to his son's dry ones. "I'm sorry. I'd … I'd like an opportunity to make things … better."

"You can't change the past," John responded coldly.

"No, but I can apologize." Charles reached out a hand and then let it drop to the bed. "I'm sorry, son. I would like a chance … If I could try again … Even simply call you …" His voice dropped off as he looked up pleadingly at his son.

Caroline glanced at John, but she couldn't read his face until he finally turned his gaze fully to her and she saw light.

"The book of my life," he said.

A slow smile spread across her face, nodding her encouragement. "Yes, my love," she said.

"Wait here," he instructed, turning back to her to add, "Please." She smiled at him.

Heeling about, he exited, and Charles merely studied his fingernails glumly as they waited for John's return. Before long, John re-entered the hospital room, dropping an open Bible onto his father's lap and pointing to the Book of Matthew. He walked back to stand beside Caroline, taking her hand. "Read that, and then you can call me," John instructed, smiling in satisfaction. He kissed Caroline's hand and then tugged her gently after him.

"Goodbye," Charles called to their retreating forms.

John paused and nodded once.

In the hall, John stopped her. "Scrabble?" he asked.

"Pardon?" she asked, completely confused.

"Shall we go home and play Scrabble?" he asked.

"No debrief?" she asked.

"No. Please. Later, but not now. Please?" he said.

"Okay. Everything's good? You're okay?" She wanted to be certain.

He smiled. "Absolutely."

"E-h-? Eh?" John queried, pointing to the letters on the Scrabble board. "That is not a word. And you definitely cannot use it on a triple-word score," he informed her indignantly.

"Check the dictionary. It's a word. I use it all the time," Caroline said.

He shook his head in mock-disgust. "Define it."

"It means, 'eh.' What else could it mean? Like, in, 'ya'know, eh?'" She adopted her best Ottawa Valley accent.

"Colonial," he accused, and she walloped him with a couch cushion. Reaching for her, he grasped the hem of her hoodie, but she ducked, letting him pull it over her head, rounding the back of the couch and then diving on him, effectively pinning him.

"Hi," she gasped.

"Ah, my favourite colonial beauty," he whispered, and she watched his eyes sparkle with humour and then darken with desire. "May I have a kiss, please? Boss," he said.

Leaning down, she kissed him deeply, a slow and thorough exploration, until she knew his mouth more intimately than his mouthwash did. His warm hands slipped beneath the hem of her T-shirt, and soon they were lost in the world of love and marriage, oblivious to Rufus watching them from the rug in front of the crackling fire. Eventually, as the fire in the hearth subsided, they escaped the chill of the great room for the bedroom, diving beneath the covers.

John pulled Caroline closer until she couldn't tell where her body ended and his began. "This all makes so much more sense than ever before. Once you put it into context," John said.

Stilling, she asked, "What in Wellington's trousers are you talking about?"

He laughed. "Now you're getting a handle on the language!"

She laughed in reply. "Well? What makes more sense?"

"Christmas," he replied, sobering slightly. "When I thought that Christmas was about presents and peace and family, it made no sense to me. There was no one in my life to buy me presents or to whom I cared to give. My family? My family was a nightmare. And peace? Frankly, darling, I am well aware that there is no peace on earth."

"But now?"

"Now I understand," he said. "It's not about any of those things. It's about the fact that the God who made the heavens and the earth gifted us His one and only Son, knowing the price He would pay."

"It all makes sense … in context," she said, shivering in the chilled cotton sheets.

"Indeed," he replied. "You cold?"

"Mmhmm. What you gonna do about it?" she asked, grinning.

He grinned in reply, proceeding to create all the heat they needed.

For only the second time in their married life, Caroline was the first to wake, sneaking out of bed to place John's presents beneath the Christmas tree, surprised to find her presents already residing there. She fingered each one and then jumped in surprise when a reprimand rang out from the bedroom door.

"No touching!" John chuckled as she stuck her tongue out at him. "It took you long enough to wake up!" he said.

She laughed, joining him and pulling him tightly into a hug. "Merry Christmas, my darling bear."

"*Happy* Christmas, my beauty. Come, let's shower and eat breakfast, and then you can open your presents."

"Are you crazy? I'll shower, but there's no way I'm waiting for breakfast. I want my presents now!" she said.

He laughed in pure joy. "Very well, boss. Your wish is my command."

She smiled brightly at him, dragging him into the shower and out again, barely touching the water in her excitement and anticipation. As they emerged dressed in comfortable clothes, John stepped toward the kitchen, but Caroline dragged him back over to the tree.

"Coffee!" he protested.

"Coffee later! Presents now!" She sat expectantly on the couch. He stood watching her. "Well?" she waited impatiently, prompting him when he continued to watch her with a confused expression on his face. "You're supposed to choose a present to give to me," she instructed.

"Sorry. I forgot that there were rules." As he reached beneath the tree, he asked, "Anything else I need to remember?"

"I'll let you know," she responded, grinning and bouncing from her spot on the couch.

"Here." John presented her with a gift.

"You have to tell me who it's from," she instructed.

He laughed. "Me."

"Is it 'from me' or 'love me'?" she questioned, her eyes full of laughter.

"Open it, woman!" he barked playfully, and she laughed again, tearing off the wrapping paper with enthusiasm to reveal a race-car-red gaming system complete with video kayaking, hockey and a James Bond game.

Her eyes filled, and he looked afraid that she would cry. Instead, she carefully placed the present aside and leapt into his arms. "I love it! Thank you. Let's play now. This isn't one of those shooting games where you're always going to win, is it?"

He laughed. He couldn't seem to stop laughing at her joy. "It's an adventure game. I'm sure I shall probably win every time, but you'll definitely have the advantage on the ice-hockey game."

"Come on, let's set it up and play," she said, clearly excited.

"What about my presents?" he teased, pulling a mock pout.

"Hmmm. Well, I suppose I could take the time to give you one." She moved under the tree and pulled out a box for him. He sat on the couch and carefully removed the paper, stopping to painstakingly refold each section in spite of Caroline's attempts to make him hurry. Finally opening the box before Caroline actually exploded in anticipation, John revealed the exact same gaming system in black, complete with a James Bond shooter and a survival game. He looked up in surprise and joined her fit of laughter, sweeping her into his arms and assuring her that he loved it.

"Can we keep the red one?" Caroline asked.

"Of course. Why don't we give the black one to the Hibberts?" he suggested. "The girls would love it."

Caroline's gaze softened. "That is a wonderful idea. And it will drive Hibb potty."

"Good word use," John said, chuckling.

The presents were put aside, and the next hour was spent playing. After a brief break for breakfast, they returned to open the mini-stix hockey, the mp3 player for jogging, the teddy-bear pyjamas, the new rugby ball and shirt, and a container of coffee-crisp chocolate bars. Soon, there was only one present left beneath the tree. John handed it to Caroline silently and then perched on the coffee table, waiting expectantly.

Opening the gift solemnly, Caroline revealed an elegant garment of deep blue silk adorned with pale pink roses and trimmed in gold thread.

"Oh, John, how did you get this?" she asked, wonder in her voice.

"I bought it in Delhi and had it made into a dress. For you," he added softly.

"Delhi? But you were there months ago!" she exclaimed.

"Yes," he confirmed as though it were obvious.

She watched him in wonder. "Thank you. It's so fine and elegant."

He handed her the gold bangles. "These go with it."

"Thank you." She kissed him breathlessly. "Thank you, my love."

"Pleasure. Would you like to try it on?" he asked. "It's almost time to get ready for Harry's supper party."

"Okay. What about you?" she said.

"My suit's in the spare room," he replied.

Before long, she found him dressed and ready, staring out the back window of the house. Turning at her approach, he grinned brightly. "You look stunning in that dress, darling," he said.

She smiled happily. "You are gorgeous, in or out of your suit."

He laughed. "Come on," he said, escorting her to the car. He grew silent again in the car on the way over to Harry Blake's house. A thin blanket of snow covered the streets and sidewalks.

"John, sweetheart? What's wrong?" she finally asked, wanting to relieve his tension.

"Nought," he replied.

"You seem nervous," she said.

Abruptly, he pulled over to the curb, stopping the car. "All right, explain this to me. I am using every technique I know to hide my emotions. I'm not tapping. How can you tell that I'm nervous?" he asked, exasperated.

She smiled. "Your eyes."

"My eyes?" he asked. His voice was strident with disbelief.

"Yes," she said. "Your eyes look almost black when you're nervous or … uh … how should I say, feeling *marital*, and they look chocolate smooth when you're calm."

"Anything else?" he asked, quirking his brow.

"Sure," she said. "When you're really upset, your face goes blank, it looks completely calm, devoid of emotion. When I first met you, you were blank most of the time. Now, though, you mostly wear a smile around your eyes."

"You know, one of the reasons they called me 'Ironheart' was because no one could ever read my internal state. I was beginning to lose confidence in myself this year, but I checked—no one else can read me. How can you always know?" he asked.

"There are a lot of things that go on beneath the surface of your eyes, and I have to admit that the workings of your mind make no sense to me, but I can usually tell how you're feeling," she said.

"How?" he asked in exasperation.

"Your eyes. Your touch. Whether you look me directly in the eyes. All kinds of ways."

He laughed, shaking his head in wonder. "I will never cease to be amazed by you." He pulled back out into the nearly empty street.

"You still haven't answered me," she reminded him. "What's wrong?"

He smiled mysteriously. "It's nothing you need to worry about and nothing you need to fix. I promise you that all will be normal again in a few hours."

"Okay. Will you tell me if you need me?" she said.

"I always need you."

She smiled and took his hand, holding it until he needed to shift gears.

The evening was brilliant. There were children running through the house, and Caroline and John found themselves in a game of Sorry! with Beth Hibbert and Harry's sister Clara, counting 1-2-3-back 4 … Charades for the adults was competitive to the point where Katie snapped at Hibb, whose feigned abject apology drew from her a laughing response and a loving swat on the shoulder.

Chuckling, Hibb accused, "This is your fault, John. My wife never hit me before she met yours. It's a bad habit to abuse your husband in this fashion."

"Go ahead then, Hibb. You tell her. I dare you!" John retorted.

Caroline fixed Hibb with the most intimidating stare and he backed away, palms up. "Not a chance," Hibb said in surrender.

"Then be a man and take what you've got coming," John concluded. Katie swatted Hibb again just for good measure, and the group broke into laughter, the tension evaporating.

Supper consisted of seven courses of the most unrelated but delicious delicacies, three of which Clara proudly announced that she had helped prepare, with Harry wholeheartedly agreeing that he couldn't have coped without her. As the conversation found a lull after the pudding, Harry delivered a nod to John, who stood, asking for silence.

"First, I want to thank Harry and Clara and Mrs. Blake for hosting this wonderful party. I have a few words to say, and Harry has graciously allowed me this opportunity." John looked around the table, and everyone watched him attentively as though the morning briefing had begun. "Two years ago, I left the UK to attend a conference in Mumbai, India. As you are all aware, I was abducted and taken to Burma for interrogation—"

"Uncle John? What's inta … inter … ?" Beth had entered the room unbeknownst to the adults.

John turned his eyes fondly to the little girl who had captured a piece of his heart. "They asked me questions, but not very nicely," he explained.

"Were they rude?" she asked, her eyes narrowed to condemn the rude beasts.

"They were very rude," he concluded, and she scowled and shook her head.

The adults chuckled around the table. Katie listened to her daughter's question and then sent her back to the other children, who were watching a movie.

John continued. "Once there, I was thrust through the door of a dingy prison cell, meeting for the first time the most stubborn … sorry, tenacious—" Caroline swatted him playfully on the leg. He grinned in response. "—compassionate and utterly beautiful woman I have ever known." He glanced down at Caroline, who was blushing deeply in pleasure. "She reached out her hand to me and, in spite of my arrogance and anger, faithfully stood by my side until I finally took hold. On the day she offered me her forgiveness, she changed my life forever." John reached down and took Caroline's hand, continuing to hold it as he spoke. "She doctored my wounds and ministered to my heart, and I began to understand that God can make us new. I realized what the Bible meant when it said, 'Therefore if any man be in Christ, he is a new creature: old things are passed away; behold, all things are become new.'

"Forced together with me for months, she could easily have hated me. I made it very easy for her. But somehow she chose to see a new man who I didn't even know existed."

Beth revealed her presence in the doorway once again, unable to keep away when her favourite "uncle" John was speaking. "Was the man invisible?"

John turned to her. "Yes, he was invisible. She had to look very hard to find him, Bethy." Beth nodded seriously, and John continued. "She has never been impressed by the ultimate spy. She seeks only a humble man seeking to crawl closer to God and closer to his wife. When she agreed to marry me, I knew that my life would never be the same. She came with me to England, giving up her home, her family and friends and even, potentially, her happiness, to be by my side. I never asked if that's what she wanted. Probably too afraid she might refuse.

"She joined the Service to be closer to me. I changed a few routines and expected that to be enough, but she wouldn't be content with simply a modified version of my old life. She knew there should be more. And I am so very grateful that she didn't settle for 'good enough.' She insisted I grow as a man, as a professional and as a Christian. And she grew to meet me. She insisted that we grow together.

"I don't even recognize the man I was before Burma, before Caroline, and yet she tells me that she could always see past my eyes to the real me, the 'new man' that God created me to be." He reached to the table and lifted his glass. "So, I would like you to raise a glass to the ultimate wife, Caroline, who has given me everything worth having."

Everyone rose, glasses held high.

"To Caroline!"

# References

Ahearn, Frank M., and Eileen C. Horan. *How to Disappear: Erase Your Digital Footprint, Leave False Trails, and Vanish Without a Trace*. Guilford, Connecticut: Lyons Press, 2010.

Andrew, Christopher. *The Defence of the Realm: The Authorized History of MI-5*. Toronto: The Penguin Group, 2009.

A-Z Lyrics Universe. http://www.azlyrics.com.

Bradshaw, John. *Bradshaw on the Family: A New Way of Creating Solid Self-Esteem*. Deerfield Beach, Florida: Health Communications Inc., 1996.

Butler, Phil. "It's Time to Play Fair With Toy Safety In China." *Everything PR* (blog). May 4, 2010. http://www.pamil-visions.net/toy-safety/214818/.

Canada Focus on the Family. http://www.fotf.ca/marriage.

Canwest News Service. "Government Vows to Curb Chinese Spying on Canada." *Canada.com*. April 16, 2006. http://www.canada.com/montrealgazette/news/story.html?id=ca90416e-fe77-4b8d-ae59-a4e9f55b6441&k=26688.

Connolly, Kate. "Germany Accuses China of Industrial Espionage." *The Guardian*. Last modified December 29, 2009. http://www.guardian.co.uk/world/2009/jul/22/germany-china-industrial-espionage.

Drew, Christopher. "New Spy Game: Firms' Secrets Sold Overseas." *New York Times*. October 17, 2010. http://www.nytimes.com/2010/10/18/business/global/18espionage.html.

"The Gospel Message—Today's Christian Videos," *Godtube.com*, http://www.godtube.com/watch/?v=77K7Y7NX#

IACP Police Psychological Services Section. *Psychological Fitness-for-Duty Evaluation Guidelines*. Ratified 2009 in Denver, Colorado.

Korba, Jack. "MGA Accuses Mattel of Toy Espionage." *Intellectual Property Briefs* (blog). American University Washington College of Law. August 19, 2010. http://www.ipbrief.net/2010/08/19/mga-accuses-mattel-of-toy-espionage/.

Lewis, Jason. "Revealed: Rover Director's Mysterious Lover Qu Li's Links to the Chinese Firm That 'Lifts and Shifts' the British Motor Industry." *Mail Online.* Last updated September 26, 2009. http://www.dailymail.co.uk/news/article-1216411/Revealed-Rover-directors-mysterious-lover-Qu-Lis-links-Chinese-firm-lifts-shifts-British-motor-industry.html.

Montgomery, John Warwick. *History and Christianity*. Minneapolis: Bethany House Publishers, 1964.

Oppenheimer, Jerry. *Toy Monster: The Big, Bad World of Mattel.* Hoboken, New Jersey: John Wiley & Sons, Inc., 2009.

Powell's Books. "*Toy Monster: The Big, Bad World of Mattel* by Jerry Oppenheimer—Synopses and Reviews." http://www.powells.com/biblio/8-9780470371268-0.

Reimer, Jeremy. "Report: Chinese Conduct 'Aggressive and Large-Scale' Espionage Against US." *Ars Technica* (blog). November 18, 2007. http://arstechnica.com/security/news/2007/11/report-chinese-conduct-aggressive-and-large-scale-espionage-against-us.ars.

"Russia, China Engaging in Industrial Espionage." *The Local.* May 22, 2010. http://www.thelocal.de/national/20100522-27365.html.

Wortzel, Larry. "Risks and Opportunities of a Rising China." The Heritage Foundation. Last modified June 22, 2006. http://www.heritage.org/research/lecture/risks-and-opportunities-of-a-rising-china.